Amanda Platell, a n̲ ̲of the *Sunday Express*. ̲

She has previously edited the *Sunday Mirror* and has been the managing director of the *Independent*. She is now Head of News and Media for the Conservative Party.

Born and raised in native Australia, is the former editor
... ... ... Amanda has spent all of her working life
in the media.

# SCANDAL

# AMANDA PLATELL

PIATKUS

'Colours' by Yevtushenko (Pg 201) is taken from *The Collected Poems of Yevtushenko*, Penguin, 1965.

Copyright © 1999 Amanda Platell

First published in Great Britain in 1999 by
Judy Piatkus (Publishers) Ltd of
5 Windmill Street, London W1P 1HF

**The moral right of the author has been asserted**

*A catalogue record for this book
is available from the British Library*

ISBN 0 7499 3119 1

Set in Bembo by
Phoenix Photosetting, Chatham, Kent

Printed and bound in Great Britain by
Mackays of Chatham PLC, Chatham, Kent

For Michael

# Chapter One

Sharon ripped open the layers of Harvey Nichols tissue paper, excited as a small child anticipating her first party dress. The gold epaulettes caught the early-morning sunshine streaming through her window in Tribune Tower as she held up the navy jacket against the fuchsia shell suit she had worn into the office that day under her long silver fox coat.

None of her old clothes would do for the crucial board meeting at nine today. Navy was not exactly her natural habitat, Sharon preferred bolder colours, but today was different. She just *had* to have her new Ralph Lauren suit. She had to look sharp, sophisticated, businesslike, even if she still could not understand why it had taken an entire week to have the necessary alterations made to the suit. No amount of bullying could get it done any quicker. And then the seamstress had had the gall to say she could have finished it sooner if Sharon and her secretary hadn't kept phoning and bullying her about making more changes.

Sharon had only called once and her secretary Roxanne was away on holiday that week. She prided herself on being decisive and exploded at the accusation of dithering. Sharon had threatened them with a double page exposé on their sloppy service. The Harvey Nichols PR woman had rather sniffily replied that she didn't think it would do them much damage as readers of the *Daily Tribune* were hardly their target clientele. At least she had agreed to open the store early so a *Tribune* courier could pick up the suit before the board meeting.

Ten minutes to nine ... she just had time to change. Luckily

Sharon had already done her basic makeup in the car. An extra touch of Ripe Mandarin blusher to complement her all-year-round sunbed tan, a little more chocolate brown lip liner, a dash of Tangerine Surprise lipstick, then the shell suit dropped to the floor revealing a red Wonderbra, suspenders and black stockings to match her black stilettos.

There was something of Marilyn Monroe about Sharon, the voluptuous proportions marred only by extensive cellulite, more lunar landscape than dimpled orange peel, on her thighs and stomach. The jacket was inched on and just managed to button up over Sharon's breasts, two large watermelons, crushed together in a brassiere a couple of sizes too small.

Sharon stroked the epaulettes as one would an adored pet, more delighted than surprised to see that the seamstress had added enough chevrons to satisfy an ambitious sergeant-major. Sharon always added epaulettes, it was her style trademark, added a bit of glamour to her editor's power suits.

Five to nine and she stepped into the narrow skirt which she had asked to be lengthened an inch. Her calves and knees were good – and she knew it – but Sharon's thighs were not a pretty sight. Then she saw it. Her scream could be heard throughout the editorial floor. The skirt had been shortened to a ridiculous length, barely covering her stocking tops, let alone her thighs. It was obscene.

In a flash she recalled the scene at Harvey Nichols the week before when she had been trying on the suit. It had been one of those moments, as she stepped out of the cubicle to admire herself in the full-length mirror, the one every woman dreads. Stepping out of a neighbouring cubicle was another woman wearing the same suit, a woman ten years younger, two sizes smaller and the person Sharon loathed most in the world: Georgina Harrison.

Size sixteen eyed size twelve with open hostility.

The two women were used to squaring up for battle inside the offices of the *Tribune* newspaper group. The intimacy of a changing room was new territory, but the basic instinct for combat was as strong as ever.

'Well, we can't both buy this, can we, babe? And I know who looks best in it,' Sharon had said archly, handing the sales assistant

2

her credit card and not waiting for Georgina to explain that she had already bought the suit the week before and was simply making sure the alterations fitted.

'That bitch! That fucking whore!' Sharon screamed in her office as she realised what must have happened. Only one person could be behind it, Georgina.

The worst insult one woman could offer another had just been dealt to her. Georgina had made her look *fat*.

'The problem is, Douglas, there are three people in my editor's chair. Now I know how Diana felt – I'm being shafted from every direction and I'm not going to put up with it.'

Holloway had expected her to be angry, but not this angry. He was glad at least that he'd chosen the Roof Terrace in Knightsbridge for the meeting. Even Georgina wouldn't throw her toys in such a public place. And, if things got a bit animated, there was no one here who would recognise them.

The Terrace was not Douglas Holloway's favourite bar. Too many unreconstructed eighties Neanderthals flashing their fortunes for his liking. it was one of London's most infamous pick-up joints and the very notion of it was anathema to him.

He preferred to be surrounded by discreet luxury and an aura of success. His favourite haunt was the Berkeley Hotel, only a few blocks but a world away. He preferred the Berkeley partly because it was fashionable, partly because it was expensive and therefore exclusive, and partly because it was close to Harvey Nichols and Becky could do a spot of late-night shopping during his evening drinks meetings, which took place most nights.

It gave him a small thrill to think that the woman he loved was even now choosing his dinner in the Food Hall of the department store, lingering over the sushi, inspecting the wild mushrooms and out-of-season blueberries, thinking of pleasing him.

Georgina was there before him – dark business suit, red lipstick, Bloody Mary, a double, extra spicy. Holloway had long suspected she only drank Bloody Marys to draw attention to her mouth. And it was a mouth worthy of attention. Not for the first time he thought, those lips were made for kissing.

He was ten minutes late and ran a trained eye over the other customers. No one he recognised. Good. It was important this meeting should remain secret.

Many saw Douglas Holloway as a cold man, harsh to the point of brutality, emotionless. As chief executive, he ran the Tribune Group with all the efficiency of a concentration camp. If people were useful, they were looked after. The weak were removed. As long as he continued to deliver year-on-year increased profits to his shareholders, the City loved him. Technically Douglas answered to the Tribune board, and ultimately its chairman. In practice, he was the boss and everyone knew it.

His climb to the top had come about after years of plotting and manipulating and he was a supreme manipulator. Douglas knew about people's insecurities, he knew about fear. He had learned how to control people through their emotions – it was instinctive to him now. What he had forgotten was that Georgina was an acute observer. For years she had studied the way he controlled people and now she was using those same techniques – on him.

Douglas was not an imposing man. Tall and slightly built with no discernible fat or muscle on his wire coat hanger frame, he had the gait of a small man, habitually taking tiny steps and always leaning slightly to the left as though carrying a heavy burden in the other hand. Only a mother could call him handsome. Yet he felt handsome, had done so increasingly as the years passed. Maybe it went hand-in-hand with growing ever more powerful. Certainly he had rarely stopped to think these days about the gawky Canadian kid from the wrong side of the tracks who could not speak to, let alone attract, a girl. He had left that far behind him.

So it was no surprise that he was approached by two women as he fought his way through the crowded bar. Both were too overtly glamorous for his taste, but their interest was good for his ego. He smiled to himself and again thought of Becky, his elegant, wealthy, perfectly pedigreed Becky.

A face full of hair was all he got when he bent down to kiss Georgina.

'A glass of still water,' Douglas instructed the waiter without looking up. 'Ice, no lemon.'

'Don't you ever drink? Don't you ever loosen up?' Georgina shot at him, irritation in her voice.

4

We'd better lighten things up here, he thought as he sat down opposite her. He could always tell when she was mad. That huge red mouth was set into a perfect bow, no hint of humour at the corners, no promise of a smile. Tonight she was strictly business.

'We must come here more often,' said Douglas smiling. 'I've already had two women try to pick me up, one at the door and the other as I passed her at the bar. See that gorgeous blonde over there? Take a look at those legs.'

'Douglas,' Georgina said, feigning exasperated weariness, 'the first is a hooker and the second's a man.'

He choked on his water and rallied enough to say: 'How do you know?'

'The brunette with the cleavage works this bar. I've seen her operating before. Very attractive and very expensive. As for the guy in drag . . . great legs, I agree, but how many six-foot blondes do you see wearing size twelve stilettos? Get real, Douglas.'

Secretly he enjoyed Georgina's teasing. She was the only person in the world, apart from Becky, allowed the privilege. They had a history of it.

Georgina Harrison, editor of the *Sunday Tribune*, had asked for this rendezvous. An urgent meeting, she had said to his secretary, not to be held in the office. Two items on the agenda – fundamental change or her resignation.

Things must be mad. At least he'd made her promise not to do anything until he'd had a chance to talk to her. Talk her out of it more like. There was enough instability in the company as it was.

The story in the Peterborough column of the *Telegraph* that morning saying she had quit didn't help matters. Holloway had either sacked, shunted or forced out twelve editors from the Tribune Group in the last three years. It didn't look good. His enemies in the rival press, and there were many, were having a field day. The headlines said it all:

TO LOSE ONE EDITOR, MR HOLLOWAY, IS UNFORTUNATE:
TO LOSE TWELVE LOOKS LIKE MISMANAGEMENT

TRIALS AND
TRIBULATIONS

Georgina and the editor of the *Daily Tribune*, Sharon Hatch, had fallen out in a big way and there was now open hostility between them. There was something about the clash of two powerful women that appealed to Holloway. In a way they were fighting over him, for supremacy in his eyes, like jealous wives jostling for position in a harem.

He had been proud to have been the first newspaper boss to have appointed women to the top two posts in the group. He'd got a lot of kudos from that, and his trust had been repaid because both were talented. But now the bitches were fighting.

The most important thing was to salvage the situation. He did not need the public humiliation of an editor walking out on him and Georgina had always been one of his few allies. He needed her around.

The *Sunday Tribune* was a tabloid newspaper, the most successful and profitable title in his stable, far outselling the *Daily* and with much higher advertising revenues. He could not afford to jeopardise his golden goose.

He had been thinking on the traffic-choked drive here how to deal with Georgina. She *had* to stay. Just play the old 'how could you do this to me, after all I've done for you' card. Make her remember her obligation to him, the way he looked after her when she'd hit the rails. It had always worked in the past. Appeal to her loyalty, be a bit angry, and very, very hurt. Vulnerable only if things get really rough.

'I can't believe you'd do this to me, Georgina,' he said now. 'You've made me look ridiculous, as if I'm fumbling.' He reached persuasively for her hand. 'How did that story leak out this morning in the *Telegraph*? Surely we can talk things through and come to a solution? You've never let me down before, please don't do it now.'

Georgina knew exactly how the story of her resignation had appeared in the *Telegraph*. She had placed it there. The diary editor was an old friend and had been happy to help. It strengthened her position. She had no intention of resigning but if Douglas thought she did, it gave her the edge in their negotiations.

'I promise I'll sort things out with Sharon. Get her to back off, leave you to edit the *Sunday*. You have my word, Georgina. I want you to stay. I need you to stay. You owe me that much.'

Georgina flinched. She'd been waiting to see how long it would take for him to remind her what she owed him, of the fact that he had literally saved her. Surely after seven years that debt was repaid a hundred times over? But Douglas Holloway was not a man to allow a debt ever to be fully repaid. Not when it was to his advantage to have her beholden to him.

Don't let him play on your insecurities, don't fall into the gratitude trap, she told herself ferociously. Weaken now and he'll win. The same old ploys. Resist. Ignore that comment. Don't show a flicker of gratitude or fear.

'I hear you, Douglas,' she said, 'but I'm not convinced.'

'You have my word,' he said, relaxing a little now. 'Sharon just wants to help, you know.'

'Help!' shouted Georgina and two waiters appeared immediately at her side. 'A glass of champagne,' she ordered. Douglas looked uncomfortable. He loved emotional women but couldn't abide it when they became hysterical – and shouting in a public place like this was verging on hysterical.

'She knows the minute I leave the office, whether it's for lunch, a meeting or a lipstick break,' Georgina continued in a low, furious voice. 'It's that creep Feretti – he's on the phone to her every minute spying on me. Two minutes after I left for the marketing meeting on Friday she was on my editorial floor, interrogating one of my reporters, trying to stir up a "hang the bastards" angle on the double murder story we were running. She was just trying to nick it for the *Daily*. There's enough competition out there with the other Sundays without having to battle with my sister paper.

'It just won't work Douglas. You can't have the editor of the *Daily Tribune* trying to run the *Sunday* as well. Unless, of course, that's what you're planning – a seven-day operation?'

'You know I've been considering that option for some time,' he said coolly. 'But I can't see a way of making it work and

7

keeping the identities of *The Daily* and *The Sunday* separate. The advertising revenue depends upon that. The bottom line depends upon it. But there has to be some cross-over, we save costs that way. That's all Sharon is trying to do – create a flow through from the *Daily* to the *Sunday*.'

Georgina knew, all the editors did, that the seven-day operation was Holloway's ultimate dream for his newspaper titles. He was planning to start the transition with the group's middle-market *Herald* titles first, then the red top *Daily* and *Sunday Tribunes*, then roll it out into his other newspapers.

Thanks to a colleague in the finance department who owed her a favour, Georgina also knew that Sharon had prepared a business plan for the seven-day venture and was presenting it to Douglas at eleven the next day. Georgina had to act fast and seize the initiative. He needed to squirm a bit longer.

'There can only be one editor, Douglas. And as if the problems with Sharon aren't enough, I've got *you* poking your nose in every five minutes with this mad idea of Mandelsoning the papers.'

Christ, this was going to be hard work, he thought gloomily.

'It's not a mad idea,' he protested. 'There's a different feeling out there, you can sense it. This is more than a change of government, it's a change in the way people see the world. Blair and Mandelson understood it before anyone else. It's style that people are impressed by, it's marketing that works. If millions of ordinary people vote for a party without policies, that has to tell you something.'

'Oh, shut up, Douglas,' Georgina said impatiently. 'You don't know what you're talking about. And let's not forget what happened to Peter Mandelson. A Minister with portfolio for less than six months before he got booted out. People voted in a government they believed would make a difference – to their jobs and their kids' educations. Sure the whole operation was superbly marketed, but there *was* substance.

'The problem is, you believe in some new Mandelsonian state, which you interpret as all style and no substance, while Sharon's positioning the *Daily* as an anti-Government paper and trying to drag the *Sunday* along with it. You can't run a newspaper properly when it's being pulled in different directions.

Either I'm left to edit the *Sunday Tribune* my way or I go.'

'Okay, okay. You have my word I'll sort things out. You'll be free to edit. The paper's looking good, Georgina. There's still a long way to go, but we're getting there. Circulation is up year on year, advertising revenue is stronger than ever. The only thing I would say to you is you must be tougher on the staff. Always remember, it's better to be feared than loved. You get better results that way.'

'Don't start quoting Machiavelli at me, Douglas, not now,' she said wearily. 'I know your theories about power. If you remember correctly, he also says that to be hated is equally dangerous.'

'You know how much I rely on you. People you can really trust are very rare and very valued in our world. Please hang in there. You're not a quitter. Don't quit on us now,' he pleaded.

By 'us' Douglas meant him and Georgina, not the *Tribune* and Georgina. They had worked together for seven years and she was one of the few people he trusted – he relied absolutely upon her loyalty and her journalistic instincts.

But Georgina was tired. The hours at the *Sunday Tribune* were gruelling, but worse was the constant undermining from Sharon. She hadn't spent time with her partner in weeks and God knows she needed a little TLC now and then.

'Why don't you just give the bloody job to Sharon and be done with it? Shut down the Sunday operation completely and save the money. Make the *Daily* a seven-day newspaper,' she sighed.

'For the same reasons I didn't give it to her in the first place, the same reasons I've explained to you many times – she doesn't have the class or the intelligence to edit the *Sunday Tribune*. It's different from the *Daily*, more up-market. It needs your touch. I cannot and will not jeopardise the success of the *Sunday Tribune*. I need you there, Georgina.'

Two glasses of champagne later, she'd agreed to stay. 'But on one condition. *I* edit the *Sunday Tribune*, *I* decide the editorial direction. If there is continued interference, I walk,' she said. 'I'll give it another two months. If you haven't sorted it out by then, I'm gone. I promise you that, Douglas.

'And there's something else I should tell you. Trevor Stephens has been dropping hints about the editorship of the *Sunday Globe*. I'll call him tomorrow and tell him it's off. For now.'

'I can't believe you were even considering going to that rag!' Holloway exploded. 'They've lost more readers in the last six months than the Tory Party did voters at the last election. You ring Stephens and tell him *tonight*.'

He reached for his glass of water, flipped his wrist in the way that so irritated Georgina and openly looked at his watch.

'Yes, Douglas, it's nearly nine o'clock, and yes, Becky will be waiting, and yes, you can leave soon. But not before I've shown you this.' Georgina pulled a perfect bound document from her black Mulberry briefcase.

Holloway looked confused. 'You said there were only two things on the agenda and I've addressed them both,' he said wearily.

'The first thing was that you either resolve the situation with Sharon or I resign. That may be two problems for you, Douglas, but it's one and the same to me. The second thing is this.' And she shoved the document into his hand. '*My* plan for a seven-day operation, only this time the *Sunday* will show the way. All the costings are there. Just read the top sheet, I know you never take in more than that.'

Holloway examined the document. The title sheet read: TRIBUNE SEVEN-DAY OPERATION – THE FUTURE

The second sheet had just four bulletpoints:

- editorial costs cut by 25 per cent
- circulation and revenue increased by 6 per cent
- advertising revenue increased 10 per cent
- overall profit increased 20 per cent

The third sheet was a flow chart indicating the executive staff structure. The top box read 'Editor-in-Chief – Georgina Harrison'. Sharon's name was nowhere to be seen.

Holloway closed the file and placed it in his briefcase. 'Very impressive. I'll get the Finance Director to check the figures tomorrow.'

'You'll find them in order.'

'Can't say I saw Sharon's name in the executive line-up,' he said smiling.

'You didn't because it's not there. All change requires tough decisions, Douglas. You taught me that.'

He got up to leave, kissed her and extracted one promise from her before he left – that she would call the staff together tomorrow and tell them she had not resigned, she was staying.

'To tell you the truth,' he said, almost as an afterthought, 'I'm a bit worried about Sharon. I think she's having a mid-life crisis, chasing her vanished youth or something. Did you see what she was wearing at the board meeting on Tuesday?'

Georgina smiled for the first time that evening.


When Douglas had left, Georgina indicated she wanted the bill, changed her mind and ordered another glass of champagne. She thought back over the meeting. It had gone to plan. The bait was set. She knew her document was superior to the one Sharon would present tomorrow, in ultimate projections and in detail. Nothing would happen for a while, but this small battle was won. She had to stay one step ahead of her rival. No room for complacency.

The thing she was most pleased about was the fact that for the first time in seven years she had not responded to the 'after all I've done for you' ploy. She was angry that Douglas went on using it; more angry still with her usual reaction, one of shame and guilt. That single brutal body blow to her confidence, so precisely aimed.

On good days she could convince herself that it was not Douglas who saved her. She'd saved herself. On bad days she felt she owed him everything.

It was his weapon, and one he used repeatedly against Georgina. For a moment the was back in that darkness, in the hopelessness of that clinic, fighting for her sanity.

The third glass of champagne no longer looked so attractive. She put two £20 notes under it and left.


Douglas Holloway had insisted that the windows of his chauffeur-driven Bentley Turbo were of tinted glass and was glad of that now as John drove the car up to the side entrance of The Terrace. Becky was safely inside, unseen, an array of Harrods and Harvey Nichols bags beside her on the back seat.

He slid inside to join her, closed the door, then reached across for her hand.

'Hello,' was all he said before placing his own hand on Becky's swollen stomach. There was no movement, only warmth, but something thrilling nevertheless about knowing his child grew there in the body of the woman he loved.

And he did love Becky. Passionately.

She was one of those elegant, willowy women who carried her pregnancy effortlessly, putting on weight only around her slender waist.

The warm bump he felt under his hand was in stark contrast to his wife Kelly's one-hundred-sit-ups-a-day washboard stomach. The thought of her waiting at home for him, exquisite and angry, made him sit back sharply.

From the size of Becky's bump, one thing was for sure. He would have to break the news to his wife that he was leaving her – soon – before a rival newspaper did.

# Chapter Two

Georgina and Sharon approached Tribune Tower the next morning at the same time but from opposite directions. Georgina headed south from her Notting Hill flat in the front of a chauffeur-driven Jaguar, dark blue, the colour of her eyes. Sharon, ignoring her chauffeur and chain smoking, travelled east from her Fulham terrace house. The specially ordered tangerine-coloured Griffith TVR matched her hair, her suntan and her lipstick. She sat in the back. Her chauffeur was forbidden to talk to her at all times.

Both women were surrounded by the day's discarded newspapers, on their mobile phones to their respective news desks, setting up stories for the day.

'Mike, can we get a steer on the gay MP who was outed last night?' Georgina began, reading from a story she had torn from that morning's copy of the *Guardian*. 'His resignation is all very mysterious. We might have another scoop on our hands, especially since he's married with three kids.'

'It seems he left his wife a couple of years ago,' Mike said. 'We've got an address for the boyfriend and Stope is heading out there as we speak.'

'Just be careful,' Georgina warned. 'If his family know, there's not a lot else to be said. It's not as though he's been deceiving anyone if they were separated. I'll be in the office in about ten minutes. Talk to you then.'

'Allenby, you fucker!' Sharon shouted into her mobile. 'How many reporters have we got on this disgusting faggot MP?'

'We've been doorstepping him since last night with a snapper,' the news editor said nervously.

'I want to know every cough and fucking spit about this guy, do you hear me?' Sharon was shouting so loudly into the phone the whole news desk could hear her. 'Those queers are all the same. Hit all the known gay haunts: Hampstead Heath, Clapham Common, all the gay bars. Put word out we'll pay big for any rent boy stuff. I want to know who he did it with, how often, how depraved. Let's nail this disgusting little fucker!'

The one thing the two women had in common was that they had both started at the bottom and fought their way up. Sharon's career began straight out of school at sixteen on the local newspaper. After mastering the beauty and shopping columns, she was quickly promoted to the news desk. She would do anything for a story – and usually did. But she was hot, a hungry young reporter with a nose for news and an innate sense of where to dig the dirt.

When she was younger, before the booze and the cigarettes had started to take their toll, she was a real looker, and sweet with it. At least on the surface. She could charm a story out of anyone, old lady or young politician alike.

The news desk adored her, their personal 'Cruise Missile' they'd called her. She quickly worked her way on to the national newspapers and made a name for herself. Sex, especially deviant sex, a speciality.

Sitting in a car at 3 am one night staking out the house of the mistress of a member of the Cabinet, it suddenly hit Sharon that this was a dead end job. She did all the hard work and her editor got all the credit. Real power was not to be had as a jobbing reporter on the road, it was in the office – the editor's office to be more precise.

In short order, Sharon turned her finely honed investigative skills to discovering a few dirty secrets about her colleagues on the news desk. One was a coke-head and the other an alcoholic, she quickly found out. Mysteriously this information, complete with photographs, appeared on the editor's desk in brown envelopes. The two hacks she'd fingered didn't last long and Sharon climbed quickly over their backs and into their chairs.

Georgina had taken a year out after university, unable to make up her mind as to what she wanted to do with her life and where she wanted to live it. All she knew was that she had to get out of South Africa.

After two years in Australia working as a cadet trainee on the *Sydney Morning Herald*, she fell in love and married. The marriage lasted about as long as her university education, but managed to teach her more about men and life than any honours degree.

When her father became ill, she returned to Johannesburg and worked there on the *Star*, as feature writer and investigative reporter.

The year she spent at home, working and nursing her father back to health after a mild stroke, convinced her she wanted out of Johannesburg, out of Africa, for good.

Post-apartheid, it was an uncomfortable place for a white woman with liberal views. She had tried to get a job on the *Sowettan*, the political newspaper which sold mainly to blacks, but was turned down.

Georgina would never forget the open contempt that had greeted her when she went for the interview.

'Why on earth would we give a job to you when there are so many of our own kind who could do it?' the deputy editor had asked scornfully.

After the pain and prejudice of the past, Georgina found herself agreeing with him. She couldn't blame him. She'd probably feel the same if their roles were reversed.

So she packed her belongings in one suitcase and headed off for London, and the place she had always dreamed of – Fleet Street.

Without friends and in possession of an accent and an assumed past that were universally disliked, she buried herself in her work. When she looked back nowadays, she could not quite understand how she had got as far as she had. Hard work, a good nose for a story, a sense of fair play, had all helped. But it was Georgina's ability to get people to rally behind her, what they had called in her school reports her 'leadership qualities', that had made the real difference.

And she had arrived in London in the late-eighties at a time when women were on the ascendant. It was fashionable to be a tough, shoulder-pad wearing woman fighting your way to the top. Newspaper bosses were aware that they were losing female readers in droves and believed the way to get them back was by employing more women in top jobs.

The fact that she was pleasing on the eye didn't hurt either.

Georgina arrived at Tribune Tower in the City at 8.30. If no longer the tallest building in London (Canary Wharf had overtaken it years ago), it was still one of the most elegant. Constructed almost entirely of glass and steel, the attenuated lines made it appear taller than its thirty-five floors. Georgina's office faced south and looked out over Tower Bridge and the sprawling, chaotic southern suburbs.

Today she was wearing red, her good luck suit. In fact, she believed any red suit brought her good luck, and there had been many. Georgina believed in luck. She knew it took more than hard work and intelligence to get what you wanted out of life, to be happy. She prided herself on her ability to recognise good fortune when it came. She was also profoundly superstitious and attributed that to her Catholic mother.

She stood looking out of the floor-to-ceiling window, twisting in her fingers the tiny gold crucifix her mother had given her as a child. In the early-morning light she caught a reflection of herself in the glass. She'd put on more than a few pounds since taking this job and didn't like it one bit. 'Curvy' her lover had said affectionately last night.

Too many late-night plates of chips, she thought, and vowed again to give them up. It's all Mike's fault, he's the one who buys them and I just can't resist. Mike Gordon was her news chief, lover of late night chips and early morning fry-ups. Georgina thought about calling Mike in first and putting to rest the rumours over her leaving. She decided it was better to leave the explanations to later, over a quiet drink.

Her only regret about placing the resignation story in the *Telegraph* was that she hadn't just manipulated Douglas, she had misled her staff and she disliked herself for that. But sometimes the end justified the means.

She had created instability and now she had to rectify the

situation and reassure her staff that she was staying. The battle had only just begun.

By 10.30 they were all in. Georgina took a deep breath, walked out of her office and stood in front of her secretary's desk. She had already briefed Steve, she always did. He stood quietly behind her.

'Would you all come here, please?' she shouted down the office. Heads looked up from whatever they were doing, many refused to move from their desks. That same look of fear and resentment on every face.

By tradition, editors always call their staff together to announce that they are leaving – all too often a euphemism for being shafted, sacked, moved sideways. Like prime ministers, the one thing editors can all be sure of is that the axe will fall on them one day. It is not a job for life, and the life expectancy of an editor is getting shorter and shorter.

'Can you all hear me?' Georgina asked. They grumbled a response. 'There have been a lot of rumours about my imminent departure from the *Sunday Tribune*. I just want you all to know that they are untrue. I have not resigned. I am not leaving. Now, let's all get on with it.'

A cheer went up as she walked back into her office, shut the door and stood facing the window again, looking down on the Tower of London. She heard the door open behind her. It was Mike Gordon.

'Nice performance George. It fooled most of them. I'm not sure what you're up to and I'm not going to ask. I'm just glad you're staying,' he said. Mike was one of the old-fashioned, no-nonsense school of newsmen.

He and Georgina had circled each other suspiciously when she first arrived. They were sure they'd hate each other, he the tough Northerner, she the South African upstart – and a woman to boot. Slowly the relationship had changed, first to one of mutual respect and then to one of genuine affection.

Georgina knew now he would walk across hot coals for her and she for him.

The moment Georgina walked back into her office, Pete Feretti, the Tribune Group's Marketing Manager, phoned Sharon.

'What's that bitch up to? Has she resigned?' Sharon quizzed him eagerly.

'No! Be down in two minutes.' Feretti left the *Sunday* editorial floor where he had his office and was in Sharon's office in one minute flat. He was known to the staff of the *Tribune* as 'The Ferret', because he could 'shoot up Sharon's arse quicker than any man alive'. He preferred to think of himself as the Ferrari of the newspaper world – fast, powerful and red hot.

Sharon was beside herself this morning, screaming and shaking with rage, her Farrah Fawcett hair bouncing around in sympathy. All pretty normal for Sharon, but he knew the signs of true rage – her skin had turned red and blotchy, small bumps appearing under the permatan surface.

She had one cigarette in her mouth, another burning low in the ashtray. The sleeves of her vivid blue Ozbek jacket were pushed up past the elbow, as if for combat, huge breasts bulging from the front of the jacket, aided and abetted by the customary too-small Wonderbra.

'Tell me she's fucking resigned, tell me she's fucking dead, tell me she's fucking out of here!' screamed Sharon, bashing her fists on the desk with every 'fucking'.

Feretti ran his fingers through his long dark curls, crossed his legs a little tighter and recounted the meeting as Sharon continued to pound the desk.

'They cheered? I want the name of every traitor who cheered, do you hear me? Every fucking traitor – NOW.' The only good thing about her rages was that they were seldom directed at him. And situations like this gave him the power to knife anyone he didn't like. He knew that one way or another Sharon would get rid of everyone here who was loyal to Georgina, however long it took.

The problem was, they had all cheered, he thought. She wouldn't like that. So he drew up his pet hate list and handed it over.

'Roxy,' Sharon screamed through the closed door. Feretti knew the summoning of her personal assistant was his signal to leave. He'd done his job. He scuttled out, buttocks clenched tightly together as though he was expecting a whack on the bottom as he left. 'Thanks, babe,' she muttered after him.

'Get me a vodka – NOW.' Roxanne took a mug and the vodka, contained in a thermos, from the cupboard and poured a stiff shot. She had been with Sharon for two years, her longest surviving secretary, and knew what measure to provide according to the crisis. 'And get that bitch Georgina down here when I'm out of my meeting with Holloway.'

When she was alone again Sharon called the *Tribune*'s Managing Director, Andrew Carson, on his private line. 'I need to see you tonight at the flat, usual time. It hasn't worked. She's staying.'

Ten minutes later Sharon was taking a seat opposite Douglas Holloway in his office, the bright blue of her jacket adding the only note of colour to the spartan room. She laid before him a hastily stapled copy of her presentation. The size of a telephone book, she'd discovered too late it was impossible to bind it. The cover sheet read:

ONE SMALL STEP FOR SHARON, ONE GIANT LEAP FOR THE TRIBUNE

Douglas flicked through the pages impatiently.

'Where's the top line?' he said, without looking up.

'Douglas, I want to take you through my plans for a seven-day operation, step-by-step,' she said, small bumps starting to appear under her skin. 'I've put a lot of work into this proposal and there's important details we need to cover.' Sharon shifted uncomfortably in her chair and with every wiggle her breasts seemed to creep a little further out of her jacket. Like her face under the thick layer of foundation, they had started to go red, a tiny rash the shape of Italy beginning in her cleavage and expanding further into Europe with every moment that passed.

'I'm not interested in detail.' He looked up. 'What's the saving on staff costs?'

'That's on page fifteen along with the restructuring of the two papers . . .'

'What is the overall saving?' he cut in.

'I'll sack about fifteen per cent of the total staff as outlined in Section 3, starting on page 16,' she said, fumbling through the document.

19

'Circulation increase?' he shot at her.

'Fifteen per cent during the first year, but that's only . . .'

'No newspaper in the UK has increased sales by that much in a year. Your sales are down on the *Daily*, just how do you propose to achieve a fifteen per cent increase?'

'Douglas I've worked it all out. New sections, new magazines, increased spend on television advertising . . .'

'And what do you suppose that will do to the bottom line? This is a business, Sharon, we're here to make money. Clearly you haven't thought this through. I've already had a far more impressive document on the subject from Georgina. I want a bottom line profit out of all this, clearly explained. Come back when you've done it properly.' He flung the document back at her and picked up the phone, her signal to leave.


Roxanne could hear Sharon approaching long before she turned into their nest of offices; the heavy thud of her footsteps on the floor, the screaming at the staff.

'Get to work, you lazy fuckers!' she shrieked at two young reporters gossiping at the coffee machine. 'If both of you don't provide me with a splash this week, I'll fucking sack you, *do you hear me*? And you, Edwards, you useless cunt. When's the last time you had your fucking name in the paper?'

Edwards flinched, as he always did when Sharon called him a See You Next Tuesday, as he preferred to say. Not for the first time he thought how unfair it was. If he called anyone that, especially a woman, he'd have every female in the place testifying before a tribunal.

'I had the splash today, Sharon,' he said defensively, and instantly regretted opening his mouth.

'It was a pile of crap,' she screamed. 'Steaming, stinking dog crap! The only reason it ended up on the front was that it was marginally less stinking than the other crap I had to shovel in.'

Her face was now inches away from his. He could smell stale cigarettes; even stronger was the stench of alcohol. She dropped her cigarette in his almost full cup of coffee and stomped off, slamming the office door behind her. Sharon's ample bottom had hardly touched her seat before she was up again and heading straight back out of her office in the direction of a young boy staring intensely at a terminal.

He couldn't have been much older than fifteen, a skinny kid in an ill-fitting, cheap white shirt and clearly one of his dad's ties. With his back to the main office, he never saw her coming.

Sharon bent down behind him and stared at the screen before spitting out: 'Who the fuck are you and what the hell are you doing playing computer games? This is a newspaper office.'

The scrawny neck spun around and two startled eyes looked up from behind thick glasses.

'On second thoughts, don't answer that,' she said. 'Whoever you are, you're sacked. Get the fuck out of here. *Now.*'

Sharon headed for her office again and this time Roxanne was right behind her.

'Sharon, that's Peter, the son of a friend of the Chairman's,' she said in a frightened voice. 'He's here on work experience during his school holidays as a favour to Sir Philip.'

Sharon uncharacteristically paused for thought. Sir Philip was the head of the Tribune board, highly respected and influential. Most importantly, he had Douglas Holloway's ear. 'Well, why didn't you fucking tell me? It's your job to keep me informed on everyone in this place. Get him in here, quick.'

'Peter, come and sit down,' Sharon said sweetly when he walked in, shoulders hunched, head bowed. 'I was just kidding out there. How are you enjoying things here?' The boy disappeared into his seat and Sharon sat on the front of her desk, bending forward to try and get some eye contact.

He looked up and into her cavernous cleavage. If he moved his head just a few inches his nose would be nestled between those phenomenal breasts. She was so close he could smell her, that salty tang of woman he had read about and masturbated imagining. He could feel his erection starting to strain the thin fabric of his school trousers.

'S-sorry, Miss?' he mumbled, eyes still fixed on the impressive sight ahead.

'What have you been doing?' Sharon coaxed, leaning a little closer and watching with satisfaction the redness creep up his neck and the bulge in his trousers twitch.

'Surfing, Miss,' he said shyly.

'How interesting. And please call me Sharon. I can't imagine you'd get much surfing done in this weather.'

'No, I surf the net and stuff.'

'Ah, so you're one of those computer whizzes, are you?'

'Please give me another chance. I know what I was doing was wrong, but I wasn't playing games out there, I was trying to access your system. I can't help myself. At school they call me Hacker.'

'Why?'

'Because I can hack into any system,' he said, at last finding the confidence to look up. Computers were all he knew about, all he felt comfortable with.

'How interesting,' she said sweetly. 'Why don't you come over here and show me what you can do on my computer?'

Sitting in front of the terminal Peter was transformed. He logged on and started drawing up files from all over the system. 'Here's the horoscopes for next Tuesday,' his fingers played over the keyboard like a concert pianist, 'a memo sent by one of your reporters to the finance department and something about the Minister for Education.' He turned around and looked up at Sharon who was peering over his shoulder.

'Well, well, aren't we a clever boy? You're brilliant, Peter. But that's all a bit too easy, isn't it? All those files are inside the *Daily Tribune* system. Can you access anything from, say, the *Sunday Tribune*?'

''Course I can, if you give me a minute.' And he swivelled back to his keyboard and started work.

'How about next Sunday's health column?' he said and it appeared on the screen.

'Too easy. Find me something they're trying to hide, if you can,' Sharon goaded.

'But how will I know if they're trying to hide something?' he asked. 'Are there any recurring words I can run a programme on?'

'Try "splash", babe,' Sharon said. 'That's journalist-speak for fucking good story.'

Five minutes later: 'How about this?' he asked, proudly displaying the *Sunday Tribune*'s splash story for the next weekend.

'Although why they put a story about the Government in the gardening queue, I don't know.'

Sharon could feel herself getting excited. 'You really are brilliant,' she squealed. 'But can't people find out you've been accessing their files?'

'My other nickname is the Lone Ranger. I leave no footprints.'

'You're so clever,' she said, rubbing his shoulders and watching his erection return. 'Now I want you to do me a teensie-weensie little favour. I want you to show a friend of mine how to do this. His name's Pete as well – Pete Feretti. He's not a journalist so it's okay. Let's say in my office at seven tonight?'

'Does that mean I can stay?' Peter asked when he reached the door.

'So long as we keep this a secret, you can stay as long as you want.'

Sharon sat back at her desk. In the excitement, she had completely forgotten her humiliation by Holloway that morning. Now the memory returned, painfully. She sat and brooded then called Roxanne.

'Get Feretti,' was all she said. Sharon smoked and waited. He minced into the room a few minutes later, the big, obsequious smile fading from his face when he saw the state she was in.

'That bitch got to Holloway before me,' she spat out.

'Got to him before you with what?'

'The fucking plans for the fucking seven-day operation.'

'Oh, no. How could she have known what you were doing?'

Sharon leaned across the desk towards him, eyes squinting either in anger or against the stream of smoke rising from her cigarette, one tangerine curl falling forward over her flushed cheeks, her voice low and menacing. 'I don't know. All I do know is I want her destroyed.'

Feretti slithered into the seat opposite and opened his hands wide. 'Whatever you want, boss. I'm your man.'

'What I want is a twenty-four-hour tail on her, in the office and out. I want to know everything that treacherous little cow is up to, everyone she's fucking, everyone she has fucked. Let's do the Full Monty on her; dig up her past, check her medical records, bank accounts, the lot. I want pictures and I want tapes. Bug her office. I don't care what it costs. From now on she's not going to fart without me knowing. And no one, do you understand, *no one*, must know what we're up to.'

'You've got it,' he said. 'I know a man who knows a man. I'll write it off on the news budget, but you'll have to sign it off.' The news budget for the *Daily Tribune* was in excess of £2 million. A lot of their stories came from sources that could not be named. It was commonplace to put through a payment for surveillance work on a story that ultimately failed to appear. You could get the best tip in the world but without proof, pictures or incriminating comings and goings, there was no story. Sometimes a stakeout lasted weeks with nothing to show for it but an entry in the budget.

'The morning hasn't been a complete disaster though,' Sharon said. 'Be in my office at seven tonight. There's a little surfer I'd like you to meet.'

'Oh, Sharon, you know how to spoil a boy. Is he cute? Is he young? Well hung?'

'Fortunately for you he's probably not even sixteen yet – fucking cute, great arse. Unfortunately for you, he's also straight.'

'They're the ones I love best! I've given more blow jobs to straights than most guys have had hot dinners. And the younger the better. Almost sweet sixteen. Can't wait. See you tonight.'

# Chapter Three

Georgina was at her desk when the phone rang, Steve saying Roxanne was on line one.

'Hi, Georgie, looking great today,' she simpered. Georgina really hated the way she did that. She knew she hadn't seen Roxanne all day so how the hell did Sharon's secretary know she was 'looking great'? The *Sunday Tribune* was located on the floor above the *Daily*. And no one, absolutely no one called her 'Georgie' unless they were friends or family.

'Sharon was wondering if you could get together sometime this morning for a chat,' Roxanne said.

On her way up in the lift, Georgina wondered which Sharon she would get today. A lot depended on what she'd eaten the night before and consequently how many slimming pills she'd taken that morning. The mood swings were frighteningly unpredictable.

Many had remarked that there was something of the evening about Sharon – a bit dim, but liable to explode into colour at any moment.

She walked into Sharon's office and immediately saw she was in for Claudia Schiffer. The sleeves were down, always a barometer to mood, and she was sitting calmly behind her desk, one cigarette in her mouth, another crushed out and still smoking in the ashtray. One of her double-or-nothing shoulder pads was slightly askew. Sharon believed that some things never went out of fashion and always wore an extra pair of Dallas-sized shoulder pads.

No sign of rage, Georgina thought. Sharon's skin, under the masses of red curls, was that amazing sunbed-induced tangerine, but no bumps.

'Darling, sit down, let me get you a coffee.' She waved her arm imperiously at the chair opposite her desk. As usual, Georgina ignored the command and stretched out on the sofa instead. It was all a game, Sharon seated in her throne on wheels, specially made in deep burgundy fake leather. She had read somewhere that it intimidated people to be looked down upon and had ensured that all the chairs in her office were six inches shorter than her own and extremely narrow, so people sat hunched and uncomfortable in them.

'What's all this I hear about you talking to the staff this morning?' she asked in her cutesy, baby-doll voice, so unattractive in a woman of her age – the wrong side of forty but admitting to thirty-three. 'No one wants you to leave, babe, especially me. Are you unhappy?'

Georgina kicked off her shoes and stretched out her legs on the sofa. Sharon's eyes narrowed, partly because the younger woman had such great legs and partly because she saw this as an act of defiance. Georgina was behaving as though she owned the place.

'You're so supportive, Sharon,' Georgina said, holding her gaze. 'I'm far from unhappy, but it's sweet of you to ask.'

'But the story saying you were leaving?'

'Don't believe everything you read in the papers. Why on earth would I want to resign? I couldn't be more secure. My paper is the strongest in the group, I'm the only editor who has delivered year-on-year growth and I have Douglas's backing. I would have thought the only editors thinking of resigning are the ones whose papers aren't performing.'

Georgina couldn't resist it. Both women knew figures for the *Daily Tribune* were down and no amount of television advertising seemed to be able to rescue the situation.

'I just want you to know that I'm behind you all the way.' Sharon said quickly, refusing to rise to the obvious dig at her own paper's performance.

Yeah, behind my back with a sheaf of knives, Georgina

thought. 'And you can count on me to be as supportive to you as you have always been to me,' she said sweetly, the smile never leaving her face but not reaching her eyes either.

'Babe, I'm only trying to help. I've been an editor for a long time, you know, and I've got very good instincts.'

For the gutter, Georgina thought. Sharon was the first female tabloid editor of a national daily newspaper, but that wasn't enough for her. Now she wanted the most successful title in the group and to be the first female editor of a seven-day tabloid. Sharon was big on firsts.

What was this charade all about anyway? Georgina thought. She knew Sharon wanted her out and Sharon knew she knew. Holloway was certain to have told her that Georgina had put forward a seven-day plan. That was the way he worked, pitting people against each other. Still they went through the motions.

'Well, I for one am glad you're not leaving, Georgina. God knows there are few enough women in this business as it is. We have to support each other.'

By the time Georgina left the office she felt nauseous – the hypocrisy of it all. Sharon was a renowned misogynist. There was not a single woman executive left working on the *Daily Tribune*. She had sacked them all.

Pete Feretti was waiting in Georgina's office when she returned from the meeting. He wanted to run through the details for that weekend's promotion, apparently.

When he left she did not notice the innocuous-looking fountain pen he'd slipped into the bottom shelf of her in-trays. Everyone knew Georgina never got through that pile and with any luck the pen would lie there unnoticed until Feretti had time to set up a more reliable bug.

The sight of Georgina's longer, slimmer limbs made Sharon reach for the slimming pills in her top drawer. She gulped two down with a cup of cold coffee and screamed for Roxanne to make her some more.

In her own mind, there was nothing personal about her

determination to destroy Georgina. It was purely business. Sharon wanted total control and Georgina was standing in her way.

There was only one thing that really unnerved the older woman: the sight of Georgina's apparently effortless slimness. She didn't diet, she didn't exercise. It wasn't fair.

Life had never been fair to Sharon in terms of body image. As far back as she could remember it had been an endless battle with the bulge. She was the Monica Lewinsky of her generation. There wasn't a diet in existence she had not tried, then given up in a wave of ravenous hunger, only to pile back on the pounds she had starved off, and more.

As a child she had tried to disguise her lumpy body by dressing like a boy.

The first time Sharon actually realised she did not want to be regarded as 'one of the boys' was when she was twelve-years-old, shopping for tracksuits at the local superstore with her two elder brothers.

Wearing boy's clothes had been part of her camouflage until then. It made her somehow less of a disappointment to her mother, who had always wanted a beautiful little girl, and more acceptable to her father, who seemed unable to communicate with her in any way other than as a boy.

The shop assistant, harassed in the busy sports store, was impatient to serve them and go off for her break. She rummaged through the racks of tracksuits and pulled two out for Sharon's brothers.

'We don't stock clothes for *larger* boys,' she said dismissively, waving a hand at Sharon. 'You'll have to try the Big Boys shop around the corner.'

It was one of those moments that cut through a child's heart like a knife through lard – slowly, clumsily, not a clean cut.

It's hard to trace back to the precise moment when a young girl realises she has a weight problem, the knowledge that in her gym shorts her legs are not quite like the other girls'. But from that moment on, it consumes.

After the incident in the sports store, Sharon went home in

tears. She ran to her mother, to feel the comfort of her embrace. There was little warmth to be had from those slender, sinewy arms; the pert breasts. The tears rolled down the child's red chubby cheeks, her swollen eyes disappearing even further into their roundness.

'Mummy,' she sobbed, 'the lady in the shop said I was a boy.' She choked again on her tears. 'And she said I was *fat*.'

Sharon had expected a passionate denial from her mother, outrage that would send her down to the shop and have that terrible girl sacked. Instead her mother led her by the hand into the parental bedroom and stood her in front of the large floor-to-ceiling mirrors covering the wardrobes.

'It may have been unkind,' she said in her painstakingly acquired middle-class accent, 'but is it true? Take a long hard look at yourself, my girl, and tell me – are you fat?'

Sharon looked in the mirror at the short, square little girl, dressed in jeans and a sweat shirt, her hair short and greasy, the big puffy cheeks, the big puffy thighs, and cried some more.

'Take a good look, Sharon,' her mother said, smoothing the creases from her own perfect size 10 frock and tidying a loose lock in her carefully bouffant hairdo. Instead of looking at herself, the image that was too painful and too familiar, Sharon looked instead at her mother, her beautiful, slim mother.

Sharon's mother Marjorie played tennis three times a week, twice with her girlfriends and once with her personal trainer, a strapping young man half her age and full of flattery. He knew how to work the Essex-Ladies-Made-Good brigade.

She was in perfect shape – thin, toned and tanned. Her makeup was immaculate: a heavy mask of bronze foundation and shimmering blusher, her eyes heavily lidded with midnight-blue shadow. Marjorie's brown hair was dyed to a golden blonde every two weeks, teased and sprayed into place five times a week.

'It's time I took you in hand young lady,' she said, grabbing Sharon by her chubby arms. Sharon always remembered that this was the closest she had ever felt to her mother. She was aware of the scent of Chanel No. 5 which almost masked the smell of cigarettes.

'We can never make you pretty,' Marjorie said, grabbing a large pinch of flesh on her cheek and squeezing it, 'but we can make you slim.'

And that was Sharon's initiation into the world of crash diets, slimming pills and self-loathing.

Georgina was on the phone when Mike burst in waving a large brown envelope at her. It was late on Tuesday morning. The news list had been unexciting, but he was excited now. She ended the call.

'How would you feel about splashing on a new Labour Minister, his mistress and two love children? This arrived today, hand delivered at reception. Take a look.'

Inside was part of a private investigator's report on the Minister, Tony Blakehurst, Mr Family Man. It was a summary of his affair with a thirty-two-year-old blonde employee, copies of the birth certificates of her two children – no name entered for the father, details of his wife and two sons. It was dynamite, especially so soon after the election and the Prime Minister's warning to all MPs that he would not tolerate sleaze in his party or his government. Yet the evidence it contained was inconclusive.

The envelope also contained pictures of Blakehurst and his wife, the usual happy family constituency shots set in their carefully tended back garden, and pictures of the mistress and her children.

'It's a great story if we can prove it Mike, but there's not enough evidence here. It wouldn't get past our lawyers. We'll just have to prove it ourselves,' said Georgina, studying the pictures of his wife and mistress. 'Isn't it weird how often the mistress looks like a slightly younger version of the wife? It's not as though she's some gorgeous nubile temptress. It amazes me how many men get away with these double lives. You'd think the wife would clock he wasn't around a lot.'

'None so blind, George,' Mike said. 'She's probably happily tucked up in Hampstead with her multi-million pound life. Why rock the boat? There's something else. Whoever sent us this must want to get Blakehurst bad. See the note at the end.'

Georgina read it aloud: 'If you require further substantiation of the story, place an ad in the Personal column of *The Times* saying *Susie, I miss you, contact me on* ... Add your private extension.'

'This is Toy Town, Mike. People don't drop off brown paper envelopes containing information that can destroy a Minister of the Government any more. It feels like a vendetta to me. Check it out anyway. It's a fantastic story if we can prove it. And place that ad.'

Brown envelopes did still arrive at the *Sunday Tribune*, but they usually contained poetry about vegetables from patients in care or diatribes about noisy neighbours or pictures of psychic pets.

'Remember that story that was sent to the *News of the World* a couple of weeks ago about the former Tory Minister and his mistress?' Mike said. 'I was talking to my mate on the news desk there and he said it arrived just like this: brown envelope, hand delivered. It was a diary of every tryst they'd had in the past three months, plus addresses and times of where they would be meeting in the next week. That's how they managed to get the video of them in bed. They rented one of the hotel rooms the couple were going to stay in and put a hidden camera at the foot of the bed. The reporter took the room again the next day, removed the evidence, then shared it with the world.'

'Revenge being a dish best served up in a national newspaper with a readership of ten million,' Georgina said and laughed. 'You're right, Mike, someone has gone to a lot of trouble to try and nail Blakehurst. Let's do the Full Monty on him. Get a private investigator on his tail twenty-four hours a day. And the mistress. Get the boys digging.'

Andrew Carson's red Jaguar XK8 was already at the flat when Sharon's driver pulled up outside. 'Come back in two hours,' she said and smiled affectionately at the personalised number-plate SHA5 as her car drove off. She took one final look in her compact mirror and walked, a little unsteadily after one too many vodkas, to the front door.

Thank God for Andy, thank God for power sex, she thought as she hitched her black mini-skirt higher, rubbed her deeply scuffed high-heeled Shelley courts on the back of her calves and pressed the front door bell. As she waited for Carson to open the door, she leaned forward from the waist and hoisted up her breasts. They were bursting out of the Wonderbra – large, pendulous orbs of flesh, tanned to a gentle orange, squeezed together to create an obscenely deep cleavage.

The routine was always the same: sex first, talk later, no food. Sharon was desperate to keep her new figure – Carson would not have wanted sex with her the way she'd looked a couple of years ago – and the slimming pills could only do so much.

Andrew Carson opened the door. He was a powerfully built man, had been a rugby player, but the years and the drink had taken their toll and much of the muscle was now covered in a layer of fat. He still looked good in a suit, cut carefully to cover the paunch. A beard covered the double chins.

Now in his late-fifties, he had been married for almost thirty years. His wife lived in Yorkshire and was completely unsuspecting of his affairs, of which there had been many. He kept a flat in London where he spent most of the week.

A workaholic and tough businessman, Carson was the General Manager of the Tribune Group. Douglas Holloway regarded him as one of his closest friends and allies there.

Sharon had hardly taken a step up the stairs to the flat when Carson's hand reached up the inside of her thigh, oblivious to the layer of cellulite that bulged above her stay-up stockings. She twisted around, slightly drunk, almost seductive.

'No knickers!' he cried, like a small boy finding a lost marble. He pushed her back on the stairs and entered her with such force she felt the side seam of her mini-skirt split.

'Oh, Andy, this is just what I need. Harder, harder,' she cried, knowing the harder he went the quicker it would be over.

Their sex life was frantic, snatched, loveless, and never conducted in bed. 'I'd feel as though I was cheating on my wife if I screwed you in bed,' Andrew solemnly told her.

So they did it in his office, her office, his flat, and occasionally, very occasionally, the back seat of a black cab.

Unusual for a man his age, he was remarkably virile. Usual for a man of his generation, he was astonishingly selfish.

Foreplay was for sissies. Oral sex was something administered *to* men *by* women. He always came, she never did, and he happily mistook her cries – three minutes after entry – for those of a satisfied mistress.

Sharon had read and perfected 'The Art of the Moan', even serialised it in a newspaper once.

Carson grunted and buried his face in her cleavage. He noticed and was excited by the smell of stale cigarettes masked by perfume, the sheen of sweat, and licked her breasts as he pounded away at her. The sex over, he stood up, zipped his trousers and stepped over her to walk upstairs.

The Kensington flat was a shrine to eighties excess: the polished black wooden floor, bold geometric monochrome rugs on every surface including the walls, huge steel-framed mirrors. The long, low coffee table, dining table and bookcases were glass and shiny chrome.

Carson walked to the black lacquer imitation Chinese drinks cabinet and poured two whiskies. They sat together on the low-slung leather sofa.

'So Georgina's still there?' Carson said. 'I know they met last night for a drink.'

'That's when the treacherous little bitch must have given him her plans for the seven-day operation. That fucking bastard! When will he realise that *I* am the only one who can edit the *Sunday Tribune*?' Sharon hissed, pacing up and down the room.

'You know what he's nervous about,' Carson told her. 'The *Sunday Tribune*'s his *Sunday Times*. It's outselling the *Daily* almost two to one and he won't risk it. Sales have increased since Georgina became editor and so have advertising revenues. Why would he jeopardise all that? You're going to have to be very clever – squeeze her out, cut off her lifelines, all your usual tricks. Question her appointments, undermine her staff, interfere a lot. That's what she hates most. Be very sweet about it when you question her staff levels and editorial budget with Holloway. Don't attack her publicly, Holloway won't have it.'

'One way or another I'll get that bitch out. I want the *Sunday*, I *will* have the *Sunday*. It will be the jewel in my tiara.'

'First things first, Sharon. Right now you've got to get Georgina out.'

'From tonight on I'll watch her every move. She won't piss without my knowing. I've got her office bugged and there's always my pet poodle Feretti to keep an eye on her. It's only when she's with Holloway I'm in the dark.'

Sharon was standing at the window now, smoking a cigarette and rolling her tongue after every drag, the way old men do savouring a large cigar. No wonder her skin's so bad, he thought. That must be her third pack of Marlboro today.

She picked up her tumbler of whisky, raised it to the moon and like a modern-day, leather-miniskirted Scarlett O'Hara, said: 'As God is my witness, I will take over the *Tribune*, all of it.'

It was all Carson could do not to laugh and he stifled an urge to say: 'Frankly, my dear, I don't give a damn.' Because he did in a way. He was fond of Sharon and admired her ruthlessness.

He remembered asking her once why she had never married, never had children.

Sharon was absolutely clear about it all – no husbands, no kids and no regrets, she had said. They were all bad career moves. Men and babies made you soft, took your eye off the ball. She was contemptuous of women who had families, believed they weren't committed, and consequently surrounded herself with male executives. Sharon had started in the business when women were lucky to be secretaries. She was a pioneer, a prophet bringing the message that women could succeed in this business. But, like Moses parting the sea, the moment the miracle of her success was performed, she closed the waters on all those following behind. She climbed the career ladder to the top then kicked it out from under her.

She was tougher than any man Carson had ever known. She even screwed like a man and he needed her now, to help him undermine Douglas Holloway. He had his own fish to fry . . .

It was early morning when Douglas called Georgina and asked her down to his office to discuss the Blakehurst story. He occupied what she called 'the presidential wing' on the thirty-first floor of

Tribune Tower. It was more like a small Manhattan apartment than an office.

She checked her lipstick and blotted the evening nose shine. The third aria of Verdi's *Il Trovatore* greeted her as she approached his office, the sunset over the City flooding the room with pale pink light. God, it made her homesick. The palette was softer, somehow washed out, but a sunset always made Georgina think of home.

The inner door to his office was open, the secretaries gone and she walked in to find Douglas alone at his desk. It was the most impersonal of offices: no family pictures, pathologically tidy, the walls lined with framed front pages of his newspapers. Looking around the room, Georgina suspected, not for the first time, that he was the kind of man who insisted his underpants were ironed and placed in colour-coded order in his drawers. There was something seriously anal about Douglas.

'Would you like a drink?' he asked and walked to the cupboard containing the hidden fridge.

'Oh, now that's a tough decision,' she replied. 'Of course I'd like a drink. Something dry and white.'

'Sparkling or still?' he asked.

'Champagne, Douglas? How generous. But isn't it a little early in the day. What are we celebrating, your acceptance of my seven-day proposal?' she said cheekily.

'I meant sparkling or still water. You know this is a dry office,' he said without a trace of humour.

'Sure is.'

'I thought we should get together and plan where to place the Blakehurst story to get the most publicity from television and radio.'

'Douglas, this is all a bit premature. We're nowhere near running the story yet, we haven't got enough evidence.'

'Well, I thought it was worth getting Becky in anyway to brief her, in case we can run it.' And on cue Becky Worthington appeared at the office door.

More Casablanca lily than English rose was how Georgina always thought of Becky – tall, slim, long legs, black shiny hair, dark grey eyes – but above all elegant, with the kind of poise money can't buy. Becky Worthington had class.

That was probably due to the fact that her father, Lord Worthington, was one of the wealthiest landowners in England, his property abutting Castle Howard in Yorkshire. But, despite Becky's privileged background, Georgina respected her. She didn't have to work and her salary as public relations executive to the Tribune titles was a pittance. Nevertheless, Becky had a sharp mind, a good commercial eye, and knew how to flog a story so that TV and radio news bulletins picked it up.

Georgina idly noticed Becky had put on a lot of weight recently and all of it around her stomach. The jacket of her Armani suit was long and flattering, yet it seemed to be straining at the front, although the short straight skirt showed off her still-perfect legs. Christ, she's not pregnant is she? Georgina thought and instantly ran through the consequences in her head. She knew Douglas was in love with Becky. He had admitted to the affair more than a year ago after Georgina had bumped into them shopping together one Saturday afternoon. But he was still married to Kelly and Mrs Holloway was not a woman to give up easily.

The more she looked at Becky, the more Georgina was convinced she was pregnant. All the signs were there – long, concealing jacket over the big tummy, breasts where there were virtually none before, that look of total contentment.

'So where are we on Blakehurst?' Douglas asked.

'We put the ad in *The Times* and Susie turns out to be a man, taking instructions from another man in the room,' Georgina said, quickly switching her mind back to business.

'The problem is, I don't think they've got any more to give us. Lots of gossip about how he spends Saturday lunch with the mistress and the kids and his wife doesn't suspect a thing . . .' Ouch! This was all too close to home. After all, if Becky was pregnant with Douglas's child, *his* wife didn't suspect a thing.

He didn't even blink – too engrossed in the story. She went on: 'I've had a team working on it all week, well, more like the entire office. I think he suspects something. He hasn't put a foot wrong, hasn't gone near the Battersea house, but back to the matrimonial home in Hampstead every night. Unless we get lucky, really lucky, we can't run it.

'It's not like one of these stories where some bimbo decides she wants the money and talks, gives us letters, tapes his phone calls, videos them having sex. His wife is respectable, even his mistress is respectable. And he's got the perfect cover to be with her. He employs her.' God, enough was enough Georgina thought, this was all too uncomfortable. She muttered something about proofs she had to check and escaped quickly.

Nine o'clock on Friday evening, Georgina stood looking out at the city night line. From her corner office on the twenty-eighth floor, she gazed down towards the dome of St Paul's, the bridges arching towards the Houses of Parliament, the buildings erratically lit.

She was thinking about her partner. God, how she hated that word, but what did you say these days? Lover, significant other, significantly someone else's, mistress, master, slave, boyfriend, girlfriend, bit on the side, bit on top? Yuck! She sat doodling for a while, trying to invent a new term, when her private line rang. Only Douglas, her family and closest friends knew that number, so she was surprised when she heard Les Strangelove's unmistakable Australian drawl. Strangelove was chief executive of the Tribune's advertising agency, McLairds, and probably the best friend Douglas Holloway had in the world.

'How ya goin' Georgie?' he said and didn't wait for a response. 'Listen girl, I've just had Tony Blakehurst on the phone. You remember, he's a mate of mine. He says one of your reporters is up at his house, wanting to talk to him about a mistress or something. What the hell's going on?'

'Les, I'm just in the middle of something. Can I call you back in five minutes?'

'You gotta call me back, Georgie, he's beside himself. You heard the Prime Minister's warning to the party about the new morality. He'll be out on his arse if you run this and he's waited so long to get into Government. Promise you'll call me back?'

It took Georgina two minutes to set up the tape recorder and check it was working. She buzzed Mike in from the news desk, briefed him, then made the return call. Les answered immediately.

37

'Les, why are you involved in this?' Georgina asked.

'So it's true. Bloody hell, Georgie, this is terrible, you'll destroy him. He's a close mate of mine. You must have met him with me some time, him and his wife? Lovely woman. And they've got two kids. What the hell is the story?'

'I'm sorry if he's a friend of yours, but he's also been a bit too friendly with a very attractive blonde who works as his personal assistant and public relations co-ordinator. And he's had two children by her. I've got the page one proof in front of me, and pages two, three, four and five. I'll read them to you, if you like.

SCANDAL OF
MINISTER, HIS
MISTRESS AND
TWO LOVE KIDS

BLAIR'S MR FAMILY VALUES CHEATS
WIFE WITH BUSTY BLONDE PR GIRL

THEY'RE SO IN LOVE, MISTRESS'
CHILDREN EVEN CALL HIM DADDY

'You're not going to run that are you?' Les was getting hysterical now. 'Look, isn't there anything I can do to stop it?'

'No, Les, there isn't. If we can prove it, we run it. This is one of Blair's senior Ministers, Mr Family Man. He's always setting up photo-opportunities with his wife and kids, when in fact he's got a mistress and two love children. It's a bloody big story.'

The line went quiet for a moment. Strangelove always had to stop talking to think.

'The real problem, Georgie, is that Tony is also a close friend of Douglas's. Let me put this plainly. The Minister knows everything about Douglas, Becky and the baby and about his business deals. If you publish, he'll blow the lot.'

'What on earth are you talking about? What baby?' she asked knowing the answer already.

'It's a big secret at the moment but Becky's pregnant.'

It wasn't unusual in this business for people to try to blackmail you, or threaten you, but this was something else. Georgina was actually less worried about Becky and the baby, that would just be embarrassing. After all, only politicians and priests lost their jobs for having affairs. No, the real killer was the hint about Holloway's business dealings. In the cut-throat world of newspaper publishing, the City admired bosses who were ruthless. It came with the territory. But any hint of corruption and their career was over. There could never be another Maxwell.

'I don't know what you're talking about, Les. All I can say again is that if I have enough evidence, I will run the story. Call me tomorrow.'

Georgina looked up into Mike's face. She'd almost forgotten he was sitting there. 'Let's just keep this between ourselves,' she said and he nodded.

'I'm taking a break for half an hour, George. Old contact of mine, the kind it's best you don't know about, has something for me. Says it's urgent.'

'I hope it's a story, Mike, because the way Blakehurst is folding around our ears, we'll need it.'

'The back-up splash is standing up anyway. We've got a copy of the leaked document outlining the Government's plans for another cut to single mothers' benefits next year. It's a bloody good story.'

'It's a good story, Mike, but not a great one. Blakehurst is a great story.'

When he'd left, Georgina played back Les's tape, still disbelieving about the clear implication. She had known Douglas Holloway for many years. He was a hard man, sometimes unfair, but never crooked. I have to tell him, she thought. His phones were on answer service. She left a message saying she needed to see him early tomorrow in the office.

The phone rang and it was Mike. 'Meet me in the Last Chance now,' he said with a conspiratorial air that almost made Georgina laugh.

'I was just packing up to leave, can't we discuss it on the phone on my way home?'

'No,' was all he said. Odd behaviour from Mike, Georgina thought as she packed her briefcase. The Last Chance was a bar around the corner from the Tribune building. Mike was waiting, a pint in front of him, a glass of Chardonnay ready for her.

'What's all the mystery about?' she asked, sitting down.

'You're not going to like it. My contact, ex-copper, the guy I met tonight . . . it wasn't a story, George. It's cost me plenty but I think you'll see it's money well spent.'

'Quit the suspense, what is it?'

'You're being tailed, around the clock. That's why I couldn't talk over the phone. I'm sure your office will be bugged too.'

Georgina sat in silence, staring at her friend.

'My contact wouldn't say who was behind it, just that it was someone close to home.'

'Sharon.'

'I know she wants you out, but this is ridiculous,' Mike protested.

'She wants dirt so she can discredit me to the board. There are a few games going on behind the scenes you don't know about. That's what the story in the *Telegraph* was all about. I didn't tell you because you didn't need to know. I found out that Sharon was presenting a plan to Douglas for a seven-day operation. A friend in finance gave me a copy of her proposal, so I bettered it and got to Douglas first. He must have told her. Of course he'd tell her. Now she's decided to play dirty. Well, two can play it that way, Mike.'

'What do you mean?'

'Get a tail on *her*, just outside the office. I'm sure she's screwing Andrew Carson. Let's prove it. See what else we can find out too.' Georgina's mobile phone rang. It was the late news man.

'George, you're not going to believe this but I've just got the early copy of the *Saturday Tribune* and Sharon's splashed on our single mothers exclusive.'

'Damn her! How the hell did she get hold of that? We had it to ourselves.'

'I've just had our source on the phone and he's furious. They didn't want the story leaked until Sunday, to coincide with the Conference in Brighton. He says no one from the *Daily Tribune* contacted him or his office. It stinks, George. We've got a leak. It was hardly changed from our copy in the secret queue. The same split infinitives and everything.'

Georgina ended the call and explained the situation to Mike. 'She's hacked into our system.'

Georgina couldn't help but admire Sharon, the way a professional boxer admires a pub brawler. There was no doubt in her mind that Sharon was a fighter, that she would never give up without being knocked out. For tenacity and strength they were well matched. They both had the killer instinct and both desperately wanted to win. Georgina knew she was smarter than Sharon and that was her greatest weapon. But smart wasn't enough. Her opponent would do anything to win. Anything. And that made her dangerous.

'I'll get the computer people in first thing in the morning to see if there are any footprints on the system, then contact Security to get your office swept for bugs,' Mike suggested.

'No,' Georgina said thoughtfully. 'Let's assume my office *is* bugged. We already know I'm being watched. If we get rid of the bug, they'll know we're on to them. Let's leave everything the way it is and carry on as normal. We're going to turn this situation to our advantage, Mike, but it's going to get dirty, really dirty.'

They sat discussing concealment strategies for their stories for more than an hour before the barman called last orders.

'Walk me to me car will you, Mike?' Georgina asked. He knew this was a signal that she needed to talk to him privately, away from prying ears. When they reached the street and she turned to him, Mike saw an unfamiliar expression in her eyes. She looked scared.

'There's something else I need you to do for me,' she said, staring up at the night sky, so heavy and low it was almost pressing on her shoulders. 'This private investigator Sharon's put on me – he'll pull everything, including my medical records, right?'

'Standard procedure, George.'

'Can you arrange for records to be wiped?'

'It's difficult, but I can get it sorted. Just tell me where and when?' It never occurred to Mike to ask her why. Of course he was curious, all his journalistic instincts prickling, but this was George. He loved her and would protect her. This he didn't need to know about.

'The Hale Clinic, my records, admitted Tuesday November 22, 1987, checked out six weeks later,' she said in a whisper. 'Mike, I don't want anyone to know . . .'

He cut her off almost impatiently. 'No one ever will know, George. You're safe with me. Come tomorrow morning there will be no record of your ever being there.'

# Chapter Four

'Wake up, sleepy head. It's six o'clock and the papers are here.' Georgina groaned, was vaguely aware her hair was being stroked, felt the soft kiss on her lips, smelt the coffee.

'Just another five minutes,' she pleaded. They played this game every morning and always ended up in bed for another half an hour. It took her that long to wake up.

She sipped her coffee then rolled over and snuggled into the warm body beside her. Belinda felt great to her, so soft and slim. But Georgina started slightly, as she always did in those early waking moments, at the realisation she was in bed with a woman.

'Ross phoned last night, left a message on the machine. He said you're having supper together. Why do you still see him, George? I thought it was all over?' Ross had been Georgina's lover for three years, until she met Belinda.

He couldn't accept that she'd left him for a woman – for another man or for her job perhaps, but not that.

Georgina sat up in bed, took Belinda's beautiful face in her hands and said: 'Ross is just a friend. I love him as a friend. I love you as a partner. This dinner is a work thing. You know I'd rather take you with me, but the newspaper world isn't ready for its first openly bisexual editor.'

'I understand, George, but you know I don't approve. How is it that it's okay for most of the men who run newspapers to be screwing anything that moves, yet a monogamous relationship between two women is scandalous?

'We've gone through this a million times and you know the reasons – prejudice, ignorance, fear. But that's the way it is. For now we have to stay in the closet. To be honest Belinda, we have to be more careful than ever. There's something I found out last night. You're not going to believe it, I can hardly believe it myself, but Sharon is having me followed.'

Belinda looked at her with an expression of utter disbelief.

'Mike found out,' Georgina went on. 'She's determined to get some dirt to discredit me with the board. I'm so sorry, darling, but you won't be able to stay over at my flat for a while.'

'I don't believe this!' Belinda said, more hurt than angry. 'First we have to sneak around like we're having a grubby affair and now you tell me we can't even sleep together? This is too much, George, you're asking too much.'

'Belinda, please, I could lose everything if Sharon gets evidence we're having an affair.'

'No, George, you wouldn't lose everything, you wouldn't lose me,' Belinda said through her tears. 'You could lose some credibility with your bigoted colleagues. But you can't lose your job. There are laws to forbid that sort of behaviour now, or haven't you heard?'

'Be realistic. I'm hardly going to take the Tribune Group to court in a high-profile sexual discrimination case now am I? This kind of prejudice is more subtle. I wouldn't lose my job, but I could forget about promotion. I'd be sidelined in a second. I'm just asking you to understand and to be more careful. I can't talk to you properly on the office phone as that's bugged as well. It won't be for long baby. Please.'

Belinda said nothing.

'Maybe when things get a bit more secure, maybe then. I don't know. Do we have to discuss it now? Couldn't we make love instead?' said Georgina and bent to kiss Belinda's breast. However much you teach them, a man simply does not know how to kiss a nipple properly, she thought as Belinda's went hard in her mouth. She loved the feel of another woman's body against her, the softness where their breasts pressed together. Slowly she moved from Belinda's nipple to her ridiculously flat stomach, then lower, kept kissing until she came, pushing her pelvis against Georgina's mouth in rhythmic movements.

An onlooker, some time later, would have found the sight of the two women wandering around Georgina's Notting Hill flat intriguing. Two feminine, good-looking women, not a hint of masculinity about their bodies or attitudes. Sexy. To many the most unlikely of partners.

When people described Belinda, they often overlooked her appearance – shiny brown hair, bright blue eyes, impish smile. The startling thing about her was her energy for life. She lived each day as if it might be her last, squeezing every drop of enjoyment from it. Being near her was like being close to a source of heat. That was what had first attracted Georgina to her.

Belinda was slim in a boyish way that was still incredibly sexy. Her breasts were small with impatient nipples always pushing out for attention. She never wore a bra, and her body was athletic without being muscular. Georgina had a lot more curves: breasts that fitted into the classic champagne glass and were still in good shape for thirty-five; she had a small waist and a classic hour-glass figure. Her breasts couldn't quite pass the pencil test any more, but they were still one of her assets. Her hair was light brown, straight and glossy, cut monthly into a sleek bob, high at the back to show off her long neck. She was no stunner, but had a power to her looks with that large mouth, the deep blue eyes, the high cheek-bones. Those who loved her found her truly beautiful.

They were Lipstick Lesbians, not a pair of overalls, pierced body parts or trace of underarm hair between them. Belinda preferred to think of them as Bi Babes, since both had had affairs with men. This was Georgina's first lesbian affair and she was warming to it.

She had always got on well with women. Unlike many of her contemporaries, who saw other women as either professional or sexual rivals, she had always had a close circle of girlfriends, both back home and in London.

When Georgina and Belinda first met they were instantly drawn to each other, but not in a sexual way. It was during a particularly bad time with Ross that the two women met at a dinner party.

Georgina at first thought Belinda was beautiful, but only in the way that she had often found women beautiful before. Throughout dinner her eyes were drawn to the lively young woman and every time Georgina looked across, Belinda was looking back.

The progress of their relationship was effortless. They became close friends, then best friends, then lovers. If Georgina was honest with herself, she could not see their relationship lasting a lifetime. But then, she could not imagine anything lasting a lifetime, especially not love. It was more a case of loving Belinda now and enjoying the moment.

Georgina had always kept her love life under wraps. No one was ever quite sure who she was seeing, but everyone would be shocked that her current lover was a woman.

Tabloid journalism had always been a homophobic world and it was not until recently that gay men had achieved some kind of acceptance there. But gay women? And a bisexual female editor? It was unheard of. Georgina knew this was one secret she had to keep, especially now that Sharon was watching her like a hawk.

After her marriage failed, her love life had been pretty harmonious. She was a serial monogamist and had enjoyed a string of long-term but ultimately non-committed relationships. She ran stories about women like her – the non-committers. They were a new breed of highly paid, intelligent, independent women who loved men but didn't really need them.

She had an instinctive radar which could pick out a fellow non-committer at fifty paces. They were the most attractive men to Georgina, because ultimately she could blame them for the breakdown of the relationship.

She had only been passionately in love once, with a man she'd met on her first newspaper. He was the one who ended it. And he had broken Georgina's heart. She married, quickly, on the rebound, and the marriage was a disaster.

Georgina was twenty-four when she met Derek Gregson in the *Herald*'s bar in Sydney. In the beginning, it was a union of unequals, she the struggling cub reporter, he the feted gossip columnist for Sydney's largest circulation newspaper. He was like a tall version of Tom Cruise: slicked-back black hair, dark blue eyes and a hole in his left earlobe where the diamond stud used to be.

Derek had a way, a very loving way, of making her feel she was lucky to have him. If she was honest with herself, Georgina did feel lucky to have him. It wasn't until the marriage was over that she could recognise his subtle abuse of her. She remembered one night when they were attending a black-tie ball for a visiting celebrity. They had arranged to meet at the bar of the hotel and when Georgina arrived Derek was holding court, surrounded by women hanging off his every word and his every available body part.

She walked in, feeling uncomfortable in the little black dress she had bought that day from the local department store. Georgina's salary hardly stretched to keeping her in work clothes, and the cheap frock was all she could afford. She felt shabby next to the other women and stood outside the circle of devotees until Derek noticed her. Her husband did not rise from his seat, just motioned for her to come over. When she was standing in front of him, he inspected her slowly then put up one hand to touch the side of her face.

'Look at you,' he said lovingly. 'Your mouth's too big, your cheekbones are too high, your hair looks as though you've just got out of bed, but put it all together and . . . I love you.'

When Georgina got her first big break on the same newspaper as her husband and was working nights, he became annoyed that she wasn't around when he needed her, which was most of the time. Derek had perfected needy. A series of exclusives put her career on a fast upward curve and she was spending more and more time away from home. Georgina was gaining confidence and Derek resented it. He wanted her dependent on him. He had married an insecure young woman, and did not like what she was becoming – independent of him. That wasn't part of the deal.

One night he phoned her in the office at what he knew was the worst possible time, half an hour before deadline. She was frantically typing the last paragraphs to the next day's front page story with her news editor leaning over her shoulder, barking instructions.

'It's your husband, Georgina,' another reporter said, handing the phone to her.

'Tell him I'll call back in half an hour,' she said as the news editor glowered at her.

'He's insisting on talking to you.'

Georgina grabbed the phone. 'Sweetheart, I can't talk now, I'm on deadline.'

'It's eight o'clock,' Derek said. 'The dinner starts at eight-thirty. You'd better be there.' He was angry and already drunk. Georgina recognised all the signs.

'I can't possibly be there by then,' she said. 'I told you this morning that I'd get there as soon as I've finished work, which will be around ten.'

'If you can't be there by eight-thirty like all the proper wives, then don't fucking come at all,' he said and slammed down the phone. It never got any better.

Derek blamed her work, she blamed his drinking. His affair with his secretary gave her the excuse to leave.

Georgina had learned very early in her life that it was incredibly difficult to combine her career with a relationship. It took a special kind of man, or woman, to put up with a partner whose job was as demanding as another lover, and as time-consuming.

Thank God for Belinda, she thought, watching her later as she moved, humming softly, through the airy living room on this gloriously sunny morning.

Douglas called her at 8 am on the way into the office. 'What did you want to talk to me about?'

Georgina glanced at the pool driver in the front seat and said: 'Not now, I'll see you when you get into the office. Call me and I'll come up.'

An hour later she was sitting in his office. It was eerily quiet, no one around, most of the lights off, Bizet's *The Pearlfishers* playing in the background. He always worked Saturdays.

'Do you realise, Georgina, that this is one of the finest operatic duets for tenor and baritone ever written? It's called "Au Fond du Temple Saint",' he said, leaning back in his chair, eyes slightly closed.

'Douglas, I remember you when your musical collection consisted of compilation CDs of opera's greatest hits,' Georgina replied affectionately. 'Whatever happened to Tenors for a Tenner or Hot to Trot Opera?'

'Let's say my appreciation of fine music has developed since then. Everyone has to start somewhere.'

'Les Strangelove called me late last night to try and stop us running the Blakehurst story. Evidently they're good mates. There's something I want you to hear,' said Georgina, and started the tape. It was set at the critical point.

'The Minister knows everything about Douglas, Becky and the baby, and about his business deals. If you run the story, he'll blow the lot.'

Holloway didn't even flinch. He looked her straight in the eye and simply said: 'Georgina, I have nothing to hide. I have never been involved in shady business deals. If you have the evidence, run the story.'

'But, Douglas, what's all this about a baby?' she asked. 'Les said Becky is pregnant with your child.' He made no reply. 'Kelly will go berserk. This will hurt her so much. You of all people know how desperately she wanted your child.'

'You're right about one thing – only I know how much she wanted my child, and the truth is not very much at all. I don't want to discuss this.'

Georgina was stunned but not surprised. It *would* hurt him, personally, and Becky, if their affair were dragged through the tabloids. But they both knew any paper would need evidence to run that story and it would be very, very difficult to prove. There was no evidence unless Becky or Douglas talked. Even Kelly's word would not get past the lawyers, who would see it as an avenging wife's attack on her cheating husband and his mistress. Douglas Holloway's profile was too high and the potential libel damages too great for a newspaper to go after him now. Most importantly, he clearly had nothing to hide in his business dealings, Georgina thought.

'The problem is, I still don't have enough to run with the Blakehurst story. It's so frustrating because I know it's true. Anyway, we've still got today to work on it, we might get lucky.

And it will certainly hold. Where can I reach you tonight if I need you?'

'I'm hosting a dinner at the Savoy. Best if you don't call. I'll be with Kelly.'

Douglas Holloway's personal life was a mess. It had always been a mess. Three marriages and two children, plus one on the way, and none of them to his wives. That's what he called unlucky.

He rarely saw his children. The son had lived most of his life with his American mother in California and the daughter was at boarding school in Scotland.

His third marriage to the mesmerising Kelly Brockwell had not always been a disaster. The skinny kid from the rented brick duplex in the unfashionable outskirts of Montreal had once dreamed of having a woman like Kelly. She matched him in height but outshone him in every other way.

Always immaculately dressed in Dior, Chanel, Gucci, Galliano, Ralph Lauren, she had a policy never to leave the house without £20,000 on her back, excluding jewellery. The skirts were short, the jackets cut low. Long straight blonde hair, cornflower blue eyes, slightly tanned, fabulous tits – she was a classic beauty.

But the thing Holloway first fell in love with were her legs. Slim and elegant, they reached almost to his waist and she had a penchant for wrapping them around him, whether walking down a dark street, in the back of his limo, or in bed.

Kelly was a model when they met, mostly catalogues and fashion shows in her native Wales. At her peak she strode the catwalks for London Fashion Week but much to her disappointment never made it to Paris or Milan.

She adored her position as Mrs Douglas Holloway and she adored Douglas. To say her husband was socially inept would be an unusual kindness. Kelly provided the social aplomb and connections he desperately needed.

And Kelly had worked hard at creating her network of influential businessmen. Men with money and power had always flocked around her and she had a way of loving and then leaving them whereby they remained friends. Most of their wives, however, had a different view of Kelly.

They were a good combination. When she wasn't networking for him or playing the perfect corporate wife, Kelly loved to shop and lunch and shop and dine out and shop and party.

They had been married for six years before it dawned on her that her husband wanted a child. Not 'thought it might be nice', or 'let's try for one', he *wanted* a child. And Douglas Holloway was not the kind of man to be denied. Kelly loved her body, loved turning heads when she walked into a room, and the thought of giving that all up, even for nine months, was abhorrent to her. After all, she'd never once seen an attractive pregnant woman. There was more than one obstacle in the way of the Holloways starting a family – Kelly was bulimic and her periods had almost completely stopped. She classed herself as Healthy Bulimic. 'I don't throw up all the time like those other sad women, I only do it when I've eaten too much,' was how she justified things to herself. She was model-thin, but never alarmingly so. Few people questioned why she sometimes spent a very long time in the bathroom after a meal.

Her gynaecologist had explained to her that unless her periods started again, which meant controlling her bulimia, she could not get pregnant naturally. Given the amount of plastic surgery she had undergone, the desire to do things naturally did not loom large in Kelly's world view. her compromise was to embark on a course of IVF, the only difficulty getting Douglas to go along with it. He hated anything to do with doctors. Finally she convinced him it was the only way.

After she had found out who was the best in the baby business, she called the Winston Clinic in London and made an appointment. The only problem with the Churchill was that it was South London. Kelly got a headache just thinking about crossing the Thames.

She took the precaution of going to see Dr Coleridge alone first, so she could understand the procedure, make it easy for her husband.

Dr Sebastian Coleridge was a tall, aristocratic man with gentle hands. He immediately put Kelly at ease.

'I wanted to come along on my own first,' she explained at their first meeting, 'because my husband is extremely busy. He is also terrified of doctors and hospitals, so I want to make it as easy on him as possible. I think we can assume from the start that his participation in this process will be minimal.'

They spent some time discussing her medical history. Her bulimia had remained a secret from her husband and her friends and Kelly had no intention of telling Dr Coleridge the whole truth either.

'From what you have told me, Mrs Holloway, the first step is to get your periods started,' he said. 'Once they have stabilised you should start ovulating again. If you do not, we will try fertility drugs.

'If we go down the path of the test-tube baby, we will take several of your eggs and fertilise them outside the womb with your husband's sperm.'

'I've read about this,' she said. 'You put the man in a tiny room with a couple of dirty magazines and he wanks off into a bottle.'

The specialist blinked briefly and went on: 'It is a lot more civilised than that Mrs Holloway, but in essence that is correct.'

'Let's just take it one step at a time.'

It took several months for Kelly's periods to return, thanks to a cocktail of drugs, but she still was not ovulating. The fertility drugs sorted out that problem.

But they created problems of their own. Kelly felt as though she had permanent PMT. It affected her moods badly and if she wasn't weeping she was raging at her life, her luck and her husband. Her breasts were sore all the time and her stomach bloated. She wasn't even pregnant and it was playing havoc with her figure. She knew she was a nightmare to live with, but it was all so unfair.

For the first time in their relationship, sex became joyless. Douglas Holloway resented having to be around on the three to five days when she was ovulating. He did not want to hear about the daily injections, the nausea, the indignity of it all. He certainly did not want to be around a temperamental woman.

Looking back, Kelly could see this was a turning point in their marriage. He was incapable of showing her the emotional support she needed. And she needed a lot.

Six months later she still was not pregnant and they decided to try for a test-tube baby.

Dr Coleridge's face was inscrutable when Kelly informed him that she was going to assist her husband in the ejaculation process. Kelly led the way into the room, which did contain a selection of soft porn magazines.

'We won't be needing them,' she said and took Douglas gently in her arms, kissing him deeply, biting at his bottom lip and running her tongue around his teeth. Kissing was one of Kelly's specialities. She had deliberately worn what she called one of her easy access dresses, a little Galliano number with a zip which started between her breasts and ended between her legs.

She gently eased the zip down and her dress dropped to the floor. Her breasts were encased in a delicate black lace La Perla bra, the tiny briefs matched of course. Bare, tanned legs, high-heeled sandals.

'Now let's see if we can make this an afternoon to remember,' she said and slowly took off his jacket and shirt, unzipped his trousers, removed his Calvin Klein shorts and gently pushed Douglas down into the arm chair. She sat astride him, nuzzling his ear, his neck, his nipples one by one, feeling his penis getting hard underneath her.

'Just close your eyes and relax,' she whispered to him, one hand still squeezing his erect nipple, the other taking a bottle of oil from her handbag and placing it beside the sample bottle on the floor. She kneeled between his legs and took off her bra, playing with her own nipples until he took the job over for her. She opened the bottle of oil and poured a slick stream between her breasts.

'Come forward a little,' she said and when he was close enough she placed his rigid penis between her breasts, held them firm with her hands on each side and moved her body up and down. She knew this man well, knew he would come quickly now, could read the early signs of ejaculation. Just as he was about to explode she reached for the bottle and placed it over his penis, capturing most of his semen.

53

'Now that wasn't too bad, was it, baby?'

Dr Coleridge had explained that the semen would be frozen and used when Kelly had next produced enough healthy eggs to be fertilised. During the months that ensued Douglas was travelling a lot, Kelly was still then accompanying him and there never seemed to be time to attend the clinic. A baby slipped off the top of their agenda and Kelly promised herself she would go through with the rest of the treatment when the time was right. She wasn't worried. They had all the time in the world.

The grey silk sheets set off Kelly's long blonde hair to perfection as she sat up in bed, looking every bit the spoiled princess.

Her devoted housekeeper was trying to tempt her with a bowl of home-made soup and, at the same time, coax her out of bed so she could clean the room. Kelly turned up her nose and pushed the tray away.

'I'm too depressed to eat,' she wailed, 'I need champagne. Get me champagne, Rosa.'

'But it's only eleven o'clock, Mrs Holloway,' she protested, plumping up the pillows behind Kelly's head.

'Then bring me some fresh orange juice as well, if it makes you feel better,' she snapped and rolled over, turning her back on Rosa.

Kelly was plotting. She always plotted in bed. Douglas had said he would be home late all week and her instincts were screaming out that he was having an affair. The late nights, the short temper, the infrequent sex. She was sure that bitch Georgina was his mistress.

Well, damn her to hell, thought Kelly. He's mine and I'm not about to give in to some jumped up reporter. Douglas wants a baby and I'm going to give him that baby. Then he'll never leave me.

Her moment of happiness quickly disappeared when she realised that was going to be a tall order as he hardly touched her any more.

How can I get pregnant if he never comes near me? she thought, depressed again.

'The eggs!' she shouted, and leaped out of bed. 'The eggs,

54

the eggs!' she sang aloud as Rosa came into the room with the champagne.

'Eggs, Mrs Holloway?' Rosa said in genuine disbelief. 'You never eat eggs.'

Kelly whisked the champagne glass and bottle off the silver tray and walked into the bathroom, slamming the door.

Her perfect body looked good even under the harsh bathroom lights. Kelly hugged herself.

'What a clever little girl I am,' she said. 'I may not have his body, but I've got his sperm. If he won't make love to me, I'll make our baby on my own.'

# Chapter Five

It was way past midnight, the office almost deserted, the debris from their take-away Chinese dinner coagulating on the conference table, the week's work done.

The flat was in darkness when Georgina got home, carrying a bundle of the first editions. She dropped the papers on the kitchen table, poured a large glass of wine and went out on to her terrace. She was unsettled. The thought of Sharon digging around in her past was frightening. There were some things Georgina wanted to remain buried.

Her private life was one of them. She had kept her new lover a secret, even from Douglas, for good reason. But Georgina knew the laws of discovery, and the need for proof of an 'unsuitable' affair. So far as anyone could tell they were just friends, no one could prove anything. The most they would get was pictures of her lover entering and leaving the flat. Georgina would have to be more careful from now on, curtains closed, no overnight stays until this thing was finished.

There was only one secret with the potential to destroy her career and, if Mike did his work well, and quickly, all evidence of that would be removed. It would remain her secret, and Douglas's.

The night was cool. A full moon was breaking through the clouds now and lit the tiny terrace making the pots of white daisies and trailing geraniums glow in the soft light. This was Georgina's favourite spot. She ruffled the top of a big pot next to her chair, as one would a small child's hair, and the scent of lavender, mint and rosemary escaped into the air. She raised her glass to the stars glowing dimly in the London sky and said: 'Here's to you, Mum.' Georgina believed her mother was there with her, watching over her. She had to believe it. She held her hands around the glass, as if in prayer, and said: 'Please don't let them find out, Mum.'

Even after nearly twenty years, memories of her mother were knife sharp. She remembered the respectable middle-class house in the all-white suburb outside Johannesburg where she was brought up, the high wall topped with razor wire to keep out the enemy. Only their enemy was within.

It seemed to Georgina that she had had two childhoods: the perfect one which had lasted until she was ten, then the nightmare one. Her mother had been so beautiful, so unashamedly glamorous, the queen of the gin and tonic set in Johannesburg. Georgina had adored her and loved learning how to apply makeup, sitting at her mother's dressing table, learning the secrets of womanhood, longing for the day when she was old enough to be just like her mum.

Then, slowly, everything started to fall apart. Instead of milk and biscuits and a loving mother eager to hear the day's news waiting for her when she got home from school, her mother would still be in her dressing gown, slumped over the kitchen table, a glass of gin and tonic in her hand.

The terrible thing was, no one talked about it. Her mother was transformed into a tear-stained drunk before their eyes, while her father became sadder and sadder. Everything around Georgina was changing, shrivelling. Even her mother was shrinking, the weight falling off her, her once full bosom flat and weary. That's what Georgina had noticed first, the soft comfort of her mother's embrace had turned hard and bony.

There was a secret, that much she knew. Sometimes late at night she could hear her parents arguing, her father saying the children had to be told, her mother begging him not to, the tears, then her father's soft tread as he walked down the hallway and fixed his wife another drink.

Then her mother went away for a few weeks – a holiday, she told Georgina. When she returned she was even thinner. Her skin was grey, dark shadows under her eyes. It was as though all the life was being sucked out of her. And the drinking got worse.

Just when Georgina thought things at home could sink no further, her mother seemed to snap around. Like the week before Georgina's twelfth birthday.

'Let's have a party, darling,' she said to her daughter. 'Fill the house with laughter again.'

So they wrote out the invitations together, planned the party food, chose the cake and bought new dresses. It felt like old times. Georgina was happy again.

She could hardly wait to get home that Friday, the night of her party. Her friends were arriving around five. Georgina raced into the house and called for her mother. There was no reply. She walked into the living room, expecting it to be decorated with the pink crêpe paper and balloons they had bought, the huge pink and white birthday cake the centrepiece of a table groaning with goodies. There was nothing.

Georgina was so shocked at first she failed even to see her mother, slumped in a floral wingback chair, her head lolling on her shoulder, groaning. She flew to her mother's side.

'Mummy, mummy, wake up! Please wake up,' the girl cried.

It was only when she knelt beside the chair that Georgina saw the tall glass knocked over on the floor, the tell-tale slice of lemon, the bottle of gin on the occasional table.

'You're drunk,' she spat, shaking her. 'You spoil everything. I hate you.' But her mother was past caring. Georgina walked into the kitchen and saw the tray of burned fairy cakes abandoned in the sink, the hundreds and thousands scattered over the kitchen floor, the balloons still in their packets on the table.

That was how Georgina's father found her, an hour later, blowing up giant pink balloons. He was home from work early to help with the party. Instead he put his wife to bed and helped clear up the mess. There would be no party that night, nor ever again.

When her father had at last finished phoning Georgina's friends to say the party was off, he came and sat with his daughter. She was still blowing up balloons as though nothing had happened.

'Stop that now, Georgie,' he said gently, taking a half-inflated balloon from her hand. 'The party's off. Mummy's not well.'

Bewildered, she looked at her father. 'She's not sick, she's drunk. I'm not a kid, you know. She's drunk and she spoiled my party and I hate her.' The child was crying now, inconsolable.

'Your mummy is sick, believe me,' he said. 'One day you will understand. She drinks to forget.'

'Yeah, forget me and forget you and forget my party.' Georgina was hysterical now, the anger and tears she had been suppressing for months wrenched from her. 'She's a terrible mummy, she's a drunk and she stinks and I hate her. I wish she was dead!'

Ten months later, she was. The secret she had hidden from her children was that she was dying of cancer, a cancer which began in her breast and spread quickly, painfully, throughout her body. She'd never wanted the children to know, believing the pain of knowing would be too great for them to bear.

She had felt it would be easier for them to cope without her if they loved her less. By the time she died the children felt they had lost their mother a long time before.

In the few days between her mother dying and the funeral, Georgina was kept home from school. She spent them at her mother's dressing table, smelling her perfume, playing with her makeup, trying on her jewellery. She felt close to her old mother here, her real mother. The scent of her was everywhere. And that beautiful picture, taken at her engagement party, the most gorgeous mum in the world. That was what Georgina wanted, needed, to remember.

There was no enlightened thinking back then about the surviving parent easing the pain and confusion in a child's mind when the other parent dies. Georgina's father was lost in his own grief. He stared at his children as though they were out of focus, a short-sighted man squinting into the distance to recognise the grieving forms of his own family. He could not see them, let alone reach them. Each retired to their own world, a world of silence, of private mourning.

The children were barred from the funeral, sent off to stay with an aunt. When they returned all traces of their mother had been removed: the pictures, her clothes, her makeup.

Months later, when Georgina woke in the middle of the night crying, her father came to her bedside.

'I can't remember what Mummy sounded like,' she cried. 'I

can't remember what she smelt like, or what she looked like.'

Even when they called out for help, their father could not comfort them. He could not even begin to comfort himself.

The next morning when Georgina woke there was the picture of her mother at her engagement party and a half-used bottle of her perfume on her bedside table. Her father said nothing about their appearance.

Like her brother, Georgina was left with her guilt and the endless questions a child tortures herself with after a parent dies. Why my mummy? Why not granny? Why not me? How could she go and leave me? Was it my fault? If I'd known I would have been kinder to her. All those spiteful things I said, will she ever forgive me?

Georgina had forgiven her mother years ago. Now, as she sat nursing her drink, she prayed again that her mother had forgiven her.


Mike was on the phone before she had even woken up. It was Saturday morning, 6 am, the light already bright through the white blind in her window.

'She's stolen another of our splashes!' he announced without so much as a hello.

'Who has?' Georgina said sleepily.

'That bitch Sharon,' he shouted as though she was an imbecile.

They had been working for weeks on a tip-off that the new mid-week Lottery Show TV girl was having an affair. Her husband produced documentaries for the BBC and was often away for weeks at a time.

Every night one of their reporters and a snapper had staked out a mansion just outside Denham. After three weeks their patience paid off.

The distinctive red Ferrari of a newly signed Manchester United striker had driven into the driveway at midnight. The photographs of the new French heartthrob were not great, the distance too much to get a really clear shot, but they were clear enough. He was even carrying the signature Louis Vuitton washbag he always took to training sessions.

He finally left the star's matrimonial home at 5 am, and she made the mistake of kissing him on the doorstep then standing there in a tiny T-shirt to wave him off. It was perfect.

As Mike explained to Georgina that morning, it was perfectly splashed all over the front page of the *Saturday Tribune*.

'She's got us again,' Georgina said. 'This has to stop.'

Kelly had many mottoes she lived by. 'Undress to Kill' was one of them. As she stood in front of the full-length mirror in their Chelsea flat, she allowed herself several admiring glances.

She knew that in her new five-inch heel Manolo Blahnik shoes she would tower over Douglas but they made her legs look incredible, and she knew her legs were his weak point. Wolford lace top black stockings and the hand-made black basque gave her newly enhanced cleavage an extra boost.

Unbelievable, she thought. Douglas didn't even notice my boob job until the bill came in from the plastic surgeon in New York. Well, I couldn't just go to anyone, we always have the best. And I just had to get Concorde home. I couldn't wait to show them off to him. But did he notice? Like fuck he did.

The little black Dior dress she'd picked up in Paris a week before was perfect – simple, understated, deeply scooped at the neckline, very short. No jewellery except for the diamond earrings he gave her as a wedding present, to introduce a little nostalgia into the night, she thought.

Kelly looked magnificent. She had that rare talent of dressing to the edge of tartiness, but never crossing into it. Douglas's driver phoned to say he was waiting downstairs to take her to the Savoy.

Well he can fucking wait, she thought. They all can. Tonight I'll make an entrance. All the other women will be looking positively Home Counties – lots of jewels around their craggy necks, bodies soft from childbirth. I'll show Douglas what he's missing.

She poured her third and final double gin and slim and kicked one of the cats that had the audacity to rub himself up against her: 'Get off me, you're not even a pedigree.' She slipped on the matching Dior coat. One last look in the mirror, no, two, then she was off.

Douglas was getting anxious. Everyone was seated at the long table in the private room overlooking the Thames. Kelly was nearly an hour late. Not another entrance, spare me, please, he thought.

This evening was particularly important to him. It was the annual gathering of the Szechwan Seven and their wives, the group of power brokers who had helped mastermind his takeover of the Tribune Group twelve years ago.

Douglas was seated at the top of the table, Kelly placed at the other end. He liked to keep as much distance between them as possible these days. Aaron Seymour, head of the famous McLaird's advertising agency, was seated on his right; Sir Philip Sharp, chairman of the Tribune Group on his left. Sir Robert Billing, now chief executive of Modtern Bank, Andrew Carson, Douglas's right-hand man and general manager of the Tribune Group, Gavin Matheson, Director of New Technology, and Stephen Reynolds, one of the brightest city consultants and door openers in town.

Douglas's personal butler was there to oversee proceedings. Everything would spoil if they didn't start serving soon. He phoned Kelly's chauffeur in the car. They were just arriving, thank God.

She had promised herself an entrance and an entrance she got. Heads didn't turn, they positively swivelled. She walked straight over to Douglas, bent over his shoulders so everyone could get a good look at her new breasts and kissed him hard on the mouth. He smelt a mixture of perfume and gin. Not a good sign.

As she walked to her seat, he took his napkin and wiped his mouth as though he'd been kissed by a leper.

The champagne was served and Douglas stood to make his speech. Everyone groaned silently. He was a terrible speaker, with the hangdog demeanour of a man who thought he didn't really belong there. Aaron Seymour had worked hard on his speeches in the past, but the French-Canadian accent was a problem, still difficult to understand after all these years. And Douglas always looked so uncomfortable.

He placed his crib cards on the table. There were six of them.

'I would like to thank you all for coming tonight, the twelfth gathering of the Szechwan Seven. We have come a long way since that first meeting in a cheap Chinese restaurant in Pimlico. The *Tribune* has come a long way.

'Profits are up and we are performing well in the most competitive price war this market has ever seen. Unlike our competitors, we answer to our shareholders. We are running a business, not a one-man display of megalomania . . .'

If I have to sit through one more of his fucking speeches, Kelly thought as she gazed around the table at the other women and started to play her numbers game. That always amused her. She was a ten and every other woman in the room was rated for their attractiveness.

Like many beautiful women, she was unforgiving towards those who were not. They just didn't try hard enough, diet hard enough, shop hard enough, in her opinion. Any woman who had a big nose, saggy breasts, thin lips, thick thighs, anything that could be fixed by surgery, got an immediate zero. No self respect. Wearing clothes that were off-the-peg, minus five points. It was better to have one great frock than ten ordinary ones.

Douglas used to love this game, she thought. Especially when I described what underwear they would have on and how much cellulite it stretched over. Now he doesn't seem to want to play any more. With anything.

Finally Douglas sat down. They all clapped politely. So they should be fucking grateful, Kelly thought. They've all made millions out of him. She looked at them now and thought, not for the first time, that Douglas would not even be here if it weren't for her.

She had introduced him to Aaron Seymour, the head of one of the most powerful international advertising agencies in the world. A brief affair with the chairman of the company had given her access. She had introduced him to Sir Robert Billing and helped convince him that her husband was the man to back. She had introduced him to Stephen Reynolds and opened doors in the City that would otherwise forever have remained closed to Douglas. For years she had wined and dined these men, flirted with them, organised lavish parties anywhere from Tuscany to Toronto, tolerated their boring wives.

They finished eating and Kelly left the table to throw up. A minute in your stomach, a lifetime on your hips – another of her mottoes. While she was reapplying her lipstick she thought, I've got to go easy on this, remember what the doctor said. But some habits were hard to break. On her way back to the room she walked past Douglas, talking to Stephen Reynolds's wife – definitely a two, Kelly thought.

'You look lovely tonight, Karen, that's a beautiful dress,' he said. Kelly couldn't believe her ears. A compliment to another woman was an insult to her. Unforgivable.

She walked up to her husband, grabbed his arm and dragged him across to the window.

'How fucking dare you say that to her?' she hissed. 'She's fat and she's ugly. She must be at least a size 12. She's had two kids. Just imagine how disgusting her tits must be. And as for that dress, it's not even designer. You didn't say one thing about how *I* looked, about *my* dress.' Her voice grew louder and louder. Carson looked over from the table, the rest made a point of not looking.

'Kelly, please don't make a scene. Not here, not tonight,' Douglas said through clenched teeth. 'Of course you look beautiful.'

'But am I the most beautiful? Tell me I'm the most beautiful woman here. *Tell me.*'

'Yes, yes. Please, can't this wait until we get home?'

From long experience he knew this was not over and wouldn't be until she had scored some humiliating point over him. Kelly was nothing if not a Payback Girl.

# Chapter Six

'Why do we have to meet at a bar? Can't you come over to my place? It's been days, I need you,' Pete Feretti pleaded over the phone when his lover called.

'No. We need to talk,' Roger said. Feretti felt his stomach tighten. Need to talk, public place, couple of hours only ... he was being set up for a fall. But he loved Roger. This couldn't end like all the others, after a few months. This was the big one, this was real.

Feretti took out his frustration on the young marketing assistant he had employed a week before.

'I told you not to show the editor that copy, you stupid bitch,' he screamed. 'Only I show the editor copy, do you hear me? I am the Marketing Manager of the *Daily* and the *Sunday Tribune*. Only *I* deal with the editor. And you fucked up on that "Win a Diana Tummy Tuck" job. You're useless – fucking useless!'

'David, where's the fucking copy on the psychic tips for O-levels promotion? This is a quality tabloid and we have to address the young readers seriously. Do I have to do everything myself? You either have that on my desk by Monday morning or I'll get Sharon to sack you.'

Feretti wasn't usually in on a Saturday. The free seeds promotion he had pulled together for that week had collapsed at the last moment.

A lot of things had been collapsing on him recently. He was still trying to recover his credibility after the débâcle of the 'Free Zimmer Frame For Every Reader' promotion. How could he have known that the 20,000 frames he had ordered through his Indonesian suppliers were only suitable for people significantly less than five foot? And it wasn't his fault that they hadn't informed him the frames were made of bamboo, painted silver. He had tried to bluff his way through it, using a very short old couple in the promotional pictures. But, after the first thousand Zimmer frames went out, the complaints started pouring in. Then the writs. One old lady had broken her hip when the frame collapsed.

The publicity had been terrible. Sharon went beserk. It was the closest he had ever come to losing his job. The only thing that had saved him was their shared history. He had been her trouble-shooter for years. Feretti had enough dirt on his boss and her underhand tricks to take her down with him.

So here he was again, trying to sort out another fine mess. Still, the day wasn't wasted. It gave him an opportunity to spy on Georgina while Sharon wasn't around and earn a few brownie points.

Saturday night and the atmosphere in the *Sunday Tribune*'s office was gloomy. There was nothing more depressing than having a great story and not being able to run with it. They would keep working on Blakehurst, but it was unlikely they'd crack it now. He had been alerted and wouldn't put a foot wrong for months.

It was about 9 pm when Feretti announced that he was leaving to have dinner with one of his great marketing contacts.

He could come and go as he pleased, he was Sharon's boy – untouchable. It was unusual for the marketing department to be located on the editorial floor, but she had insisted upon it.

Feretti and Sharon had a lot in common. In his early thirties, Pete spent almost as much time at the beauty treatment centre as she did. They were into everything – whatever was the newest in electrolysis, line-reducing treatment, collagen injections, seaweed wraps, tanning. The thing Sharon liked most about him was that he would sell anyone down the river, do anything to further his or her career. He was devoted to her and to himself.

Feretti was HIV-positive but still healthy, relatively. He had told no one. This was the only secret he'd kept from Sharon. He was also a bully and universally despised.

The moment he left, the others started in on him.

'If that bum puncher says one more time how he'd like to give one of my reporters the best blow job he's had in his life, I'll kill him. So help me God.'

'Duplicitous little queer! Do you know he's going round telling people you'll be out of here by the end of the week, George?'

'Look, he says that every week. We all know he's a snake, but that's got nothing to do with his being gay. He's just a loathsome person,' she replied wearily. It was an uphill battle fighting the homophobia in the office and right now she had enough battles to fight.

Feretti always took a black cab when he headed for Hackney. He changed before he left – lav chic, he called it – tight leather trousers, white T-shirt, silver belt. But that would have to wait. Tonight he was meeting his lover first for a drink.

He was still a good-looking man, a bit ravaged, but his hair was dark and long, the semi-permanent colour hid the few grey hairs and made him look younger than his thirty-five years. Only five foot three. Cuban-heeled boots made him appear taller and, despite an expanding paunch, his body was still in good shape.

When he reached the bar in Soho, Roger was nowhere to be seen. He arrived half an hour late. Not a good sign.

'Look, Pete, things are just getting too complicated. I need some space. You're crowding me too much,' he started.

'Darling, I'll do anything. If you want to see less of me, that's okay. Just once or twice a week at my place. I can cope with that. You know I love you more than anything. You're the one I've waited all my life for, please don't destroy us,' Pete pleaded.

'No, it has to be a complete break.'

'Is your wife suspicious? We can be more careful. Please, Roger, I love you. Don't do this to us. You know how much I want to please you.' And his hand went to Roger's lap and stroked his crotch.

Feretti's love-life was as two-faced as he was. Anonymous encounters in Hackney's public lavatories supplemented his longer-term relationships (three months was the longest so far) with married men. There was also Paul, a 'special friend' of long standing, but more of a confidant than a lover these days. The best sex Pete had was usually with strangers. He prided himself on giving the best head in London. The Penis Pleaser, he called himself.

'No. There's no way of breaking this to you gently, Pete, but I've fallen in love – with a girl. It's over.'

'I don't believe it! You wouldn't leave your wife for me, but you're leaving her for some slut you just met?'

'Who said anything about leaving my wife?'

'But I love you, Roger. This is just a fling, I'll wait for you.' Pete's hands flew to his face and tears fell, making his pink-rimmed eyes even pinker. He left in floods.

He sobbed the entire journey to Hackney Green. As the cabbie dropped him off, he checked his wallet. Plenty of twenties. He walked the short distance to the men's public lavatories and chose his favourite cubicle.

After unzipping his trousers, he took out his penis – hard in anticipation – wrapped a £20 note around it and waited.


Douglas was the last to arrive at The Ivy for lunch on Sunday. His brother Daniel and his wife Jacqueline were already seated at the table drinking champagne, for which no doubt Douglas would pick up the bill.

Daniel was a Professor of Psychiatry at the University of Montreal, specialising in dysfunctional families, and had done some really interesting work in the area of 'under-fathering'. He was often in London giving talks at one conference or another.

The waiter came over to the table to get Douglas's drink order.

'Your brother, sir?' he enquired. 'Quite a family resemblance.'

'Though he's not nearly so rich and not a total bastard,' Jacqueline said quietly under her breath, but loudly enough for Douglas to hear. As with almost everything to do with his sister-in-law, he chose to ignore it.

'And how is the wonderful Douglas?' she enquired. 'Still slaving away at that nasty little newspaper group, ruining people's lives?'

Though almost pretty, Jacqueline's face was tinged with bitterness. She'd been meant for something better than this – a sweet, ineffectual husband, two kids, huge mortgage, struggling on an academic's salary. She was expanding with every year and the fullness of her flesh thankfully softened the harsh disappointment in her eyes.

Compared with the other couples they knew, their lives were not too bad. Compared with the wealth and glamour of the elder brother's life, theirs were dogged by lost opportunities and unfulfilled potential. Every time she met Douglas, Jacqueline was stung by just one thought. Why wasn't it me? One of Kelly's designer outfits cost more than she spent on a holiday for the whole family. It just wasn't fair.

There was a real closeness between the two men, but Jacqueline was openly hostile to her brother-in-law.

Douglas looked uncomfortably casual in navy blazer, white shirt, grey trousers, black suede lace-ups. He was one of those men who only seemed at ease in a suit. 'How's the book coming along, Daniel?' he asked.

'It's almost finished. At least I've got a title now – *Emotionally Absent Fathers*. It's fascinating, you know, Douglas, what I've come to understand about our own upbringing from . . .'

Jacqueline switched off at this point and scanned the restaurant for famous faces. Conversation between the brothers always went the same way. Daniel trying to explain how their own father, like most of his generation, had let them down, failed to teach them how to be men, his brother dismissing it all as psycho-babble; Jacqueline saying Daniel wasn't doing much of a job with his own sons, being away on the lecture circuit so much; he trying to demonstrate to her the difference between physical presence in a child's life and emotional presence.

Finally lunch was over. Jacqueline wanted to shop and Daniel was dragged off behind her.

The chauffeur was waiting outside the restaurant and once inside his car, Douglas gave himself over to thoughts of his father.

I don't blame you, Dad, he thought. He remembered the first time he had tried to explain to Becky about his father and his family and Daniel. She had listened patiently.

Papa did the best he could but he was never around, always trying to scrounge enough money to make ends meet. By the time he was thirty-four he had five children and a wife to support. I hardly remember anything about him when I was a child, except him taking me to the hospital when Daniel was ill with rheumatic fever. Things were tough for us when we were kids.'

He'd never needed the term 'wrong side of the tracks' explained to him as a child. The railway line that cut between the genteel, tree-lined, upper-middle-class area of Montreal West and his home in Ville St Pierre said it all.

Every day as he left the shabby brick duplex his family rented Douglas was reminded of which side of the tracks he came from. The poor side. The rare times he saw the kids from the English community, they rammed his poverty down his throat. They would come in gangs every year to buy firecrackers from the local back-street stores. In Ville St Pierre you could buy anything illegal, at a price. The oppressed French Community traded from rundown shops, hardly any paint left to peel off, grimy windows, dark interiors.

The wealthy kids taunted the young Douglas and his brother whenever their paths crossed. 'The Devil lives here,' they would scream as they passed by in the street. 'How does it feel living with Satan? How does it feel being poor as sin, you French bastards?'

The brick duplex was blistering hot in summer, its low ceilings capturing the intense humidity and turning the rooms into saunas. It was like a scene from an early Elvis Presley movie: the dirty, dusty streets, a heat that never relented, people asleep in sweat-stained vests on the verandas – even the dogs were permanently tired. In winter, with only one fireplace to warm it, the apartment was bitterly cold. As he grew up, Douglas vowed that he would escape the relentless poverty.

The sight of his father leaving the house at 7.30 each morning in his work clothes, carrying a packed lunch and a heavy heart, was another determining factor in his young life. Papa worked his guts out for ten hours a day to bring home barely enough to feed and clothe his five children. But he was unskilled and work at the local factory was all he was qualified for. Holloway's father was determined that all his children would have an education, receive the chance in life he'd never had. Only that bit of paper, an education, would give them an escape route.

Their back yard was a treeless, joyless plot of land, surrounded by a broken picket fence. The only relief was the clumps of flowers Maman grew around the kitchen window: marigolds and hollyhocks in summer, violets and snowdrops in early spring.

In those back streets the young Douglas Holloway learned to fight, and to barter, and to survive.

I want to be a good father this time, he thought to himself. I don't want to repeat the mistakes my father made. I've made a mess of my relationship with my first two children, I won't do that again. But there's so much I have to sort out first.


There were two reasons Kelly wasn't at lunch that day. First, she couldn't stand Jacqueline. *So* provincial. Second, she had an important lunch date with her old friend Kate. Kelly needed advice. More importantly, she needed to find out if her husband was having an affair with Georgina. If anyone knew, Kate would.

She was on to her second Virgin Mary when Kelly arrived, dressed completely in black – tight Capri pants, low-slung gold link belt, pumps, low top, leather fitted jacket. All Chanel.

'Will there be a third for lunch, madame?' the waiter asked her.

'No, just us.' She bent to kiss Kate on both cheeks. Kelly always reserved a table for three when there were just two lunching. The third chair was for her jacket. Always too expensive to leave in a cloakroom, and anyway, who the hell got to see it there? The extra chair gave her the opportunity to drape her jacket and display the label.

Kate was a columnist for *The Times*. She knew everyone, all the gossip, and Kelly trusted her. Kate had that amazing diarist's talent of making everyone believe she was their best friend when in fact she was pumping them for information.

'You know I was telling you how things weren't exactly great between Douglas and me, the sex and everything? Well, I've been putting a few things together.' Kelly paused to take a sip of champagne.

'He's hardly come near me sexually for months – now he's moved into the spare bedroom. When he's home he never talks to me, he's on the phone the whole time. And he's started taking more business trips. He's *never* home, and he doesn't ask me to go with him any more. I'm sure he's having an affair and I know who with.' Kelly didn't even notice that Kate, who never drank, had called the waiter over and ordered a double Bloody Mary.

Sooner or later I knew Kelly would find out about Becky and the baby. The whole world knows, she thought. She had been dreading this moment. Her husband John said that if she was a real friend she would tell Kelly, but what did men know about these things? Kelly would only blame her, turn on her, and she was a formidable enemy. She would find out for herself in good time.

And that time was now.

'Kelly, are you sure you're not just imagining things? Douglas has a lot on his plate at the moment,' Kate started.

'Don't give me any of that crap! It's that bitch Georgina, isn't it?'

Thank God, she still didn't know the truth! Kate breathed again.

'Georgina? You must be joking. I'm sure it's not her.' Well, at least *that* wasn't a lie. 'She and Douglas have been friends for years, you know that. No, I'm sure it's not her.'

'Who's she seeing then? Her private life is always so mysterious. She never talks about anyone except her *partner*. That means it has to be a married man,' Kelly said cynically.

'I just know it's not Georgina. I'll try and find out who the mystery man is. I'm seeing her next week for lunch anyway.'

Their order arrived: smoked salmon and scrambled eggs for Kate, a green salad for Kelly.

'I just can't believe he'd leave me, Kate. I've worked my arse off for him, been the perfect corporate wife. You remember what Douglas was like when I first married him. He didn't know

72

anyone, had no connections. I gave him all of that. I opened up a world to him that had been slamming its doors in his face for years. He was nobody. And the business contacts I've made for him and the endless boring dinners I've sat through, playing the perfect hostess!'

'I don't know how you do it,' Kate agreed. 'It would bore me rigid.'

'I do it because I love him and because we're a team. That's what marriage is to me. I know a lot of people think I'm just a silly little trophy wife, but it isn't like that. I've helped Douglas build that business because I'm the one with the network of influential friends and contacts.'

'I'm sure he appreciates that, Kelly.'

'He's got a fine way of showing it! Well, don't think I've giving him up without an almighty fight, especially not to that little slut Georgina. I've got a plan to win Douglas back, an unbeatable plan,' Kelly said. She leaned closer to Kate and said in a conspiratorial whisper, 'promise you won't tell anyone?'

'Of course I won't, Kelly, I'm your friend.'

'I've gone through with the IVF treatment. At this moment I am carrying Douglas's child,' Kelly said triumphantly and patted her pancake flat stomach.

Kate first choked on then coughed up tiny bits of smoked salmon and scrambled egg in a most unlady-like manner. She reached for her Bloody Mary and swallowed hard.

'Have you told him yet?' she managed to get out.

'Not yet,' Kelly said smugly. 'The doctor says the first six weeks are the most dangerous, that's when I'm most likely to lose it, so I'm not telling him until I know it's safe. It was awful, Kate, especially having to go through it all alone. Thank God Douglas donated some sperm a year ago. I just told the doctor he was away on business and we wanted to proceed. Simple. Won't Douglas be surprised?'

'Kelly, I don't know what to say,' Kate said. 'I hope it works, I really do.'

'What, the pregnancy or the marriage?'

'Both actually.'

'I'd do anything to keep Douglas. I've never loved a man as

73

much as I love him. We're so right together. You've been married to John an eternity, how do you do it? Your sex life must be fab.'

Kate shrugged her shoulders and thought: How do you explain to a woman who has always lived off her looks and her sexuality that a relationship is more than just sex and glamour? That a baby will not cement a broken marriage? She decided not even to try.

'I'm sure you'll sort things out. There was a great serialisation of that new book *Mid-Life Sex Crisis* in the *Mail* today. Why don't you get a copy of that?'

# Chapter Seven

Douglas waited in his limousine until the receptionist called to say the doctor was ready for him. He hated sitting around in waiting rooms. He ran up the three flights of stairs to Dr Reg Stevenson's rooms. It kept a man fit.

He never felt quite comfortable sitting opposite Doctor Reg in his old-fashioned surgery: the ancient leather wingback chairs, the medical books piled on every surface and Reg's red braces peeking out alarmingly from under his jacket.

Doctors' surgeries and waiting rooms reminded him of those horrible days when he was a child and his asthmatic brother Daniel would be rushed to the doctor's and then often into hospital. The waiting, the fear.

Doctor Reg's voice brought him back. 'How's the *Tribune*, Douglas? How's business going?'

Every appointment with Doctor Reg took at least forty-five minutes, and Douglas's medical records read, in part, like a personal diary. The doctor always asked about work, kept a note of his current wife and/or girlfriend, and always asked after them.

'And how's Kelly?'

'That's partly why I came to see you, Reg. It's sort of a problem with my marriage, but, um, not actually any more. Do you remember I was having that little problem a while ago when I couldn't really, um, perform very well with Kelly? Not that I want to any more, perform with her, I mean. I've fallen in love with someone else. Now I want to make sex . . . I mean, make love with her, not Kelly, and, um, I'm afraid, the old problem will come back.'

Doctor Reg gave him a reassuring smile, put his elbows on the desk and made a steeple with his hands.

'Douglas, are you trying to tell me that you're impotent, that you can't get an erection, or that you just fear the old problem will return?'

'I guess it's more the fear really. Sometimes when I'm really tired, Becky – she's the one I'm in love with – has to work quite hard to get me going.'

'Dear, dear, we can sort that out. The condition you are suffering from is quite common among men over forty-five. It's due to lower levels of testosterone in your body and means you can't always get a spontaneous erection, even when mentally stimulated. Can your penis still be stimulated manually or orally?'

Douglas mumbled yes, or something close to it.

'There's something quite new on the market, a process by which you apply patches impregnated with testosterone which allow the hormone to be gradually absorbed into the body. They're very expensive, but very effective. They last for about thirty-six hours and you place the patch on a hairless part of your body, usually under the upper arm.

'And of course, there's always Viagra.'

'How soon before they work?' Douglas asked.

'The patches work within about twelve hours. But you must be careful never to put two patches on at the same time. Viagra starts working within the hour and the effect lasts for several hours.'

Douglas was meeting Becky for dinner tomorrow night at the mews house close by her flat which he'd secretly rented. Thirty-six hours from now. He was cautious when it came to his health and his performance, and was taking no changes with Becky. He decided to take both the Viagra and the patches and give them a test run before he met up with her. He wanted to be sure just what the effects would be, and preferred to try that out on his own.

I'll put one of the patches on before lunch today, see how it works, he thought. If the patches can't do the trick, I'll use the Viagra tomorrow night.

*

Georgina always looked forward to her lunches with Madge, the *Tribune*'s legendary agony aunt. Now well into her late seventies, her mind was still as sharp as a hungry cub reporter's. She saw everything, had seen everything. Her career advice was as much sought after as her personal counselling and she always offered Georgina both.

'Darling, you look wonderful,' Madge said to her as the maître d' helped her into a chair at *her* table, always the same one by the window with the clearest view of Tower Bridge. Madge was recognised everywhere she went, the Queen Mother of the newspaper world.

Her black hair, although thinning, had never been allowed to grey and was swept back off her still handsome features. Madge's hair had always been her trademark – bouffant in the sixties, coiffured in the seventies for a slightly sleeker look, back to big hair in the eighties – along with the cigarette held aloft in a silver holder and her rapier wit.

'Now tell me about all this nonsense that's going on at the *Sunday*?' she said.

'Madge, it's a bloody nightmare. I think Douglas has gone mad. He's obsessed with Labour spin doctoring. Sees it as some kind of sign that the world is changing,' Georgina sighed.

'Don't tell me! I had lunch with him last week and he was going on about the Mandelsoning of the Tribune Group.'

'So you've heard it too. Tell me it's not me that's going mad?' Georgina implored.

'My sweet, Douglas is a very, very clever man, but sometimes he gets things wrong and when he does he gets them massively wrong. He's convinced that marketing is the way forward. That the way we present the titles is more important than what's in them.'

'It seems like a great excuse for more cost-cutting to me.'

'Well, that's why the idea is so appealing to him. He not only slashes editorial costs in the process, because the journalism isn't such a priority, he also believes it will pull in more readers. The lure of the slick sell. I told him he was mad when he explained it to me. I know Mandelson quite well and Douglas even asked me if I would approach him to write a column for the *Daily*. I know what the answer to *that* would be!'

'But, Madge, he's losing sight of what's really important: the readers. They're not stupid. Douglas's whole argument is based on a false premise – that the Labour Party was elected without policies. In fact, they promised people a better Britain, better education, better health care, the things people really care about now. They weren't mesmerised by the slickness of Blair, they believed his promises.'

Madge raised her glass of champagne, the first of many, and said: 'Let's forget about all that for a minute. Here's to you and the success of the *Sunday* darling. Now how are you getting on with the ghastly Sharon?'

'Actually, that's one of the things I wanted your advice on,' Georgina said. 'It's all getting rather nasty, I'm afraid. I discovered a couple of weeks ago that she's having me tailed, trying to dig up some dirt on my personal life to discredit me before the board. And I'm sure my office is bugged. Our stories are mysteriously appearing in the *Daily* as we work on them. She must have tapped into our system.'

'So what have you done about it?' Madge asked, raising her glass to lined but perfectly made-up lips.

'Fighting fire with fire. I've put a tail on her, outside the office. Someone I trust. And we've started holding mock conferences. We never discuss the big stories in my office. I now understand the term "corridors of power" as the corridors are about the only place it's safe to talk. My best defence is to keep on producing a great newspaper. It's the figures that will count in the end. And the profits.'

'Does anyone in the office know about Belinda?' Madge probed.

'Only you. I don't think what we still affectionately call Fleet Street is ready for a bisexual editor.'

'I'm not sure you're right about that, Georgina. Look at all the big stars who've come out and all the Labour politicians. The days have long gone when people can be sacked because of their sexuality. I sometimes think it's you who want to keep Belinda a secret, because you can't really handle it yourself.'

Georgina looked away from Madge's eyes, they saw too much. 'Maybe you're right. Maybe I'm not ready to come out. Things with her are quite difficult at the moment, I'm not sure where they're heading. To admit publicly to her is like making a commitment and I'm not sure I'm ready for that. There's no one else I can say this to, but I miss having a man. It's hard to explain . . .'

'You don't have to, my sweet. The important thing is that it is almost impossible for Sharon to "out" you. We all know the laws of disclosure. She'd either need pictures of you in bed together or a signed affidavit from Belinda, both of which are highly unlikely. The real problem you have here is Sharon. She's one very mixed up woman.

'The thing she really wants is public acclaim,' Madge went on. 'I'm not one to gossip about my colleagues,' and she leaned closer to Georgina, 'but I remember talking to her years ago after we serialised a book on birth order in families and the effect that had on the particular child. I'd never heard Sharon talk much about her childhood, but when she told me that she was the third of four children, two elder brothers and a sister who was the youngest, I started to understand more about what drives her.

'Evidently the sister was slim and pretty, like the mother, while Sharon was plump and plain. Her mother virtually ignored her except to put her on another crash diet or course of slimming pills, and her father didn't know how to cope with what she became: a sulky, overweight tomboy. She's always had to fight for attention, to scream to get heard, which is why she's so loud and obscene now. It gets her noticed.'

'Her brothers were very bright and went on to become a lawyer and a doctor, *professionals*, and she felt eclipsed by them. He was quite wealthy you know, Sharon's father. Something in hardware. Not very grand, but rich.

'He practically ignored her but adored the younger daughter, who from all accounts was very beautiful. Even Sharon's best friends could not call her a beauty. Consequently she feels she has to prove something to her family and to herself, that she *is* someone. That's what makes her so objectionable.'

'It's an explanation, Madge, but hardly an excuse. There comes a time when you have to stop blaming your parents for making you what you are and take responsibility for your own actions.

Sharon has all of the worst characteristics of a man and none of the saving graces.'

'Never forget how cunning she is, Georgina. No one ever thought she would get the editorship of the *Daily*. She worked for years, undermining poor old Rogers. She became the first woman editor of a national daily, but that wasn't enough. Nothing is ever enough for her. Now she wants another first, to be the first woman editor of a seven-day operation. And you know why she wants the *Sunday Tribune*. Because it's the most profitable part of the business.'

'I know,' Georgina said wearily. 'We make more money in one day than that *Daily* does in three. Our sales are rising while hers are declining. Doesn't that tell you something? That we're getting it right on the *Sunday* while she's screwing up the *Daily*?'

'I'm not one to gossip about my colleagues,' Madge repeated, '*but* you know she has a bottle of vodka in her bottom drawer *and* she's high on slimming pills most of the time. Have a word with the lovely Roxy. She has a passion for your news editor and for cheap champagne. He'll get a few secrets out of her and probably won't even have to sleep with her.'

Their main courses arrived. Madge always had the same thing: a large piece of fresh fish gently cooked in butter.

When they'd finished the maître d' personally took away her plate and returned ten minutes later with a beautifully wrapped doggy bag. 'Supper for Henry madam and please give him my compliments,' he said. Henry was Madge's cat and almost as legendary as she was.

Pete Feretti came flouncing into Sharon's room and flopped down dramatically on the sofa.

'My life's over, no one loves me,' he whimpered.

Sharon looked up from the pile of page proofs on her desk and smiled to conceal the intense irritation she felt. She knew she would have to suffer ten minutes of this before they got down to business.

'Darling, Pete, *I* love you,' she said in the sweetest tones she could muster. 'And so does Paul.'

'Paul doesn't count,' he said sulkily. 'He's been with me for years. We're more brothers than lovers now. And, anyway, I don't fancy him any more.'

He wept a little, Sharon consoled him a lot, and finally she asked: 'So how are we going on our little trailing exercise baby? What's that bitch been up to now?'

'Not a lot really,' Feretti said, disappointed. 'The bug in her office works like a dream, but it's all so boring. Work, work, work. Her conferences are so dull – nothing like yours, boss. And she's so soft on everyone. She gets in around nine, usually lunches, doesn't drink much, no sign of drugs, leaves the office anywhere between eight and midnight, sometimes has a few drinks after work with that brute Mike Gordon in the Last Chance or else a late dinner, usually with friends, then home.'

'What about her phone calls?' Sharon said impatiently, lighting another cigarette.

'They're all being taped. Nothing but work or friends. There's one particular friend she spends a lot of time with, a woman called Belinda Green. She even stays over at Georgina's flat sometimes.'

'Yes, yes, yes. That's it!' Sharon screamed, 'She's a fucking lesbian. I want photographs of those fucking dikes fucking, do you hear me?'

Feretti squirmed uncomfortably in his seat. 'Actually, Sharon, strictly speaking lesbians don't fuck.'

'Then get me pictures with vibrators, sex toys, anything. Get me *evidence*.'

'Unfortunately, Georgina's flat is really difficult to photograph. It's on a busy road on a red route. We can't even park and sit to observe the place. And the windows have shutters, so you can't see into the place. All we can observe is who goes in and out, and when. There's nothing to pin on her yet.'

'Damn her to hell!' Sharon shrieked, pounding both her fists on the table. 'Your fucking life won't be worth living if you don't get some dirt on her, do you hear me?'

The new fashion editor was terrified when she got the call from Sharon's PA to be in the editor's office at six that evening. So terrified she had to call one of her closest fashion agents and get a new outfit sent over to Tribune Tower.

At 5.30 pm Tara was in the ladies', rechecking her makeup. Was the new purple, almost black lipstick too much? she asked herself again. At least it matched the nail polish. The fine wool black Gucci trousers hung on her hip bones, leaving just an inch of bare midriff before the strapless Lycra top. The leather of the black jacket was so soft, Tara was worried just bending her arm would damage it permanently. And it had to go back tomorrow. She was used to clomping around in heavy four-inch platform shoes, so the high-heeled Jil Sander sandals were an ambitious choice.

Tara had been with the *Sunday Tribune* for almost a week, poached by Sharon from *Marie Claire*. For some reason Sharon had not had a lot of luck with fashion editors, but she had been assured that this was the hippest young fashion expert around.

She presented herself at Roxanne's desk at exactly six o'clock and was told to wait. By eight she was still waiting, her black nail polish almost completely chewed off two fingers.

There was commotion in the office, people running in and out, doors slamming, everyone ignoring her.

She nearly jumped out of her seat when she heard Sharon scream from inside the office: 'She's a fucking lesbian.'

How could they have found out? Tara thought with a sinking heart. Her former editor's advice had been clear. Whatever you do, do not reveal your sexuality. Tabloid newspapers are no place for gay women. They'd have a field day.

She was just about to grab her handbag and run when she heard Sharon again.

'You'd better fucking believe it, Allenby. The adorable little Georgina is a fucking queer. I got it from a good source.' Her tone was triumphant. 'A carpet-munching queer. Spread it around. Now fuck off.'

The burly news editor rushed out of Sharon's office, his trade-mark big trousers flapping as he dodged his way through the rows of desks. The reporters joked that his floppy pants were necessary to cover the fact that he was always shitting himself. Nappy pants they called him. 'The boss is ready for you now,' he said. It was almost nine o'clock.

'Sweetie pie,' Sharon cooed. 'How wonderful to see you. Just thought we'd have a little girlie chat. Sit down and have a drink.'

'Roxanne, where's the fucking wine?' she shouted through the closed door. Her secretary appeared a minute later with two very chilled bottles of Jacob's Creek Semillon Chardonnay. Someone had told Sharon New World wines were fashionable. Only ten years out of date.

Tara slid into and almost off the nearest leatherette sofa and took the proffered plastic cup.

'I just thought we'd get together and have a chat about the direction the paper should be taking with fashion,' Sharon said, lighting another cigarette.

'As you can see, I'm very interested in the subject. I love designer clothes, but then I can afford them. The *Tribune* readers ... well, frankly, they're working-class. We have to remember they're all poor and have no taste, so keep it simple and cheap but looking a million dollars. And make sure the models have tits. Men look at the fashion pages too. I won't have a picture of a model in the paper unless she's at least a 36 double-C. Make it look classy. What are you planning for next week?'

Tara took another gulp of wine. She looked again at the red Christian Lacroix jacket Sharon was wearing and wondered why she had bought it two sizes too small. And she could have sworn it didn't have walnut-sized gold buttons and epaulettes when she'd seen it at a show last year.

'I was thinking of doing a preview of the sales,' she said nervously. 'Sort of Cheap and Chic.'

'Great idea,' Sharon said, dragging hard on her cigarette and fluffing out her tangerine curls. 'Now, as you know, I have a very high profile and it's important I always look stylishy. Now and again I will need you to get some clothes in for me ...'

Tara had expected this. Most editors used their position to get a few favours from the big fashion houses. They usually paid, but at a huge discount.

'I saw this stunning little suit in Harvey Nichols the other day, Calvin Klein, lilac, short skirt, soft double-breasted jacket,' Sharon said. 'Could you get it in for me?'

'No problems. What size?'

'An eight, of course,' Sharon shot back, indignant she should even ask.

Tara did a quick conversion in her head. American eight equalled English size twelve in Calvin Klein. 'Um, excuse me, Sharon, is that an American eight?'

'No, you stupid girl, English,' she said and sucked in her stomach. 'And I want it with epaulettes.'

Tara's heart sank. What the hell was she to do? Sharon would be lucky to fit into a size twelve. And epaulettes. How could you put epaulettes on a Calvin Klein suit? She left the office in a complete state. My career is over, what will I do? she brooded.

The next day she was contemplating packing her things and just leaving. One more call, she thought, and dialled the number for Calvin Klein's UK distributors.

'Zara, it's Tara,' she said. 'Darling, I've got the most terrible problem. I'm going to get the sack and I've only been fashion editor of the *Tribune* for one week. Not even that. My career's over. My life's over.'

'Don't tell me: Sharon's asked you to get in some clothes and she's told you she's a size eight?'

'How on earth did you know?'

'She's been doing it for years. Don't worry your pretty head about it. All we do is take out the size twelve label and sew in an eight. It was even more ridiculous before she lost weight and we had to put size twelve into a size eighteen. And epaulettes? She wants epaulettes, I suppose. Four rows? It's *always* four rows.'

Tara sank back in her chair. The relief was immense. She looked down at her black nail polish and saw there was only one nail intact. It was only then that she remembered what she had overheard outside Sharon's office.

If there's one thing we 'fucking lesbians' can do, she thought, it's fucking stick together. All employees, including editors', home numbers were listed in a book on the news desk. Tara looked up Georgina's. She didn't have the courage to identify herself, but a quick message on Georgina's answer machine at home salved her conscience.

Maybe tonight she could recapture some of the old magic, Kelly thought as she lay in the bath. At least Douglas would be home.

I'll cook something special – I'm sure I've still got time to order in from the Savoy, she decided.

He came home around midnight. The light supper was beautifully laid out on the table, candles hurriedly lit as she heard him come in, champagne on ice.

Kelly was wearing a white baby doll négligée, low at the front and almost transparent, her long blonde hair plaited loosely down her back and tied with a white satin ribbon. Douglas went to kiss her on the cheek and she turned her mouth to his. There was no response.

She slid her arms around his neck and he immediately grabbed them and held them at her sides.

'No, Kelly, that won't work. I'm tired, I'm going to bed.'

'But, Douglas, I've cooked dinner for you!' He looked over at the table, she'd never cooked a thing in her life, looked back at her in that ridiculous nightie and thought: How did I ever get into this mess?

'I've already eaten,' he said as he walked upstairs to his room. He had now moved into the Ralph Lauren bedroom, as Kelly called it. All the rooms had names – the Mulberry study, the Versace bedroom, the Designer's Guild bedroom, the Purves and Purves sitting room. They were straight out of a designer's shop display. Kelly just walked in, fell in love, with *everything*, and ordered the entire room. Furniture, curtains, carpets, ornaments, the lot.

Kelly heard his bedroom door slam. She slumped onto the sofa, head down, arms dangling between her legs, like a designer rag doll.

What am I to do? she thought, opening the bottle of champagne and thinking hard. She had him at home, this was a rare opportunity, and she was not about to be put off. Douglas was going to be a father and she knew it was crucial that he believed the child was conceived naturally. If he thought she had gone behind his back with the IVF treatment, he might never forgive her.

Kelly waited until his light went out, enough time for him to be sleepy, took off her négligée, opened his door and slipped into his bed. She felt for his penis and almost whooped with joy when she found it hard.

85

Before Douglas realised what was happening, Kelly was astride him, rubbing his penis, her hair now loose over his stomach.

'Get off me,' he ordered. Kelly looked down, almost fearfully. She'd never heard his voice so cold.

'But, Douglas, you're so hard, you want me, I know you want me. Just close your eyes and enjoy it, baby,' she whispered. He did close his eyes, more out of sheer frustration than desire. The moment he did he was lost. Kelly had a scent that was pure animal. He had noticed it the first time they were in bed together. She knew it and never wore perfume. She called it her love scent. Right now he was suffocated by it.

Within seconds she had guided his penis inside her. She thought nothing of her pleasure, only his. She took one nipple in each hand and squeezed them roughly, the way he always liked, and moved rapidly and deeply over him. His head went back and he gasped as she took him deeper and deeper inside. It was a matter of minutes before she felt the pulse at the base of his penis, then the throbbing.

When she lay down beside him she realised the noise escaping from his mouth was not a moan of pleasure. He was groaning. 'That wasn't for you,' he said incomprehensibly and gently pushed her away from him.

Damn those bloody patches!

Georgina did not recognise one of the voices on the answer machine when she played back her messages that night.

The young woman's voice was apprehensive, even frightened, and the message short.

'Not that it matters to me really, or that I care, but Sharon Hatch is trying to smear you. She thinks you're a lesbian. Well, good luck to you if you are. We girls have to stick together. Just thought you should know.'

Georgina dialled 1471. The caller had withheld their number.

# Chapter Eight

Pete Feretti was already at his desk when Georgina arrived at 8.30 on Tuesday morning. He followed her into her office and threw himself face down on the sofa, quietly sobbing.

'Roger's left me, my life is over!' he snivelled. This was all Georgina needed. She was in early to prepare for a meeting with Douglas and the money men over the *Sunday*'s editorial budget.

'I should have known. My psychic told me last week there would be great upheaval in my life, that I'd lose someone close to me. I thought it was my mother, I hoped it was her, but it was Roooogeeeer.'

Georgina stood looking down at him. It was at once impossible to console a man you despised, yet difficult not to be touched by someone in such pain.

Then she reminded herself he had been in similar despair two months ago when Dennis had left him, and a month before that when Steve had. Men just left Feretti. Most people avoided him. He had no close friendships.

'I'm sorry, Pete, but I have to be in the board room in five minutes,' she said, collecting her files. 'I'll see you after conference around twelve. Can't imagine this meeting will take too long.'

Feretti sat up sulkily, long black hair ruffled and his pale grey eyes swollen to slits. 'Ooooooh, noooo, I've cried on my new silk shirt. I'll have to go and buy another one,' he said to Georgina's departing back.

After she left, he moved swiftly to her desk and riffled through her bottom tray, still full of letters dating back months. He found the fountain pen and slipped it into his pocket and replaced it with another identical one before letting himself out of the office. Mission accomplished.

The atmosphere in the boardroom when Georgina arrived could only be described as tense. She glanced at Douglas and her heart sank a little.

He had one of those faces that hid nothing. He could be almost handsome in some moods: the eyes cobalt blue, flecked with grey, the skin a warm shade of pink. His hair was thinning, but you only noticed when he looked down – he was fifty-four after all.

His lips, vaguely feminine in their fullness when he was relaxed, had all but disappeared today. Today it was going to be one of those days.

The meeting had been called to discuss another round of cuts on the editorial budget of the *Sunday Tribune*. Andrew Carson sat on Douglas's right, the Finance Director, James 'Fatty' Oakland, on his left.

'Where the hell is Sharon?' Douglas said. 'If she can't be bothered getting here on time we'll start without her. She's been briefed anyway. I've been looking at your staff levels,' he shot at Georgina, 'and there are too many journalists on the *Sunday*. Most of them are no good, they're just drones. They do as little work as they can and get pissed all the time. I only want multi-skilled, multi-talented young people working here.'

Georgina often wondered who Douglas had the most contempt for – the readers of the *Tribune* or the journalists who produced it. It had been twenty years since he'd worked as a journalist himself and in those years everything had changed.

There were fewer of them for a start, the number working at the Tribune Group had halved, they all had strict contracts and most of them worked a twelve-hour day. Of course there was still some "dead wood" as he liked to call it, but precious little these days.

'Where are the plans for the restructure?' Carson handed

Douglas a pile of documents and he distributed them around the table.

The door was flung open and Sharon burst into the room, cigarette in her mouth, coughing, followed by her hapless PA, carrying her files. 'Sorry I'm late but that moron of a driver took me through every fucking traffic jam in London. Remind me to get rid of him, Roxy. And get me a coffee and some more cigarettes. So, have we got to the sackings yet?'

Sharon was dressed for combat. She had added her own touches to the bright orange Ronit Zilkha suit – big, shiny black buttons and extra shoulder pads. The skirt was short, the fitted jacket a size too small with a deep neckline from which her bosom oozed, just a hint of black Wonderbra peeking out.

'Sharon and I have already discussed the staff numbers at the *Daily Tribune* and she's been very helpful in giving an overview of the *Sunday* operation. I believe we should sack about three-quarters of the existing staff and recruit twenty-five multi-skilled operators instead,' Douglas said, glancing at the figures in front of him. Sharon and Carson exchanged looks.

Georgina did a quick mental head count. There'd been 150 journalists on the paper when she arrived three years ago: there were now 85. Sack three-quarters, that's 60, leaves 25. Recruit 25, making a staff of 50.

'You must be joking, Douglas,' she said in disbelief. 'That's half the staff we had three months ago and one-quarter the staff on the *News of the World*. How do we compete with the market leader if we've got no journalists? Even the *Sunday Mirror* has more journalists than that. You know how Sunday tabloids work, for God's sake. They're labour intensive. For every four stories we work on, only one makes it into print.'

'Most of that lot you have there are useless fuckers,' interjected Carson. 'Sharon has kindly drawn up a possible hit-list of journalists and a list of potential recruits. *She* doesn't seem to think your team's so great. And there are a number of opportunities to share staff across the *Daily* and *Sunday* titles. Why, for example, do we need two gardening writers? You share an astrologer, why can't you share the other specialists and cut costs?'

Sharon sat smiling, one arm crossed over her huge breasts, the other holding a cigarette on high, triumph in every line of her.

'Because the whole principle behind keeping the two titles separate is that they have different personalities,' Georgina explained. 'If you want to maintain that difference, you need separate specialist writers.'

'I don't want any arguments on this. You all know what I want for the papers – a streamlined operation. No reporters, only writers. A small team of executives who brief all writers, and they write perfect copy, to length, so all sub-editors are redundant. it's quality journalism we're after here. And every writer should be able to write about everything – no more specialists.' Douglas was warming to his theme now.

'No more drones, no more drunks. All the production journalists will draw pages electronically, put the copy in the page, write the headlines, scan the pictures and send the page. That cuts out half the production staff.'

'Are you seriously suggesting, Douglas, that the writers' copy is not even checked?' Georgina said in disbelief. 'That it's just poured into the page untouched. And then that the production journalist . . .'

'Page editor,' he corrected.

'. . . the page editor works on it on screen, proofs it on screen, then sends it to the print sites without the editor even having seen it? You cannot be serious!'

'What I am about to say is highly confidential,' he said. 'The streamlining of the newspapers is part of a master plan, my master plan for the entire Tribune operation. In the end, and I know this will take some years, I want multi-skilling of journalists to be taken to its ultimate extreme. Why employ one journalist to cover a story for our radio stations, several for our newspapers and one for each TV station? One man or woman should do the lot, and once they are properly trained they will be *able* to do the lot. Just imagine it. One man with a tape recorder and a video camera producing the story for all media.'

Everyone in the room sat in stunned silence.

'We must create a super-race of journalists,' he ranted.

As they went on discussing Douglas's proposal, it was clear that no one around the table shared his vision. He became angrier and angrier.

'Let me remind you who is in charge here. This is my dream. I will not compromise. These cuts are the start of the future. Just do it.' And he walked out.

Sharon whispered something to Carson then rose to leave. She stopped behind Georgina's chair and said: 'If it's all too much for you Georgie, I'll help you out with the sackings. Some people just aren't cut out for tough managerial roles.'

I walked into that one, Georgina thought to herself angrily as she left.


'Lock the fucking door!' Sharon screamed as the second hand on the wall clock hit eleven. Her office was almost full with journalists, mostly men, most in Marks and Spencer suits circa 1985, with matching shirts their wives had bought them, the blue striped ones with the attractive white collars.

'But Greg isn't here,' said Steve Dainson, the news deputy. Greg Allenby was the *Tribune*'s legendary news editor. His nickname was 'Raging Bullshit' because he could bullshit better than anyone else in the business. And he could rage. All of Sharon's key people could, though never at her. A bullying complex was mandatory in all her executives.

'He was on the phone when I got up,' Dainson faltered. It was debatable which he cared about most: defending his immediate boss or avoiding the inevitable humiliation that came with presenting the news list. 'It must have been really important.'

'Nothing is more important than my conferences,' Sharon shouted. 'I don't give a fuck if he's here or not, we'll have conference without him. He knows we start dead on eleven. I will not tolerate this fucking sloppiness any more. His news lists are always crap anyway. Right, let's get on.'

Sharon, like most daily newspaper editors, held two conferences a day: one late morning to discuss the likely stories and one late afternoon to decide which stories had worked and where they were placed in the newspaper.

She sat behind her huge desk which was scattered with proofs and newspapers. An exceptionally large bunch of yellow, red and pink carnations and chrysanthemums stood in a bright orange plastic vase. Flowers gave a woman class, Sharon believed, emphasised the feminine side. An oversized ashtray was already full to brimming and there was ash scattered all over the desk. The journalists lolled on the fake leather sofas placed around the room. They had to loll because the synthetic leather was so slippery.

'Right, Steve, let's see if you can do better than that useless sod of a news editor,' she said. Everyone had a copy of the pre-prepared news list.

'There's a great story we've got an exclusive on. Blair plans to have his son Euan head a Save Our World conference in London next year. You know, save the environment, give the children a say in their future,' Dainson said. 'The Government will organise and fund the conference and they're inviting representatives from all over the world . . .'

'What a pile of crap!' Sharon burst in. 'No one gives a fuck about the environment, only a bunch of namby-pamby greenies. Next.'

'Ah, well, there's a really good development in the recent cash for questions scandal, another exclusive. We've discovered that . . .'

'Yesterday's news,' Sharon interrupted again. 'How many times do I have to tell you our readers don't give a fuck about politics? Give me stars, give me Royals, give me scandals, give me showbiz. Or give me your notice.'

There was a frantic rattling of the door handle and everyone turned to look.

'Fuck off, Greg,' Sharon screamed at the locked door and burst out laughing. 'Your list is a pile of crap as usual.' She tore up the news list and chucked it at the bin. 'That's what I think of it. There's not a single thing here I'd put in the paper. Start again and get those lazy cunts of reporters working for a change. I want a completely new list ten minutes after conference. Right, features, what have you got?'

'You know the new hole they've found in the ozone layer, I thought we could get together a piece on the Orgasm Zone, you know, where people in the world have the best orgasms,' said Sally Brink, features editor. 'We'd call it the OoohZone and do a map showing where people have the best sex in the world.'

'Now that's more like it,' Sharon said excitedly. 'That's what I call a feature. Get it ready today. I'll run a flash on the front page, saying, "Finally, the truth about the OohZone Layers." Get it? Layers . . . people getting laid.'

'It might be a bit difficult getting all the research together in a day,' Sally said, and regretted it the minute she opened her mouth.

'Call yourself a fucking journalist?' Sharon shouted at her. 'Just make it up. I want it for the spread today. Phil, can you get some really tasteful pictures of couples screwing? No pubes, no nipples, no dangly bits. Keep it classy. Oh, and you'd better throw in a black or yellow couple, just to show it's international. But make the bull picture a white couple.' Phil Plattmann, picture editor, made notes of the instructions. 'What else, Sal?'

'It's the thirtieth anniversary of the Andrex puppy tomorrow and I thought we could do something on that.'

'I've got a great idea,' enthused Dainson. 'We'll track down the original puppy, do a photo shoot – you know, now and then – and get Bill to write a funny interview with the dog.' Everyone groaned and waited for the barrage of abuse. The only good thing about having Dainson in the conferences was that, due to his sheer stupidity, he usually bore the brunt of Sharon's tirades.

'Do you have any idea what the average life expectancy of a dog is you fucking moron?' she demanded. 'Do you really think the readers want to see a picture of an exhumed Golden Labrador? I can see it now, our perfect family sitting around the kitchen table eating their Coco Pops, reading the *Tribune*. Then little Jimmy starts bawling because there's a picture of a dog that's been dead and buried for fifteen years!'

Dainson never seemed the slightest bit embarrassed by his gaffes. Sharon valued him because he came up with the wackiest ideas, and some of them even made it into the paper. 'What about an interview with the dog from beyond the grave?' he blurted out.

'Now you're talking! Get Mystic Merve to write it, lots of stuff about what it's like for dogs in heaven, they'll love all that. All our readers believe dogs go to heaven.' Mystic Merve was the *Tribune*'s answer to Mystic Meg, a male Meg-alike. He was a creepy looking man with straight black hair and piercing red eyes, thanks to tinted contact lenses, who spoke in a soft eerie voice and was in touch with 'The Other Side'. He was actually a pretty useless middle-aged reporter called Peter Foukes who lived with his wife and three children in Essex, but he was too expensive to pay off so Sharon had had the brilliant idea of turning him into Mystic Merve.

They ran through the picture schedule, then sport. 'That's it, get out the lot of you,' she barked. 'And get that useless cunt of a news editor in, *now*.' Allenby almost fell into the room when the door was unlocked.

'The news list was crap, crap, crap!' Sharon shouted at him as he slid down on one of the sofas. 'Anyway, I need to talk to you about something more important.'

'Yes boss,' Allenby dutifully replied, running his fingers through his beard and dislodging part of his breakfast.

'I've been watching Blair really closely since he came into office and there's one thing he's doing that's really clever,' she said, calm now.

'Yes, bow?'

'He champions lost causes,' she said. 'Think about it. First the Government reopened the inquiry into Hillsborough, then it opens Number 10 to the poor and the homeless – even though Norma Major had been doing that for years. Then it makes a big fuss about the cover-up over Gulf War Syndrome and injects £2 million pounds into research – hardly enough to keep a research unit going for a year, then the Foreign Minister puts her backing behind that eleven-year-old girl who was raped and murdered in Normandy last year. You see the pattern?'

'Ah, yes, boss, kind of,' Allenby said, looking down at his battered brown Italian slip-ons.

'You useless cunt, you don't see it at all. It's almost as though someone's gone through a pile of old newspapers and picked out all the really emotive events. Then they announce they're opening up the case, reinvestigating, campaigning against injustice. It's just a great big fucking rolling publicity stunt. It costs the Government nothing to put a junior minister in charge of the case and gets loads of free publicity. And those sad fucks out there buy it. They think the Government cares. It's fantastic.'

'So, you want me to go and trawl through the last few years and find some deserving cases?' Allenby said with a knowing smile.

'Yes, yes, yes. I want all the unresolved murders, especially if they're young girls and were raped or brutalised. Lots of womb tremblers. Then we can retell the whole story with all the gory details, re-interview the parents, boyfriends, pictures of the bedroom that hasn't been touched since the night little whoever didn't come home. We set up a campaign to find the killers, demand action from the Government, run petitions in the paper and present them to Blair. The full whammy. Minimum effort and no cost to us, maximum publicity and feelgood factor.'

'You're a genius, boss.'


Sharon was in good spirits when she arrived for lunch at the Blueprint Café, overlooking Tower Bridge. She was forty-five minutes late. Sharon believed it was important to keep people waiting, to remind them how important she was.

After such a successful morning with Operation Ripper, as she affectionately called the body disposal document she'd presented to Douglas, she was ready for more.

Rebecca Kershaw looked a mess – long mousy hair which hadn't seen a hairdresser for years, scuffed shoes, no makeup, rows of rings piercing the rim of her ears and a nose stud. With all the money I pay her, you'd think she could at least put on a clean jumper, Sharon thought. Rebecca was Douglas's second cousin, now twenty-five and a talented journalist. Sharon had employed her as a freelance since she'd first started working in London.

'Rebecca darling, you look wonderful. I always envy women like you who look so lovely without a scrap of makeup,' Sharon said as she sat down. The waiter brought her usual vodka and orange.

Sharon's friendship with Rebecca was no happy coincidence. Douglas's cousin was a gossip and terribly indiscreet about her relative's private life. It was all good material.

Rebecca ordered a salad, Sharon had fish and chips, her one decent meal of the day, and by the end of lunch had commissioned six pieces for the *Daily* and *Sunday Tribune*.

'I'll call Georgina when I get home and tell her what I'm doing,' Rebecca said, still innocent enough to believe that an editor should be informed as to what she had bought for her paper.

'Don't worry about that, chook, I'll speak to her. She'll love the story about the woman who was repeatedly raped by her three brothers then went on to have the baby with two heads.'

'They were Siamese twins, they had two bodies too,' Rebecca objected.

'You just go to Indonesia and get the story, Rebecca, leave the details to me. Will the TOT piece about that Manchester woman be ready this week?' TOT was Sharon's term for a Triumph Over Tragedy story, otherwise known as Womb Tremblers.

'It's pretty depressing,' Rebecca said, big eyes filling with tears. 'The poor woman sat there surrounded by dozens of pictures of her children, five of them dead and the sixth and last in hospital and not expected to last the week. And she's just been diagnosed as having breast cancer.'

'Sounds great,' Sharon said enthusiastically. 'Just remember to keep it up-beat.'

She delighted in commissioning stories behind Georgina's back. She always agreed the fees with Rebecca, always paid her double or triple the going rate for features on the paper, and Georgina could do nothing about it. The relationship was historical and Sharon always justified it on the grounds that the features were to run across both titles. There goes your budget for the week, bitch, she thought in the car back to the Tower.

The contribution sheets went first to Georgina for signature, then to Sharon, who usually 'forgot' to sign them.

Once in her office, she opened Rebecca's file on screen to see how much she'd been paid. In the last nine months it amounted to £120,000 – more than any other staff writer or columnist on the titles.

Could be a bit embarrassing for Douglas Holloway if that gets out, she thought with a smile. This was turning out to be a good day.

A large belch reminded Sharon she'd pigged herself at lunch.

'Roxanne,' she screamed through the closed door. Her PA scuttled in. 'Mummy was a bit naughty at lunch and needs some of her little babies.' Roxanne returned with two small white and blue capsules.

'Sharon, you have to be careful, you've already had two today,' she said as she handed them over.

'Don't you fucking dare tell me what to do! You're just a fucking overpaid secretary. I'm the boss. I call the shots. Now get the fuck out of here.'

Rebecca still didn't feel happy about not telling Georgina what she was working on, so she called her that evening. What could Georgina do after all? Sharon had commissioned them, and set the fee. And, after all, Rebecca *was* Douglas's cousin.

The money was great, but with half of her work ending up on the spike, she wasn't getting a high enough profile.

It was late when she called and Steve had left for the day. The call was picked up by Paul Column, the assistant editor for features. He put Rebecca on hold and raced into Georgina's office.

'Quick, I've got Rebecca on the phone,' he said with mock urgency. 'She already spoken twenty words and at her rate that comes to about £1,000.' Everyone in the office was appalled at the fees Sharon paid her.

'Shut up and get out,' Georgina said to Paul affectionately, throwing her stress ball at him. She took the call.

'Rebecca, first I haven't got the space to run a quarter of these stories and second, I don't want half of them,' Georgina said firmly.

'That's not my problem. Sharon commissioned them and you're going to have to pay, whether you use them or not. And I need a new by-line picture taken. Can you send a photographer to my flat on Tuesday at 7 pm?'

Paul wandered back into the office. 'So what are we up for this time?'

He was young, late-twenties, but had a seasoned civil servant's understanding and acceptance of the things he couldn't change.

'You know she was on to me first, saying how she'd discussed the stories with Cousin Douglas and Cousin Douglas thought they were wonderful and Cousin Douglas thought we were ripping her off.'

'You must be fucking joking!' Georgina exploded. 'She's paid more than anyone in this office. You know that better than anyone because her fees come out of your budget. I don't believe Douglas knows anything about it.'

'Why are you so loyal to that bastard, George? You're the only person I know who sees any good in him. He's a cold, calculating prick. I wouldn't put anything past him.'

'You don't know him like I do. Let's have a drink to celebrate your newly busted budget.'

Before she left, Georgina phoned Douglas.

'I need to see you.'

Walking into his office ten minutes later, she was steaming. 'Do you realise, Douglas, that Sharon is commissioning Rebecca without my knowledge?'

'Rebecca who?'

'Your delightful, semi-skilled cousin, the lovely Rebecca Kershaw, freelance journalist, remember her? She's a decent enough journalist, Douglas, but Sharon is paying her way over the odds, more than twice what I pay anyone else unless it's a splash. It's ridiculous. I pulled her contributions sheet today and she's earned well over £100,000 in less than a year. It could be very awkward for you.'

Douglas's face whitened. 'I don't know anything about it. I don't want to know anything about it. If Rebecca is employed here, it's nothing to do with me. If she's being paid too much, that's nothing to do with me either. Just sort it out.'

'I can't sort it out if Sharon is commissioning her directly. Douglas, you *have* to get involved.'

'I'm running a company here, I can't be bogged down in detail.' It was his standard reply when he couldn't face up to a problem. Georgina left the room.

'I've got something for you,' Sharon said when she finally got Andrew Carson on the phone. 'You'll find it very, very interesting. Your place, tonight?'

She had been teasing him about her latest findings on Douglas for some days now. It was the only way she had been able to get his attention. Andrew had this rather unfortunate habit of disappearing from time to time, and she always punished him for it.

She had been sitting on the new evidence, savouring its impact, for when he was focused one hundred percent on her again.

His distraction had been caused this time unusually by his wife. He was visiting her in hospital most nights after a hysterectomy. Fucking attention-seeking hysterical-ecotomy, Sharon had thought. The lengths some women will go to to get affection.

She tried to avoid his grasp when she arrived at the flat, but he pushed her roughly up against the door and buried his face in her cleavage for a few moments, like a greedy little boy. She hated the way he made those raspberry noises when he put his face down between her breasts, like a pig feeding at the trough.

'Ouch, Andy!' she squealed, as he pushed her harder up against the door and jammed her back into the keys he always kept in the lock. 'The keys are sticking into me,' Sharon complained, 'it's stupid to leave them there.'

'Security,' he mumbled, his face still immersed in her breasts. 'Safer there, spares upstairs,' as though reciting a mantra. There had been a small fire in his flat one night years ago and he couldn't find the door keys in the panic. Thereafter he'd always left a set in the door and a set in a box on the hall table upstairs.

He tried again to lift Sharon's skirt. 'No, Andy, for once there's something more important than sex. It's not that I don't want you, it's just that what I have in my briefcase is even more delicious than my pussy.'

She took off the CD – The Beach Boys Greatest Hits – and

inserted the tape. 'Get me a drink, Andy. There's something I'd like you to hear.'

They sat together on the black leather and chrome sofa as the tape started to play.

'The real problem, Georgie, is that Tony is also a close friend of Douglas's. Let me put this plainly. The Minister knows everything about Douglas, about Becky and the baby, about his business deals. If you publish, he'll blow the lot . . .'

Carson leaped up from the couch and whooped with delight. 'Yes, yes, yes.' He turned to Sharon and grabbed her by the shoulders. 'You fucking little genius,' she said, kissing her roughly.

The next move was more like a rugby tackle, and about as gentle. He dragged her to the end of the sofa, threw her face down first, raised her miniskirt and took her from behind. It was over so quickly Sharon couldn't even get up a good moan. He was too excited even to notice.

'How the hell did you get that?' he growled into her ear, then lifted her off the sofa, kissed her again, almost lovingly, and they both sat down. At least he hasn't smudged my makeup, Sharon thought.

'You know she was working on the Blakehurst story all last week. Well it turns out Les Strangelove, Douglas's friend, is also close to Blakehurst, and he called Georgina late Friday night begging her to hold the story. Typical of the cow, she refused to hold it out. All that crap about integrity. In the end she didn't have enough proof, that's why it didn't appear Sunday. You know I'm having her office bugged, so I heard it today when Pete brought me in the weekend's highlights.'

'So the lovely Becky is carrying Douglas's child? Very interesting,' Carson said. 'I've suspected for ages they were having it off. Now we have proof. Good girl. Becky isn't married, so we can't cause any trouble there. I wonder if Kelly knows about it? Find out. Take her to lunch, see if she's suspicious. But whatever you do, don't let on that you know. Knowledge is power – we'll hold on to this for a while.'

'I've got something else for you, Andy. Rebecca Kershaw's fees. Make interesting reading.' And Sharon pulled a computer print-out from her briefcase.

'Great work, Sharon. Now we need to do the Full Monty on Douglas and Becky,' he said.

Carson, a one-time supporter of Douglas Holloway, had become increasingly disenchanted with the way he was running the company. He, like many of the board members, had become a millionaire since Douglas took over the helm, but the company was stagnating.

With the bottom-line benefits of brutal cost-cutting now in the pockets of the directors, several of them were just waiting for the opportunity to oust their chief executive.

They were not sure how much further he could take the company. His last two purchases, a chain of provincial newspapers in New Zealand and a TV station in South Africa, had been beset with problems and unseen costs.

Carson looked over at Sharon affectionately. And you're the person to help me get the dirt on him, he thought. Keep my hands clean.

She was flushed with her success, or the whisky, or the slimming pills, and put her head in Carson's lap. Face up for a change.

'And I've come up with a great name for our Douglas file – Drop the Dead Douglas,' she said, and they fell into each other's arms, laughing.


After Sharon had left, Carson poured himself another whisky. He would need more than an affair, a love-child and overpayment of his cousin to get rid of Douglas. They were damaging pieces of evidence, but far from mortally wounding. I need to set a trap, he thought, something that will discredit him commercially, throw his judgement into question, destroy his credibility with the City and the important shareholders.

He opened his briefcase, his Red Box. With the amount of documents and briefings he took home every night, he was like a government Minister, drowning in paper, he thought bitterly. It would be different when he was running the Group.

Leafing through the week's agenda, he saw there was a meeting set up with Graham Kuper, the South African businessman and entrepreneur. Like many small-state multi-millionaires, he was desperate to get a stake in a major international media group. Opens a lot of doors, looks prestigious. Kuper had about £50 million to play with and was in London to discuss whether it was worth investing in the Tribune Group.

Carson sat back in his chair, holding the whisky glass in both hands, as if in prayer, or in thanks. He had met Kuper years ago. Bit of a shady character. He looked at his watch. Two o'clock in Capetown. What the hell? He picked up the phone and dialled the home number of the deputy editor of one of the local rags, Stuart Peteyson.

They had worked together years ago and Peteyson owed him. Peteyson was then a young gun foreign correspondent in central Africa, Carson his news editor, both working on the *Telegraph*.

He could still remember the scene. Carson had called Peteyson back to London to discuss his living expenses, which were double the former correspondent's. Leafing through the hand-scrawled expenses sheets (always a bad sign, like bad writing in a French exam, hoping the examiner wouldn't see the holes), Carson immediately recognised a fiddle.

One of the many perks of being a foreign correspondent was being able to employ a maid who cleaned the offices. In Peteyson's case his office was based in his apartment. He had trebled the amount paid to the girl. Entertainment with unknown and indecipherable dignitaries accounted for the rest. Then Carson spotted it. The actual restaurant and hotel receipts had been altered. Cleverly but not carefully enough. The slight pen stroke that turned a £79 bill into £179. Hardly detectable.

He looked closer at a couple of the receipts from what was clearly Peteyson's favourite eatery. They were photocopies of blank receipts, filled in with what Carson suspected was Peteyson's fair hand. he looked at his signature on the bottom. There it was, the give-away 't', not crossed but looped. The bastard had been forging his own expenses.

When Peteyson walked into Carson's office several days later he had already worked himself up into a rage, like a boxer preparing for a fight. He leaped up from behind his desk, slammed down his fist and shouted: 'What kind of fucking fool do you take me for?'

He then flung the entire stack of expense sheets at the young hack and continued to rant.

'Altering receipts, forging bills, false accounting. This is embezzlement. Theft. I could fucking throw you in jail for this Peteyson, you stupid, stupid cunt.'

Carson walked back around his desk, stood with his back to the reporter and picked up the phone. 'Get me the Head of Security, in my office now.' He slammed down the phone and turned to Peteyson. 'You've got about four minutes, the time it will take that over-paid moron to get here, to tell me what you've been up to. I either get the truth or we'll press charges against you. This is a criminal offence. Fancy a few years in a nice open prison, do you?'

Peteyson broke down, tears mingling with the tiny rivers of perspiration already running down his face. Carson could smell the sweat of fear, could almost taste the saltiness in the air. This tactic always worked, especially with the younger ones.

'Mr Carson,' he sobbed and fell into a chair, burying his face in his hands, shoulders shaking. 'It's a woman, a hooker. Met her at the local winebar, didn't know she was on the game, thought she loved me, said she loved me. It's all gone so terribly wrong. She's threatening to tell my wife, blackmailing me . . . pictures . . . she's got pictures. Her pimp was videoing us. Oh my God, please help me.'

It was a slightly more lurid version of the usual kind of trouble young correspondents got into. Carson had seen it all before. At least it was a woman and not a young boy like the Egyptian correspondent a few years ago.

He had no intention of turning Peteyson in, but wanted to see him squirm. And it was always useful to have people in your debt, especially bright young journalists like this. He could be important one day, if Carson saved him now.

'I can't do anything about your wife, you stupid fucker, but I might give you a second chance. Pick up those expense sheets.' Peteyson scrambled around on the floor on his hands and knees, collecting the scattered sheets, then handed them to Carson. He took out a red folder from a drawer, placed the sheets in it and filed them in a locked cabinet. 'You put one foot out of place and

I'll burn your fucking arse. Do you understand me? Now get out of my fucking sight.' Carson never mentioned the incident again. He didn't need to. It hung between them every time they spoke. The huge debt, the obligation.

Peteyson's voice was sleepy now at the other end of the line.

'Hope that's not another fucking hooker you've got in bed with you Peteyson,' growled Carson.

'Andy, how are you? Just a second.' Carson heard him scramble out of bed and walk with the portable phone to another room. 'What can I do for you? I assume that at two o'clock in the morning you haven't called to ask about my health.'

'I need a favour, Stuart, on the quiet. Do some serious digging for me on Graham Kuper, see if he's got any skeletons. I'm looking for hidden dirt. Anything that's out in the open or been referred to before is of no use to me. Do the Full Monty on him. And quickly. Oh, and regards to your wife.'

He slammed down the phone and went to bed.

# Chapter Nine

'Champagne to celebrate, eh, Georgie?' Les Strangelove said and waved the waiter over. 'The house champagne will do. Expenses aren't what they used to be.'

They were lunching at Le Pont de la Tour, at Les's invitation. It was one of his favourite restaurants, though Georgina was not so keen. She thought it was over-priced, over-stated, over-rated. She preferred her restaurants and her food simple.

Georgina had met Les years ago through Douglas. Mostly she liked him. At fifty-five he was one of the most successful 'suits' in the advertising business. He had the naïve charm of Paul Hogan and the mind of Clive Anderson, kept an all-year-round tan and was still craggily handsome.

Although he had left Perth at the age of five and come back to live in the East End with his English parents, Les still had the most distinctive Australian accent. He decided early on in his career that his blue eyes and boyish charm were not a sufficiently unique selling point in the highly competitive world of British advertising.

So Les took elocution lessons from a drunken old Australian at his local pub. He dressed almost exclusively in RM Williams, the now fashionable Australian bushman's outfitters, and bought a cardboard box full of old Australian settlers' pictures when he was out in Sydney on business twenty years before. These were now lovingly framed and scattered around his mansion in Moor Park, a wealthy suburb just outside London. Any visitor was given a Cook's tour around his ancestral homes: 'the old shack my great-great-grandfather built – he was a convict, you know, the corrugated iron shed that was my home as a boy . . .' It was all very convincing.

Les had the rare ability to schmooze without being nauseating. He was invaluable to McLaird's for his network of powerful friends. His policy was: 'Good work can't save a bad relationship, but a good relationship can save bad work.' And he'd had plenty of opportunities to prove that throughout a long career.

'I can't thank you enough for holding out the Blakehurst story, Georgie,' he said. 'It was such a relief when I opened the *Sunday Tribune* on Saturday night at Kings Cross.'

'Les, I told you on the phone and I'll tell you again – it wasn't the old mates act that kept it out. We just didn't have enough on him to run it. We're still working on it and if I get enough evidence I will run it.'

'Yeah, yeah, say what you like. All I know is that we're *very* grateful. So grateful in fact that my friend has arranged a little thank you present. Just drop into Tiffany's any time, they're expecting you. Private room, anything you want. Within reason, of course.'

'I can't believe what I'm hearing. You're trying to bribe me,' she said in disbelief.

'Easy on, Georgie, it's not a bribe, just a little thank you.'

'But there's nothing to thank me for. I didn't hold it out for you or to protect anyone else. Blakehurst has nothing on Douglas. He's clean. In fact, I'll show you how close we came to running the story of your friend's little indiscretion.'

Georgina reached into her large handbag, pulled out a roll of proofs and handed them to Les.

'I'd open that carefully if I were you. We don't want anyone seeing, do we now.' Les looked at the pages – they were full colour proofs of what would have been page one of the *Sunday Tribune*, the pages two and three spread, and the pages four and five spread.

A smug-looking Blakehurst was pictured with his mistress on the front page beside the headline:

SECRET SCANDAL OF
TOP MINISTER'S
SORDID SEX SHAME

106

Inside were pictures of the Minister and his wife, more shots of the mistress, their love nest, his home in Hampstead.

'You couldn't ... you weren't ... you won't,' Les spluttered, and then began to have what appeared to Georgina to be an epileptic fit. He choked on the bread he was eating, poured champagne all over his face and suit trying to get it to his mouth, and started gasping for breath.

It was when his eyes started popping that she got really worried.

'Should I get a doctor, Les? Waiter! Quick call a doctor. This man is having a fit or a stroke. Get someone quickly.'

As Les slid down in his chair, a man two tables away rushed over. 'I'm a doctor or used to be,' he said, and laid Les on the floor, loosened his tie and cleared his air passage with his fingers.

'It's just a piece of bread stuck in his throat,' he said eventually. 'He does look as though he's had a nasty shock though. Just sit quietly and breathe deeply,' he said to Les, who was now upright in his chair again, still clutching the proofs to his chest.

Georgina vaguely recognised the small woman huddled inside a black leather jacket in the lift with her. She thought for a moment, trying to place her. There was nothing memorable about her: badly cut frizzy dark hair, hardly any makeup, a face so lined she could be anywhere between thirty-five and forty-five.

'God, this lift takes forever,' Georgina finally said. 'You're Myra Prescott, aren't you? That was a fantastic piece you wrote in *Me* about adopting the Romanian orphan. How is the child? She was waiting for some operation wasn't she?' *Me* was the new magazine launched a few months ago in the *Tribune*'s stable mate the *Daily Herald*.

Myra beamed a grateful smile at Georgina as she took off her jacket. 'It's so hot in here, and the lift seems to stop at every damned floor,' she said. 'Tania's brilliant, the light of my life. I've been sending money for the heart operation she needs. It's a nightmare, waiting until she's well enough for surgery. I'm desperately trying to adopt Tania, but the authorities don't seem to think a single mother earning £85,000 a year and living in a big house in Islington is what's best for her. It's heartbreaking. I've been through hell and back, and I expect to return there many times before this is over.'

The lift arrived at Georgina's floor and she stepped out, followed by Myra, even though it was several floors away from her office.

'It's incredible, really,' Georgina continued. 'You can't tell me it's better for the child to live in a filthy orphanage, with no one to take care of her properly, than to come and live with you. I hope you're writing another piece as a follow-up.'

'I'd love to,' she said, her eyes welling up with tears, 'but I'm afraid, if I do, I'll never be able to adopt her.' Myra dug deep into her handbag for a tissue and wiped her eyes. Georgina noticed for the first time how incredibly dark they were, as though the pupils were constantly dilated.

'Is there anything I can do,' Georgina offered, 'put a bit of pressure on the authorities by doing a piece in the *Sunday Tribune*, which is distanced enough from the *Herald*.'

'Oh, Georgina, would you do that?' Myra asked. 'You're brilliant. Here's to women helping each other. Here's to the sisterhood.'

'Give me a call and let's see what we can do,' Georgina said and Myra waved goodbye.

Odd woman, she thought. It was only when Myra lifted her arm to wave that Georgina noticed the nervous red rash on the other woman's arms.

Douglas decided to walk the six blocks to his solicitor's office. It was a beautiful evening, following a perfect summer's day and the heat haze was now picking up the first pink shades of sunset over the City. Julian Stockwell met him in the foyer and they walked together to his office.

'I don't have long Julian, my driver's picking me up in thirty minutes for dinner at nine,' Douglas began. 'I just wanted to check on a few things. Have you been over the details of the Delaware company with the accountants? I need to be sure everything is in place.' Stockwell ran the London end for American attorneys Johnson Questing.

'Everything is in order,' he said. 'I have spoken to the five trustees of Rosebud Inc. personally. There is now about £3 million in Tribune shares in the company and £1 million in cash, earning good interest. It's safe.'

Before his marriage to Kelly, Douglas had sought advice from his solicitor and accountants. He loved her dearly but after two costly divorces, wanted to protect what he had worked so hard for – just in case things didn't work out. It had seemed impossible then but, if it came to it and he and Kelly divorced, he did not want her walking away with his fortune.

The impossible had now happened and he was extremely glad that he had taken the necessary precautions. Of course he would be fair, look after her, but he was not prepared to lose everything. And if he left her for another woman, he knew Kelly would fight to the bitter end for every penny.

She was still young and, even he had to admit, extremely beautiful. She would marry again, probably to someone richer than him. It wasn't fair that Becky and his child should go without because of Kelly's extravagance and his mistakes.

Now it was certain he would divorce, he needed to know that things were in place.

Douglas had retained his dual citizenship. His mother was French-Canadian and father American, so it was relatively easy to set up a company in the tax haven of Delaware in the States. The five trustees were lawyers, the sole beneficiary his brother Daniel. It was all completely legal and gave Douglas the opportunity to avoid some UK tax on a chunk of his earnings. Technically the trustees were there to run the company, to oversee and manage his interests, but in reality he took care of that.

'As instructed, your brother is the sole beneficiary of the company,' Stockwell confirmed.

'I may want to change that, Julian. I'm about to have a child and would like to start making the necessary arrangements to name him or her as chief beneficiary. How long will that take to set up?'

'I'll have to contact the trustees and tell them of your intentions, then at the next board meeting it can be ratified. I don't see any problem. As the board meetings only take place twice a year, we could either wait until September or arrange an emergency meeting. Given the distance some of the trustees will have to travel, that could take a month or so.'

'There's no hurry, but I'd like it sorted by September. There's just one other thing. In the event of a divorce, how safe is the house in East Heath Road? How safe from Mrs Douglas, I mean.'

'You took my advice at the time, Douglas. It's as secure as it can be.' He remembered the earlier meeting. Stockwell's advice had been to put the house in someone else's name. It was a stroke of genius. Kelly would find out about it eventually, but she would have one hell of a job getting her hands on it, especially as the 'owner' was not even a British citizen.

'It is preferable if you transfer ownership of East Heath Road to a foreigner, someone you trust implicitly. Then it will be more difficult for Mrs Holloway to claim half of it,' his lawyer had said.

'But I'll be giving her the flat in Chelsea, isn't that enough?' Douglas had retorted angrily.

'Working in the business you do, you must be aware of the divorce laws in this country. Your wife is entitled to half of everything you've earned while you were together. From what I see here, the greater proportion of your wealth has been acquired during the period of the marriage. I would therefore advise you to place as many of your assets as you can outside Britain, as quickly as possible.'

There was only one person in the world Douglas could trust with this – Daniel. Douglas had made his brother promise he would tell no one of the arrangement, especially not his wife. Daniel had reluctantly agreed.

It was Friday afternoon and the *Sunday Tribune* was in the normal state of anxiety pre-publication day. On a good week, you ended up with a choice between a couple of potential splashes, holding your breath that a rival newspaper didn't break the story before Sunday. This was not one of those weeks. There were two possible splashes, both of them second-rate.

Some journalists describe the process of making ordinary stories look interesting as 'making shit shine'. Others refer to the process as 'tricks with light'. Either way, they needed all their tricks this week. Georgina had to choose between two stories for the splash:

CHERIE MERCY
DASH SAVES
DYING CHILD

or

HEEVES WIFE
SECRET TRYSTS
WITH TOY BOY

'These days Cherie is always rushing to someone's bedside to save them,' Mike said grumpily. 'She just trying, and failing, to be the new Diana. Who cares?' He'd been working on the Heeves story all week, one of the junior reporters' tip offs.

'You know the problem with Heeves, he's not an A-list name. He only gets four million ratings and it's Friday night on Channel 4. Not our readers,' Georgina said. 'I'll give it a spread inside, pages two and three. The pictures of Mrs Heeves and her toy boy will work better in colour on three.

'Steve, get Dave and Pete in so we can look at the front page,' she said to her PA. Dave came in with his layout pad and they set to roughing out the splash.

Georgina always wondered but never asked how Dave got hold of these pads. They were tools of the old hot metal days and Douglas had banned them from all the papers. It was supposed to be a paper-free office. It'll soon be journalist-free the way Douglas is going, she thought.

Georgina was deeply unenthusiastic about the results of their scrutiny, secretly hoping that a big story would break tomorrow and save them from splashing on either of these.

As they were finishing, Mike came back into the office. 'We've got a problem, I need to talk to you alone.' When the office had cleared he said: 'We've got another leak. John Allen from Newslink Agency just called me and asked what our Heeves story was. He'd had a call from someone on the *Mail on Sunday*.'

'How the hell do they know what we're working on? That story didn't even hit the system until an hour ago.'

There was definitely a spy in the office. Week after week a story they were working on would appear either in the *Sun* on Saturday or the first editions of the *News of the World*. But they'd never had a potential splash leak before.

'I want a list of everyone working in the office today and the names of everyone who has handled that copy. It's been in a secure file until an hour ago. I just can't believe someone would do this!'

Mike left and Georgina called Security.

'Is there any way we can trace the outgoing calls from the *Sunday Tribune*?' she asked the acting head of security. 'And the incoming ones. I need to find out if anyone has called the *Mail on Sunday* office today.'

'That's easy,' he replied. 'We tape all calls incoming and outgoing. I'll do a computer check. Have you got a particular number you're looking for, even a prefix? It'll take less time that way.'

Georgina could not believe what she was hearing. She had called Security as a matter of routine, she hadn't expected them to be able to *do* anything.

'Are you seriously telling me that all the calls coming into the Tribune offices and all going out are taped, all the time?' she asked.

'We've always done that, I thought all the editors knew. It's just a precaution.'

This unbelievable, and probably illegal, Georgina thought after he left. I'm being bugged from every direction. First Sharon, then the company. Every single phone call I've made from here has been taped.

Sunday morning and Georgina was exhausted. She'd been too tired to see Belinda last night and they'd ended up having the usual row about how she put her job before their relationship. They both had short fuses but also short memories when it came to domestics.

Belinda had taken it badly when Georgina had sat her down and explained that, because of Sharon's investigation and the tail on her, she could not stay overnight at the flat, as she had been warned when Georgina found out about Sharon's investigation.

'This is ridiculous,' she'd exploded. 'As if your job doesn't rule our lives enough already, now I can't even sleep with you.'

Georgina had been patient. 'Sweetheart, it's only for a while, just until this mess blows over. It doesn't matter if we're seen out together, or if they follow you to my flat. So far as the world is concerned, we're best friends and spend a lot of time together. They can't prove a thing. But if you stay over, they've got evidence, of a kind.'

In her heart Georgina was rather relieved they had been forced to spend less time together. She loved Belinda, but sometimes wondered if she loved her enough. And there was still a little part of her head that couldn't get around the fact that her lover was a woman.

Georgina was in bed when Belinda arrived at her door at 10 am with an arm full of croissants still warm from the patisserie around the corner, fresh coffee and a large bottle of orange juice. She prepared a tray, grabbed the newspapers which had already arrived and went back to bed.

Georgina was sitting cross-legged, wearing nothing but a white vest, reading the papers. Belinda brought in two cafetières of coffee.

'Caf or decaf?' she asked.

'Give me real coffee and plenty of it,' Georgina said. 'I don't know how you can drink that decaf muck. It's like sex without genitals.'

Belinda placed the tray on the floor and slipped in behind her, legs straddled around Georgina's, arms around her waist, hugging her from behind. She started kissing her neck, her hands on her breasts now, twisting her nipples, then one hand worked its way slowly down between her legs. She held Georgina tightly until she came.

'You sure know how to please a girl,' she said, lying back in her arms.

Finally they managed to get out of bed and go for a run around Hyde Park. 'Can I borrow one of your white T-shirts?' Belinda asked after they'd finished showering together. It was one of the many advantages of having a female partner, thought Georgina. Sweeter orgasms and you got to swap clothes.

In faded Levis 501s moulded to her bottom and a white T-shirt, Belinda looked fabulous. She could have had £20,000 worth of designer clothes on her back and she couldn't have looked better.

It was a clear, almost hot summer day as they went out to Georgina's car, her pride and joy. She had searched for ages to find it, a perfectly restored Mercedes Pagoda 280 SL convertible in pearl white. They took the top down and jumped inside. Georgina stroked the walnut dash: 'Good morning, baby' and they set off.

Belinda leaned across to kiss her lover and stopped when she saw the expression on her face.

'For God's sake, Belinda, not here,' Georgina shouted over the revving of the engine.

They arrived at John and Peter's place at two for lunch. They were Georgina's oldest friends in London and among her dearest. John was now Assistant Editor Features on the *Daily Tribune* and Peter a successful author and freelance journalist.

A cork popped the moment they walked into the kitchen and sat down at the big kitchen table overlooking a wonderful, madly shambolic garden. The sun was shining.

'Here's to you, pet,' John said, handing Georgina a glass of the wonderful fizz they imported from Burgundy. 'And to our new house guest – Piddles.'

'Oh, John, you can't call her that, she'll know you're taking the piss. Give her a proper name,' Georgina said as the tiny stray cat rubbed up against her legs, jumped into her lap then stepped territorially on to the table.

'Water pistol alert,' Peter said, reached over to the dresser and aimed a long squirt of water at the tabby kitten. She leaped off the table as though hit by lightning and looked around crossly for the culprit.

He went around and petted the soggy moggy, then said to Belinda: 'It's aversion therapy. I read it in the *Telegraph*'s pet column. It trains them to stop doing unspeakable things and they don't associate the shock with you. Clever, isn't it?'

By the end of the first bottle, they were talking shop.

'I've been hearing some worrying things, George,' John said as he poured her another glass. Georgina ignored the sharp look

114

Belinda gave her. 'Sharon has offered jobs on the *Daily* to two of your reporters. And she was telling Joe Philips the other day that there are a lot of redundancies in the pipeline, that they'll sack a lot of specialists and run them across both titles.'

'I know what she's up to,' Georgina said. 'She's doing it under the pretext of Douglas's master-plan to purge the titles. I know most of the people she's offered jobs to, but when I front her about it she just denies it. Douglas assures me he's got her under control. I was talking to him about it yesterday when he came around for his Presidential Meet the People tour and he said not to worry about it. "You worry about the newspaper Georgina and I'll worry about the politics",' she said, imitating his French-Canadian accent.

'I know she wants me out, but she hasn't shown her hand to Douglas yet. All I get from him is the old "Sharon will never edit the *Sunday Tribune*. She doesn't have the intelligence or the style to do it" line.'

'Just be careful, pet, watch your back. And especially watch that snake Ferret. He really is the most treacherous monster. It's guys like that that give gays a bad name.'

'And you have as good a reason to be worried, as do I,' Georgina said. 'I haven't been able to tell you guys on the phone, because they're all bugged. I'm not even sure about my home line. I'm also being tailed twenty-four hours a day.'

John's eyes widened in disbelief. 'That bitch! She's really after you now.'

'*And* my office is bugged *and* someone is hacking into my system and stealing stories for the *Daily*. Thank God for Mike. I've known about it all since the beginning, so I have the advantage. The real victim in all of this is Belinda,' said Georgina, taking her hand. 'Imagine Sharon's glee if she had proof that I was having an affair with a woman.'

'But George, you know the laws of disclosure,' Peter said. 'Unless she has photographs of you actually having sex together, or a confession from Belinda, there's no proof.'

'We're not talking about the proof required to publish a story Peter,' she said wearily. 'We're talking about evidence to produce to the board to discredit me. Pictures of Belinda arriving at my flat

115

and leaving the next morning, a few choice snaps of us hugging in the window, would do the trick.'

'She could never produce that sort of thing in a board meeting, surely,' Peter said.

'It wouldn't happen like that and you know it. Sharon would make sure they got into the hands of the directors and there would be no trace of her behind it. Anyway, the important thing is that I am aware of it. Newspapers are a dirty game, but I never thought they'd get this dirty.' Georgina reached for her glass and this time Belinda put out her hand to stop her.

'You're driving, sweetheart,' she said softly. This was Belinda's code to her to say: 'Stop'. She worried most about her lover at times like these, when the pressure was really on. Georgina never got drunk, never again. They exchanged glances and she asked Peter for a coffee.

Georgina was silent during the drive home. Belinda held her hand and left her to her silence. She knew this mood, what had brought it on, and when to leave her lover to her own demons.

Belinda was one of the few people on earth whom Georgina had trusted with this pain. Douglas knew, of course, but only because he had rescued her.

It was during a routine 'Well Woman Check' compulsory for all employees of the *Tribune* that she learned something was wrong. Seriously wrong.

The doctor had examined Georgina's breasts, then examined them again. She had found a lump. The mammogram confirmed their fears.

The next few weeks were a nightmare of waiting – the appointments with the specialist, the operation to remove the lump.

And for Georgina there was another nightmare: the memory of her mother's disease. The fears she had managed to force back into the deepest depths of denial began to creep forward, slowly, maliciously, consuming every scrap of normality like the cancer that had consumed her own mother.

For the first time in her life, Georgina came face to face with the pain of a loss she had never had the chance to resolve. She found herself regressing, waking in the middle of the night desperate, for some sense of her mother, as she had done as a child. That first night she woke, Georgina went into the spare room where her past was stored and took down an old yellowing makeup case. Impatiently she emptied the contents on to the floor and searched.

When she found what she was looking for, she went back to bed and placed the old photograph on the bedside table. It was the picture of her mother, young and beautiful and laughing at the world, on her engagement day. Next to it Georgina placed an almost empty bottle of perfume, so old the contents had darkened to the colour and consistency of stale espresso coffee.

Next to them both she placed a bottle of gin.

Night after night Georgina would lie in bed listening to her mother's favourite operas, sipping endless gin and tonics, trying to remember the woman in the photograph and push away memories of her as she began to die.

Georgina became obsessed with the thought that she would die like her mother, the pain eased only by alcohol. In a way, she was recreating that truth.

Even when the test results finally arrived, Georgina did not believe their conclusion. Non-malignant tumour. All she could register was tumour, which must mean cancer. Non-malignant was a benevolent misnomer. No cancer could be non-malignant. Sooner or later they all killed.

Sleep became another enemy. Georgina went to see her GP and he prescribed sleeping pills.

For weeks she functioned at work. Each night it was the same routine. Douglas was the only one who noticed something was very wrong. He called her into his office one evening.

'George, I think you need a break,' he said awkwardly. They were closer back then, friends more than colleagues.

'The last thing I need at the moment is a break,' she said, flopping into a seat.

'Look, maybe no one else will tell you this but you look terrible,' he went on. 'You've lost so much weight and you look exhausted all the time. I know you've been worried about the tests, but they're clear. You don't have cancer. Is it something to do with your mother?'

Georgina looked away as her eyes filled. She could feel the streetlights picking up the tears and making them shine. The whole room turned into a kaleidoscope, fragments shifting and distorting as she turned her eyes back to Douglas.

He walked from behind his desk and kneeled before her, taking both her hands. 'It's okay, George,' he said softly, then the tears came. She held on to his hands as though they were a lifeline, all that connected her with the real world. He stood up and brought her to her feet, then walked her gently out of the office.

Douglas hailed a cab and took her home, holding her as she wept. No word was spoken as they went into her flat. He led her into the bedroom, took off her shoes and pushed her back on the bed, wrapping the duvet around her like a cocoon. Sitting beside her, he stroked her hair as a father would until she fell asleep. It was past midnight before he left.

Georgina woke in a panic. It was one in the morning, her eyes glued together with dried tears and mascara. She would never understand why, but that night the burden of living through the fear and the pain became too much. She was tired, deathly tired. All she wanted was to sleep for a very long time.

The gin sloshed into the bottom of the tumbler. No need for tonic or lemon tonight. The top on the sleeping pills unscrewed easily and she poured a handful into her palm and slowly swallowed them.

When at first she woke in the silent, pale room, Georgina thought she was at last home, in her real home, Johannesburg. The woman leaning over her smelt so fresh, like a mother. Georgina opened her eyes slowly and saw that this was no bedroom.

It was only later, much later, that she realised how close she had come to death, and that Douglas had saved her. Some instinct had made him turn back to her flat that night.

She owed him a great debt. Over the years she would repay it many times.

Mike came into her office as Georgina was getting ready to leave. She was standing staring out of the window, another unforgettable sunset, thinking of a million things – her mum, her home, the fine mess she was in.

'Fancy a quick South African Chenin Blanc?' he asked. It was code that he had something to tell her in private, away from the spying eyes and ears of the office. Georgina hated South African Chenin Blanc.

'Love to,' she said and they walked out of the office together. The Last Chance was packed and they made their way to a booth at the back. Mike only just stopped short of holding her elbow as they squeezed through the crowds. On the short walk there, he had, as always, made sure he walked on the road side of the pavement.

She had teased him about this when they first started working together. 'You may be my boss, Georgina,' he had said, 'but you're still a woman and I was taught to treat women properly.' Secretly she loved the show of gallantry. It reminded her so much of her father.

Georgina sat down and Mike asked her to take care of the envelope he had been carrying. 'Stick it in your handbag for a minute,' he said and went off to get the drinks. On his return, Georgina took the bag to the ladies' and opened the envelope.

Inside was the summary of the private investigator's report on Sharon. Her car was regularly parked outside Andrew Carson's flat twice a week, Monday to Friday only as he returned to the country late on Friday or Saturday morning. Length of stay – usually three hours.

Under the summary was a sheaf of photographs, the kind of long-lens pictures the newspapers were no longer allowed to use. But these photographs were not for publication, just circulation, and then only as a defence weapon.

There was a time and date recorded on each print – Sharon entering the flat, Sharon leaving the flat. Then she came to it. The series of photographs Georgina needed. Sharon was standing at the window, a tumbler of whisky raised to the heavens either in salute or prayer. The next show was of her in the same position, Carson at her shoulder. The next he had his face in the side of her neck, his hand down the front of her Wonderbra. The next she had twisted toward him, her face obscured, skirt up to her waist, a flash of red suspender belt, no knickers, and Carson's hand on her bottom.

That will do nicely, Georgina thought as she replaced the photographs in her bag and went to rejoin Mike.

'Not bad,' she said, smiling mischievously as she sat down. 'But don't pull our man off yet. We're going to need as much evidence as we can get.'

'He told me on the phone that Sharon also has expensive tastes in cigars.'

'But she doesn't smoke cigars, or not that I've ever seen?' Georgina said, puzzled.

'Nor did Monica Lewinsky,' Mike said; she fell about laughing.

'Come to think of it, Carson's a big cigar man . . .'

'So was the President.' And Mike spilled his beer, he was laughing so much. 'There's also some interesting stuff on Ferret,' he said. 'It appears he's been doing a bit of a George Michael in some men's lavatories in Hackney. We haven't got any pictures yet. It seems Pete has a fairly eclectic taste in men – or should I say men and young boys? I've instructed the PI to keep back until he has something really good. Some jailbait, if you get my drift.'

'So he's in to boys as well, is he?'

'The younger the better it appears. Apart from Carson, there's no one else in Sharon's life. She goes home alone and leaves alone.'

'Well done, Mike. This is great. Looks like we're in with a chance, after all.'

# Chapter Ten

Douglas and Becky wandered hand-in-hand around the house in East Heath Road. It was almost finished. A magnificent Gothic building in Hampstead directly overlooking the Hea0th, it was now unrecognisable from the wreck they had viewed six months ago. Only Becky had seen its potential then.

She had heard that the property was coming onto the market. It was more than half-finished when the owner, a very wealthy pop star with surprisingly good taste, died of a heroin overdose. He had employed Silverstone architects to gut the house, which had been badly converted into apartments in the sixties, and to design a completely modern, minimalist home.

From the outside, it looked like any other multi-million-pound Hampstead mansion, the Gothic detail restored perfectly. Inside it was completely white, with pale bleached wooden stairs joining the four floors. One entire wall of the house, from floor to ceiling, had been stripped back to its original rough red brick.

Becky had spent hours, and committed £2 million, with architects John and Sebastian Silverstone, transforming it into an ultra-modern, showpiece home. Half of the fourth floor had been removed to make a huge, double-height central living area and the roof over it was made entirely of glass. A large mezzanine study overlooked it, with a terrace coming off the other wall.

Only one room was complete so far, the second of five bedrooms on the third floor. White walls, bleached Californian oak floors, floor-to-ceiling windows overlooking a private garden, a large Impressionist painting on the wall above the French antique bed.

'We might as well christen it as we're here,' Douglas said as he took Becky's face in his hands and bent slightly to kiss her.

'Wait,' she said, reached over to the remote control on the bedside table and directed it towards the far corner of the room. The 'Champagne Aria' from *Don Giovanni* began. They had a soft spot for Mozart, especially *Don Giovanni*, as this was the first opera they had been to together. This aria, about living life to the fullest, without a care for anything, had become 'their song'.

Douglas smiled, and started undressing Becky. He loved the white cotton knickers and bras she wore, the swell of her stomach, the full breasts. There was something pure about Becky. She always smelt as though she'd just come out of the shower, her skin had never seen the sun and was as soft and pale as a child's. He entered her gently, more gently now as she was carrying his child. She wrapped her legs around him and rocked with his movements until first she came, then he did. Their sex was intuitive, loving, and almost always missionary position.

After years with Kelly and her sex book techniques, it was a relief simply to love a woman. He was not the sort of man who enjoyed knee-trembling sex on the stairs, or not after the first few months anyway.

From the moment Douglas realised he loved Becky, he had lost interest in his wife sexually. Well, most of the time anyway. In the early days he could manage both, but now it was as though his cock had an in-built fidelity switch. And it was Becky he was faithful to.

Douglas rolled over, keeping a protective arm around Becky, and took in the beauty of the room. He thought for a moment about the bedroom he had grown up in. Cramped and shared with his brother Daniel, it was in an annexe at the back of the shabby brick duplex his parents rented.

He sent up a silent prayer to whoever was watching over him. After years of struggle, he now had the life he wanted – a powerful job, money, a woman he truly loved, and this baby.

But it wasn't perfect yet. There was still Kelly and the inevitable divorce. He was prepared for it to be vitriolic and had gone to great lengths not to let his wife find out about his new home.

He knew she would learn the truth eventually, but could not

find the strength to be honest to his wife, simply sit her down and say the marriage was over, he was in love with someone else. All his experience told him that this would in the end be the least painful course, but he couldn't find the courage to face her. He thought about the pain he would cause Kelly when she found out about Becky. The second twist of the knife would be the discovery that his lover was pregnant.

He knew he would simply walk out one day. Kelly would come home and find him gone. She would find out about Becky and the baby from a friend or a gossip. He wanted to tell her himself, to be kind, to be honest, but he knew in his heart he would walk out of her life as quickly as she had walked into his. Emotionally he was a man without courage, and he despised himself for it.

Douglas decided to phone Georgina later that night. He'd been worried for some time that things were getting out of control between her and Sharon and he needed to create a breathing space. He also needed room to start implementing the cuts he had planned on the *Sunday Tribune*. Better while she was away.

There was too much unrest within the Group as it was. He was fighting on too many sides. More dangerously, the enemy was now within his own fortress. There were too many factions and he knew if they were attacked from outside, those factions would join forces against him. A conversation yesterday with Zack Priest, the Company Secretary, had worried him.

'Douglas, there are some things I must point out to you. There are rumblings among some of the board members. I suspect Andrew is stirring things up and using Gavin as his cover,' Priest had warned.

'I don't believe Andrew would be disloyal to me, Zack. Gavin perhaps, but never Andrew. We created this thing together. You're way off beam there. I'd trust him with anything. Look how useful he's being on the Kuper deal. He's taken the lot off my back and is handling it personally so I can concentrate on the television side. What have you heard about Gavin?'

'He was holding court at the American Bar earlier this week. Some of his old mates from the *Express*. He was saying that you'd

123

lost touch, weren't investing enough in the quality of the newspapers, the journalism. That now all the cost-cutting was done you were fumbling, out of your depth.'

'What else?'

Zack took a deep breath. Both he and Douglas knew that Matheson was not the only one critical of the last two acquisitions he had made. Circulation was falling on all the titles except the *Sunday Tribune*, advertising rates were slipping. They only maintained their yields by discounting space and increasing the ad ratio in the papers.

'He went on about how you had failed to turn the company into a serious multi-media player, how we were being left behind by the other newspaper groups. How the Tribune Group was now seriously in danger of a hostile takeover from one of the larger television companies,' Zack said quietly.

'That duplicitous bastard! How can we get rid of him?' Douglas was seething now.

'You can't. He's an executive director of the group.'

Douglas was stung by the betrayal. Matheson was useful to him, so he had always tolerated him, but even one rogue director was dangerous. And Matheson had clout. The City loved him. His profile was almost as high as Douglas's. He had to put out the fires within his own camp.

He had thought long and hard about what Zack had said about his friend Andrew Carson. Was it possible he too was disloyal? After all they had been through together? All they had achieved? Douglas did not have many friends, especially not men, but Carson was the closest he had to a brother outside a blood tie. Douglas simply could not believe he was disloyal.

One thing was clear in his mind: he had to stop the in-fighting between his two female editors, especially as it now appeared in one form or another of the rival press's gossip columns on almost a weekly basis. It reflected badly on him, looked as though he couldn't control his own editors. He had already formulated a plan to foster some calm.

'Georgina, there's a special project I need you to look after for me,' he began when she answered the phone. 'I'd like you to go to Australia for a couple of weeks. There's a newspaper in Perth we're looking to buy. You know that part of the world. You'll have to go to Sydney to meet the owners. Maybe take a week's holiday as well.'

'What's up, Douglas?' she said suspiciously. 'You don't offer holidays, you cancel them. And I don't know that part of the world. There's a bit of a difference between South Africa and Australia. What's so important about a little rag in Oz? I only worked there for a few years, I'm hardly an expert.'

'You're the closest thing I've got and I thought you'd appreciate the break,' he said. 'We're coming into the summer slump so it's a good time to be away. Get back fresh for the autumn assault. Just think about it. You'd be doing me a great favour and you deserve a holiday.'

Georgina had mixed feelings about his offer. Things were difficult between her and Sharon. A break from the constant back-biting, the constant surveillance, was appealing. So was the thought of a holiday. It would also put a bit of space between her and Belinda. Things weren't working out quite as she had hoped there.

But could she afford to leave the paper for three weeks? Would it still be there for her when she came back?

Georgina and Mike had arranged to meet early that morning for a breakfast meeting since it was impossible to discuss anything in the office now Sharon had it bugged.

'How are things going with the Foreign Secretary story?' Georgina asked when their coffee arrived.

You could always read Mike's face like a book. He had his 'big exclusive' face and his 'we've just lost our big exclusive' face and today he was wearing the latter.

He had been working for weeks on a tip-off that the Foreign Secretary, Jack Edgerton, had a love child by a Thai prostitute. Edgerton had been especially vocal in his demands for tougher measures against single mothers and heavier penalties for fathers who deserted their children. Himself happily married with four children, he was in the self-righteous Blair mould and a devout Catholic to boot.

The tip-off had come from another Thai prostitute who had claimed the woman, Ling Sinwaeni, had had an affair with

Edgerton when he was still at university and she was fourteen.

The go-between had produced pictures of a very young but very recognisable Jack Edgerton, arm in arm with Ling, plus pictures of her and her daughter in the brothel. There were also copies of Ling's bank statements proving Edgerton had paid money into her account for about five years.

Mike sighed and said almost tragically: 'No good, George.' Losing a big story was a blow for most of them and this would have been a big one:

SCANDAL OF
RANDY JACK'S
THAI LOVE CHILD

'We've proved that he sent money to the Thai hooker and her child for years, and the pictures of them together are genuine.'

'So what's the problem?'

'I got a stringer out in Thailand, someone I trust, to find Ling and it looks as though she's been set up. The hooker who gave us the info was just out to make a quick buck. The father of Ling's baby, so far as she can ascertain, was another university student who was with Edgerton backpacking through Asia. Our man never touched her.'

'Why was he paying money into her bank account then?' Georgina asked.

'It appears our sanctimonious Foreign Secretary has a kindly side. His friend died of a drugs overdose less than a year after they went to Thailand and, according to Ling, Edgerton helped her out for a few years. It's still a great story. "Foreign Secretary pays to raise Thai hooker's love child".'

'You're talking in headlines again, Mike,' Georgina said teasingly. 'Actually, I've got a better idea. Copy all the pictures and keep them somewhere safe, along with the go-between's statements. This is what we've been waiting for – the story that will blow Sharon out of the water.'

'I'm not with you?'

'Don't put anything in the system, but keep it all together. Sharon has been lifting our stories from us for weeks and we know

126

she never checks anything. She assumes we've already done the hard work, and we always have. So far. When the time is right, we'll plant this little sting – but this time it won't be us that gets stung.'

Douglas, Carson and their finance director, James 'Fatty' Oakland, travelled separately in chauffeur driven cars to the Ritz for the meeting with Graham Kuper. Cost cutting was okay for the troops, but it was important that the prince and his barons maintained a certain style.

Each man was lost in his thoughts. This was an important meeting. Fatty was contemplating the improved bottom line that Kuper's millions would bring to the Group, and the big bonuses and increased share options they could legitimately award themselves next year if things went well tonight. He looked lovingly around the interior of his new Rover 800. Even with a big bonus, he wouldn't upgrade this yet. He'd always dreamed of having a car with walnut veneer, and the British racing green he had chosen made him feel like a racing driver, even though he had a chauffeur most of the time.

Douglas was calculating how he could deflect Kuper's interest away from the group's main titles and television interests and instead entice him into taking a major shareholding of their loss-making mid-market title. It would require flattery and cunning to manipulate this man. Douglas's special subjects.

Last to leave Tribune Tower was Andrew Carson. He believed it always created a good impression to be seen as too busy to leave the office on time, with urgent business only he could handle. He leafed through the fax Stuart Peteyson had sent from Capetown that morning to his flat and smiled again.

The dossier read:

*Graham Kuper, 48, born Capetown.*
*Two children by first marriage, amicable split, one child to second wife Sandra. No sexual scandals.*
*Currently worth £200 million.*
*Chairman of North Zigaron Airlines, Chief Executive of SAE, South African Entertainments.*

*Keen to buy into international, UK-based media group.*

*Motive primarily status and international standing, seeks influence news network would provide.*

*Prior media coverage hostile. Tough businessman suspected of dirty tricks campaigns against commercial rivals and attempts to 'influence' government to change monopoly laws in South Africa. Nothing proven.*

*No formal charges ever made by media. Closed down small scandal magazine which hinted at impropriety by suing them and winning massive damages.*

*Government source privately claims Kuper is suspected of supplying aid to Sierra Leone rebels in attempt to destabilise government and win favour with rebel government in return for favourable trading agreement.*

*Am working on last. Dangerous.*

Carson re-read the last two paragraphs. This could be it.

They all went directly to Kuper's suite and chatted over drinks before the serious business began with dinner. Douglas hated this bit, the social chit-chat. Without Kelly there, he found it difficult to strike the right note of informality. It was in situations like this that he most missed her. She was a perfect counter-balance to his own social awkwardness.

His PA Julie had prepared the usual personal profile on Kuper – wife and children's names, special interests, pet hobby-horses. Since this was the first meeting, though, he could hardly ask his usual first question: 'How's your charming wife?' He remembered from his notes that Kuper was fanatical about cricket and managed a question about the forthcoming test between South Africa and the West Indies. Carson was a real cricket enthusiast and the men weighed up the pros and cons of the respective international sides, which took them through to dinner.

They ate in Kuper's private dining room overlooking the Thames.

'I would have thought with your international stature as a businessman you would be more interested in taking a major share of our broadsheet titles, Graham,' Douglas began as the smoked salmon parcels arrived. 'They have a more serious voice in the business world, the corridors of Parliament. They are a more influential platform for a businessman such as yourself.'

'I don't require a newspaper to talk to people of influence,'

Kuper replied testily. 'The real power lies in talking to ordinary people, influencing the perception of the masses. That's why I find the *Tribune* so appealing. What do you have now, over three million readers a day? Now that's power.'

'Actually we have nearer nine million readers a day of the *Tribune*, each purchased copy being read by 2.2 people,' said Fatty. 'And twelve million on Sunday.'

'But they're just the working classes,' Douglas said scornfully. 'They have no power, no voice, no influence. They don't count. A far more powerful group in British society is the middle classes. The Tribune portfolio of newspapers is broad, we have more than the red tops. The *Daily* and *Sunday Herald*, our mid-market titles, have a readership of just under five million. If it's a real voice you want, and a significant one, the *Herald* is the best vehicle. It would be extremely difficult, but we may be able to convince the major shareholders to turn the *Herald* into a separate company, under the umbrella of the Tribune Group.'

Fatty shifted his considerable bulk in his chair, some might have said nervously. Douglas hadn't warned him this was coming. In moments of great stress Fatty had a most unpleasant habit. He didn't even know he was doing it, but he was doing it now. His forefinger crept up to his right nostril and started digging about, then slipped almost unnoticed into his mouth. He chewed.

Douglas continued: 'Of course it would be more cost-effective to leave all central services, finance, management, printing, circulation and distribution, with the *Tribune*, but maintain editorial and commercial independence for the *Herald*. More prestigious for the owners too, dare I say.'

'I hadn't thought that possible,' said Kuper. 'It's an interesting idea, a very interesting idea. How quickly could you get a proposal to me? Tomorrow?' Heads turned to Fatty who stopped chewing immediately.

'I'll get working on it tonight,' he said. The crafty fox, he thought to himself. Douglas was planning this all along.

Carson hardly said a word. It was going too well.

Georgina had been weighing up the consequences of setting up a sting for Sharon on the Foreign Secretary story. It was a tactical move and she wanted to wait for the right moment. Her mind was made up for her when she started reading her delivered copy of the *Tribune* that Friday in the flat.

They had been working on a story all week about the Monarchy. The Prime Minister's influential Demos group was about to release a report recommending important changes to the way the Monarchy operated. Mike had got hold of a leaked copy.

It wasn't necessarily a splash for the Sunday, but it was a good story and they had planned to run it over two pages inside with a You The Reader Decide hotline.

The most controversial element of the recommendations was a proposal that the Sovereign, whoever that happened to be, would be forced to stand down at sixty. The problem was the Royal Family had a record of longevity and a seventy-year-old Monarch just wasn't appealing any more to the general public.

It would avoid a repetition of the awkward hiatus created by Queen Elizabeth, with a rapidly ageing Prince Charles waiting in the wings, becoming more and more eccentric as the years passed. The theory was that it would keep the Monarchy young, more relevant and more appealing.

That theory was now explained in detail in the *Daily Tribune*. It was a complete lift of the story Mike had been working on. There was no doubt of it.

Georgina reached for the phone as it rang. She waited to hear Mike's voice then said: 'It's time to move. Get our little green curry into the system.'

They both knew how easy it was to tap their phones and had decided on the code words 'green curry' in one of their sessions at the Last Chance. Mike replied with a 'Yes, yes, yes' that sounded like a poor-man's version of the orgasm scene in *When Harry Met Sally*.

# Chapter Eleven

Sharon's chauffeur dropped her off at home after midnight. Even before she put the key in the door she could hear Rocky meowing impatiently. He pushed himself hard against her legs as she walked in, demanding attention. Sharon scooped up the old black and white moggy in her arms, hugged him to her face and inhaled deeply that wonderful scent of cat. It was so comforting.

Few people knew of the existence of Rocky. She thought it was bad for her image. The last thing she wanted people to think was that she was a sad woman living alone with her cat. He had wandered into her house in Fulham eleven years ago, one ear badly chewed and half his tail missing, and it had been love at first sight.

An envelope, marked 'Urgent, Private and Confidential', had been pushed under the door. She looked around for any other packages, or letters. There were none. How could they forget? she thought bitterly. Perhaps there will be a message on the answer phone.

A glass of wine first. The refrigerator was empty except for two oranges, a bottle of Spanish fizz and half a dozen bottles of Jacob's Creek Semillon Chardonnay. I *will* resist the chocolate fudge ice-cream in the freezer, she told herself sternly, then shut the door and stared hard at the picture stuck to the front of the fridge with a couple of Grommit magnets.

It was almost impossible to believe that the woman pictured on a beach wearing a lime-green bikini was Sharon. The face was bloated and there were about six chins supporting the jaw. The big fleshy forearms were crossed in front of the body in an attempt to conceal – the stomach full and hanging over the bikini pants, tell-tale shadows over the cellulite, thighs wide and heavily hung with saddle-bags. It looked like one of those ghastly 'Before' snaps run alongside pictures of 'the new slim you' in dieting magazines. In fact that is exactly what it was – Sharon 'Before'.

Sharon glared at the picture and repeated her mantra: 'I will never be fat again, I will never be fat again,' and poured herself a glass of wine. She walked through to the sitting room, a triumph of chintz over taste, and sat in the Colefax and Fowler pink rosebud chair beside the phone.

The first seven messages on the answer phone were from work, all problems, the next was from her friend Liz reminding her about their Girls' Night Out on Saturday. In fact, it was always just two girls, Sharon and Liz.

There were some drawbacks to her single life and Chinese meals in Chelsea on a Saturday night with a girlfriend was one of them. Carson always returned to the family home at weekends.

The next call was the one she had been waiting for. 'Hello Sharon . . . oh, can you hear me. I hate these machines dear, I never know what to say. It's your mother, calling to wish you happy birthday. Now don't forget you're coming for lunch on Sunday. Everyone will be here. Please come Sharon. Your father was so cross when you didn't make it last time. We haven't had the family all together for ages. Did I tell you Samantha has a marvellous new job *and* a new boyfriend. Is there someone you'd like to bring dear? Oh and please wear something nice, you don't have to dress up for us. Your father sends his best wishes.'

Sharon sat back in her pink chintz room, the heavy floral curtains drawn, and fought back the anger. In one message her mother had poked around in every open wound, wounds that had been inflicted in childhood and never healed. She hated the family 'get togethers' which provided the stage for her siblings' triumphs. Both her brothers were married and had children. Her sister had been married, and divorced, twice and had also produced the required two grandchildren. They all had respectable jobs. Her mother disapproved of the way she talked and the way she dressed. Her father disapproved of almost everything about her. She was eclipsed by her beautiful younger sister Sam. She had always been Dad's favourite, Sharon thought bitterly.

In her parents' eyes she was a failure. No husband, no children. They ought to feel proud of me, she thought, proud of what I've achieved, but no, nothing I do is good enough. She'd lost count of the 'new boyfriends' her sister had brought home after her second marriage had collapsed, but did they care about that? Her darling little sister had produced grandchildren, she was soft and flirty, she was the kind of woman her father could identify with and be proud of.

He couldn't even be bothered to come to the phone. 'Sends his best wishes' indeed. What about his love? Sharon knew from an early age that she could never compete with her sister's beauty so she'd tried to shine in other ways, by being a success. But that was the boys' territory. A doctor and a lawyer. *That* was success. Her father thought there was something deeply disagreeable about his elder daughter's profession. And she had failed at the things he considered important in a woman – marriage and motherhood.

She walked back into the kitchen, took out a bottle of wine and went to sit in her garden. This was another of Sharon's secrets, she loved gardening. The wildly coloured petunias spilled out of pots, pink, purple, white, crimson, and the marigolds formed an irregular border down either side of the lawn. The garden looked like a floral reincarnation of the contents of her wardrobe: masses of bright colours erupting everywhere, pots too small to contain their profusion of flowers.

Rocky jumped up on her lap and squinted at his mistress lovingly through the cigarette smoke. What a way to spend my birthday, she thought, alone with my cat and a bottle of wine.

Not for the first time, Sharon considered the sacrifices she had made for her career. Did she have any regrets? Only at moments like this, birthdays, Christmas, did she feel the loneliness. Work really did satisfy her most of the time in a way no relationship ever had.

There had been a series of boyfriends, she had even been engaged once, but men were always so demanding. It was difficult for them to understand that she actually preferred staying late at work to going off and seeing a movie or having dinner or even

133

sex. While she had reaped the benefits of the feminist movement in her career, the sexual revolution had passed Sharon by. As a child she'd received little physical affection, so she did not miss it now. Stories had come to her far easier than orgasm, and sex on the whole was rather a disappointment. Only one man had been able to bring her to a climax, and he was married. The truth was, she didn't miss it. Work was like sex for her – the thrill of the chase, of a story, the excitement of teasing it into the paper, then the ultimate satisfaction of seeing a scoop on her front page. Yes, better than sex. Or at least better than the sex she was used to.

But she did need to feel desired. That gave her power. And the relationship with Andrew Carson, as with a couple of other married men in the past, satisfied that need. They wanted her and that was enough.


There was a sack of discarded newspapers on the floor; a pile almost as big lay unopened on the table. Breakfast was always a chaotic affair in Georgina's flat as she rushed to drink coffee, read the day's papers and get ready for work. It was Friday morning and the phone rang every ten minutes.

Belinda had arrived unannounced at around seven in the morning and Georgina could not quite work out why she felt so irritated by her being there. It wasn't just the fact that it was not altogether normal for a friend to visit another so early. She felt Belinda was pressurising her.

She walked around the table and slipped into the chair behind Georgina, straddling her. She nuzzled her lover's neck and slipped her hand down the dressing gown to stroke her breast.

'Not now, Belinda, I've got to get to work,' Georgina said.

'Sweetheart, I need to talk to you,' she said, and returned to her side of the table, poured another cup of coffee. 'There are a few things I need to clear up and I won't see you tonight or tomorrow.'

'Can't it wait?' Georgina asked irritably.

'No, George, it can't. You're always racing off. I never get to see you these days. I just need ten minutes. I want to sort out what we're doing this weekend. Suzy has invited us over for Sunday lunch and there's a big party on at Jason's on Saturday . . .' Belinda was interrupted by the phone ringing. It clicked to answerphone and Georgina recognised the voice of her news editor.

'Don't answer it,' Belinda said tersely.

'Don't be so childish, I have to answer it, it's my job,' she said and picked up the phone. When she had finished the call, Belinda was still waiting at the table.

'As I was saying, George, there are some things I need to talk over with you.'

'For Christ's sake, do you have any idea how busy I am today?' Georgina said. 'I don't have time to discuss our weekend arrangements. Can't you just for once think about me and not yourself?'

They stared at each other, one angry, one almost in tears. Belinda dropped her chin, blinked hard, refused to cry.

'And can't you see what that job is doing to you?' she asked gently. 'It sucks you dry. By the time you get home, there's nothing left of you. You're physically and emotionally drained.'

'Look, I'm under a lot of pressure,' Georgina said. 'The problems with Sharon are coming to a head and it's all getting very nasty. I'm fighting on every side. I don't think you have any idea what that feels like. I spend a minimum of twelve hours a day in that place, often eighteen hours, making decisions, sorting out problems, keeping people happy, fighting.'

'But, George, what's in it for you? What's left of you? Don't you ever stop and think there might be another way to live your life? You're a clever, talented woman, you could do anything.'

'But this is what I want to do,' she said impatiently. 'You knew that when you met me. If you were a little more supportive and a little less self-absorbed, things might improve between us. Don't blame the job because our relationship is in trouble.'

'You can't see it, can you? It's the job that's making you incapable of having a real relationship – with anyone.'

Sharon had the private investigator's first report on her desk. It had arrived at her home late last night, but in her birthday gloom she had barely glanced at it. She opened it again.

*Day One:*

*Chauffeur arrives 7.32 am. Douglas leaves flat 7.45 am, carrying overnight bag, immediately gets on carphone – digital, can't be intercepted.*

*Breakfast at the Howard with Aaron Seymour, head of McLaird's advertising agency. Leaves 8.30 am. Arrives at Tribune Tower 8.48 am.*

*Lunches with Zack Priest, company secretary, in his office. Leaves Tribune Tower 7.48 pm. Meets Sir Stephen Hughes, non-executive director of Modtern, at the Berkeley Hotel. Drinks only. Leaves 8.33 pm.*

*Walks two blocks to the Fifth Floor Restaurant, Harvey Nichols. Dines with Suzanne Fielding, Head of Programming Fosters TV. Leaves at 9.48 pm. Chauffeur drops him off at locked gate to back alley in Devonshire Place.*

*Alley serves mews houses in Devonshire Place and Devonshire Close. Cannot ascertain which house he enters.*

*Day Two:*

*Chauffeur arrives 7.33 am, Douglas leaves at 7.49, carrying overnight bag, straight on carphone . . .*

It was the same every day, only the names of the people he met for breakfast, lunch, drinks and dinner changed, Sharon thought.

She called Carson. 'I've got the first report and the fucker hasn't put a fucking foot wrong,' she said. 'All he does is work, work, work. One thing's for sure, though he didn't stay with his wife most of last week. Our friend says it's impossible to see which fucking house he goes into when he's not sleeping at his Chelsea flat. He *acts* as if he's being tailed.'

'Nothing is impossible,' Carson said. 'He'll make a mistake, slip up somehow, and you'll be there watching him. Make sure you're tailing both of his chauffeurs. What about the report on Becky?'

'She's on holiday at the moment at home and things are pretty quiet. She stays in all morning, lunches with her fucking society friends or people from that fucking useless agency we employ. We've got to find a way to get rid of those parasites.'

'All in good time. You've got to learn to be patient.'

'There's something else. She has a steady stream of people arriving in the afternoon, some of them with swatches of fabric. The silly rich bitch is probably redecorating.'

'Maybe. Get their car registrations checked out anyway. And have them followed.'

'The tail on Georgina hasn't thrown anything up yet,' Sharon began.

'We've got bigger fish to fry than her,' Carson snapped back swiftly. 'Get rid of Douglas and there *is* no Georgina. Forget about her for now.'

Sharon had no intention of forgetting about Georgina, now or ever. This had got personal and she was going to bury her rival – personally.

All her instincts told her that this Belinda woman who was always at the flat was Georgina's lover. The difficulty lay in proving it. She never slept over and there was no show of affection in public. No proof. Yet.

One night that week Douglas did go home to Kelly. This time there was no baby doll négligée, no dinner ready. It was just after 10 pm and she was sitting up waiting for him, an almost empty bottle of champagne in front of her.

It was five weeks since Kelly had been impregnated and everything was fine. It was very early and the most dangerous period was not yet over, but she was confident now. She was carrying her husband's child and wanted to tell him.

'Douglas, darling, come and sit with me for a minute,' she said. 'I've got some good news for you.'

'I'm tired and certainly not in the mood to talk,' he said. 'Anyway I've got a few calls I have to make.'

'Please, Douglas, just sit with me for a minute.'

'I told you, I've got things to do,' he said angrily. 'I don't have time to hear about your latest shopping trip.'

'I haven't been shopping, don't be nasty. Please, just sit and talk to me for a bit. Please, darling. It's important.' She was pleading now.

He walked straight past her and into the study, picked up the phone and started talking.

Something in her head just flipped. He was mid-sentence when the phone was ripped from his hands and Kelly started screaming.

'Don't you dare ignore me! Who the hell do you think you are? I said I wanted to talk to you.'

Douglas turned his back on her. She hated this more than anything else: to be dismissed. All thought of the baby went out of her head and the one thing that had been possessing her all week burst out of her.

'And where have you been all week? You've been with that bitch Georgina, haven't you?' Kelly was past tears. There was hatred in her eyes as she picked the entire phone up and threw it at the wall.

Then she started hitting him. Not slaps but fists, first into his face until he raised his arms to protect himself, then anywhere she could lay a punch.

Kelly ripped open the silk shirt she was wearing, exposing her newly perfect breasts. She cradled them in her hands, twisting the nipples until they were hard. 'Take a look. Go on, look, you impotent little bastard! She doesn't have tits like this. She's not beautiful like me. She's *nobody*.'

He stood, ashen-faced. It was Georgina he was talking to when she'd ripped the phone from his hands. Had she heard? He would deal with that tomorrow.

Kelly stopped hitting him and unzipped her skirt. She threw it at him and stood there, shaking, naked except for a pair of Manolo Blahnik stilettos. He turned away.

'Look at me, you fucking bastard. You'll never have anyone as beautiful as me. I'm the sexiest woman you've ever had, you told me that. Maybe you need a little reminding just how sexy I am.' She started a slow dance, like a high-class lap dancer. She moved provocatively towards him, shaking her blonde hair softly from side to side with each step. Douglas started to back away, came up against an armchair, half sat, half fell down into it.

Kelly moved towards him again, placed one leg to either side of his, then bent low from the hips and laced her arms around his neck. He was smothered in silicone.

'She'll never love you like I do. Douglas, just look at me. Tell Kelly you love her. Tell your baby you'll never leave.'

For the first time in months, he felt something for his wife. Not love but pity, the kind you feel for a hopelessly injured puppy left

138

on the side of the road. Helpless pity, because he knew there was only one way to end her suffering, and that was to leave.

He walked to the bathroom and returned with a dressing-gown, wrapped it gently around her shoulders and led her back into the sitting room.

'Douglas, I'm sorry,' she began when she had calmed down. 'It's just that there's something I wanted to tell you, and I needed to see you. Something wonderful, I couldn't tell you on the phone.'

'There's something I have to tell *you*,' he started, feeling a rare rush of courage and conscience. He sat down beside his wife and took her hand in his. 'I don't quite know where to start.'

Kelly knew she was in danger. This was the first time he had touched her in weeks and it didn't feel good. It was partly the way he was holding her hand, the way you touch someone who is ill or dying. She could see the pain in his eyes. Every instinct told her to retreat and regroup. If she let him continue he would end up leaving her. She felt it in the pit of her stomach.

'No, no, no!' she cried. 'Don't tell me you're leaving. Don't tell me you don't love me. I'll be good, I'll make it work. Just don't ever leave me.'

She lifted his hand to her face and placed it against her cheek. He could feel the warm tears. He knew it was cowardice, but couldn't face her with the truth. Not now, not when she was in such a state. He did what he always did in tough situations. He avoided it. Deal with that one tomorrow, he thought.

# Chapter Twelve

Douglas had a lot on his mind – Becky and the baby, Kelly, the traitors on the board, the deal with Kuper, the merger with Fosters TV.

He knew he had to leave Kelly, and soon. He owed it to Becky and to their unborn child, but he just couldn't face up to confrontation. Better to do it gradually.

The meeting with the Chief Executive of Fosters, Stan Billmore, was set for Tuesday week. Douglas had worked tirelessly to get the business proposal finalised, trusting no one within the company except Zack Priest. It was too risky.

Priest was one of the few board members who would retain a seat in the planned merger. He and Carson and Fatty.

Initially, Douglas had been against keeping Carson in the dark over the details of the merger. He did not believe that his long-time friend and ally was working against him. Andrew Carson had saved his skin a number of times in the past, so he'd had every opportunity to stitch Douglas up – and he never had.

But Douglas bought Priest's logic that the fewer people who knew about the details the better. Every director who worked on the project had a secretary who had friends and could rarely resist a quiet gossip over a few glasses of wine. The reporters on his titles always tried to make friends with bosses' secretaries. They were goldmines of information.

And if there was one thing Douglas had learned, it was that everyone who knew a secret told one person. The old 'I was told not to repeat this, so I'll only say it once' logic. For the moment it was about containment.

It was crucial now that the Tribune Group broaden its media base. His critics were right about one thing: the other newspaper groups had left them behind in terms of their television expansion. Apart from a share of three minor terrestrial TV companies, their electronic media portfolio was slim. The newspapers were highly profitable, especially with the economies he had brought to bear through saving cost-cutting, but it was not the future. Print was a declining market, especially for his titles. The future was television.

He could see it now: Tribune Communications, a multi-media print and television company, with him as the Chief Executive of the controlling board. A scaled-down version of the Tribune board would be maintained, along with the Fosters TV board, and a controlling Tribune Communications board running the entire company.

Convincing Fosters and Billmore that he should stand aside for the younger Douglas would be the difficult part. But Billmore was well into his sixties now and couldn't possibly expect to run a young, dynamic company. No, I am the only man for the job, Douglas thought. Billmore will surely be happy taking on the role of Chairman. He could stay as Chief Executive of the operational television board, for the time being anyway, although both subsidiary boards would have to be scaled down.

The restructuring of the Tribune board would provide Douglas with the opportunity to oust Gavin Matheson and anyone else he suspected of less than one hundred per cent support. His time was coming.

But his more immediate problem was those two troublesome women. Keeping them from each other's throats was taking up too much of his precious time. He needed them both, at least for now, but if they forced him to decide between them, it would be a purely commercial decision. Sentiment was a luxury he could not afford.

Carson was about two minutes away from orgasm. Sharon could always tell because he paused briefly, savouring the moment, his face flushing to puce. At least she could see his face tonight. She was getting sick to death of the 'Roger Over The Sofa' number he had grown so fond of lately. Hadn't she read somewhere recently that a man was losing interest when he couldn't look you in the face during sex? Must do a feature on that.

Fuck! It was uncomfortable on the kitchen table, she thought, not forgetting to increase the pitch and regularity of her moans. And the glass top was so slippery.

A grunt from him reminded Sharon that it was time for her to climax. It wasn't hard to fake the cries tonight. The base of her spine had been rubbed almost raw by the pounding.

'So what was so important you had to see me tonight?' he said, zipping up his flies a few minutes later.

Sharon eased herself off the table, tucked her breasts back into her jacket, pulled down her purple suede miniskirt – there was no undressing with Andy – and took the file from her briefcase while he got the drinks.

'Those people who turn up at Becky's place – they're all interior designers or architects of some sort. The interesting one is John Silverstone, architect to the rich and fucking famous. I had them followed and the one place they have in common is 13 East Heath Road, Hampstead. It's a fucking drop-dead, huge mansion, that's being done up.'

'You'll have to run a check on who owns it.'

'What do you think I am, fucking useless? It wasn't easy to find out. Bet you can't guess who owns it, Andy?' she said provocatively, grabbing his crotch. 'Go on, guess.'

'I'm in no mood for games,' he growled.

'So now you've had your bit of fun, you're not interested in games? Ask me nicely who owns it. Say "pretty please".' He put his face so close to hers she could smell the whisky on his breath, see the veins at his temples bulging.

'Tell me who owns the fucking house, Sharon,' he said through gritted teeth, then menacingly put his hands around her throat. She had never seen him quite like this before and was both frightened and excited. He looked as though he really wanted to hurt her. At last she had got a response from him. He does care, she thought, then blurted it out.

'The house belongs to one Daniel Holloway,' she said in triumph.

Carson was quiet for a moment, taking it in. 'I think it's almost time to move on Kelly. It's obviously Douglas's place and for some reason he's put it in his brother's name. Probably to keep it out of Kelly's clutches. Find a way of letting his dear wife know that there's a mistress and another love-child on the way, and a multi-million pound mansion. But keep yourself clean. It must not be traced back to you, Sharon.'

As he spoke, Carson became more and more animated and more and more aroused. He took her hand and placed it on his crotch. The excitement of the chase was infectious and he grabbed her again, this time leading her with a sense of urgency into the room next door, his study.

Carson's personal computer came alive with one keystroke. He was so excited he forgot his usual ritual of making Sharon look the other way while he called up the Internet and keyed in his password. Sharon took note – BRAVO. How appropriate, she thought.

The screen came alive with scenes of pornography. Two men were screwing an appreciative woman with breasts even bigger than Sharon's. Carson grunted as he bent her over the back of the chair and entered her roughly. Within minutes he had collapsed on top of her, the only sounds his deep panting and the cries of the woman on the computer screen.

Carson led her back to the sitting room, sat back deep into the leather sofa and put his arm around Sharon's shoulders.

'There's something else interesting too,' she said, pleased with this rare show of affection from her lover. 'I pulled Georgina's holiday and sick leave record at the paper and she was off sick for a month, years ago. It was weird, because her records had been wiped from the computer. I had to get a favour from one of the old timers in the personnel department to go back through the written records stored out at Finchley.'

'Don't lose sight of the real target here,' he said. 'If we get Douglas, we get Georgina. This thing with you and her is verging on the obsessive.'

Sharon took another slug of her whisky and coke, diet of

course, and continued as though Carson had not spoken. 'My journalistic instincts tell me something is wrong here. Who takes a month off work unless they've had a breakdown or cancer or something? Or maybe drugs. Whatever it is, I'll move heaven and earth to find out what was wrong with Little Miss Fucking Perfect.'

In the cab home that night, Sharon was in a rare reflective mood. Was she obsessed with Georgina? Was it jealousy or good old-fashioned journalistic rivalry?

There had been times when she had thought they could make a great team, Sharon as editor and Georgina as her deputy. They complemented each other. Georgina was good with people and got more out of her staff, but Sharon had the toughness and ruthlessness she lacked.

They both had a good nose for a story, while Sharon had better contacts to provide those stories.

Deep down she knew she wished she had some of Georgina's class. However hard she tried, she was not an elegant woman. The expensive clothes, the fashionable address, the car that cost more than most people's annual income, it didn't add up to the one thing she had always wanted to be. As her mother had told her many times: 'You can buy style, my dear, but you can't buy class.'

And the mere sight of the attractive younger woman swanning around the office in her understated way was enough to make Sharon ill. As a journalist she knew she was Georgina's superior, but as a woman – it irked. Sharon could do without the daily comparison. She had got there first and she would out-last the bitch. With Georgina gone she would be unique again, the only woman editor. No comparisons, no competition.

There was no way they could ever work together. Georgina had to be destroyed.

Sharon believed in favours, doing them, and calling them in. She phoned her old colleague Jason Rhodes on *Bazaar*. He was chief writer now, and he owed her.

'Jason darling, there's a little favour I need to ask you,' she said, without any preamble.

He had been expecting this call. It wasn't the first, but his 'debt' to Sharon would take some paying. Two years ago, he had lost his head over a young lover, loosely connected to the Royal Family. That's what had made it a story. Sharon had phoned him in the office. She knew everything – where they met, how they had sex, all the sordid details – and she was planning to run it. There could have been criminal charges. But she held it out, as a favour to an old friend. He never discovered that Sharon did not have a shred of proof for the liaison and would never have got the story past the lawyers. The threat and the fear were enough.

'So how is your little friend, what's his name? Willy, Stevie, Charlie? Is he fourteen yet?' Then Sharon explained what she needed doing.

'And the interview must take place within two blocks of Tribune Tower at 10 am on Wednesday, July 23.'

Kelly was flattered when the call came from Jason Rhodes at *Bazaar*. He wanted to do a big piece on her and Douglas, the most glamorous couple in publishing, with 'at home' shots. He was away in Los Angeles for a fortnight so the interview was set for July 23. Only three weeks to get ready.

She immediately phoned Nicky Clarke. 'I don't care about your waiting lists. Get Nicky on the phone – now. I must see him that Wednesday morning at 8.30.'

The receptionist patiently explained again that there was a four-week waiting list to see Nicky, no exceptions, and she didn't have an appointment. He was fully booked.

'Don't you know who I am? I'll fucking get you sacked over this,' Kelly said and slammed down the phone. It would have to be Michaeljohn's, she thought, and started dialling.

Then she phoned Champney's and booked herself in for two days before the interview. The works: body massage, seaweed wrap, wax, facial, new nails. And the clothes . . . She'd have to get something new, like a whole new wardrobe. Dior or Chanel for the formal daytime shots, Gucci for the informal at homes. What if they wanted a formal picture? That long red Valentino frock with the plunging neckline she'd seen the other day was perfect. So much to do, so little time.

Kelly decided not to tell Douglas. By the time the story appeared he would know she was pregnant, would be delighted about the baby and things would be right again. She'd do the interview herself, then Jason could call him in the office for extra quotes. Her husband hated these celebrity-style interviews, but Kelly was desperate to do it. She still had that set of pictures taken of them professionally a year ago for Kelly's birthday. That would be enough of them together.

The interview in such a high-profile magazine appealed to her not inconsiderable vanity. But it was important for another reason. Douglas could hardly dump her after she'd told the world how happy they were, and about the baby they were expecting. It would make him look ridiculous and she knew that was one thing he hated above all else. It would also be a slap in the face for Georgina. I'll show that jumped-up little reporter who's in control here, she thought.

Feretti flopped down on the sofa in Sharon's office. 'Roger called me last night at home. He said he misses me and wants to meet up for a drink. Well, I told him . . .'

Sharon wasn't listening. She never listened to Feretti drone on about his lovers. It was always the same, but she had to indulge him. He was useful.

It was early-evening and Feretti finally got up from the sofa, went to the cupboard and poured himself a drink, and one for Sharon.

'So how is that bitch doing downstairs? Any gossip?' she asked.

'I'm not speaking to her,' he said huffily. 'She turned down my idea on Psychic Recipe Cards. You know, Gravalax From Beyond the Grave. It would be a wonderful promotion. She's got no style. And you remember that idea Which Willy, where we run shadowy pictures of famous men's willies and get the readers to match them up? We couldn't use real pictures of their dicks, of course, but I've got a collection at home. Pin the Sausage on the Star. She thought that was tasteless. *Tasteless!*'

'Any news on what was wrong with her when she took that month off?'

'I've talked to people who were on the paper then, and

nothing,' he said. 'It's all quite a mystery. She had some sort of cancer scare, but then got the all-clear or so it seemed. The next anyone knew she had disappeared. She never told anyone where she was and no one asked.'

'Get the investigator to check on the flowers Douglas sent during that period. He always uses Paula Pryke in Islington. They'll have a record. If she was in hospital, he would have sent flowers. At least that will tell us where she was and we can take it from there.

'Any mutterings about the ten fucking useless contract people I sacked?' asked Sharon. The ten reporters worked four days a week on the *Daily* and did a fifth shift on the *Sunday*. She had offered them an ultimatum – either they worked exclusively for her and dropped the extra shift or they would be sacked.

'They're all very upset about that, especially dear Georgina, friend of the poor underpaid, overworked reporter. The problem is, none of them blames her, they all blame you.' The moment it slipped out Feretti regretted it.

Sharon shot out of her seat and rounded on him, pushing her jacket sleeves up as she screamed. 'Fucking blame me? Fucking blame me! She's the fucking editor, they should hate her for it,' she shouted, jabbing her finger in the air with every 'fucking'. Feretti was too terrified even to brush the cigarette ash from his shirt when it fell.

'I want the name of every fucker who blamed me.' Here we go again, he thought, and picked up the pad she threw at him. Now, who's been nasty to me recently?

It was Friday night, almost the end of the working week on a Sunday paper, and Georgina was exhausted. The streets of London had slowed to a crawl and she looked out of the car window at the crowds of people pouring out of the West End theatres. Oh, to have a life, she thought, not for the first time.

A couple, probably in their early-twenties, were entwined, oblivious to anything around them, his hand grasping her bottom, she holding his head as they kissed. The sight of them, the strong arm around the girl's back pulling her into him, made Georgina long, for a moment, for the passion of a man. Would she ever feel that again? Did she want to?

It was all so difficult with Belinda at the moment. The concealment, the frustration, the rows. If I were dating a man, at least I'd be able to go home to a little comfort, she thought wistfully. It had been a rough day.

The sacking of the ten contract reporters had hit her hard. She had argued with Sharon for weeks that it was a mistake, but in the end couldn't stop it. They worked part-time on the *Daily* and Sharon said they either worked for her and her alone or she'd sack them. Even with the double-shift rate they were paid for a Saturday, they couldn't afford to give up their day jobs.

If this was the implementation of Douglas's master plan for the Tribune titles, it was only the beginning. First they would lose their Saturday shifts, then their *Daily* work. Georgina believed his concept for a streamlined operation was a mistake. She had told him so, privately.

'It's suicidal, Douglas. Can't you see what you're doing? All our titles are losing circulation and it's because we don't invest in the journalism. The readers have become much more critical consumers. The only papers that are doing well now are the ones that invest in the newspaper, in the staff.'

All Georgina could think of was flopping into her sofa with a very large, very cold, glass of wine. Her mobile shrilled. It was Belinda.

'You sound exhausted,' she said. 'What's happened?'

'Just the usual battles. Sharon got rid of ten of my reporters today. One of them has just been told his wife has breast cancer. He's had such a rough time, it's just inhuman. And it's not only that. They're all first-class operators and I need them.'

'I'm really worried about you, George. You're slogging your guts and, and for what? Everyone knows Douglas is losing it. The Tribune is the most fragile of the newspaper groups. There are rumours everywhere that Gavin is working to get him out, rumours of a merger. You'd be better off getting out now,' Belinda said.

'That's one of the reasons I can't go, because I know he's in trouble.'

Georgina's relationship with Douglas was a complicated one. She often wondered whether she would have stayed working with him for so long if it hadn't been for the fact that he'd found her that night. Many times she had wanted to leave, but he always managed to talk her around. Beneath the logic was the implication that she owed him. They had worked together for half her career.

They had a lot in common. Both from working-class backgrounds and both foreigners in London, they'd needed to prove themselves. Douglas was driven, increasingly, by his need for power. The money wasn't important to him, except that it brought him position in the world. He believed in hard work, then more hard work.

'All you need is to know where you want to be. The getting there is easy. You have to want it passionately, need it,' he'd said to her in the early days. 'But you must also understand the nature of power and be ruthless enough to do what is required to keep it.'

'Doesn't it ever bother you, some of the things you've done, the people you've sacrificed along the way?' she had asked.

'I have always believed that whenever possible you should behave honourably, but sometimes a man has to do things which others regard as wrong. You can't be good all the time or you'll lose. People take advantage of you, see it as weakness. Sometimes the end justifies any means.'

'But power without glory is also dangerous, Douglas,' she had argued. 'If the people around you don't respect you, you're vulnerable to attack because no one will come to your defence. You really are quite Machiavellian about all this, aren't you? My little Paper Prince.' After that it was always a private joke between them.

'Douglas, don't you ever stop and think to yourself how lucky you are, what happiness all this has brought?' she had asked him on another occasion.

'Luck has nothing to do with it. The harder I work, the luckier I get.'

They had always disagreed about this. Georgina believed in fortune. Sure it was important to have intelligence and to work hard, but that ability to recognise good luck when it came your way, to embrace fortune, that was a real gift. And fortune had played a large part in both their lives.

Belinda broke her train of thought. 'He's just using you, George. How can you believe in him when he lets Sharon get away with murder, undermining you all the time? Take those reporters she sacked today. It's unacceptable. You know she wants the editorship and the way she's going she'll get it. Douglas must know what's going on. Why doesn't he stop it?'

'He has assured me that my position as editor of the paper is secure. He's the one who put me there in the first place. I trust him. He must have his reasons for letting her do the things she's doing right now. He may be many things, but he's not disloyal. He won't betray me. Douglas is an honourable man.'

'Believe that and you'll believe anything,' Belinda said impatiently. 'Look, sweetheart, why don't you come over here tonight? At least for a while.'

Georgina was almost home now and the thought of driving over to Belinda's was not an appealing one. 'Not tonight, I'm really tired and . . .'

'Just forget it then,' she snapped and the mobile went dead.

# Chapter Thirteen

The merger with Fosters TV was crucial to Douglas. As he sat in the back of his limousine en route to the Howard Hotel for the meeting with Stanley Billmore, he allowed himself a few minutes to consider just how important it was. Of one thing he was sure: unless he could pull this deal off, or a major acquisition of another television group, his days as Chief Executive were numbered. Men like him were judged on performance. Only he knew that he had taken the company as far as he could. Unless he could expand the Tribune Group, the profits for 1998/9 would be significantly down and he would be out. Nothing was surer.

The financial press had been less than kind of late. The feature piece on him in the *Observer* last week was well-researched, well-argued and damning. The writer had asked the question everyone was now asking, openly or in private: after milking dry the fatted calf of Tribune newspapers, what next for Douglas Holloway? The City was watching and waiting for his next move and it had to be a dramatic one. It had to be a merger, with him at the helm. He *had* to be seen as the orchestrator of the next step in the Tribune Group's growth.

He remembered the press coverage in his first few years at the *Tribune*. Douglas had ruthlessly restructured the archaic operation and transformed it into a modern, efficient company in less than two years. In the City, where hard men are admired, he was regarded as one of the hardest. Profits were up year on year, bottom-line costs slashed, the old inefficient print working practices outlawed. He had turned the company around, but now it was time to move on, to prove to the cynics that he was more than just a cost-cutter, he was a manger with vision, someone who could grow with a company. That was the challenge now and only a merger with Fosters would silence his critics.

The deal with Fosters was simple – a merger of two great media empires. Douglas wanted to keep the two companies operating separately creatively, but to backroom source all shared facilities and therefore cut overheads and increase bottom line profits.

Stanley Billmore and Douglas met at 10 am in a private room at the Howard. Tactically it was important that this meeting did not take place on either man's turf.

With Douglas was Zack Priest, and Stephen Reynolds, Financial Consultant. Billmore had brought his Financial Director, Angus Ferguson.

The large boardroom table was set with pads and pencils, bottles of water and glasses. The coffee was brought in immediately they arrived. Douglas took a sip and wanted to spit it out. Why was it that no matter how expensive the hotel, conference coffee was always weak? The men took their places on opposite sides of the table.

'As you will see from the document I biked to you yesterday, Stanley, the merger would involve setting up an umbrella company, Tribune Communications, with a separate board,' Douglas began. 'We would still maintain the Tribune board to run the print operation and Fosters board to run the television operation.'

'I have no problem with the proposed structure,' Billmore said. 'Nor with the scaled-down version of each operational board. It makes sense to cut costs there and I accede to your greater knowledge as to which of the Tribune board members should go. However, there are still a number of stumbling blocks, the first being the name of the new company. Given that Fosters is the larger company and, more importantly, the direction of the new company will be into electronic media, one would argue that it should be called Fosters Communications. I don't believe my board would be prepared to move on this point.'

Much as he would have loved the new company to be called Tribune Communications, Douglas knew in his heart that he was unlikely to win. Which was why he had put it on the agenda. There had to be some seemingly big issues he could concede in order to get what he really wanted – his own position within the new company.

'I speak for my shareholders when I say that this is a serious point for the company,' Douglas said. 'The *Tribune* has been in operation for almost fifty years, it is a heritage to be proud of, and one which gives the new company great credibility.'

'But newspapers are rapidly becoming a thing of the past. We wouldn't be sitting here today if the Tribune Group did not need help, financially, to move into the future,' Billmore argued. 'I will of course refer this back to my board, when the time is right, but I think I can give you their answer now. It's either Fosters Communications or nothing.'

'You indicated to me last night that you think the board will accept the financial deal,' Douglas said. Both Zack Priest and Billmore's financial director nodded assent.

'There are no obvious problems there, but of course we must now formally present the deal to our boards and shareholders. There is one other issue though, which I would prefer to discuss with you in private.' The other men left the room. Douglas and Billmore faced each other alone across the massive table.

'The role of Chief Executive,' Stanley Billmore began. 'It's no secret that I have made a lot of money out of this business. I'm nearly sixty-nine and I would be happy to stand aside and take on the role of Chairman of *Fosters* Communications. But I am not confident that the board would accept you as the new Chief Executive. You've made a lot of enemies in the past few years, Douglas. What did that *Observer* article at the weekend describe you as – "the most hated man in British newspapers"?'

Douglas's face went as white and cold as marble. His lips tightened and he paused for a few moments to regain his composure. 'Every successful man makes enemies,' he said. 'It is better to be feared than loved. I've taken tough decisions and a lot of people have been hurt along the way. They are decisions which had to be taken. I have no regrets. I am sure the members of your board will look at my achievements and not listen to my critics, most of whom are jealous, frustrated former hacks writing poisonous stories aimed at hurting the Tribune Group.'

'I agree. Powerful men make enemies. But is the *respect* there Douglas? You can't answer that and neither can I. What I must do is make it clear to you now that all I can guarantee you is the role of Director of Publishing on the main board, perhaps that of joint-Chief Executive. More than that I can't say. Perhaps we should call the others in now.'

The men continued to discuss minor details of the deal. No more was said about the role of Chief Executive. Round one complete, both men still standing, Douglas down on points.

It wasn't difficult for the private investigator, Grant Travers, to confirm that his quarry was meeting with Billmore inside the Howard Hotel, but confirm it he must. Billmore, who pulled up in his Jaguar five minutes after Douglas, was instantly recognisable. The man with him would be identified later from the long-lens shots he had taken. Priest and Ferguson, who had arrived separately, he knew.

We'll have to blag it, Travers thought and called his office. Within minutes one of his secretaries put the call into the Howard switchboard.

'Good morning, this is Julie Stephens, Mr Douglas's personal assistant. There will be an urgent call for him in about thirty minutes. There was some talk that he may change meeting rooms. Could you please confirm which room he is in?'

'Yes, Miss Stephens,' the receptionist replied. 'He has taken the room you originally booked, Room seventeen.'

The second call from Travers's office followed ten minutes later.

'This is Steve from Fosters TV courier office,' Travers's assistant said to the receptionist. 'I have a set of documents for Mr Billmore. He's expecting them. Which room should I address them to?'

'That will be Room seventeen, first floor,' she said.

Travers's report was dropped off at Sharon's home late that night. She opened it immediately – odd to get a report mid-week, must be something happening.

The summary made interesting reading. She called Carson at his flat. The music was loud, Boz Scaggs, and Sharon was sure she could hear a woman's voice in the background when he gruffly answered the phone.

'Who the fuck is with you, Andy? I can hear someone else there,' she said, for a moment forgetting why she'd called.

'Don't be fucking stupid, Sharon, it's the TV. What's happening?'

'One of Travers's people dropped a report off tonight. Guess who that treacherous little bastard Douglas spent three hours with today at a private meeting room in the fucking Howard?'

'Don't play games, it's late.'

'One Stanley Billmore, chief executive of Fosters fucking TV. And he had his Financial Director with him. That slimy cunt Zack Priest was there too, and Steve Reynolds.'

'That's great. We've got something now. We'll talk tomorrow.' Sharon was *sure* she heard a woman's voice again in the background.

Carson replaced the telephone. Douglas had said nothing to him about this meeting. They had discussed, even at board level, the need for the Tribune Group to broaden its base, ideally to merge with one of the major terrestrial television companies and enhance their portfolio.

Now it appeared he was pursuing the deal behind the board's back. Or certainly behind my back, Carson thought angrily. Someone within the Finance department must be pulling the figures for him. That wouldn't be too hard to find out.

The phone call with Carson had left Sharon feeling deeply uncomfortable. What if he did have someone else?

He had always made it clear that he would never leave his wife. She understood that and, in a strange way, accepted it. He had two lives, one with her and one with his family. Sharon had two lives, one with him and one with her work. She didn't see anyone else, didn't need to.

He had never said he loved her, but she wasn't looking for commitment. That really didn't bother her. If there was another woman though – *that* would bother her.

Thinking about it now, she wasn't at all sure how to front him

155

about it. What rights did she actually have? They had never talked about their relationship, it had just happened, then went on happening.

The first time they'd had sex, at a Think Tank in Somerset, set the tone. It was the last night of the conference. The senior Tribune executives had spent the weekend trying to plan the future and the final dinner was a long and liquid affair. Long after most had retired to the library or to bed, Andrew and Sharon had ended up playing pool together. She was wearing a skin-tight La Perla dress, short and red with a built-in push-up top. As she leaned over the table to play her shots, Carson could not take his eyes off her. Half-way through a game he took her hand and almost dragged her back to his room.

He closed the door then pushed her up against it, burying his face in her deep cleavage and pushing the tight skirt up above her hips. He was inside her before he uttered a word, pounding away up against the door. All he said was: 'Christ, Sharon, I've waited a long time to do this.' For her it was dangerous and exciting.

They both knew what they wanted and they took it.

But what did she want now? If there was someone else, would there still be room for her and was she prepared to share him with another mistress?

Sharon arrived home around 10 pm, her only consolations an affectionate Rocky rubbing himself against her legs with fervour and an early copy of next day's *Tribune*.

After feeding Rocky on his favourite fresh Marks and Spencer prawns – someone needed to be spoiled tonight – she took a bottle of Spanish champagne from the fridge, one glass and settled herself down in her favourite pink chintz chair.

The smell of the multi-coloured spray carnations in big vases all around the room was soon engulfed by Marlboro smoke.

'It may be lonely at the top, but it's fucking satisfying,' she said to Rocky as he sat licking his paws on her lap. Seldom had she had as much pleasure as when discovering the story about the Foreign Secretary and the Thai prostitute in the *Sunday Tribune*'s horoscope file.

'The fool even had the pictures scanned into the system,' she said to Rocky who looked up adoringly. 'And she thought she was hiding them. Nothing is hidden from me, nothing.'

RANDY JACK
HAS SECRET LOVE
CHILD BY HOOKER

was the front page headline.

EXCLUSIVE PICTURES INSIDE – SEE PAGES 2, 3, 4, 5

Sharon took a deep drag on her cigarette and leaned further back in her chair. What a fool Georgina was to leave a story like this lying around in the system where anyone could find it. And trying to hide it in the horoscope queue was a pathetic attempt at concealment. You're out of your depth, baby, Sharon thought, smiling, and soon you'll be out of the *Tribune*.

The exclusive went on to describe, in lurid detail, how Jack Edgerton had met the pre-pubescent Ling Sinwaeni on a backpacking holiday while he was still at Cambridge.

She was a simple farm girl when they met. He made her pregnant then abandoned her. Ling was now working as a prostitute in a seedy bar in Bangkok, having sex with brutal foreigners while her fourteen-year-old daughter, Jack Edgerton's child, slept behind a curtain in the same room. It was only a matter of time before she too sold her body.

Edgerton looked young and arrogant in the pictures, where he was seen clutching an unbelievably young Ling, the jungle behind making a perfect backdrop. Run side-by-side with pictures of him at Cambridge, there was no mistaking his identity.

The banker's draft bearing his name was faded and crumpled, adding evidence to his shame.

Beside the pictures of Ling and her daughter the *Tribune* had run the latest happy family snaps of Edgerton, his wife and children – Mr Family Values.

In the interview with Ling, she claimed Edgerton cruelly abandoned her and their child after promising to marry her and bring them both to England to start a new life. Well, she *did* start a new life – as a prostitute. It was the only way she could feed her baby after the money he sent ran out.

There were two copies of bank statements, each for £2,000, that Edgerton had sent her all those years ago. Proof enough.

Sharon scanned the pages again, deeply satisfied. No need for those prats at the office to know that, she thought. She went to her handbag to get her mobile phone. If they got a result they became complacent and she planned to call them and change – no, improve – every page of their exclusive for the final editions. No doubt the lazy fuckers would all be in the pub by now, half-pissed. Well, she would just drag them all out of the pub and back to work.

'What the fuck,' she said aloud. Her mobile phone was normally in the side pocket of her handbag. She stuck her arm deep into the huge burgundy leather bag, much as an eager vet would insert his arm into a cow's backside, feeling around, searching.

She cursed herself when she remembered last using it at her desk and went to the phone in the sitting room only to see the answer machine flashing red with messages.


By the time Sharon started reading her early copy of next day's *Tribune*, Mike had already called the *Daily*'s news desk. The trap had been sprung and the plan was that he would alert them the moment the first editions ran.

But his first call was to Georgina.

'Mission accomplished, George,' he said. 'The first edition of the *Daily Tribune* has splashed on the sordid tale of the Foreign Secretary and his love child.'

'Well done, Mike,' she said, 'but our mission is not yet accomplished. Do you know where Allenby is?'

'One of three pubs drinking to his success. It won't be hard to track him down.

'Allenby, you fool!' Mike bellowed convincingly when he found his fellow news editor in the pub. 'We couldn't stand the Edgerton story up. We contacted his office and it turns out Ling was the lover of his best friend at Cambridge. They met when they were backpacking, but Edgerton himself had nothing to do with the girl.'

'If you think I'm falling for that crap, you're more of a fool than I thought,' Allenby screamed above the noise of the pub. 'You'd do anything to kill one of our stories.'

'Listen to me very carefully,' Mike insisted. 'I've already put a call in to Douglas Holloway and the Company Secretary. You'll have your arses sued by Edgerton. Ling Sinwaeni denies the story. It was put to us by a hooker who saw a money-grubbing opportunity.'

'But the pictures and the bank statement . . .' Allenby wailed.

'Completely authentic. Edgerton met Ling and sent her money after his friend died. It wasn't his baby. We have a statement to that effect in the office. He has been nothing but kindness to her, nothing but a friend. You'd better get the presses stopped and the story pulled or your life won't be worth living.'

Allenby knew his life wasn't worth living anyway. Sharon would blame him for this, even though it was she who'd found the story in the *Sunday*'s computer system.

He tried calling her first, on her mobile, no answer, then at home. In the end he left a message and waited for her to call him.

It hardly made any difference as Douglas ordered the presses to be stopped in the middle of the first run. Only a few thousand copies had made it on to the streets around London and *Tribune* drivers were desperately trying to retrieve all the copies before they went on sale. It was impossible. Just one copy sold could mean a massive court case.

To libel a happily married senior member of the Government would cost the Tribune Group hundreds of thousands of pounds and, as Allenby knew, cost more than one of them their jobs.

Early copies of the first edition are picked up either at Kings Cross Station or the print sites and delivered to the newsrooms of every national newspaper each night. Rivals pore over each other's exclusives, seeing which stories they have missed and which they want to lift from other papers and place in their own later editions.

The moment the Foreign Secretary story dropped, newsdesks across London were calling Edgerton's press officers. The apparatchiks of senior members of Government are always available, especially for a story like this.

The denials from the Foreign Secretary's office came almost as quickly as the threats of legal action against the *Tribune*.

To minimise the damage, Douglas had instructed that a page-three apology be run in all editions of the *Daily Tribune* after the original story was pulled from the first edition. It was damage limitation on a scale unprecedented in Fleet Street history.

The whole fiasco had made the *Tribune* look ridiculous and Douglas hated nothing more than being made to look ridiculous.

He saw Sharon at 8 am the next day.

Unusually sombre in a black suit, she stood, uninvited to sit, for half an hour while he ranted at her, her head slightly bowed, soft tangerine curls falling over her pale face. Even the sunbed tan let her down today.

'This is the most unprofessional piece of journalism I have ever encountered,' he shouted at her again. 'You are a disgrace and you have brought disgrace on the *Tribune*'s name. Not to mention a lawsuit that will break records in this business.'

Sharon finally raised her head and spoke, quietly. 'Douglas, I agree with everything you say. I have only one course of action, much as it pains me. To sack the person responsible.'

'What do you mean the person responsible? *You* are the editor. *You* are responsible,' he said coldly.

'Of course, I take overall responsibility for the mistake,' she began again. 'But I rely on the integrity and ability of my senior executives. Allenby was the one who brought me the story and authenticated it. He must go.'

Douglas Holloway had thought long into the night about the action he would take. With their annual results looming, it would be damaging to him to have to admit publicly that one of his most senior editors was incompetent. They needed a sacrificial lamb and he knew he could count on Sharon to provide him with one, slitting its throat personally if required.

By noon, as the formal writ for damages arrived on Douglas's desk from Edgerton's lawyers, Allenby had been sacked and escorted off the premises by two Security guards. He was dismissed by Sharon personally. It took less than two minutes and he was gone.

Afterwards she sat at her desk, trembling. She had smoked thirty Marlboros and it was not even twelve o'clock. Ash was scattered thickly over her desk. Sharon thought for a moment it looked like the cremated remains of her news editor.

There was a soft knock at her office door and Feretti walked in. He was shocked by the appearance of his friend and walked around the desk to hug her. He held her quietly for what seemed like a long time and she sank into his embrace.

It was only when he pulled back and looked into her face that he saw the change in her. The momentary vulnerability had gone, replaced with a look of utter determination.

'We've got to get that bitch,' she spat out. 'No one humiliates me and lives.'

'What do you want to do, boss?' he asked eagerly, glad that the old Sharon was back.

She sat back in her seat, the harsh midday sun falling unflatteringly on her deep cleavage, revealing the crepiness around her neck and breasts.

'Have you turned up anything on the florist or which hospital she was in?'

'The florist doesn't keep records back that far,' he said. 'I've tried the delivery company they use and the same with them. I'm drawing a blank.'

'Well, think of a way, you useless bastard,' she shouted. 'Or you'll end up the same as Allenby.'

Carson stayed clear of the interrogation over the Edgerton fiasco. Unusually, he was not available when Douglas called him late the night before to discuss the matter.

Carson was more interested in finding out who had been working with Douglas to provide the figures for the Fosters TV business plan. It took him just one hour to locate the source within the finance department. Carson arrived at the Tower at 8.15 am, called in the head of the information technology department, and explained the problem.

'Clearly, Joe, what I am about to discuss with you is highly confidential,' he began. 'Only the Chief Executive and I are involved in this investigation. As you know, Mr Douglas is away in New York for a couple of days and he wants the problem sorted before he returns.'

Joe Winter was flattered. He had only once been called to the General Manager's office and that was to receive an almighty bollocking for a failure in the fax transmissions from the editorial floor to the print sites.

'I understand, Mr Carson,' he said. 'Anything I can do, you've got it.'

'For reasons which will become clear, no one – and I mean no one – must know of this investigation,' Carson continued as Winter nodded sagely. 'You will report directly to me and I will pass on the information personally to the Chief Executive. I believe someone within the finance department is leaking highly confidential information to an outside company.' Carson heard Winter's sharp intake of breath. 'He has supplied information relating to the current status of the Tribune Group and details of our loans and liabilities. How can we find him?'

Winter looked relieved. 'That should be easy, Mr Carson. Only the Finance Director and a handful of his executives can access that information on the system. I can pull the records from the last few weeks and see who has been accessing the material. That's, of course, unless it's someone who is hacking into the system either from another department or from outside. It will take longer to track that back.'

'Start with the people who have access to the information from within the department,' Carson said. 'I'm sure it's an inside job.'

Before nine o'clock, Winter was back in his office, holding a stack of computer print-outs. 'The only person who has accessed that information within the last two weeks is Stephen Binder,' he said. 'I've got all the print-outs here. He's your man.'

In ten minutes Binder was in Carson's office.

'I'm not going to beat about the bush. As of this moment you are under investigation by the company for corporate fraud.' Binder was speechless. What little colour he had in his typical washed-out accountant's face had drained away the moment he saw the anger in Carson's.

'Mr Carson, I don't understand,' he managed to get out. 'Fraud? Me? I've never done anything I wasn't asked to do either by my Finance Director, you or the Chief Executive.'

'It's the Chief Executive who instructed me to take this action.

You are in a lot of trouble, sonny. Do you realise what happens to accountants who are suspended for passing out confidential company information? Your name will be mud, you will never work in this town again. Do you understand me?'

Binder opened his mouth to speak but nothing came out. 'Do you deny that you have been preparing a report on the finances of the Tribune Group?' Carson shouted at him.

'No, sir.'

'Do you realise that that information is highly confidential?'

'Yes, sir. But . . . but I was doing it for Mr Douglas sir, he asked me to do it,' Binder pleaded.

'Well, sonny, it was Mr Douglas who told me to suspend you. He thinks you're up to no good, overstepping the mark, perhaps providing a bit of information to the other side as well. Information that could be damaging to us. It wouldn't be the first time this sort of thing has happened. I want your full report on my desk in ten minutes. I have promised the Chief Executive that I will have dealt with the matter before he returns tomorrow. I will decide whether you are suspended immediately pending a full investigation into the affair. And I would advise you not to speak to anyone about this matter. If you do you will be instantly dismissed.'

Well before lunch Carson had the Fosters/Tribune merger document on his desk.

# Chapter Fourteen

The interview was going well, Kelly thought. She was glad she'd decided on the pale pink Dior suit and low pumps. The skirt was just above the knee but very tight so it rode beautifully up her thighs when she sat down. Jason was suitably impressed when she walked in, but also seemed nervous. They were in the lounge of the fashionable Simpson Hotel.

'Not much is known about how you first met Douglas,' Jason began. 'It was in New York, wasn't it?'

'It was so romantic. Douglas has such a sweet side to him. We met at a publishing party. He was there, talking to some financiers about a project,' Kelly recalled. 'He's usually quite shy with women, but he walked straight up to me and said I was the most beautiful woman he had ever seen. He had to take me to dinner, immediately. So we left the party and had dinner that night, and breakfast the next morning, then lunch, then dinner. Every day he was there. And he was such a gentleman, he never touched me. We just talked, got to know each other.

'By the end of the week, he'd asked me to marry him.'

'That's not the Douglas Holloway most people know,' Jason commented. 'It's that other side of him that people really want to read about.'

'I'd be lying, Jason, if I said he was the easiest man to get on with. His work is so important to him. I see my role as one of total support. It may sound old-fashioned and lots of career women will hate me for saying this, but that's how our marriage works. I travel everywhere with him, making sure everything is right. I even pack a couple of packets of his favourite coffee when we travel. It's those little things that are important.'

'And children, Kelly, why have you never had a family?' he asked.

'To begin with Douglas didn't want a family, he just wanted it to be the two of us. This is completely off the record – I think he was jealous, didn't want to share me with anyone, even a child. Now we've decided to start a family and we're trying really hard,' she said, giving him a stage wink. 'Hopefully by the time this article is ready to run, I'll have some good news for you.'

They chatted on for another half hour then Jason looked at his watch. It was 11.05 am, time to move in for the kill.

'So tell us about the new home you're moving into Kelly. It sounds magnificent.'

She looked confused. 'What new home?'

'Come on, Kelly, you can't keep a place like that secret – the £5 million mansion at 13 East Heath Road. Douglas bought it as a wreck almost six months ago. I believe it's almost ready to move into now. The work on it must have set you back a fortune. Who was the interior designer?'

Kelly's beautiful face froze. She looked at him as though he'd just asked her to perform oral sex on him, right there. Jason went on: 'And I understand Becky Worthington has acted as consultant on the refurbishment. Surprising, really, since she's eight months pregnant.'

Kelly's mind was working slowly, like one of those bad dreams where everything moves in excruciatingly slow motion. Becky Worthington, she'd met her a number of times at Tribune functions ... daughter of some Yorkshire landowner ... she'd been in their home ... single, scrawny, aristocratic, small tits ... she'd left several messages on Douglas's answer machine in the past, nothing for a while ... and now this house ... and a baby.

Kelly grabbed her Dior handbag, excused herself and went to the ladies'. She called Kate on her mobile.

'I can hardly hear you,' her friend said above the noise of a restaurant. She was lunching with one of her best contacts and was in the middle of a great story for her diary. The last thing she wanted was a long, needy call from Kelly. 'Can I phone you back?'

'No, you can't,' Kelly hissed. 'It's not Georgina, is it? It's Becky Worthington. And her baby is his!'

'Oh, Kelly, I've just found out myself,' lied Kate. 'I don't know if it's true, they're just rumours,' she lied again. The line went dead.

She tried to call Kelly back but her mobile was switched off. Damn the timing, she thought as she excused herself from the table, headed for the ladies' and jabbed in the number of her editor on the diary.

'Tristan,' she said when he answered, 'we've got to run with the Holloway love child story tomorrow.'

'But I thought we were saving that until Kelly found out?'

'I have it from an impeccable source that she just has,' Kate said conspiratorially. 'I'll file in ten minutes from the car, back in the office in fifteen. You've already got the background piece in the system I did last week. Offer it up to the editor. It'll make a perfect set piece up front in the paper, maybe even the front page. Charles should have done all the picture research. Just make sure I get the fucking byline – an *exclusive* byline.'

Kelly strode back to the table where Jason was sitting, picked up his tape machine, removed the tape and dropped it into his coffee. 'There will be no interview. You print one word of what I've said and I'll sue the arse off *Bazaar* and you personally,' she said, and walked out.

It took ten minutes for the cab to reach Tribune Tower. She took the lift and walked straight into Douglas's office.

'Where is the bastard?' she said to his personal assistant, Julie.

'Mr Holloway's in a board meeting, Mrs Holloway. He won't be long. I'll get a message to him if it's urgent.'

'It's so urgent I'll take the message myself.'

'You can't do that . . .'

'And who the hell is going to stop me?' Kelly said walking down the corridor to the meeting room. As she burst in, all heads turned to her. Carson was addressing the meeting and stopped mid-sentence.

166

She was ice cool and stood at the top of the table, as if ready to present a paper. 'Members of the board, I would like to take a little of your time to tell you about the character of the man who is leading this company, my husband, Douglas Holloway.'

He scrambled to his feet. 'Don't you come near me, you lying cheating bastard,' Kelly warned him. He picked up the phone and said to Julie: 'Get Security in – quick.' He tried to usher Kelly out, but she pushed him aside.

'He has been cheating on me for months with the daughter of Charles Worthington. Douglas and Becky are about to have a child. Unfortunately, I too am carrying my husband's child. You're a hypocrite, Douglas, a liar and a cheat. And I know everything about your love nest.'

Everyone in the room was silent. It was a moment of exquisite embarrassment. Two Security guards walked in awkwardly and took Kelly's arms.

'Don't you dare manhandle me. You might hurt the baby.' She went to leave the room, turned at the door and said: 'Now you tell me, is this man fit to run a public company?'

Douglas had, like so many men with mistresses before him, repeatedly assured Becky that he no longer had sex with his wife. It was important to her. She could just about cope with the fact that they were sometimes living under the same roof, so long as she was sure there was no intimacy. He had not told her about that single night, after he'd tried the patches. There was no need. What he didn't tell her, couldn't hurt her he'd thought. Now this.

How the hell had Kelly got pregnant? he thought to himself angrily. How unlucky can I be that I sleep with her once in months and, miracle of miracles, she's fertile. He remembered how desperate he once was for a child with her, but that was past history and he did not like revisiting the past.

Perhaps she'll miscarry, he thought. Perhaps she's made it up to try and get me back. Whatever the future held, of one thing he was sure. The story of the boardroom scene and Kelly's pregnancy would be all over town within hours.

The timing was a problem. The last thing he needed right now with the Fosters deal so close was to take time out to see Becky. But he had no option.

Douglas called his mistress as soon as he was back in the office.

'I have to see you, darling,' he said when she answered. 'Meet you at the Savoy Grill at one.' Normally he wouldn't go near the place, it was too Establishment, but the Grill would be full of people who recognised them both. He knew Becky had too much self-respect to cause a scene in public. It was the coward's way out, but then he was no Braveheart when it came to women.

She was waiting in the far booth when he arrived half an hour late looking serene and elegant in an oversized camel Maxfield Parrish suede jacket and black trousers. At eight months, it was now impossible to hide her pregnancy and Douglas had to admit, she looked wonderful on it. She kissed him and took his hand.

The middle-aged waiters in white linen aprons, the ostentatious trolleys laden with antique silver serving trays and domes, the over-fed businessmen all reminded him why he seldom came to this place.

'What is it, darling?' she said immediately. 'You look terrible.' He held tightly to her hand as if letting it go would mean losing her forever, even when the wine waiter came to the table and took his order for a bottle of still water, large, no ice.

The booths around the room were already full, mostly with politicians and businessmen, all people who knew Douglas.

'There's something I have to tell you, but first you must remember one thing – I love you,' he began. 'I love you more than anything else in the world.'

'I know that, darling,' Becky said, smiling up into his eyes.

'Kelly is pregnant,' he blurted out.

She looked puzzled. 'Well, that's wonderful, Douglas. It didn't take her long to find someone else. Good luck to her. Hopefully now she'll let you go. Anyone we know?' She stopped smiling the moment she saw the pain in his eyes. 'Who is it, Douglas?'

'I made one stupid mistake, Becky. I promise you it was only the once,' he said imploringly. 'She seduced me. I couldn't stop it, I just lost control. I'm so sorry.'

Becky slowly withdrew her hand from his and placed it in her lap. In the silence that followed she tried to take in what she had just heard. She felt a chill in the pit of her stomach. She was pregnant with Douglas's child. Douglas's wife was pregnant with his child. He'd always told her Kelly didn't want children, that he didn't love his wife. He'd always said he didn't have sex with her. He'd told her lies.

How many of her friends had warned her about Douglas? 'I bet he tells you he doesn't sleep with his wife. Just be careful, Becky. Every husband tells his mistress that,' they had said repeatedly. But Douglas was different. She had trusted him. She had believed him.

Now all she wanted was to curl up in a ball, to ease the pain in her stomach.

'You lied to me,' she said finally. 'I will never forgive you for this.'

'Please, Becky! I love you, I made one mistake,' he said. 'I'd give anything to turn back the clock, to make it right. Please, please, just tell me you forgive me?'

'I can't tell you that because, unlike you, I'm not a liar,' she said coldly. 'I do not lie to the people I love.'

'Becky, we'll get over this,' he began again desperately. 'We've got to think about the baby. I'll do anything, please.'

'It seems to me you've now got two babies to think about, Douglas. Everyone will know Kelly's child is yours,' she said quietly, 'everyone will know that you betrayed me. How could you do this to me, Douglas? How could you humiliate me like this? How often have you lied to me? How often have you slept with your wife? How did it feel getting straight out of her bed and into mine? Was she better than me?' A tear trickled from the side of her eye.

'Becky, it only happened once, I promise you, one terrible mistake,' he pleaded. He tried to take her hand again and she pulled it back sharply. She had never pulled away from him before. It felt like she was ripping out his guts.

'Don't touch me,' she said coldly. 'I'm not sure I ever want you to touch me again. Now, if you don't mind, I'm leaving. I think I'm going to be sick.'

Douglas watched her as she went, elegant and dignified as ever. This was the woman for whom he had waited all his life. He did not intend to lose her through one stupid mistake. The thought of not having her and their child in his life brought back the old terror. The one he'd felt as a child when he'd thought he was losing his brother Daniel. Losing Becky would be as tragic.

I'll let her calm down for a while, he thought to himself. Send her armfuls of Casablanca lilies and wait until tonight.

Becky walked out of the back entrance of the Savoy and down on to the Embankment. When she reached the huge Egyptian obelisk, guarded on both sides by sleeping lions, she sat down and stared at the muddy waters of the Thames.

For the first time since giving up smoking at the beginning of her pregnancy, she wanted a cigarette and a bottle of wine. Her stomach ached even more than her head. She'd always felt grief as a pain in her stomach, ever since she was a little girl and lay frightened in the rambling castle that was her home. Too many shadows, too many demons. Now she felt suffocated by new shadows, new demons.

She had been raised to believe in duty. The marriage of her wealthy parents had seldom been a happy one but her mother had explained to Becky why she stayed.

'It has never occurred to me to leave,' she used to say. 'I am a wife and mother. A lady accepts her lot and carries on. That is my duty. I do not expect happiness, only peace, and I have that here. I have my home and my family.'

The Worthingtons were one of the oldest and wealthiest families in North Yorkshire. Becky's pedigree, a traditional upper-class education at boarding school, then the finest finishing school in Switzerland, had made her an extremely eligible young woman. Her parents expected a good match, but she had surprised them all by taking a job in a public relations agency and turning down all the aristocrats who pursued her. She wanted to live in the real world, have a career, fall in love, live a little dangerously. Then she met Douglas Holloway.

Her parents were contemptuous of his newfound wealth and affectations. The Savile Row suits and hand-made shirts, the 1957 silver Bentley, the English butler – it was as though he was trying to buy his way into the Establishment. There was nothing more ridiculous than the sight of Douglas on the occasion Sir Charles had invited him on the estate's pheasant shoot, kitted out in his brand new plus fours, beautifully tailored shooting jacket and cap. Sir Charles couldn't count the number of times Douglas had told him that *everything* had come from Holland and Holland, the Royal Family's supplier, even his hand-made over and under shotgun. They feared he saw their daughter as a trophy, his entrée into a level of society he could never hope to reach on his own.

Becky had a lot of her mother's common sense about her. As she sat under the shadow of the Ancient Egyptian relic she considered her options. She could leave Douglas and raise the baby on her own. Or she could forgive him. She knew men were weak. As a child she would hear her parents arguing over her father's latest indiscretion. That was life. Men cheated and their wives took them back.

All she knew now was the pain of his betrayal. She couldn't think straight, needed to be with her mother, needed time. Becky hailed a cab and took it all the way to her parents' estate in Yorkshire.

Daniel was in town, this time without Jacqueline, and Douglas had asked Georgina to drinks that evening. He had been unable to get hold of Becky since lunchtime, but left a message on her mobile phone that he'd meet her at the house at ten. It was probably a good idea for her to have a few hours to cool down, he thought again.

It was difficult for Georgina to refuse to see him after what he'd gone through today at the board meeting.

Feretti raced into her office after lunch with the news. 'You'll never believe it, Georgina,' he said gleefully. 'Kelly Douglas stormed the board meeting today and slugged Douglas. She screamed at him, accusing him of having an affair *and* a baby with Becky Worthington. *And* she's pregnant too. Can you believe it? Then she trashed the place, throwing reports everywhere, turning over chairs. She just went mad. They had to call the police.'

Poor Douglas, she thought. Even if only half of what Feretti said was true, it must have been ugly. How on earth did Kelly find out? They had been so careful. And what was this about her being pregnant? What a mess. Douglas must be mortified.

'Why do you take such delight in other people's misfortunes? You actually get pleasure out of it, don't you?'

'Well, Sharon thought it was hysterically funny. When she told me, I couldn't stop laughing. He deserves it,' Feretti said and flounced out to tell the world.

So when Douglas called, Georgina felt she had to meet him. She phoned Belinda, to say she'd be late for dinner. They were eating out tonight with friends.

'Look, Georgina,' Belinda had begun. 'I don't have a problem with you working late, I understand you don't want to let Douglas down tonight, but you're letting *me* down. I'm tired of you arriving as the coffee is served. I'd rather go alone.'

'Please don't give me a hard time about this!'

'I'm not giving you a hard time, I'm just sick to death of being treated like the little woman. You're never around, always working, always tired. And when you do bother to drop home, I'm supposed to take care of you. It's like being married to a male chauvinist.'

'Yeah, and I feel like I'm married to a nagging wife,' Georgina said and hung up.

Douglas gave her a lift to the winebar where they were meeting Daniel. They drove in silence. She knew him well enough to let him be when he descended into these moods. There was a darkness inside him, always close to the surface, and when he stepped into the shadows there was no reaching him.

Daniel struggled to hold a conversation with his brother. 'I know what happened,' he said. 'Kelly phoned Jacqueline. It must have been awful. At least now it's all out in the open.'

'I don't want to talk about it,' Douglas said. 'All I want to know is how she found out. Someone has betrayed me.'

Daniel thought this was probably not the time to point out that his brother had betrayed both his wife and his mistress. Finally Daniel left, but Douglas didn't budge. Unusually for him, he ordered another bottle of wine.

'Stay for a bit, Georgina?' he asked. 'I didn't want to hurt Kelly, things just got out of hand. She doesn't deserve this. I meant to tell her, I've been trying to for weeks, but every time I started, it ended in a scene and I just backed off. What a mess!'

'Why did she phone Jacqueline? I thought they didn't get on?'

'I guess Kelly felt comfortable talking to a woman who hates me almost as much as she does now.'

'But why, Douglas? What is it between you and Jacqueline? Why is she so hostile to you?' Georgina had asked this question many times before, but he'd never answered it.

'Promise me you won't ever tell anyone this, but Jackie was my first serious girlfriend, the first one I ever slept with. We met at university and fell in love. You know what it feels like the first time. She was beautiful then, so full of laughter and optimism. You wouldn't recognise the girl I fell in love with in the sour woman you see today. Then she got pregnant and I guess I didn't handle it very well. I didn't want a baby. Certainly didn't want to get married, I was only nineteen.

'We were talking about what to do. She was determined to keep the baby. We argued about it for days and in the end I said if she wanted it that much, I'd stand by her, support her, but I wouldn't marry her. A few days later she turned up at my rooms in a complete state. She'd had an abortion, didn't even tell me first. It was all horrible. Jackie said then she'd never forgive me for what I'd made her do: kill our child.

'She married Daniel to get back at me, to hurt me. And it worked. That's why I left Canada. I couldn't bear to see them together. Thirty years later I've screwed up again. I'm not even sure I believe Kelly's pregnant. I wouldn't put it past her to make the whole thing up.'

'*Could* she be pregnant by you, Douglas?' Georgina asked gently.

'It's highly unlikely, but yes, it is possible,' he said and stared hard at a spot somewhere over her head. 'Anyway, I'll sort things out with Becky somehow. I have to go now. I promised her I'd be at the house by ten.'

Georgina poured herself a glass of wine the moment she got home then put on a Cowboy Junkies CD. She thought about the paper and Douglas's offer of a break in Australia. It was tempting. She could return via South Africa and see her family, go out into the bush, get things into perspective.

The tensions at work were beginning to show. The new Group

leader writer, appointed by Sharon, was writing to her brief, trying to position the *Sunday Tribune* as an anti-Government, old-fashioned values newspaper. Not a word had appeared as yet, as Georgina re-wrote it from top to bottom.

Douglas's determination to play paper spin doctor was pulling the paper in another direction. The paper was still being edited by three people. It was being hung, drawn and thirded every week.

And things weren't going brilliantly with Belinda. Perhaps a break would do them good. The front door bell broke Georgina's train of thought. She opened the door and Belinda staggered into the living room. She drained Georgina's wineglass in one go and went to the fridge for a refill.

'You might have had enough of that, sweetheart,' Georgina warned.

'Don't you *dare* tell me how much I can drink!' Belinda said, slopping wine on the floor. She lit a cigarette and stood, drink in one hand, legs braced as if for battle.

'Have you eaten? I can fix you something,' Georgina offered.

'Shows how much attention you pay to anything I say. I've been out to dinner. You were supposed to be there too, remember? I waited and waited. You said you'd come along. You were with someone else, weren't you?' Belinda was paranoid that Georgina would leave her for a man. The subject came up every time she got drunk. And she was seriously drunk tonight.

'Sweetheart, I was with Douglas and Daniel. I'm not seeing anyone else. I just want things to work out between us. Look, there's something I need to discuss with you. Douglas has asked me to go out to Australia to look at a newspaper he's thinking of buying. It would take about a week, then I'd go home for a week on the way back and see my folks. What do you think?'

'Why are you bothering asking me?' Belinda said, taking another large gulp of wine.

'With everything that's going on at the moment, it seems like a good time to stay clear. Sharon's been publicly humiliated by the Thai prostitute story and will have to keep her hands clean for a while. She's not in a position of strength and she knows it. I also know she's digging into my past and watching every move I make. If I'm not here she can't tail me and at least we're safe until all this blows over.'

'You've clearly decided to go. Just do what's right for Georgina, you always do. Don't bother about me. Do you know your problem? You don't really care about anything but yourself and that stupid fucking newspaper. It's all you, you, you! Well, I'm sick to death of it.' Belinda crumpled to the floor and started to cry.

Georgina went over and sat beside her, cradling her in her arms, rocking her gently. 'It'll be okay, sweetheart. I'm here, I care about you.'

'But you don't love me, George, do you?'

It was only after she had poured her lover into a cab that Georgina stopped to think about Belinda and what this affair was doing to them both. It certainly wasn't making either of them happy.

They had been happy, hadn't they? Those early days were bliss. Living in the real world had proved harder. Georgina knew that she loved Belinda, but she hadn't loved her enough to acknowledge her, except with a couple of her most trusted friends. The fact that they were gay and more likely to accept the relationship had been the main reason for coming clean with them.

Georgina felt trapped, but not by love. Rather by guilt and a desire not to hurt the woman she had held so tenderly in her arms. But where was it going? Deep in her heart she knew she could not answer the question Belinda had asked of her.

For the tenth time that day Becky's phone was on answer machine. She has a right to be upset, Douglas thought as his driver headed towards the mews house in Devonshire Place where they met in secret. Once he had her in his arms, he would be able to talk her around.

The house was, unusually, in darkness when he arrived. Becky always left the front lights on for him even if she was too tired to stay up. Recently she had been very tired and was often in bed by 10 pm. He walked into the bedroom and it was empty. There were no signs in the kitchen that she had been there. No note. He began to panic. Think, Douglas, he said to himself sternly, if she's not here where is she?

He walked the small distance to Becky's own flat. Again he encountered emptiness, but nothing compared to the emptiness and fear now creeping into his heart.

He sat down in the antique French armchair by the phone and opened her address book. It was well past 1 am but he didn't care. The first call was to her sister, Sarah.

'Sarah, it's Douglas,' he began, without so much as apologising for waking her so late. 'Is Becky with you?'

'Oh, it's you, is it?' she said scornfully. 'No, she's not here, and I doubt whether I'd tell you even if she was.'

'Please, Sarah, I've got to find her. Do you have any idea where she is?'

'No, I don't. Why don't you leave her alone? Haven't you hurt her enough?' she said and hung up.

Douglas systematically worked his way through Becky's address book, calling every friend she had. No one had heard from her. Finally he called her father's house.

'Sir Charles,' he began, 'I'm trying to find Becky. Is she with you?'

'All I can tell you is that she is safe,' Sir Charles said angrily in his stiff Etonian tones. 'She was with us this afternoon, in a terrible state, but left this evening. I have made no secret of the fact that I considered you to be the most undesirable of partners for my daughter. You have simply confirmed my worst fears. You are a scoundrel, sir.'

'Please, Sir Charles, I have to find her, it's . . .' The line went dead.

Sir Charles had no intention of telling Douglas that Becky was asleep in her old bedroom at home.

Douglas walked slowly into the kitchen and poured a whisky, a large one. He took off his jacket and noticed his armpits were soaked. The sweat smelt of fear.

Only one thought occupied his mind: he must find Becky. He picked up the phone again and called Georgina.

She looked at the bedside clock as she grabbed the phone, feeling that familiar dead panic grip her. Her greatest fear was a call from home to tell her one of her family was ill, or worse. At 3.30 in the morning it could only be bad news. She was relieved to hear Douglas's voice.

'I know you think you can call your employees any time of the day or night, Douglas, but this is ridiculous,' she said. 'Do you have any idea what time it is?'

'Georgina, I need your help, you're the only one I can trust,' he said. She had never heard that tone in his voice before. It was pure panic.

'What is it, Douglas?'

'I've lost Becky, you've got to help me find her. Have you got someone you trust completely? Someone who's good at tracing people? What about Mike Gordon?'

'I'd trust him with my life,' she said, 'but what's going on? Do you think she's been in an accident?'

'No, she's just disappeared and I have to find her. She can't have flown anywhere because she's eight months pregnant, so she can't have got far. Get him checking everything – train stations, Eurotunnel.'

'It will be like finding a needle in a haystack, Douglas. She could be anywhere. I'll need her car registration, credit card details, names and addresses of all her closest friends, family, anything that will help track her. I'll get Mike on it straight away.'

'Thank you,' he said and hung up. Georgina was struck by the thought that this was the first time she could ever remember Douglas thanking her.

# Chapter Fifteen

Kelly had waited up all night for her husband to come home and face her after the board meeting fiasco. She had called his office hundreds of times and every time the answer was the same – he was in a meeting and would not be out for some time. His mobile was on answer service. Sooner or later he has to come home, she thought, even if it's just to collect his things.

She wasn't sure what she wanted to say to him, whether to rage or to plead.

It was long past midnight the night after the board meeting when the phone rang. Thank God, it must be him, she thought, and grabbed the phone.

'Kelly, it's me.'

'Douglas, we've got to talk,' she said quietly. 'I never wanted you to find out about the baby like this. I'm . . .'

'So far as I'm concerned there is nothing to talk about. I'm divorcing you.'

'*You're* divorcing *me*?' she said incredulously. 'You're the one who's been having an affair. You're the one who's got his mistress pregnant as well as his wife. You really are the most arrogant man.'

'Kelly, I didn't phone you to discuss the matter,' he said coldly. 'The marriage is over. I have a proposition to put to you about your baby, one that's simple enough even for you to understand. The deal on the table is this – you get rid of the baby, tell everyone you made it all up about being pregnant, and I will pay you an additional £1 million on top of the divorce settlement.'

He waited and heard only silence. 'Kelly, are you there?'

'Let me get this straight, Douglas,' she said slowly. 'You are willing to pay me £1 million to get rid of my baby?'

'Be sensible for once in your life. You've never wanted children, Kelly. A baby will just get in the way of your new life.'

'And what new life is this?' she asked slowly.

'I want a divorce and I *will* marry Becky. Think about it. I will give you £1 million to terminate the pregnancy, on top of everything else. It's a very generous offer. You've got a few weeks to decide, before it's too late.'

He had worked out with his lawyers that to support the child until it reached eighteen-years-old in the style to which Kelly had become accustomed would cost him nearly a million. He knew as soon as it was out of nappies the baby would be dressed in Baby Chanel, then there were nannies, school fees, holidays. This unwanted child would cost him a fortune. To spare Becky the public embarrassment of his wife's pregnancy, he was willing to deal now. Douglas believed he could deal on anything.

'I can't believe you're doing this to me,' Kelly said quietly and hung up.

Immediately she called Kate. A sleepy voice answered the phone.

'Kate, it's me.' Kelly never said who she was, expecting people to recognise her voice immediately. 'Something terrible has happened, can you please come over?' she said and cried softly into the phone. 'I can't bear to be alone, not tonight, not now.'

'Kelly, it's one-thirty in the morning,' Kate said patiently. 'The children are asleep. I can't get up and leave now. I'll come over in the morning.'

'No,' Kelly sobbed, 'I need to see you *now*. You're supposed to be my friend.' The sobbing continued. 'Please, please, come over. You've got a nanny, she can look after the kids.'

Kate could tell by the sound of her voice that Kelly was desperate. She herself was now wide awake and her nose was twitching at the prospect of a story. 'I'll be there in twenty minutes.'

Kelly was sitting on the floor when she arrived, still in her white Hermès dressing gown, the front door to the flat unlocked. Even now, hair all over the place, face streaked with mascara, she looked appealing. Kate went over to where she was sitting, like a

179

crumpled doll, took her in her arms and soothed her as she would one of her own children.

She felt so sorry for Kelly. It had been inevitable she would find out about Becky and the baby, but Kate had always hoped Douglas would have the courage and the decency to tell his wife himself. That would have been bad enough. Now Kelly was pregnant. As she babbled the whole story out, the interview, the discovery about the house, her husband's affair and the baby, the board meeting, Kate knew Douglas had not found that courage.

Every twenty minutes or so she disappeared to the bathroom to scrawl down the details of the story Kelly was pouring out. In the end it was the details, so quickly forgotten, that made great copy.

'And there's something else, Kate,' she said finally. 'I can hardly believe it's true myself. Douglas just called and offered me a million pounds to have an abortion.' She was completely calm now, staring straight ahead, unseeing. 'He wants me to say I made it all up, to save Becky the embarrassment of the world knowing he was still sleeping with his wife.'

'Oh, Kelly, I'm so sorry,' was all Kate could say. She knew her friend was given to exaggeration, that she embellished stories to make her world seem more exciting, but the sense of betrayal, of sheer disbelief in her voice told Kate this was true. And she could easily believe it.

'He used to love me so much, where did it all go wrong?' Kelly asked, neither waiting for nor expecting an answer. 'How could I have been so stupid? All the signs were there. I always thought it was Georgina and she was no real challenge. She could never steal Douglas away from me. He always said he despised those upper-crust women. Oh, Kate, what am I going to do? The terrible thing is, I still love him.'

'How did he find out you were pregnant?'

'I tried to tell him the other night but we ended up having a huge fight. The first thing he knew about it was at the board meeting. I just blurted it out when I found out about Becky and the baby. Oh, Kate, that's the last way I wanted him to find out. I thought this baby would bring us back together again. But then, I didn't know his mistress was pregnant too. Everything has gone so terribly wrong.'

'Is tonight the first time you've spoken to him since the board meeting?'

'Yes, he called about half an hour ago, just before I phoned you. His voice was so cold. He's never spoken to me like that before. No emotion. I still can't believe he wants me to get rid of the baby. That's what shocked me most.

'It's all so confusing. I only got pregnant to try and keep him. You know I never really wanted this baby. But now I'm carrying a child, my child, I couldn't do anything to harm it. I never thought I'd feel this way. . .' Kelly broke off and began to cry, quietly. 'And I'll never see Douglas again.'

'Sooner or later he'll have to come home. You'll just have to wait, Kelly.'

'You don't know him like I do,' she said. 'When he leaves someone he cuts all ties. It's as if they've died. He never talks to his former wives. If they call, he gets his secretaries to deal with them. It's something that used to worry me in the early days. You know, that nagging feeling – if he can treat them like that, could he do it to me? But I thought I was different. He said he'd never loved anyone the way he loved me. I was the woman he'd waited for all his life. And now he's found someone he's probably saying exactly the same thing to, and she'll believe him like I did.'

'You're both upset now, wait until things cool down,' Kate said without a trace of conviction in her voice.

'No, once Douglas falls out of love with you, you cease to exist,' Kelly said sadly. They talked on into the night and finally fell asleep on the big navy Ralph Lauren sofas in the sitting room, a collection of empty bottles on the table between them.

Kate woke with a start and jumped to her feet at the sight of two men in overalls standing in the doorway. Early morning light was flooding the room. She was about to scream but Kelly beat her to it. Both men took a hasty step back into the passage and the elder of the two spoke first.

'Please stop screaming,' he said, waving a piece of paper at Kelly. 'Are you Mrs Holloway? We've got authority to be here, honest. Look at this.' And he gingerly placed the paper on the coffee table before taking several steps backward.

Kate came to her senses first and picked it up. 'It's a form of authority, signed by Douglas, for these men to come and take his personal possessions,' she explained slowly to Kelly, not quite believing it herself. 'They're from a removal firm.'

'Mr Douglas's secretary gave us a set of keys, said you knew we were coming,' the man explained apologetically. 'Look, if it's a bad time, we can come back.'

Kelly rose from the sofa and said sweetly: 'Would you mind awfully coming back in a couple of hours? I just need time to have a shower, then I'll help you.'

As soon as they had gone, she jumped in the shower and changed into a pair of old jeans and a T-shirt. Kate made fresh coffee and they sat at the kitchen table looking out over the garden. 'I'm okay now, Kate,' she said. 'Thanks so much for coming over, but you'd better get home.'

'If you're sure you're all right?' she said, relieved and surprised by Kelly's calmness. The moment she left, Kelly went out into the garden and opened the shed. it took her a few minutes to find what she was looking for: the canister of hydrochloric acid the gardener had bought to clean off the brickwork. She remembered he had warned her not to touch it, especially not to get it on her clothes. How ridiculous she thought now, this is the first time I've even been in my own shed. She pulled on garden gloves and carefully filled a spray gun with the acid, then walked calmly back into the flat.

Her first instinct was to destroy Douglas's beloved, hand-made suits and she went to his closet. There they were, all navy pin-stripe, twelve of them. No, she thought, that's too eighties, and closed the door.

She then went back into the Versace sitting room and stood before Douglas's alphabetised CD collection. One by one she opened each case and removed the disc, giving each a short blast of acid before replacing it in its cover.

When the removal men arrived two hours later, she politely showed them in. 'Oh, and I'm sure he'll want his CD collection,' she said, leading them into the front room. 'Douglas loves his music. Some of these CDs are collector's pieces. I couldn't bear to think of him without them.' The men were surprised by her calmness. Wives didn't usually behave like this. Within half an hour they had collected all the client's belongings and were glad to be out of there.

'Beautiful-looking woman,' the elder man said to his workmate as they loaded the last packing box into the van. 'Did you notice a funny smell in the flat though? She must have been decorating.'

Douglas was in the middle of a meeting when Julie knocked softly on the office door.

'Could I interrupt you for a moment?' she said and closed the door again. He went out into her office and she handed him the phone. 'It's Sarah, says it's urgent, about Becky.'

He grabbed the phone. 'Sarah,' he said quickly. 'Where is she?'

'She's in labour,' Becky's sister began. 'The baby's early and there are problems. God alone knows why but she's calling for you. She's at York General.'

Douglas dropped the receiver. 'Get John around to the front of the building immediately,' he barked at Julie. 'Find out when the next fast train to York is and call me on the mobile. Otherwise I'll drive.'

It took almost half an hour to reach Kings Cross Station, Douglas cursing the traffic, London and his driver in equal measure. During the two-hair train journey he phoned the hospital repeatedly to find out how Becky was doing. The sister on duty refused to put him through, so Sarah kept him updated.

The moment the taxi swung into the hospital drive he was out, sprinting through the doors, shouting at the woman behind reception to ask where the maternity ward was. He ran down the corridor and finally found the sister in charge of the ward.

'You'll have to scrub and gown up before you can go in,' she said curtly. When he was finally taken into the delivery room Douglas went straight to Becky and took her face in his hands, kissing her frantically. Only then did he notice the pain in her eyes, the sweat running down her face and staining the green hospital gown.

The doctor and nurses were oblivious to his presence. There was so much blood.

'BP's dropping,' a nurse sitting beside the monitor shouted.

'Becky darling,' Douglas said helplessly. He was used to solving

183

crises, not observing one. 'How is she, Doctor? How's the baby?'

Becky's face contorted, she let out a low cry.

'Can't you do something for the pain?' Douglas shouted at the doctor.

'The baby is premature, we're doing everything we can for it,' the doctor shot back at him. 'Unless you shut up, I'll have you removed.'

'Come on, Becky, push harder, we're almost there,' the nurse encouraged her. After what seemed another eternity a tiny baby was being held aloft by its feet. Douglas held his breath until he heard the first scream. By the time the baby was cleaned and placed in his exhausted mother's arms, the father was crying tears of relief.

He stroked Becky's wet hair. 'Everything will be all right now, darling,' he whispered. 'I'm here. I'll never let anything hurt you again.'

Douglas kept Georgina waiting for nearly fifteen minutes before the door to his office opened and Zack Priest walked out, carrying a stack of documents.

The meeting had been scheduled for the day before, but Douglas had mysteriously disappeared. For the first time Georgina could remember, he was uncontactable for an entire day, even on his mobile phone. When Georgina called his driver, she was told he was in a meeting. Some meeting, Georgina had thought, that occupies him so completely for so long.

He was sitting at the top of his long conference table, white shirt, Hermès tie, silver cufflinks. Whereas all of his twelve navy pinstripe suits were hand-made by Prince Charles' tailor, as he was fond of telling her, his designer shirts always looked as though they were made for a bigger man. Somehow he never quite got it right.

The table was littered with papers which he was hurriedly collating.

'What have you got there, Douglas? Another plot to take over the world,' she said teasingly. His face went bright red. They were in fact the plans for the merger with Fosters TV, but he had no intention of telling anyone about that, not even Georgina.

'You look terrible, Douglas,' Georgina began. 'And what was

184

all the mystery about yesterday? You'd go beserk if I disappeared for an entire day.'

'Personal crisis,' he said briskly. Whatever had taken him away, he clearly had no intention of discussing it. 'I've had an itinerary drawn up for your visit to Australia,' he said. Georgina had told him yesterday she would go. 'I really appreciate your doing this. You'll fly in to Sydney and meet up with the major city institutions who own the *West Gazetteer*, then go over to Perth to see how the paper operates. Julie has booked the flights for you on to Johannesburg. Here are the last five years' business plans and performances and a biography on all the people you'll be meeting,' and he shoved a folder down the table at her.

'I need another favour, Georgina. Before you go, try and find out who told Kelly about the house, Becky and everything. It's too much of a coincidence that she found out now with all the problems I'm having on the board and all the criticism of the Group in the trade press. It's just an instinct, but I think someone's out for me. You'll probably think I'm paranoid, but I get the feeling I'm being followed. Maybe I'm the one who needs a break.'

'I'll do what I can, set something in motion, but don't hold your breath. You've got a lot of enemies Douglas, a lot of people who would like to see you lose all this,' she said. 'The place is alive with rumours that you're losing support within the board, that Andy and Gavin aren't backing you any more.'

'I know, I know,' he said impatiently. 'The situation is serious but not critical. I am close to securing a deal which will silence my critics, then I'll deal with Matheson. I still don't believe the stories about Andy. It would suit some people's purposes to make me mistrust him, divert my attention from the real traitors. You have to understand the way people's minds work when they're fighting for power. Make me mistrust Andy and it weakens my power base. I lose my Chief Operator and spend my time watching my back and planning his downfall. I won't fall for that. I trust Andy like a brother. The key thing whenever there is a bid for power is to anticipate the battle. It's easy to cure the problem if you catch it early. If you leave it until it's fully blown, it's easy to diagnose but difficult to cure.'

'Don't lecture me on Machiavellian principles, Douglas. I just hope you diagnosed the disease early enough, and accurately.'

'If all goes according to plan, I'll have those duplicitous bastards out of here so quickly they won't know what happened.'

'What are you plotting?' she asked.

'I'm sorry, Georgina, I can't tell you. With any luck it will come off before you get back from Australia.'


Carson was back at his flat waiting for the call from Stuart Peteyson. He'd phoned earlier in the day to say he had the goods, but Carson had said it was too risky to take the call in the office. He paced around the room. The phone rang. It was Sharon. He had decided not to tell her about the Kuper situation. With this he trusted no one.

'Darling, I have the naughtiest, naughtiest idea. I'll be round at your flat by nine. I want to take you for a little drive,' she said.

'I'm not in the mood for games,' he shot back.

'This isn't a game, it's a fantasy come true. See you at nine. Come down when you hear the horn.' Sharon was worried. She couldn't put out of her mind the sound of a woman's voice in the flat when she had phoned the other night. If Carson was seeing someone else, there was only one way to get him back before it was too late. She would seduce him back. Sex was the key and she had put some planning into tonight's little venture.

It wasn't just their relationship Sharon wanted to protect. He was the key to her taking over the *Sunday Tribune*. She couldn't do it without him. She had to secure her place. There was only one way to get Carson eating out of her pussy, and that was more pussy. After tonight things would be put right.

His phone rang again almost immediately after Sharon's call.

'Andy, it's Stuart. Stand by the fax. I think this is everything you need on Kuper. I've used a government contact of mine. He's very reliable but I've had to pay big money for the information.'

'Will it stand up in court?'

'I have copies of the bank transfers from Kuper's bank account to one General Laurent Mosika, the rebel leader in Sierra Leone. We're talking millions of pounds in donations to the fighting fund. It doesn't sit well with all the pictures of starving and brutalised children we've seen on the news recently. The latest estimate of deaths of women and children alone is almost ten thousand and most of that put down to the rebels plundering and starving out the villages as they pass through to the city. The scenes are horrendous. He's one of the most brutal leaders Africa has seen. I've also laid my hands on a letter Kuper sent to Mosika two months ago outlining his *requests* for co-operation in setting up a major newspaper and satellite network there once he is in power, which can only be a matter of weeks now.'

'How the fuck did you get that?'

'You taught me well and remember, this is Africa. Money buys you anything here if you know where to go. I traced the disgruntled former mistress of Kuper's right-hand man. He ditched her for a younger woman, kicked her out of the apartment he'd given her. She's back in the brothel he picked her up from and very, very bitter.'

'I need the original letter and copies of the bank statements immediately. Fax over what you've got now, but I must have the originals. And no one must know about this Stuart. Your life depends upon it.'

More likely yours does, Peteyson thought as Carson hung up.

When the faxes arrived minutes later Carson read and re-read them. This was it. All he needed. The rest was up to him.

He was locking the faxes away when a car horn blared downstairs. He opened the window and saw Sharon getting out of a black cab. Or was that Sharon? Same body, but the woman walking to his front door was wearing a very obvious long blonde wig.

'Returning to our Essex roots, are we, Sharon? You'd pass for a second division footballer's girlfriend in that,' he said as he opened the door. He took a step back when she walked into the light of the hallway. 'What the hell is going on?' he said. 'You look like a fucking hooker.'

'Fancy fucking this little hooker in the back of a cab then?' she suggested. 'You always said it was one of your fantasies.' She took him by the hand and dragged him into the waiting cab.

'Just drive us around,' she said to the cabbie. As Carson sat down, Sharon took the jump seat opposite and sat with her legs apart. Only now did he fully take in her outfit: tiny Lycra black dress so low it barely covered her nipples, breasts oozing out at the top, stockings and suspenders, high-heeled gold sandals, black-red lipstick, and that wig. He sat transfixed.

Sharon reached into her handbag and slowly extracted a long slim box which she opened, removing a very large cigar. She rolled it around in her mouth, licking the end, as she had so often done with Carson's penis.

'I think we'll save this for later,' she said seductively. 'I know how much my baby loves cigars. And, if it's good enough for the President, it's good enough for my baby.'

Sharon leaned across, undid his flies and was pleased to see he already had an erection. She got down on her hands and knees and took his penis in her mouth. When he was rigid, she straddled him on the back seat. It was slightly more difficult than she'd imagined.

Trust her luck to choose a cab with no suspension. Every time it went over a pothole in the road, her head hit the roof, but Andy didn't seem to notice. He was grunting like a fat boar at a trough, forcing himself higher into her. It was over quickly, as she'd anticipated. She told the driver to stop, readjusted her skirt and they got out together. Sharon threw a £50 note into the driver's window.

'Let's go out for a drink, Andy,' she said. 'No one will recognise me in this.'

Her wig was slightly askew, mascara smudged into panda eyes, red lipstick all over her face. (God knows what my underwear looks like, he thought.) She wore a big, satisfied smile.

'I wouldn't be seen dead with a woman like you,' he declared loudly, and hailed another cab. He climbed in, shut the door in her face, took a wad of notes out of his wallet, wound down the window and tossed them to her. 'This is how the fantasy ends,' he said and signalled to the driver.

Sharon was desperate. This was not how their little fantasy was supposed to end. Something was badly wrong.

Carson was treating her as though she was of no account. She'd been an idiot, giving him too much without any guarantees. He was in a position to destroy Douglas, yet her place was not secured. She had taken him at his word. Fucking fool, she screamed at herself. Then: nobody treats me like that and gets away with it.

Mike was just returning to the table with another round of drinks when a crumpled-looking woman sat down in his seat. The Last Chance was packed, as usual.

'It's Myra. Hello, George,' she said as Mike placed two glasses of Chablis on the table. 'Thanks,' Myra said, taking the glass and sipping its contents. 'Actually, I prefer red wine. Would you mind getting me one?'

Myra lit a cigarette and started gulping the white wine Mike left on the table. Georgina couldn't help but think how odd it was that this woman she hardly knew had just arrived uninvited at her table, taken Mike's seat then sent him off for a glass of red wine. But she seemed so stressed out, dark eyes darting around the room, then back to rest on Georgina's face, that red stress rash visible even in the soft light of the bar. During the conversation Georgina noticed that Myra never actually looked her in the eye.

'Men, they're only useful for getting drinks and paying the bill – and the occasional fuck,' Myra said, her eyes unnaturally wide.

'Actually, Mike's a great friend of mine ...' Georgina said, stiffening.

'Forget about friendship with men, it doesn't exist. The only true friendship is between us. It's women like you and me, Georgina, who can take control. As a team, we're unbeatable. Forget about people like him, they're insignificant people.'

'It's the "*insignificant people*" like Mike who get the papers out, Myra, and as I said before he's ...'

'Actually, I'd love to come and work with you on the *Sunday Tribune*,' Myra went on, oblivious to the coolness in Georgina's voice. 'You have a vacancy for a deputy editor, I read it in UKPG. We'd be fantastic together.'

'But you don't have any experience in newspapers,' Georgina said as politely as she could. 'Your background is magazines. It's rather a big job to even contemplate taking on without a track record.'

'Fuck the experience!' Myra spat. 'You're not seeing the *big picture*.'

'And what, exactly, is that?'

'You and me together! Think of the PR opportunities, the coverage we could get. The only two women to run a national newspaper, together, sisters! The campaigns we could run to increase our profile.'

'Running a successful newspaper is not just about PR, Myra and it's not about *our* profiles ...' Georgina began, and was relieved to see Mike returning to their table with a glass of red wine in one hand and a spare chair in the other. He sat down next to Georgina.

Myra gave him her sweetest smile and placed a hand on his arm. 'You're a sweetheart, thanks,' she said, then turned to Georgina. 'I just wanted to grab you for a moment to talk about Tania.'

'How is she?' Georgina asked, glad they could get off the subject of Myra's ambitions. 'Is she well enough yet for the operation?'

'They're still waiting for a suitable kidney donor,' she said and her face crumpled as the tears began to fall. 'I'm sorry, but this is tearing me apart. I love that little girl so much. I can't bear to think of her in that terrible orphanage. I'll talk to you tomorrow, George, if you don't mind.' And she rushed off.

'What the hell was that all about?' Mike asked, after Myra had left.

'I've only met her once before,' Georgina said, 'in the lift of all places and she started telling me about the Romanian orphan she wrote the piece about in *Me*. You must remember the story, it was run as a cross-ref in the *Herald* news pages a couple of months ago. I could have sworn Myra told me then that the child needed a *heart* operation.'

'There's something weird about that woman,' he said. 'She looks like she's on drugs or something. Did you see her eyes? Plastered! And that dandruff! I've never seen anything like it, like someone's dumped a bag of wood shavings on her shoulders. Don't trust her, George.'

'Oh, Mike. Stop being so melodramatic,' Georgina teased, thinking that there was no way in the world she would trust her.

'And so unkind. She's clearly stressed out of her head. It's probably because of the child.'

'I'm serious. I've heard a few things about her. She's desperately ambitious and has really fucked over people in the past. One of the subs on the *Tribune* used to work for her on her last magazine and they called her Hindley because she likes torturing people and tries to bury all her mistakes.'

'That's a terrible thing to say! She can't be all bad if she's trying to adopt that orphan,' Georgina said.

'*If* being the operative word. Let's wait and see if it ever happens. Just don't trust her, George,' Mike said, making a mental note to run a check on the orphan Myra was supposed to be trying to adopt.

# Chapter Sixteen

It was early evening and Georgina was briefing her team when Douglas called and asked her up to his office. 'There's someone I'd like you to meet.'

The inner door to his office was open, the secretaries gone and she walked in to find Douglas cradling a tiny baby in his arms.

'Georgina, I'd like you to meet Freddie, or should I say Frederick. Let's hope he doesn't speak with a French-Canadian accent.' Douglas laughed and raised the baby close to his face. He chuckled, Freddie smiled, she thought 'What, the hell . . .', and before she could ask the only question she wanted answered, Becky Worthington appeared from the private bathroom in the corner of his office suite.

The Armani trouser suit concealed the fact that she had given birth only a week before.

'This is Becky's baby,' Douglas said, without a hint of embarrassment.

It touched Georgina deeply to see Douglas with his child. There was a softness she had never seen before, but always knew existed. Such a stark comparison from the reptilian façade he adopted at work.

Until now the only outpouring of emotion she had witnessed from Douglas was towards his two fine old cats, Tristan and Rupert. Georgina, like her mother, believed that a man who loved cats couldn't be all bad.

But this was a man in love, and not just with the baby's mother.

'Becky has come in to be briefed on the African appeal we're setting up in the *Daily Tribune*,' Douglas said without looking up. 'You'll have to carry it through into the *Sunday*. It's a great PR opportunity.'

'Since when has the *Tribune* got involved in appeals?' Georgina asked incredulously. 'I can't count the times you've told me that black babies, even if they're dying, don't sell newspapers.' She stopped and thought for a minute. This was very unlike Douglas. She'd better find out whose idea it was before she put her foot in it any further. After all, it could be Becky's brainwave. Douglas shifted uncomfortably in his seat and looked up at his mistress, who could not meet his eyes.

Only hours earlier there had been a terrible row between them.

'We almost lost our own baby, Douglas,' Becky had said. 'How can you cynically exploit the suffering of other children to sell a damned newspaper?'

'Look, it wasn't my idea. The marketing people think it's a good tactic. We need to do something to take attention away from all the bad press the group has been getting. Anyway, we've made a commitment now and we can't go back on it. You're still on maternity leave, so you don't have to handle the campaign.'

'That's not the point and you know it, Douglas.'

'Becky, if it makes you happier, I'll give a donation myself to the fund.' She had looked at him enquiringly. 'All right, a big donation.'

Sensing Douglas's discomfort, Georgina changed tack. 'Take me through the rationale.'

'The Tribune Group has been getting a lot of bad press lately,' he said. More like *you've* been getting a bad press lately, Georgina thought. 'All that trouble with the recent sackings on the *Herald*, we're being criticised for caring more about money than people. This gives us a chance to show that the *Tribune* cares, that it has a heart. It's important for a paper to have a heart, never forget that, Georgina.'

'You don't have to convince me and I'm happy to get behind the appeal, but you can't go crazy on it,' she said. 'The last time the *Daily* ran a picture of starving black babies on the front of the

193

paper they lost 30,000 copies on the day. We're a red top tabloid newspaper.'

'How can you measure a few copies of the newspaper against the value of saving children's lives?' he said, looking down into Freddie's tiny face. 'We'll kick it off next week with a wrap-around special edition with a special eight-page pullout on the crisis, lots of pictures of starving babies, detail the atrocities, interviews with mothers who have lost children, women who have been raped and brutalised by rebel soldiers. The appeal will kick off in the *Daily*. It's all organised.'

'My colleagues are trying to set up a deal with Fosters TV,' Becky said. 'It would be a joint-venture, so we'll get coverage every night on the news as well. The situation in Sierra Leone has reached crisis point and I think it's a good thing for the *Tribune* to be involved. It creates the right impression for the titles. We've all seen after the Labour victory that your average reader cares about what's happening in the world. They're not so insular. I think it will work. There's some excellent footage coming through now. I've got it set up on the video.'

She turned on the tape with the remote control, then sat next to Douglas. The first scene was of a young girl, probably in her early teens, with a large blood-soaked bandage wrapped roughly around her head. Her huge eyes were lifeless, almost as lifeless as the limp baby she was cradling in her arms. Both were clearly on the point of death, a look of complete hopelessness in their eyes, flies crawling all over their faces. The film cut to scenes in a make-shift hospital where tiny bodies were lying on scraps of material on the floor. The reporter was saying that of the forty children there, only a handful were expected to make it through the night. Most were starving to death, separated from their families. Then it cut to mass graves being filled in, piles of spindly bodies clothed in rags thrown carelessly on top of each other, trying to stop the spread of disease raging through the refugee camps. They were scenes of utter desolation.

'We're planning to do a TV commercial for the appeal,' Becky said. 'McLaird's have a great idea to use this footage and cut it with scenes of British children playing happily. We haven't decided on the music yet, but we're trying to get clearance to use The Cars' track "Who's Gonna Take You Home Tonight?" You know, the one they used at the end of the Live Aid concert. There would be no words, just the juxtaposition of the starving children and our own. Then at the end there's a black screen with the words "The *Tribune* Cares – Do You?"'

'It sounds very powerful,' Georgina said. 'Whose idea was it, Douglas?'

'Actually, it was Andy's.'

Mike was waiting for Georgina when she returned to her office, wearing the excited glow that always meant a story. He placed a large white envelope on her desk, winked and said: 'Take a look at these.'

Georgina removed more than a dozen large colour prints. The first showed a blonde woman parking Sharon's car outside Carson's flat with a black taxi waiting behind her car. The sequence then saw her standing at the front door in the most luridly tarty dress. Then Carson joined her and they both got in the taxi. The pictures of them in the cab looked as though they were having sex. The accompanying report from the taxi driver confirmed they were.

'Jackpot!' Georgina said. She looked up at Mike and smiled the widest smile. Replacing the photographs and report in the envelope, then locking them in her briefcase, she took his arm.

'I think this calls for a drink,' she said and they left the office together in fits of laughter. On the way to her car Georgina turned to him.

'Thanks, Mike.'

'For what? I've really enjoyed nailing that bitch.'

'No, thanks for everything. I'm off to Australia in a few days, but there's something I have to do before I go. The only thing Sharon understands is aggression – so I'm going to present her with our little body of evidence. The last thing you can do for me is keep all the originals of the photos and the statements somewhere safe. If anything happens to me, I want you to use them.'

'I hardly think that's likely when she sees them,' Mike said, laughing.

'She'll stop at nothing to discredit me, especially now. It will take her a long time to live down the Jack Edgerton libel, but never underestimate Sharon Hatch. Just keep watching our patch, and my back, while I'm in Australia.'

'Oh, and another thing I forgot to mention,' Mike said. 'Remember that bizarre meeting we had with Myra Prescott in the Last Chance?'

'How could I forget?' Georgina said, recoiling slightly at the memory of the conversation.

'She's been trying to get matey with Sharon of all people, but she's having none of it.'

'Sharon is the least likely sister Myra will ever find,' she said chuckling.

'And she's also crawling all over Andrew Carson. But, more interestingly, I ran a check on the child Tania. Remember the Romanian orphan she's supposed to be trying to adopt?'

'Yes, the child with the heart, or was it kidney, problem?' Georgina said, trying to remember what Myra had said last.

'Well,' Mike said, pausing for dramatic effect, 'Tania died a month after the story about her ran in *Me*. She didn't have a heart *or* a kidney condition, she died of pneumonia. And there is no record anywhere that *anyone* filed for adoption, let alone Myra Prescott.'

'What, you mean she made it up?' Georgina said incredulously. 'I can't believe anyone would make up something like that.'

'You'd better believe it, George. I told you not to trust her.'

'Believe me, I never did. All my antennae were up from the moment I met her,' she said. 'But to invent something like adopting a Romanian orphan, it's so calculating.'

'I was talking to the sub that used to work with her and he said her other nickname was "goldfish".'

'Because of those big bog eyes?' Georgina asked.

'No, because evidently a goldfish has a memory of less than two seconds, due to its tiny brain. So it swims along, bumps into the side of the glass bowl, turns around and by the time it gets to the other side of the bowl it's completely forgotten there's a glass wall there. It only exists for the moment.'

'Weird. Somehow I think the Hindley nickname may be more appropriate.'

Sharon had been intrigued when Georgina called and suggested they meet for a social drink, outside the office, that night after work. There was nothing social about her relationship with Georgina, but she had to know what she was up to.

Both women prepared for the meeting in identical toilets, separated only by one floor and the array of makeup each had positioned in front of her on the wash basin.

Sharon's makeup bag was not dissimilar to a carpenter's tool box. The square bag opened at the top, then folded outward revealing compartments like steps, each level full of old brushes, broken lipsticks, half-used eye shadows and tissues stained with brown, green, black, but mostly orange.

Georgina emptied her black Mac bag, little more than a slim pencil case. The lipstick, there was only one, was Nude, after which she applied a layer of lip gloss and gave a quick brush to her shiny hair.

At the same time Sharon was applying a thick layer of dark brown lip-liner a quarter of an inch outside her normal lip line. This she filled in with Apricot Envy. The Vaseline jar provided a healthy shine on top. Hairspray and more hairspray. Perfume, lots of it.

Soft grey eye shadow and deeper grey kohl for Georgina, Black As The Night shadow and black liquid eyeliner for Sharon, finished off with a dusting of Tangerine Sunset powder.

Fucking fool, she thought, thinking that meeting outside the office will give her any safety. She pulled out her state of the art tape recorder, checked it, and slipped it back into her handbag.

In the back of the taxi on the way to their meeting point Georgina ran over again the conversation she had had with Mike before she left.

'Remember, she'll be taping you, so tape her,' he had said for the tenth time. 'Don't admit to putting a tail on her, say the pictures and statements arrived in the office. Keep it short and to the point. Get in and out as quickly as possible.'

The women arrived together at the Howard and chose a quiet table in the corner. Drinks were ordered and hardly touched. Georgina's charcoal grey suit was a perfect foil for Sharon's bright green, set off with a low-cut orange camisole. Even Georgina had to admit, there was something wonderfully Pamela Anderson about those breasts and Sharon's confidence in parading them.

'Do you want to put your tape recorder on the table, or will it work just as well in your handbag?' Georgina began when the waiter left their table.

Sharon fluttered heavily mascaraed eyelashes in a parody of innocence. 'I have no idea what you mean,' she said, clasping her handbag protectively to her exposed breasts.

Georgina lit a cigarette and offered her one. 'Thanks, babe, but I'll have one of these. Each to their own.' And Sharon pulled out a packet of Marlboro Reds.

'Silly me,' Georgina said sweetly, 'I was given to believe you prefer cigars these days. Very large cigars ...' Sharon shot her a look, half anger, half the closest thing Georgina had ever seen in her to fear.

'We might as well get straight to the point,' Georgina said.

'About your *health* break in Australia,' Sharon interrupted. 'I hope you'll be ... better ... when you get back.'

'No, Sharon, about the tail you've had on me for the past months.'

'I have no idea what you're talking about. Clearly the rumours about you have been underplayed. You're obviously suffering from a serious persecution complex as well as everything else.'

'Let's not waste our time, Sharon. I've something to show you.' Georgina produced a large folder from her briefcase and handed it across the table.

Sharon took the folder, opened it and started leafing through the photographs. 'So Pete Feretti's a queer,' she said derisively. 'Tell me something new. George Michael's done it all before. Old news, baby. If you think that's going to damage me, you're even more naïve than I thought.'

'That's just the warm up session,' Georgina said. 'Keep going, Feretti is nothing compared to what follows.'

'You fucking bitch ... you fucking whore,' Sharon whispered under her breath.

'So you've got to the pictures of you half-dressed, then even less dressed, then engaging in activities one should not engage in with a married man, have you? Carson doesn't take a good picture does he? But I guess the same could be said of you, especially the ones with the cigar. Did you dream up that little sex act yourself or steal it from Monica Lewinsky?' Sharon looked up, the anger in her face producing a red flush that started at her neck and tried to break through the deep brown makeup on her face. 'Don't stop now, Sharon, you're only just getting to the interesting stuff.'

The last sequence of photographs was of her arriving at Carson's flat wearing a blonde wig and almost wearing a skin-tight Lycra dress, him greeting her at the door, them leaving in a taxi, some very blurred pictures in the back of the taxi, and a very succinct statement from the driver as to what had taken place in the back of his cab, how much he had been paid and by whom.

'What do you want?' Sharon demanded defiantly.

'Stop stealing my stories, stop queering my pitch, back off my staff. I don't want to use this information but I will. Believe me I will. What you have in your sweaty little hand are copies. Keep them. The originals are with someone who has express instructions that if there is any real threat to my job, any smearing of me anywhere, they are to be handed over to every national newspaper in the country.'

'They'd never be able to use them, you fucking fool,' Sharon spat out.

'I'm perfectly aware of that, Sharon, but they'd have enough evidence to do a story on The Editor, the Managing Director and the Monica Connection. Enough to discredit you and make you a laughing stock. More importantly the pictures will go to all the board members of the *Tribune*. You know as well as I do how they value a high moral tone. Either you or Carson would have to go and, as Clinton proved, the girl always goes first.'

'You wouldn't fucking dare!' Sharon exploded. 'They'd sack you for tailing me.'

'My dear Sharon, whatever made you think I put a tail on you? These pictures arrived in an envelope at the office. I have no idea where they came from. Even you would have to admit, Sharon, you have a lot of enemies.'

Georgina did not wait for an answer. She buttoned her jacket, stubbed out her cigarette and took a package from her handbag. 'Small gift for you and lover boy,' she said, and left.

Sharon waited until she had gone, ordered another glass of champagne, changed her mind and ordered a bottle, then slowly untied the black satin bow. Inside was one giant Havana cigar.

Why am I taking all the shit for this? Sharon thought. Her first instinct was to call Carson and warn him, then she stopped herself. He hadn't returned any of her calls since the night of the taxi ride, had gone to ground again.

If he had dumped her, as she was beginning to suspect, she could do worse than try and set up an alliance with Georgina and Douglas. Without Carson's support, she had nothing. He could dump her tomorrow and she'd have no comeback.

On the other hand, she was still in a position to save Douglas Holloway, if she dared. High risk, she thought, and a smile began to spread across her face.

Sharon called the waiter over. He cut the end off the cigar she handed him and held a silver lighter to it as she placed it in her mouth and sucked.

The flight to Sydney was interminable, even in business class. Georgina wished she could be sensible, drink only water, eat sparingly, do lots of walking up the aisles. The moment the pre-takeoff champagne was offered, her resolve disappeared.

She took the *West Gazetteer* document out of her briefcase and started working. It was a profitable business: huge classified advertising revenues seemed to be well run, at least on paper. The staff was big, by the Tribune Group's new streamlined standards, but the salaries were more modest. It would be an interesting venture.

She rummaged around in her briefcase for the biographies of the shareholders, pulled it out, and found a large red envelope in the middle. Belinda's handwriting.

'My sweetest Georgina,

When your face
appeared over my crumpled life
at first I understood
only the poverty of what I have.
Then its particular light
on woods, on rivers, on the sea,
became my beginning in the coloured world
in which I had not yet had my beginning.
I am so frightened, I am so frightened,
of the unexpected sunrise finishing,
of revelations
and tears and the excitement finishing.
I don't fight it, my love is this fear,
I nourish it who can nourish nothing,
love's slipshod watchman.
Fear hems me in.
I am conscious that these minutes are short
and that the colours in my eyes will vanish
when your face sets.

*Yevteshenko*, 1960

I feel your face has set. I love you but I must leave.
Forever yours,
Belinda

Georgina closed her eyes and felt a warm tear slide down her face.

She had not wanted it to end this way, yet there seemed an inevitability about it all now. The further she travelled away from London, the more she was convinced that the relationship had to end, for both their sakes. She loved Belinda, but not enough. She knew that now, as she had the choice either to make things right again or allow them to die.

Along with the pain, Georgina felt the cool and calming breath of relief.

The view from her eighteenth floor room of Sydney's Regent Hotel was awesome. That wonderful coat hanger of a bridge on the left, the Opera House down to the right, the ferries scurrying across the vivid blue water. Georgina tried the flat in London again but the answer phone was on. Again she left a message, not knowing if Belinda would get it.

The meeting would take place over lunch, at the Mosman's, one of Sydney's finest seafood restaurants perched over Mosman Bay.

'The view is magnificent,' Georgina said to Walter Hearn on her right, Chief Executive of the Zennicle Bank, one of the major shareholders of the *West Gazetteer*. Peter Graham was his counterpart at Co-Op Corp, the other major owner. It was an informal meeting to test the water and their desire to sell the newspaper.

'You will know the history of the *West*,' Hearn said. 'The most profitable newspaper in the southern hemisphere. It publishes Monday to Saturday and is the State's only title. There was a rival newspaper once, but it didn't last long. To be honest, we make a nice little return on our investment and would only be interested in selling if the offer was exceptional.'

They continued discussing the business over lunch, neither declaring their hand.

'There is one issue that concerns us,' Graham said in the tone of voice businessmen use when something actually concerns them greatly. 'We have worked very hard to create and maintain an image as the caring bank. We pride ourselves on the fact that we do not invest in companies or countries which exploit either people or the environment.'

Graham refilled Georgina's glass. He looked slightly uncomfortable but continued. 'Looking at your company's industrial relations track record, I would need a guarantee prior to proceeding that you would not slash the work force the way you have done on your own titles in Britain. The press and print unions here are still quite powerful and we at Co-Op Corp would not welcome the kind of adverse publicity that would follow a massive blood-letting. It would damage our other interests, selling off to a brutal new owner.'

Georgina knew this was an assurance she should but could not in all honesty give. The *Tribune*'s takeover policy was slash and burn, to reduce overheads and increase the bottom line profits. The easiest area to cut was staff costs and Douglas's view was that you cut the staffing levels to the bone and then beyond. If things started to collapse, you could always recruit, but at a much lower salary level.

'I haven't had a chance to see the operation on the ground,' Georgina said, clearly avoiding the implied question. 'You have to get in there and see the newspaper running before you can make any judgments about staffing levels.'

'Unfortunate name that boss of yours has, Georgina,' Graham said. 'We Australians have become a bit sensitive about the way the British generals sent our boys to slaughter in the wars, you know. Douglas Haig and Ian Douglas were together responsible for the deaths of tens of thousands of our lads. Treated them like gun fodder. Damned unfortunate name.'

Hearn decided to play the role of diplomat and steer the conversation in a new direction. 'So after today you're off to Perth to see the operation,' he said. 'There have been a lot of changes there recently. We've just put in a new management team. Steve Hanson, the editor-in-chief, will show you around.

'If you get a chance, you must see some of the countryside south of Perth,' he added. 'The wine-growing area around Margaret River is getting an international reputation. And the beaches there are some of the finest in the world.'

'What a shame. I'm only there for two days, then off to Johannesburg to see my family, so I'm afraid I won't have time,' she told him.

Carson was sitting opposite Douglas in his office when the Company Secretary came in.

'We're just discussing the Kuper deal, Zack. Take a seat,' Douglas said. 'Andy's done a great job. Kuper's prepared to put

£30 million in to buy 45% of the *Herald* titles. The Tribune Group will run all support operations – finance, printing, circulation, distribution.'

'Kuper is adamant that the papers should be independent editorially. That gives him more stature: joint owner of the *Herald* and all that. Sounds better at parties,' Carson said, and they all laughed. The vanity of newspaper proprietors!

'He also wants a separate advertising and marketing team, but the rest he's happy for us to run,' Carson continued. 'We'll simply cross-charge the *Herald* for all other support, taking 55% of the cost ourselves, and 45% to Kuper's group. It will certainly help our bottom line to offload nearly half of the losses on the titles.'

'It sounds like an excellent deal, Andy,' Priest told him, 'but can I sound a note of caution? There's some talk that Kuper's not everything he seems to be. Some shady business deals in the past. There was a piece in a South African magazine that accused him of bully boy tactics with the Government, trying to get around their monopoly laws.'

'That will be the *Eye Saw*. It was a poor man's version of *Private Eye*, full of business gossip. Kuper sued the magazine for running that piece and won an out-of-court settlement so big the rag closed. Nothing has ever been proved against him. I've checked him out thoroughly. Flies too close to the wind sometimes, but what self-made billionaire hasn't? You have my personal assurance he's clean.'

'Thanks again, Andy,' Douglas said. 'It's been a load off my mind, your handling this deal. You won't go unrewarded.'

No, I won't, Carson thought to himself. But you have no idea how great my reward will be.


The tour around the offices of the *West Gazetteer* produced no surprises. It was a well-run operation, bit of fat, especially on the editorial staff, but it worked. Georgina had been slightly distracted by news on the television that morning that there was threatened strike action by the air traffic controllers at all major airports in South Africa. She was desperate to get home and see her father and brother. Please God, let me get there, she thought.

She was back in her hotel room packing when news came

through that the strike was on. Georgina slumped on the bed and wished she could cry. No tears came, only frustration. She tried Belinda again, no answer, took out the bottle of whisky she'd bought for her dad and started to drink it.

By morning there were still no flights to Johannesburg, so she hired a car and set off for this magical place, the Margaret River.

The travel agent at the hotel booked her into a small house overlooking the ocean in a place called Yallingup. What the hell? She had nothing else to do and nothing to lose.

# Chapter Seventeen

'Lock the fucking door!' Sharon screamed as the second hand on the wall clock hit 11 am. There were only two things you could rely upon in the *Tribune* office – first, that the door to Sharon's office would be locked at eleven and second, that she would scream: 'Lock the fucking door!' The usual executives were sliding off the sofas, flicking ash into half-empty plastic cups on the floor, drinking putrid coffee out of similar plastic cups, sometimes confusing the two.

'But Dave isn't here,' said Steve Dainson, the deputy news editor, opening two slats of the horizontal blinds with his fingers and peering out, like a dirty old man spying on a young girl. 'He's put the phone down – he's standing up – he's coming,' he said desperately. Dave Leiber was the hastily appointed news editor, Allenby's replacement. In looks and demeanour he was a dead ringer for his predecessor.

'I don't give a fuck if he's standing on his fucking head,' Sharon shouted. 'I wait for no one. Steve, news list.'

She leaned back in her real leather chair, only editors and managing directors got real leather chairs at the *Tribune*, and fixed her eyes on Dainson who was trying unsuccessfully to hide behind the huge vase of pink, red, yellow and tangerine gladioli on her desk.

'What are we doing about the Westminster by-election?' she asked.

Dainson started to shuffle the two pages of his news list, knowing as he pretended to scan the stories that there was no

Westminster item. Oh Christ, he thought to himself as he felt that hot sweaty patch break out on his back. He quickly considered his options and had no trouble deciding the course of action.

'Dave must have forgotten it,' he said. 'I know I reminded him this morning. Must have slipped his mind. Anyway, I've got a great idea. Why don't we ring the Palace press office and find out which way the Queen is going to vote? Then we can run a huge front page saying "Queen Dumps Tony".'

It was one of those moments. The room was as silent as an undertaker's chapel. Dainson knew that silence, he'd made a gaffe. But what the fuck was it? If in doubt, proceed full-speed ahead.

'Okay, we'll ask the whole Royal Family and get Mystic Merve to predict which way the corgis will vote and then we can have a big picture of one of them lifting its leg on Blair,' he stumbled on, looking around the room appealing for some support, any support.

'Will someone put this moron out of his misery?' Sharon ordered, clearly enjoying his embarrassment.

The political editor just raised his eyes to the heavens. Sally Brink, features editor said, in a very small voice: 'I don't think she's allowed to vote, Steve. Isn't she in charge of the Government or something? You remember, she always goes to the opening of Parliament with Phil in one of those horrid frocks. Not Phil – the Queen, I mean.'

'Honest mistake, anyone could make it,' Dainson blustered. 'I still think the corgi idea would work. Or why don't we get a bunch of Royal Family look-alikes and ask them how they'd vote, then just pretend it's the Royal Family?'

'Out! Get out of my fucking office – all of you,' Sharon shrieked, 'and don't come back until you've got a decent list of ideas. Do I have to think of everything myself? And get that useless news editor in, *now*.' Dave Leiber almost fell into the room when the door was unlocked.

'Sharon, I'm really sorry, but I had the most amazing woman on the line,' he said when everyone else had left the room. 'She claims she had an affair with Earl Spencer. You know, Diana's father . . .'

'Of course I fucking know who he is. This had better be good,

Dave, or you'll be the shortest surviving news editor in Fleet Street.'

'Sorry. Well, she says she had an affair with Spencer thirty-two years ago. She worked in the pub on the estate and he used to drop by sometimes after the shoot to have a drink with the gamekeeper. That's how they met.' He paused for dramatic effect, revelling in what he was about to say. 'She claims the affair lasted for about six months and she has letters to prove it.' Another pause as he sat back in his chair, running his hand over his jowls. 'She claims he made her pregnant and that she now has a child, a daughter, who was born five years after Diana, living in a small council flat in Birmingham.'

'Yes, yes, yes!' Sharon shrieked, and leaped up from her desk, punching her fist in the air and showering Leiber with cigarette ash. 'Princess Diana's Secret Sister. The Princess and the Pauper. I can see tomorrow's front page now.'

'Hold on a minute Sharon,' he said. 'We haven't even met her yet. I don't know if the story will check out.'

'We're hardly going to get any fucking trouble from Spencer,' she said sarcastically. 'How long has he been dead? And I can't imagine Charles Spencer or his sisters volunteering for a DNA test to prove the woman wrong, can you? The great thing about this story, if it checks out at all, is that it's virtually impossible to prove and just as impossible to disprove. We all know that even dead Diana sells newspapers – and an illegitimate sister, living on in her memory . . . It couldn't be better. Everyone has been scrabbling around trying to find the new Diana. Well, we've found her. Lucky for us the Earl is dead. He's the only one who could sue us. When are you seeing her?'

'She's coming into the office this evening. I got her on the first flight down. She's bringing the letters and pictures of her daughter who, she says, is a dead ringer for Diana.'

'If she isn't now, she will be when our make-over people get through with her. This is fucking fantastic, Dave. Bring her in to see me the moment she gets here.'

Mrs Stella Anderson arrived at the *Tribune* offices shortly before 6 pm clutching a plastic folder of pictures and scraps of paper and was whisked straight into Sharon's office. Leiber and his deputy were waiting for her, coffee and sandwiches on the desk.

'Mrs Anderson, how lovely to meet you,' Sharon said sweetly, coming out from behind her desk to greet the woman. 'I know how difficult this must be for you, but you're doing the right thing. Would you like a sandwich?' Sharon was superb in these situations, all motherly and caring.

'Thank you, Miss Hatch,' the woman said. 'I wasn't expecting to meet you.'

'Please, call me Sharon. Now sit down and tell me all about it.'

Stella Anderson was a pretty woman in her late forties, plump in a reassuringly mumsy way. The floral frock and pink cardigan looked like her Sunday best. Judging by her bright blue eyes and pink-painted mouth, the full breasts and soft curves, it was clear she had once been a very lovely woman. She took a tissue from her bag and held it to her mouth, eyes blinking tearfully.

'I was never going to tell anyone about this,' she began in a thick Birmingham accent, 'but things have got really hard for us. For me and Emma, I mean. I've tried my best to bring her up a good girl and provide for her but it wasn't easy as a single mother, especially in those days. I had to leave my job when they found out I was pregnant.' Sharon stood up and went across to the woman, slid her arm around her shoulders and held her for a few moments. She had read recently in a review of a Clinton biography that 'touchy feely' worked at putting unfortunates at their ease.

'I know how difficult this must be for you,' she said. 'Just take it slowly and start at the beginning.' Sharon had seated the woman as close to the hidden microphone as she could, to make sure the tape would be clear. 'Remember, this is just between us for now. If you don't want to go ahead with it, we'll drop the whole thing. Just tell me everything. Who is Emma's father?'

'The Earl Spencer, Princess Diana's father,' Stella said, and stifled a sob.

'And tell me when and how you met?' Sharon coaxed.

'I was working at the Hope and Anchor, the local on the Earl's estate,' she continued. 'I was only sixteen and didn't know much about . . . men and things. He was so kind to me. They used to come in sometimes after the shoot, the Earl and his gamekeeper, to talk about how it had gone and how the pheasants had flown. Shooting talk, you know. We kind of got friendly and one night he was still there after closing time organising something for the next shoot and said he'd take me to my room. It wasn't safe, a young girl like me walking around on my own. My room was above the stables across the yard. Everyone else had gone. I guess I was flattered, him being so rich and all. It happened the first time that night. He came into my room.'

'What actually happened, Mrs Anderson?' Sharon probed gently.

'He had his way with me.'

'He raped you?' Sharon exclaimed, trying to keep the excitement out of her voice.

'No, he didn't rape me. I didn't know what was happening. I was a good Catholic girl, didn't know anything about what men did to women I was . . .' another sob '. . . a virgin.'

'So, he took advantage of you, a poor innocent young girl?' Sharon sympathised.

'I guess that's what he did, Miss Hatch, yes. It went on for about six months. The Earl was so kind. He used to bring me presents, stockings and jewellery and things. Then I found out I was pregnant. Well, I didn't realise, it was one of the other girls who spotted it. I didn't know how babies were made.' She stopped talking briefly and, her eyes filled with tears. 'I told the Earl and he was so angry. He told me to leave the village, that I was a bad girl and it wasn't his child. He gave me some money, £100, which was a lot then and I left. I was so ashamed.'

'Do you still have any of the presents he gave you?'

'Had to sell them for food. There's nothing left except a few letters he wrote me. I moved back to Birmingham and had the baby, then got work at a pub, the Stag. Emma lived upstairs and we managed somehow. We always managed somehow. The thing is, Miss Hatch, I've never been able to give my girl anything but love and now for the first time she's asked me for something and I want to be able to give it to her. But all I have is the story. One of my friends told me a newspaper might pay me for it. Is that true, Miss Hatch? I've always read the *Tribune*, my dad used to buy it, it's our newspaper, so I came here first.'

'You've done the right thing. And what is it that your daughter has asked you for?'

'Emma loves dancing, just like Diana did. I couldn't afford ballet lessons, it was hard enough just keeping a roof over our heads and food on the table, and often we went without that. She was a professional dancer, worked over in Paris for a while, but she fell and hurt her knee. She needs an operation to be able to dance again and our local doctor says she'll have to wait two years on the NHS, because it's not urgent. She can't wait, Miss Hatch, she's living with me in a council flat in Birmingham and it's killing her. I need £50,000 for the operation and to give us a fresh start. She deserves that.'

'That's a lot of money Mrs Anderson,' Sharon said gravely, knowing full well the *Sun* or the *Mirror* would pay twice that for the story if it held up. 'Have you brought the letters and pictures of Emma?'

Stella Anderson placed the shabby plastic envelope on the desk and took out a series of photographs. 'This is Emma as a baby, then when she was thirteen in a ballet outfit she borrowed from a friend at school. Oh, she so wanted to be a ballerina, but the cost of those lessons ... and anyway, she was too tall. This one was taken at her twenty-first birthday party, this one at her wedding. That husband of hers was a real sod, pardon my language. Left her after four years, ran off with another woman. Broke poor Emma's heart it did. This picture was taken when she was dancing in Paris. I don't hold with those skimpy outfits, but Emma said they had to wear them. And all those feathers. How do you dance with all those feathers on your head?'

Sharon looked at the pictures in disbelief. The young woman who looked back was tall, with a great figure, short blonde hair and blue eyes. In the picture taken on her wedding day she had her chin down and gazed up soulfully from under her long fringe. She looked remarkably like Diana, albeit a poor man's version. With a couple of hours of hair and makeup she could look almost aristocratic.

'Now the letters, Mrs Anderson, could I have a look at them please?' Sharon asked, containing her excitement with difficulty.

'They're in the folder,' she replied, then looked forlornly at the empty plastic sleeve. 'Oh my God, no! They must have fallen out on the plane. No, they must be here – help me find my letters.' A frantic search of the office ensued but they were nowhere to be found.

'Steve, get a couple of reporters to check the flight Mrs Anderson came in on, and the taxi that brought her here,' said Leiber. '*NOW*.'

'I've got photocopies of them at home. Will they do?'

'We'll send a couple of reporters back on the flight with you this evening to get them,' Sharon said. 'And if you don't mind, we'd like to put you up in a quiet hotel for a few days, at the *Tribune*'s expense of course. Emma too. It will be a nice treat for you both. The reporters can do the full story then.'

'Oh, that would be lovely,' Stella said gratefully. 'After a lifetime of heartache, maybe now I'll be able to do something good for my little girl. You can't imagine how it broke my heart to see Diana on the television, all that money, and my poor Emma dressed in rags. And all the time they were sisters.

'I used to pray that one day my Emma would meet Diana and they would become friends. Then that terrible accident. Poor Diana, poor Dodi. Now Emma will never meet her sister, but maybe some good can come of all this.'

'Let's hope we can help you to redress this awful injustice,' Leiber said sanctimoniously.

'I don't want a new dress, I want £50,000.'

The moment she left the office Sharon walked up and hugged her news editor. 'This is it, this is the fucking big one,' she cried. 'The father of the Princess of Wales seduces underage barmaid, gets her pregnant then cruelly dumps her. She struggles to bring up her daughter alone in a council flat while Diana was brought up in splendour. They both marry young and end up dumped by their cheating husbands. One life ends tragically in a tunnel in Paris, the other is just beginning in the *Tribune*.'

'Hold on Sharon, we've got to check all this out,' Leiber said, rubbing the back of his neck anxiously.

'I know we have to fucking check it out, you moron. But I feel it's true, I *know* it's true. Did you see those pictures? By the time we've finished with her, she *will* be Princess Diana. And that picture of her as a teenager in the ballet costume – it's just like that picture of Diana as a girl. Remember the one from her private collection that was first published in the Morton book? This is too good to be true.'

'That's what worries me,' Leiber said, stroking his jowls again. 'And the missing letters. Anyway, we'll check it all out: the pub on the estate, birth certificate, the photocopies of the letters, the lot. I've got to admit, there's a strong resemblance.'

'Just make sure you get her and her daughter into a hotel where no one can find them,' Sharon warned. 'And I don't want them moving from their room until we publish. No phone calls, no contact with the outside world. Keep them safe. Let's get a tame genealogical expert to authenticate the family resemblance and a handwriting one to check out the letters. We must be able to get a copy of the Earl's signature from a book or something. And get Roxy to transcribe the recording of the meeting. If the worst comes to the worst and they bottle out, we've got the pictures and can run with the story anyway.'

Becky was bathing Freddie when Douglas called to say he would be home early and wanted a quiet night in. She was immediately alarmed, partly by the tone of his voice and partly because he never came home early, unless he was ill, and that seldom happened. He was one of those men who saw illness as weakness.

The move into East Heath Road had come earlier than Becky had expected. They had been planning to wait until a couple of months after the baby was born and he had broken the news to Kelly. Then Becky and the child would move in first, plus the nanny, and Douglas would follow after a suitable interval. He didn't want Kelly to think he was moving out on her and in with another woman, even though that was exactly what he was planning.

But everything had changed so dramatically – and rapidly. Becky had heard stories about Kelly's appearance at the board meeting, but it was difficult to tell fact from rumour and Douglas did not want to talk about it.

She had also read a rather lurid account of the event in a newspaper diary. How the hell did they get details like that?

Becky suspected her friends protected her from the truth, on this occasion and others. Douglas had called her in the hospital the day after Freddie was born and said he was arranging the removal immediately. By the time she came out of hospital, after a few days' rest, East Heath Road was ready. All that was missing was Douglas's CD collection. She guessed Kelly had kept that out of spite.

Despite Becky's attempts to get him to talk about it, Douglas refused to discuss the situation with his wife.

'I've left Kelly to be with you,' he had said. 'That's all you need to know.'

'But what about the baby, Douglas? She must be distraught,' Becky worried.

'I don't know because I haven't discussed it with her. Nor do I intend to.'

'After all those years, how could you just walk out? Surely you owed her the courtesy of telling her face to face what was going on?'

'The subject is closed. You've got what you wanted: me, this house and our child. That's all I want, too. She almost destroyed us once. Let's just leave it, please.'

Although she never raised the subject with Douglas again, Becky could not stop thinking about it. Like millions of women before her, who had been a mistress then seen off the wife, a small part of her brain kept asking the nagging questions: If he could treat her so badly, will he do the same to me one day? He loved her once, will he fall out of love with me and find someone else? What kind of a man walks out on a marriage and a baby without even explaining things to his wife?

And like millions of mistresses before her, she decided not to think about it – too much. She had him now, she would be different, that's all that mattered.

Becky had done her best that night to make the kitchen cosy. She had cooked Douglas's favourite – grilled chicken, skinless of course, a green salad (he had read somewhere that greens prevented the onset of prostate cancer) and a bottle of 1983 Pauillac Chateau Lynch-Bages. Modest cheese plate to follow. The candlelight softened the kitchen. She had agonised over whether they should eat here or at the dining table on the first floor. But sitting at the opposite ends of a table for twenty was hardly intimate and she felt like a serving maiden sitting next to him.

The kitchen was a showpiece, like everything in the house, but the aluminium cupboards, sink and American freezer made the room seem cold. The marble floor and glass table didn't help either. They ate at home alone so rarely and she wanted this meal to be relaxed. Douglas had been working like a maniac lately and all the signs of stress were there.

He arrived late, kissed her, and asked after Freddie. 'He was asleep hours ago,' said Becky. Like so many work-obsessed fathers before him, like his own father, Douglas went into his son's room and gently kissed the sleeping child. His few moments of quality time.

Becky poured him a glass of wine as he sat down. 'What's up darling, hard day?'

'I had another meeting with Billmore. The Fosters deal should be done within a fortnight. It's all going well.' He hated discussing business with his women. 'For some reason I can't help but feel worried about it, though. Something's wrong, Becky, but I can't put my finger on it.'

'You're just stressed, darling. We need a holiday.'

'Not until I have this deal signed and I've got rid of those bastards on the board. Then the announcement. Maybe we can go away together afterwards, for a few days anyway. The launch of the African appeal should help ease the situation. The ads are great.'

'Aaron called me this evening to say they're so pleased with their work on the TV ads, McLaird's are submitting them for the Basch Awards. Isn't that wonderful?'

'Awards don't win you readers,' he said grumpily.

'Something else is bothering you, isn't it.'

'As if I didn't have enough to worry about, the papers from Kelly's lawyers arrived today. She's hired Mitchell Montague. You know, the palimony lawyer. You'd think we could just sit down between us and sort this out. I've already offered to give her the flat and a lump sum of £1 million. She just laughed and hung up the phone.'

'She's hurt at the moment, you can't blame her for lashing out. I'm sure she'll be more reasonable after the initial shock has worn off.'

'You don't know Kelly. She won't rest until she's had her pound of flesh,' he said. 'How the hell did she find out about this house, and Freddie? We were so careful. Someone's stirring up trouble for me, Becky, I just know it. The problem is, I can't for the life of me work out who it is. Who wants to hurt me that badly?'

Andrew Carson was sitting at the dining table in his flat, surrounded by bound documents, neatly arranged in piles. He picked up the top copy of the first pile, a detailed two-year account of every penny the *Daily* and *Sunday Tribune* had paid Douglas's relation, Rebecca Kershaw, plus comparative earnings of other freelances in the same period. Alongside each of the stories Rebecca had submitted was a record of the fee paid, nearly a third of the stories had the word 'spike' written alongside them. In newspaper terms this means 'not published'. He replaced the document on top of the eleven other copies on the table.

Beside the next pile was a stack of twelve tapes, unmarked. He took the top document. It was a full transcript of Les Strangelove's conversation with Georgina over the Blakehurst story. The first page contained only one quote, set in 18 point bold type.

# 'The Minister knows everything about Douglas, about Becky and the baby, about his business deals. If you run the story, he'll blow the lot.'

Following the transcript were colour photocopies of the pages Georgina had originally laid out, the ones she had shown Les Strangelove.

At the end of the transcript were the words:

# 'For reasons unknown, the *Sunday Tribune* failed to run the story.'

The third document was more pictorial, more colourful and the one that had taken the longest to compile. Carson had had to pull in a lot of favours to get all the pictures. The first page was a mock-up of the *Daily Tribune*'s front page with a screaming headline:

SERIAL SHAGGER

and a sub deck saying:

# *Douglas's morals are in the gutter, like his newspapers*

Underneath it was a picture of Douglas, leering at the camera like Jack Nicholson playing a psychopath. The next page contained pictures of him with his three wives plus a paparazzi shot of him in the street with Becky. The third page was full of head shots of women, all captioned, all former girlfriends. There were twenty pictures in total. The final one had a picture of him with the now-famous Tory red eyes superimposed over it. The headline over the top read:

THEY COULDN'T TRUST
HIM . . . SHOULD YOU?

The fourth and most damning file contained Kuper's bank statements and correspondence with General Laurent Mosika, supplied by Peteyson earlier that week. Unlike the other piles, there were thirteen copies of these documents. Carson took a brown envelope from the drawer and put one copy in it, then placed a pre-prepared address sticker on the front.

Private and Confidential
To be opened by addressee only

Peter Smith
The Editor
The Sun

He then carefully placed one of each of the documents, plus tape, into separate brown envelopes. Twelve complete packages in all. He took out a roll of typed names and addresses and stuck one on each envelope. There was one for every *Tribune* board member, excluding Douglas Holloway. Carson even addressed one to himself.

# Chapter Eighteen

Georgina did not even notice the ramshackle shack she had rented at first. All she saw was its setting. White sand reached up almost to the veranda of the rammed earth hut, the bay sweeping off to the right, piles of ancient rocks lashed by the ocean to the left. Behind her were miles of virgin bush land. It was perfect. The air was full of the sound of crashing waves and the song of birds.

She walked inside and saw the house consisted of one big room, kitchen along one side, a big old sofa in the middle, positioned to take in the view over the ocean, and a double bed. The bathroom was at the back. No curtains, just a huge window overlooking the bay. A couple of old wicker chairs on the veranda. The smell of eucalyptus and sea salt.

It was late afternoon. a cool clear day and relatively warm despite the fact it was mid-winter. She bravely peeled off her clothes and plunged into the icy ocean. It was like purging her soul. There wasn't another person in sight, the beach was hers, the *Tribune* and all its problems a million miles away. She began to relax for the first time in months.

After her swim, she opened a bottle of Cullens lightly oaked Chardonnay and sat on the veranda. The bird song increased with the fading light. A wily black wagtail landed on the chair next to her and shook his tail angrily. She laughed aloud at his cross white eyebrows and decided he was reprimanding her for her laziness and that she should go for a walk in the bush before the light died.

There was a rough track leading from the house along the coastal ridge and she set off. About two miles along it she came across another shack, similar to her own, with a wiry old man sitting out front. He wore a battered bushman's hat, boots and shorts, unremarkable looking except for his companions. Georgina stood transfixed. He was surrounded by a family of magpies, one sitting on his forearm as he stroked its neck and made strangely realistic bird sounds. He was talking to the birds. It was too intimate a scene to interrupt, so she made her way silently back to her shack and settled in for the night.

She woke in the dead of night in a terrible sweat, for a moment not knowing where she was. She'd been dreaming. It was a hideous dream, she'd had it often before. She was standing in her office when the tower began to tremble. People were running around screaming: 'We've been hit by a plane, the building's collapsing.' She clung to a pillar in a corner of the room, desperately trying to stay alive as the floor fell from beneath her.

Georgina could never sleep properly after this dream, so rose a few minutes before 5 am, dressed and set off along the path she'd discovered last night. The morning light was pale, the bush full of the sound of birds. Turning a bend she saw a group of kangaroos feeding. They stopped and raised their heads, smelling but not yet seeing her. She stood motionless.

'They won't move if you don't,' she heard someone say behind her, in a slow Australian drawl. Startled she turned around to see the old bird man standing there. Her sudden movement spooked the kangaroos and they loped off to a safer spot.

'You're the man with the magpies,' she said.

'Yeah, Brian's the name. They call me Brian the Bird Man,' he said with a chuckle. His face was deeply creased from years of smiling and squinting into the sun, his skin tanned a dark brown despite the hat.

'Hi, I'm Georgina.'

'Come and meet my family.' He headed off down the track to his hut and she followed, wondering for a brief moment what the hell she was doing trailing after some strange man in the bush in the middle of nowhere. But she felt completely at ease. As soon as they arrived she heard bird song, then seven or eight black and white birds flew down to greet them.

'This is my family, George,' he said. One of the birds hobbled towards him then flew up on to his shoulder. 'This is Biggles. Biggles, meet George. Had to fix his foot – was hurt real bad, that's why I call him Biggles, because he can't land. Magpies are my favourites. Like the way they value families. See that smaller one over there? That's Sharleen. She's the mother of the two young 'uns, her teenage sons. Her husband's the big bastard, Bruce.'

Brian went inside the hut, came out with a handful of mince and started feeding them. Biggles refused to take the meat offered to him. 'Don't turn your bloody beak up at it, mate, it's all you're getting today. Miss Lynne doesn't approve of me nicking the prime beef mince, so you've got pork today. See how the parents feed first? Then the uncles and aunties. In magpie families there's only one couple who have conjugal rights, the rest just look after them.'

Georgina heard a commotion from inside the hut. 'What's that noise?' she asked.

'The patients squawking for a feed. Come in and see.' Inside the hut one entire wall was stacked with bird cages. About a quarter were occupied by Brian's menagerie of birds. 'This is the hospital. People from miles around bring me birds when they get hurt. I heal them, then let them go. That's how I got to meet Biggles. Kinda took a shine to me and never left. Brought his whole bloody family. Miss Lynne, that's the wife, don't approve, so I spend most of me time down here.'

'Do you mind if I come back this evening?' Georgina asked.

'Dawn and dusk I'm here. You're welcome.' And so a friendship began between the old bush man and the city girl.

Kelly was in widow weeds. She'd chosen black for her meeting with the legendary Mr Montague. Today she was wearing Chanel, a tiny sleeveless dress and matching jacket trimmed with white, her hair was twisted and pinned at the back of her head, long strands hanging loose.

His New York office was exactly as she had anticipated, very modern and very expensive. Their first contact, by phone a week ago, had been perfunctory. Today they were getting down to business. He led her into the office and sat her at the seat opposite his huge glass and steel desk. A vase of Casablanca lilies stood at one end. Lilies gave her terrible hay fever and she took a small white linen handkerchief from her Chanel handbag.

'I'm sorry, Mr Montague,' she said, sniffing and pointing at the lilies, 'hay fever.' Kelly had done a lot of crying lately and the flowers were a welcomed cover for her red eyes. 'We might as well get straight to the point. I want this over with as quickly as possible.'

'I understand how painful this must be for you, Mrs Holloway,' he began.

'I doubt that very much,' she said softly. 'The reason I have come to you is because you are the best. And I do not want the press having a field day over this divorce. I'm not being greedy, I just want a fair deal for us.'

'"Us", Mrs Holloway? I can assure you that my fees will be paid by your husband. You have no need to worry about that.'

'The "us" I was referring to is me and my baby,' Kelly shot back. 'Right now your fees are the last thing on my mind.'

'I'm sorry, I had no idea. That does rather cast a different light on things. You'll be looking for a lump sum and support for your child and yourself for life, then?'

'No, I want somewhere to live and basic maintenance for my child. That's it. I want nothing more to do with Douglas Holloway as long as I live.'

'I'm afraid it won't be as simple as that.' The lawyer leaned back in his soft leather and steel chair and put the tips of his fingers together. 'The father has a right to see his child. Any court of law would uphold that.'

Kelly stared out of the window at Manhattan and for a moment could only think that this was the same magical skyline that had been the backdrop to her first meeting with Douglas. Strange that the setting for their divorce should be that of their first romance.

'I think that, given the fact my husband offered me £1 million to abort our baby, I can safely assume he'll want nothing more to do with it,' she said in a flat voice, placing her hands over her stomach protectively.

For a few minutes they sat in silence, the only sounds the faint whining of the wind against the huge windows and the low hum of the air conditioning.

'The reason I have come to you is that I want Douglas to know I am serious about my desire to have this over with, quickly, with a minimum of fuss. If he refuses to do that, I'll drag him through the most public and damaging divorce case ever seen. If he tries to get anywhere near my child – ever – I will destroy him. Do I make myself clear?'

It was Friday evening at Tribune Tower. Pete Feretti burst into Sharon's office singing, 'I'm in love, I'm in love, I'm in love,' and danced around the room, hugging himself like a teenage girl with a crush.

'Not now, Pete, I'm busy with this fucking editorial for Sunday. So how's the little bitch taking to my new leader writer?' Sharon said.

'Well,' he said in a stage whisper and leaned across the desk, half-closing his eyes against the cigarette smoke, 'she didn't tell me, but I found out from Ian on the subs' desk. *Madam* rewrote it on Saturday, from Australia. Said the rantings of an anti-liberal, anti-Government moron had no place in the *Sunday Tribune*. You know how precious she is about her darling working class readers.'

'She what? She fucking what? If that bitch so much as touches a word of my leaders again, I'll destroy her,' Sharon screamed. She leaped up and came around the desk, putting her face inches away from Feretti's. 'I want to know immediately if she tries to touch a word of it again. Do you understand me?' He flinched, partly from the force of the words, partly from Sharon's excruciatingly bad breath, and nodded. 'Now get the fuck out of here, I'm working.'

After he left she lit another Marlboro and sat back in her chair. It wouldn't be long now. The Drop the Dead Douglas dossier was ready, she'd copied it all herself. All she had to do was be patient. Only a fortnight to the next board meeting – Douglas's swansong and Georgina's last day as editor.

And now the *Daily* had one of the biggest news stories for years. The timing was perfect.

★

'Okay, let's go. What do we have?' Sharon said. They were seated at the small conference table in her office, its surface covered with pictures of Emma, sofas littered with pictures of Diana and her father. The story had been kept under wraps and the only executives who knew about it were present – Dave Leiber, news editor, Steve Dainson, deputy news editor, and Phil Plattmann, picture editor.

'So far things have checked out pretty well, but not conclusively,' Leiber said. 'We found an old codger who used to be a beater on the Earl's shoot and he remembers the lovely Stella. Confirms she used to work at the Hope and Anchor at the time she says. Apparently he had a crush on her, all the blokes did. She was a real looker, huge tits, lots of curves, but she wouldn't have anything to do with them. He said she and the Earl were "friendly" but couldn't confirm more than that. Then she mysteriously disappeared and the last he heard of her was that she'd got knocked up and was living with the sprog in Birmingham.'

'Great, anything else?' Sharon said, the colour rising in her skin. She leaned forward in anticipation, heavy breasts resting on the table, cigarette smoke blowing in Leiber's eyes.

'There's no father's name on the birth certificate,' he went on. 'We found an old lady who lives next to the Flag in Birmingham who remembers Stella. She arrived with a baby and worked in the bar for some years. Said her husband had died and left her with nothing. She was an only child, so there's nothing to follow up there, and both her parents are dead. So's the local parish priest. We don't have a lot, except her word, but nothing we've found disproves her story.'

'What about the letters?' Sharon asked.

'They're more notes than letters, actually. We gave them to a handwriting expert with a copy of the Earl's signature. He can't say yes, can't say no. They were pretty tatty, crumpled and stained then photocopied, so it's impossible to prove one way or the other. They're only signed S, so we can't even check the signature properly, but they're obviously from a lover.'

'And what has Emma had to say for herself?'

'She didn't know anything until a couple of years ago when she found her mother crying, clutching the picture of the Earl she

224

always kept in a drawer by the bed. Until then Stella had always maintained that Emma's father was killed in a road accident, but she would never talk about him. She was always obsessed with the Royals and at first Emma thought she was just upset that Diana's father had died. It was only when Diana herself did that Stella finally cracked and told her daughter everything.'

'Right, I want lots of copy about how Emma idolised Diana, watched her getting married on the TV, kept every clipping of her, went to Kensington Palace after she died and to the funeral,' Sharon ordered.

'But she didn't say that,' Leiber protested.

'She will.'

'The lawyers aren't too happy about the whole thing Sharon,' he warned her.

'Fuck the lawyers. If we held out every story they went gutless on we'd never have a fucking exclusive. Everything checks out.'

'The other thing is Stella and Emma want all the money pre-publication. Twenty-five thousand on signing the contract . . .'

'Haven't they even signed the fucking contract yet?' Sharon screamed. 'You morons! I want that contract tied up tonight. Do you hear me?'

'Then twenty-five thousand on the eve of publication, or they'll take the story to the *Sun*,' he continued. 'It seems our little Emma is a bit more worldly when it comes to knowing the value of this story than her mum. What do you want me to do?'

'Get the contracts signed – *immediately*. You screw up on this one, Dave, and you'll be out of a job so fast your fucking head will spin. Do as they want. This is the first big story you've brought me. I will not lose it. Now get out, the lot of you, while I go over the pictures with Phil.'

Phil Plattmann was one of Sharon's few confidants. They had worked together for years and she trusted him.

'What are your instincts on this one, Phil?' she asked when the door closed behind the others.

'So far as I can see, we're in a no lose situation. We have affidavits from the mother and Emma, all the facts checked out as far as they can be. The only way of disproving the story is if

Charles or one of the sisters takes a DNA test, and that's hardly likely.'

'I'm not completely convinced by Mrs Anderson's innocent act,' Sharon said. 'But we're going to run with it. I desperately need a big one now. How are the pictures coming along?'

'Great. Emma looks like Diana and after the make-over she will *be* Diana. I've got a copy of Diana's wedding dress to put her in, plus knock-offs of a couple of her other famous outfits for the photo shoot.'

'Let's get Emma to do a copy of those fab pictures of Diana in *Tatler*. You know, the sexy ones. Really ham it up. And you've got pictures of the pubs and the council flat?'

'We'll have all of them here by tomorrow. She's not a natural blonde you know.'

'Nor was Diana,' Sharon shot back.

'The photographer who's been holed up with them saw her walking around the hotel suite in a white bra and G-string,' Plattmann said. 'Did you know she's got a tattoo on her thigh?'

'Christ, that's all we need! Di's secret sister has tatts. Cover it with makeup in the lingerie shots,' Sharon ordered.

# Chapter Nineteen

The Stag, affectionately known as the Stab because so many journalists' reputations were shredded there, was heaving with exhausted hacks. It was the closest pub to Tribune Tower and as they finished work for the day, the journalists often stopped in for a pint or two, or three or four. Wednesday was an early night for Mike Gordon and he was at the bar buying a round when the chief sub Nick Richardson came up behind him.

'You'll never guess what the *Tribune*'s splashing on tomorrow,' he whispered in Gordon's ear.

'Don't tell me Sharon's got a story at last?' he laughed back. 'I don't believe it. Here, take these and tell me at the table.' He handed over four pints. They squeezed their way through the smoky room and sat down with a crowd of *Sunday Tribune* journalists.

'Well, I'm not telling tales, not really, because it's already printing and we'll see it for ourselves in a couple of hours,' Richardson said. Early copies of the newspapers were delivered to the Tower each night at around 11 pm. 'Sharon claims to have found Diana's secret sister.'

'Bloody hell, that's a good story,' Mike said, taking a huge gulp of lager. 'I knew she had a big one because I heard on the grapevine that the lawyers have spent all week trying to stop her running it.'

The problem with newspapers is that they leak like sieves, both internally and externally, and many editors have a paid spy on a competitive title to tip them off when a big story is coming.

'I just hope it's not another Hitler Diaries,' said Richardson laughing. 'Okay, let's play newspaper cock-ups of our time. I bet I win this one. A tenner, everyone, and the one who gets the most *published* cock-ups takes the lot.' They all reached into their wallets and took out £10 notes to place in the middle of the table.

'My game so I start. The *Mail on Sunday* tracks down the Nazi war criminal Martin Bormann in Argentina, sends a crew to expose him, runs it front-page, and it turns out to be an Argentinian taxi driver,' Richardson said, laughing so much he spilt beer all over the kitty. 'One to me.'

'The *Sunday Mirror* running the gym pictures of Princess Diana and having to settle out of court for a small fortune,' said one of the reporters.

'What about the *Sunday Mirror* running the pictures of Rod Stewart out on the town with a mystery blonde,' Richardson blurted out before anyone else could get in, 'and it turned out to be a very poor Rod look-alike. He was at home with his missus on the other side of the world. Big settlement. Two to me.'

'Best one recently, the *Sun* carrying the video with Diana romping with – now which one was it?' another reporter said.

'Hewitt, it was Hewitt. Or rather it wasn't Hewitt and it wasn't Diana either. Lack of detail, no points.' The late desk man walked in with the papers at that moment. The *Tribune*'s splash said it all:

SCANDAL
OF DIANA'S
SECRET
SISTER

Emma's and Diana's faces stared out from the front page. The resemblance was remarkable.

THE PRINCESS AND THE PAUPER

was the headline across pages two and three, with pictures of poor Emma as a child, then a teenager, then a bride next to corresponding pictures of Diana and her privileged life. A picture of the Spencers' palatial house was placed next to one of the council flat in Birmingham where Emma was brought up.

DIANA'S DAD HAD SECRET AFFAIR
WITH 16-YEAR-OLD BARMAID

was the headline across pages four and five, with pictures of the Hope and Anchor where the affair began, the Crown where Stella fled when Spencer abandoned her and pictures of her as a voluptuous young woman with a baby in her arms.

LITTLE EMMA LONGED TO BE A
BALLERINA JUST LIKE DIANA

ran across the spread with a picture of Emma in her borrowed ballerina outfit and Diana in hers.

It was a tabloid triumph.

Champagne corks could be heard popping inside Sharon's office. The hacks outside worked on; only a privileged few had been called in to celebrate.

'Now tell me who's the fucking best editor in Fleet Street?' she screamed.

'You are, boss,' they said in unison, but newcomer Leiber bellowed it the loudest. Plattmann was there, and Dainson, and Ferret.

'Shut the fuck up!' Sharon screamed above the noise and grabbed the remote control for the TV. 'Our ad's on.' She pushed the volume up to maximum just as Emma came into view. She stumbled slightly as she walked up the steps of a decrepit council block.

'My name is Emma. I am Princess Diana's sister,' she said, glancing up soulfully from beneath her fringe. The film cut to her sitting on a bare single bed in a dingy room, plaster peeling from the walls, no curtains at the broken window.

'This was my bedroom. It's a far cry from the luxury enjoyed by my sister.' Cut to her walking outside Kensington Palace.

'Diana was my idol. Too late I discovered she was my sister. Now I will never meet her. Read my incredible story, only in the *Tribune* tomorrow.'

The camera then cut to a scene of a rather attractive, albeit large, bottom walking briskly through the offices of the *Tribune*. The woman was waving her arms and barking instructions to eager-faced hacks. She turned, tangerine curls bouncing, and stared intensely into the camera.

Across the bottom of the screen the words: 'The editor of the Tribune – Sharon Hatch' flashed up in bold red type. They were positioned neatly across Sharon's breasts which were, remarkably, covered.

'As a woman, I completely understand Emma's agony. Share her pain and the story of the Princess and the Pauper, Emma's incredible story, only in the *Tribune* tomorrow.'

Sharon turned off the sound and screamed: 'Fucking brilliant! We did it, we did it. Here's to the extra 250,000 copies we'll sell tomorrow.'

Leiber was the first to break the silence. 'Great idea to put you in the ad too, boss,' he simpered. 'You looked fantastic.'

They had all been aware the ad was being made, as the film crew had shot all the footage of Sharon racing down the office during peak production time – 'to get the atmosphere of a working news room, the excitement'. The women journalists had been particularly annoyed as they had been forced by the director of the ad to undergo full hair and makeup and were then seated in full view of the cameras.

Secretaries from the entire group had been roped in to make it appear as though the *Tribune* was completely PC and had lots of women journalists.

'It was our new ad agency's idea, but I fucking love it,' Sharon said, standing proud and victorious behind her desk like the captain of a ship, cigarette smoke rising into the air, champagne glass in the other hand. 'I sacked the other agency because they just didn't get it. This paper is about *me*, Sharon Hatch, and it's time the fucking world realised that. *I am the Tribune*.'

The phone on Sharon's desk shrilled and Leiber picked it up. 'Well you'd better bloody find her or don't bother coming back because you won't have a fucking job to come back to,' he shouted.

'What's up?' Sharon asked.

'That useless prick Davies has lost the girl.'

'What do you mean, lost the girl?' Sharon shouted back. 'There are two reporters minding them, how the hell did he lose her? They weren't supposed to let either of them out of their sight.'

An hour later the phone rang again. This time Sharon picked it up. 'Tell me that again, very, very slowly,' she said sounding chillingly calm. 'First you lose the girl, then you lose the mother? Find them now or you're both sacked.' And she hung up.

'There's something wrong here Dave,' she began. 'I can understand Emma giving them the slip – she's been holed up in that dump of a hotel for more than a week. But the mother. Why would she scarper?'

'Davies said Emma wanted to go for a drink in the bar, alone. He followed her but she left with a man. When he tried to stop them the guy got really heavy and threatened him. How did the mother get away?'

'Through the hotel window it seems. For God's sake, get on the phone now and put a block on the second payment. If something's up, at least they'll only have half the money.'

'I can't do that, Sharon. Emma insisted on a bank draft and the deal you agreed was we paid the second £25,000 on the eve of publication. That was 5.30 today.'

Georgina was on her regular evening visit to see Brian and his magpies. He had told her nothing of his life, said it wasn't important – he had after all introduced her to his 'family', the greatest of compliments. And he'd asked her nothing of herself. It was wonderful being anonymous, slobbing around in a pair of old shorts and a T-shirt, no make-up. The guys back in the office wouldn't recognise her.

After two days in this unexpected paradise, the air traffic controllers' strike was over and Georgina should have flown home. But something held her here, and not just the sheer beauty of the place. She called her family, told them she had more work to do, and stayed.

They were sitting on the veranda, later than usual, a bottle of one of the local wines between them, Biggles on Brian's shoulder, when a dusty four-wheel drive pulled up in front of them. 'Dad, what the hell are you doing? Dinner's ready and Mum's throwing a wobbly. Get in,' the young man driving the vehicle said, leaning across to open the passenger's door.

'Don't be so bloody rude, Ned, can't you see I've got company? Miss Lynne will have to wait, or have a guest for dinner.'

It was only then that Ned seemed to notice Georgina. He gave her a huge smile, tilted the brim of his hat and said: 'Sorry, I didn't see you there. Get in, you can come too.' So Georgina and Brian piled into the car. They drove in silence along the dirt track for about thirty minutes. Suddenly the bush gave way to immaculate rows of vines, like dark green corduroy stretching off in the distance.

At the end of a track a huge house was visible in the fading light. As they drew closer Georgina turned to Brian and said: 'What an amazing place.' The house was surrounded by vineyards and huge whispering gum trees. It was made of rammed earth blocks, the second floor supported by huge bush poles logged from the local forests.

'It's made of the same material as the place I'm staying in,' Georgina continued, turning to Brian. 'I've never seen blocks like that before.'

'They've been making them for a while now,' he said. 'Literally, they just ram the earth together into huge blocks. That's why the houses blend in so beautifully with the bush. Notice the colour? It's the same as the soil around here. We try to use all local materials for building now, like the bush poles. They're made from local trees as well.'

The front of the house was entirely glass. A woman in an apron was standing at the open front door.

'About bloody time,' she said to Brian as they pulled up. 'What time do you call this?' And stopped on seeing Georgina.

'Miss Lynne, this is my friend George. George, Miss Lynne,' he introduced them.

'Wasn't expecting you but you're welcome anyway. Always

enough to go round. We're eating out back,' the woman said to Georgina and walked through the house and out into the garden behind. A long wooden table was stacked high with food, benches to either side. Four men were sitting there in their work clothes, drinking wine from tall glasses.

'Matt, Pete, Steve, Greg, this is George. Get her a drink,' she said to the men. 'Sit down, tea's ready.' And she returned with a plate of barbecued T-bone steaks. There were huge bowls of potato salad and coleslaw already on the table, home-cooked loaves of bread and a bowl of tomato and onions.

'Whose place is this, Brian? Do you work here?' Georgina whispered. Steve, sitting opposite, laughed out loud.

'It's Brian's bloody place! He's the most famous wine maker around here.'

'I don't do much any more,' Brian told her quietly. 'My son Ned's taken over most of the running of the place. I prefer magpies to grapes these days.'

'You and your bloody magpies, Dad,' Ned said affectionately. 'You know, sometimes I think he cares more about them than Mum and me.'

'Tell me about the place,' Georgina asked him. 'What type of wine do you produce here?' As she watched him talk about the property, she could see his father's features echoed in his young, unlined face. He had the most beautiful, dancing eyes, grey in this light, blond hair falling over his eyes without a hat to keep it in place. He was as tall as his father but more powerfully built, sleeves rolled up to reveal forearms ridged with muscle from hard work, not working out in a gym.

There was a simplicity about him that Georgina found compelling – no showmanship, no cheap chat-up lines, no false flattery. He just talked intelligently about his passion, the grapes and this beautiful countryside.

She wished for a moment that she'd brought her bag and could dash into the house to apply a bit of mascara, and that her shorts weren't quite so grubby.

'I'll pick you up early tomorrow and show you around the spread if you like,' he offered.

Looking into those eyes, she was surprised to find herself

233

feeling oddly light-headed. Georgina held Ned's gaze longer than she needed as she nodded her acceptance, then tore her eyes reluctantly away as his mother started to ask what a city girl like her was doing so far from home.

Sharon was straightening the epaulettes on her navy Ozbek jacket when the circulation manager came in around 5 pm with the day's estimated sales figures. She ripped them from his hands.

'Brilliant! Fucking brilliant. We're up 260,000 copies,' she whooped. 'It would have been more if you'd boxed out more copies. What's the extra print run for tomorrow?'

'We're putting out an extra five percent again,' he said. 'Hopefully day two will carry through.'

'Hopefully? This is one of the best fucking stories you'll see in a long time.'

'I've heard whispers that the *Mirror* has a big box out tomorrow, up seven per cent. They must have a big one.'

'Nothing they have can possibly compare with my exclusive,' Sharon said, standing proudly in front of the huge colour blow up of the day's front page, already framed and hanging on the wall.

Leiber was leaning over Sharon's shoulder as she sat at her desk rewriting the next day's leader column, oblivious to her cigarette.

'Okay, how does this sound?' she said.

CARING ROYAL
FAMILY MUST
MEET DIANA'S
LOST SISTER

Princess Diana was the most-loved Royal for one main reason – because she cared, about the poor, about the suffering, about the abandoned.

*Through no fault of her own, Diana's family has caused suffering to an innocent woman and her child.*

The *Tribune* has exclusively revealed the existence of Diana's secret sister, a young girl who was abandoned by her father and brought up in abject poverty. She has suffered, just as her innocent mother suffered.

In memory of Diana, it is time for the Royal Family to look compassionately at another needy victim.

Charity begins at home. Meet Diana's sister, love her as she loved countless others, for this is no stranger.

*In the name of the Queen of Hearts, open your heart to her sister. Had she lived, Diana would have done so.*

'And we get the exclusive on the meeting,' Sharon said with glee. 'Get it put in, Dave, and bring me the *Mirror* as soon as it lands. Let's find out what pathetic fucking story they've got.'

Two hours later an ashen-faced Leiber walked into Sharon's office holding an early copy of the next day's *Mirror*. He couldn't bring himself to speak, just placed it on the desk in front of her.

EXCLUSIVE:
PORN SHAME
OF DIANA'S
'SECRET SISTER'

screamed the front page headline next to a picture of sweet Emma, naked except for a tiny gold G-string and tiara, wrapped seductively around a pole, her large tattoo prominently displayed.

NAUGHTY EMMA LOVES BEING
SPANKED WEARING HER TIARA

was the headline across pages two and three with video-grabs of what was clearly a soft porn film. There were 'Censored' stamps all over the pictures. The copy explained that as this was a family newspaper, it could not possibly reprint the pictures in full, but the video was available for £7.99 plus post and package. Impatient readers could listen to the Princess' 'sister' 'moan in pleasure while being spanked with a riding whip by two big black men' on a premium phone line.

Leiber stood with his head in his hand, praying to be anywhere else in the world at that moment.

Sharon read and re-read the *Mirror*. She couldn't take it in. The whole story had been a lie from start to finish, she thought – Stella, Emma, the letters – a complete fucking con. And she had fallen for it. Emma was no more Diana's sister than she was.

'Shafted,' she muttered under her breath, then screamed: 'Those fucking cunts have shafted us!' She looked up at Leiber. 'You have one chance of saving your fucking job. Find out who set me up. Do you hear me!'


Andrew Carson sat at his desk in Tribune Tower, almost stroking the signed papers in front of him. It was the Kuper deal, £30 million in exchange for 40% of the *Tribune*'s stable mates, the *Herald* and *Herald on Sunday*. The South African businessman would sit on the board of the Tribune Group, as a non-executive director.

In less than a week the deal would be announced and ratified at next Wednesday's board meeting. Carson could hardly wait. He was so close.

The appeal to save the starving children of Sierra Leone would launch on Monday – the very starving children Kuper's millions were helping General Mosika to massacre.

Carson had covered his tracks well. No one but he and Peteyson knew where the dirt on Kuper had come from and Peteyson would never talk. His career depended on it. Douglas had played straight into Carson's hands by allowing him to handle the Kuper deal personally. And the Sierra Leone Appeal was nothing short of a master-stroke. Of course Douglas would piece it all together in time and see the path leading back to his trusted Managing Director, but by then it would be too late. His credibility would be shot. No one would believe him. The damage would be done.

All Sharon knew about was the Les Strangelove tape and the Rebecca Kershaw accounts, but those items would not be the ones to topple Douglas. They would just add to the evidence against him, evidence which proved conclusively that, even if he was not corrupt, he was not capable of running a public company.

Sharon could not pin anything on Carson. It would be his word against hers. She would have to admit that she'd had Georgina's office bugged. And, after all, she was the one commissioning Douglas's cousin. In the end Carson might have to admit they'd been having an affair and he had ended it. A woman scorned had no credibility. His wife would take it hard, but she had never left him before when one of his indiscretions had been found out.

He stopped for a moment to do something he rarely did: think about his wife. She was fifty-six-years-old and her figure had never recovered from the four children she had carried. Hazel was a mother and a home-maker and he'd always suspected she knew he played around. But she was wonderfully old-fashioned – marriage was for life, for better or for worse, and if he sought his pleasures elsewhere, she could at least be grateful she did not have to bother any more.

Picturing Hazel in her sensible walking shoes and support tights, Marks & Spencer jumpers, pearls, and mid-calf tweed skirts, he laughed to himself. No, he thought, she was unlikely to want to go it alone in the singles market. If his affair with Sharon blew up, Hazel would stick by him, even make a point of turning up with him at Tribune functions like a loyal Tory wife.

What a fool Douglas was to trust him with the Kuper deal! The go-getter of old would never have left something as important as this to anyone else, would never have skated over the detail. It just confirmed what Carson had believed for a long time. Douglas had lost it, he was starting to make mistakes. And this mistake would cost him his company.

Carson ran through the timetable in his head again, the countdown to destruction.

Feretti walked up the steep path to the men's lavatories, cursing the extra pounds he'd put on recently. It made his black leather trousers so tight he could hardly breathe. He sucked in his stomach a little more and ran his hand through his shoulder-length black hair. Needs a cut, he thought. I'll sort that out tomorrow. He felt the bulge of his wallet in his back pocket, thought of the pile of twenties, and the bulge in the front of his trousers grew bigger.

It was after midnight, later than usual, when he entered the men's lavatories, selected his favourite cubicle and stood waiting with the door open.

A young man staggered in and towards the urinal, unzipping his trousers clumsily. He was beautiful. Six foot at least with the body of an athlete in faded Levis, white T-shirt and a black shiny shell suit jacket. Nice bit of rough, Feretti thought. Bit younger than usual and not really my type, too Essex, but so cute.

He came out from his hiding place, still holding his erect penis in one hand, and stood close behind the young man who was aiming badly at the back of the urinal.

'Hi, gorgeous,' Feretti said. 'Do you come here often?' The young man spun around, spraying him with urine. He looked first at Feretti's face, then at his penis which was pointing up at him.

'What the fuck?' he said, and shoved his own penis inside his jeans. 'Keep away from me, you fucking queer.'

'So you want to play hard to get,' Feretti said in a soft, coquettish voice. 'Well, I'm hard, so come and get it.' And he moved closer. It all happened in a flash. The young man reached inside his jacket and in a second the long blade of a flick knife was in front of his face, catching the light from the fluorescent tube overhead. Feretti looked at it in disbelief as it was raised above his head and brought down with expert precision, one slice, from his ear to the front of his throat. He kept staring at the young man and saw now that the knife was red. He felt something warm pouring down the side of his neck, on to his shirt. He raised his hand to his neck and felt the gaping wound.

For seconds they stood staring at each other in disbelief. The young man screamed and ran from the toilets. Feretti stood there, his vision slightly blurring, looked down at his white shirt and saw it was red. Damn, I'll have to go out and buy another one, he thought, then staggered forward. The room had tilted to a 45-degree angle and he tried to straighten himself, stumbled and fell forward, head smashing against the base of the urinal.

He opened his eyes and felt the cold tiles under his face. The last thing he saw was a river of blood running from his head down the trench of the urinal. His hand was still clutching the twenty pound note wrapped around his penis.

Perhaps because he'd been HIV-positive for several years, perhaps because he's seen so many of his friends die painfully in the eighties, Pete Feretti had talked often about his funeral. It had become a dinner party game.

The setting – it *has* to be Westminster Cathedral, with the coffin drawn by six white horses, just like Diana.

The music – a choir singing 'I Vow To Thee My Country', 'Goodbye England's Rose' and his favourite, to be requested by his lover, Carole King's 'Will You Still Love Me Tomorrow?'

The congregation – full, to standing room only, with everyone who ever loved him, all grieving inconsolably.

As with most of Feretti's life, only some of his dreams came true. The funeral took place on a still, warm day in the East End of London. The sky was a milky blue, born of pollution and an ambivalent sun. The church was set back from the busy highway and surrounded by a huge park, now untended and home to a dozen homeless old men. It was almost as big as Westminster Cathedral.

Inside it had the unloved, rundown feel of so many big churches in the inner cities, neglected by absentee parishioners. It had been cut in half by a temporary partition, to make it feel less empty. On the altar was a huge vase of white lilies, arranged by his long-time, many would say long-suffering, partner, Paul.

He was sitting slumped in misery in the first pew to the left, a portable cassette player his only companion. To his right, on the other side of the aisle was an old woman, her head hanging down. She too was alone, with her thoughts and her sorrow. Her only son lay in the coffin in front of her. She had told no one about the manner of his death, she was too ashamed.

As the priest walked down the aisle towards the altar, Paul pressed the start button on the cassette recorder and Elton John's voice began singing – 'Goodbye England's Rose'. The two people who had loved Pete Feretti most in the world grieved privately, soundlessly, during the brief service.

As the coffin was carried out of the church by six strangers, Paul started the music again. His copy of *Tapestry* was old and the taped version of 'Will You Still Love Me Tomorrow' had picked up all the crackles and amplified them.

Paul softly sang along to the words, remembering the nights he and his lover had sung it to each other. Mrs Betty Feretti shuffled out behind the coffin, remembering the little boy she had lost.

No one noticed the glamorous figure wearing dark sunglasses and wrapped in a fur coat sitting at the back of the church. She had sat rigid throughout the impersonal service, the only sign that she was a mourner rather than an onlooker the tears running down her cheeks. She slipped out quietly as the brief service ended. Within twenty minutes Sharon was back at her desk.

# Chapter Twenty

It was two days since Ned had taken Georgina around the property. Since then they had spent almost every moment together. He went to great pains to explain to her how the grapes were grown, why theirs were so special and produced the finest wine in the district.

His father had been one of the wine making pioneers in the region, tearing up the pastures where once dairy cows had grazed and planting them with row upon row of vines. It had taken ten years of hard graft before they began to see a profit. Brian had been determined to make it work and now after twenty years they were reaping the rewards. Two gold medals at the last Australian Wine Growers judging, one for their Sauvignon Blanc, one for their Chardonnay.

They were sitting in the shade of an ancient silver tree by a creek, magpies singing in the branches, when Ned first kissed her. It was so different from Belinda's kisses, the force of his mouth took her by surprise.

His hands moved urgently over her body as he pushed her down on to the rug. They lay there and kissed like teenagers, exploring each other's smell and taste, not saying a word. Suddenly Georgina got a fit of the giggles.

'What's so funny, George?' Ned said, clearly hurt.

'I can't believe I'm lying under a gum tree snogging an Australian like I was sixteen-years-old,' she said, then saw the confused expression in his eyes. 'No, it's wonderful. I'm laughing because I'm happy. It's a million miles from my life back home.'

'If it makes you happy, stay.'

'What do you mean, stay? Everything's so simple to you. I have to go back. My life is in London.'

'Your life could be here with me.'

'Oh, Ned, you hardly know me.'

'Enough to know that I love you. Georgina, I've never met anyone like you. You told me last night how unhappy you were at the paper. You said you'd love to write a book. Well, do it. Have the courage to chuck it all in and start again. That's what my dad did. He hated the dairy farm, so he tore it up and planted vines.'

'You make it all sound so easy. I've spent all my working life in newspapers,' she said. 'I don't know if I could just give it up. It's in my blood.'

'But it doesn't make you happy,' he said. 'I'll build us a house with a big veranda overlooking the ocean. You could be happy here, George, I know it.'

'So you want me to come and be your little bit on the side?' she said teasingly.

'No, I want you to be my wife.'


They spent Georgina's last night in the rammed earth hut where it had all begun. Ned had arrived carrying a basket full of fresh crayfish and king prawns and chilled wine in his lean, tanned arms.

The wine was warm by the time he finally let Georgina get out of bed. He was as hungry for her as any man had ever been. He grabbed her the moment he walked in, kissing her hard, stopping only to rip off her white T-shirt and unbutton her Levis. Burying his face in her neck, he began kissing Georgina, making his way to her breasts as he fumbled with the clasp on her bra. His kisses were rough, partly from his stubble and partly from ferocity, as his lips greedily sucked on her nipples.

She let out a small cry, part pain, part pleasure, and Ned quickly looked up. 'Don't stop, don't ever stop,' she breathed as the direct line of sharp pleasure shot from her nipples down to between her legs. She was wet and hot, ready and longing for him.

Ned pushed her on to the bed. She felt like a rag doll. He was the first man who had ever made her feel so vulnerable. His clothes were on the floor in seconds. Yanking off her Levis, he buried his head between her legs. His tongue found its small, hard target and licked until Georgina felt her body flinch. She pushed his head away and tried to sit up.

'Stop!' she pleaded. 'I want to come with you inside me, I'm so close.'

There was no arguing with this man when it came to sex. He smiled mischievously and rolled on to the bed next to her. 'Get on top of me,' he ordered. Her guard was down. As soon as she was astride him, but before she had time to guide his penis into her, he slipped down between her legs and pulled her on to him. Within seconds she had climaxed.

Georgina took his face in her hands. 'You're a bully,' she said smiling. 'But I love you.'

'I know,' he said, pulling her down on top of him. His kisses were tender now, exploring her mouth with his tongue. She reached down for his penis and marvelled again at the size of it.

'Whoever said size doesn't matter is a bloody liar,' she teased, as she took him in her mouth. He let out a small groan, then pulled away from her. 'What are you doing?' she asked as he rolled out of bed.

'The lady said she wanted to come inside me, and so she will. I need to calm down a bit first though.' Ned returned with two glasses of wine, naked and still with a huge erection. He handed her a glass, then took her by the hand to the battered old armchair beneath the window. 'Sit,' he said, then proceeded to kiss her – first her face, moving slowly to her breasts, stomach, then his favourite destination, between her legs.

Georgina could feel the heat return and lowered herself in the chair. Ned was kneeling at her feet, within seconds he was inside her, his penis filling her as though it had been made expressly for that purpose.

There was passion but no gentleness in their lovemaking now. He pulled her on to the floor, and on top of him, squeezing her nipples hard as she threw her head back and climaxed again. Then he was on top of her, one of her legs hooked over his arm so that he could reach further inside her.

Georgina could tell he was close to orgasm as he slowed his

movements inside her, his face a mask of control, savouring the moment. Then he squeezed his eyes tight and dropped his head, shuddering into her.

A long time after Ned had collapsed on the floor next to her, one arm still flung over her breasts, Georgina thought of Belinda. She had expected to feel strange with a man inside her after all those months with a woman, but nothing had ever felt so right.

Now that she looked back on the relationship, her time with Belinda felt like a period of calm in a storm, a time of healing, of forgetting men and her need to have a relationship – and children. She could see now that she had been opting out.

Georgina rolled on top of Ned and kissed him hard. 'I love you,' she said again as he dozed. She drew a line with one finger from his eyelid to the corner of his mouth. She did love this raw, passionate Australian, but it had all happened so quickly. How could I seriously be giving up everything for an Aussie wine maker I met two weeks ago? she wondered again.

She was scared of how she would feel in two months' or two years' time, scared that she might have fallen in love with the Australian bush and sunshine rather than the man. But, despite the fears, she knew she had never felt so passionately about anyone or anything in her life, and for the first time in many years was prepared to take a chance.

My love is this fear, she thought, remembering the poem Belinda had sent to her, and she kissed Ned again. The closeness of her body, still wet with him, and the smell of her began to arouse him again. She grabbed his penis in her hand and gave it a squeeze, then jumped up.

'Later, later,' she said teasingly, and just managed to escape his grasp as he reached for her.

They ate on the rickety wooden veranda overlooking the ocean and watched the sun go down together. It was perfect – too perfect.

Georgina always felt like a kid when she arrived home in Johannesburg, full of excitement, charging ahead of the other passengers to get through Customs, steering her luggage trolley like a racing driver.

Her dad was standing waiting as he always did, immediately opposite the automatic doors, grey head bobbing above the crowd. The hugging ritual was always the same too. Her dad pushed through the crowd and embraced her much as he had when Georgina was a child, in a gigantic bear hug.

'Have you been waiting long?' she asked.

'Eighteen months and three weeks,' her father said and a young girl who had been watching them wiped away a tear.

Georgina had decided to stop in and see her family on her way back to London. Everything had happened so quickly. She needed a couple of days to get centred again, draw on that strength she only ever truly found at home.

The flight had been long enough for her to think again about the magnitude of what she was planning to do. Somehow it was easier to believe in the miracle of this new life when she was in Ned's arms. He had held her so hard at the airport she felt as though he was crushing them together forever. A few hours later it felt more like he had squeezed the life out of her, and that frightened her.

On the flight her heart and her head appeared to be having a fundamental disagreement. There was no doubt that she felt great love and passion for Ned, her heart was sure of that, but to give everything up for that love?

And did she really think that she could move from London, her life and her friends, and live in splendid isolation in the bush with this beautiful man? All Georgina knew was that she was prepared, probably for the first time in her life, to gamble on happiness, however high the stakes.

The luggage loaded, they got into the car and Georgina heard the snap of the locking system.

'Don't ever get in a car without locking the doors,' her father said for the thousandth time. When they stopped at the first set of traffic lights, he rode the clutch with his foot hard on the accelerator, ready for quick getaway. They felt most vulnerable when stationary, the threat of ambush still foremost in people's minds here. 'Your Aunt Jean has stopped driving completely now,' he said. 'People, especially women, just don't feel safe any more. You hear of all these terrible things happening ... people attacked when they stop at the lights. The other day a woman was driving along and this big van just turned in front of her and blocked the car. You have to be so careful.'

As they pulled into the drive of their family home in Brixton, Georgina was reminded of just how different it was from the Brixton she knew in London. The low white-painted stone house was surrounded by a ten-foot-high solid brick wall. The spikes at the top, which had been painted dark green, made it look like a parody of a picket fence. Security doors swung open when her father pointed the alarm device at the box and they drove quickly in, the gates slamming shut behind them.

They had only been home ten minutes when the intercom crackled and Georgina heard her brother's distorted voice: 'Anyone home? It's Eddie.' Her father checked the video screen and opened the gates, then the front door. Half a dozen little feet came thundering into the front room. Georgina's three nieces, Charlotte, Rebecca and Violet ran to her and chorused; 'Auntie Georgie, Auntie Georgie, you're back! Did you bring us any Sylvanians?'

'Come on, you girls, your auntie's not a present-buying machine,' Georgina's brother said affectionately and bent to kiss her. 'How are you sis? It's been too long.'

Caroline, his wife, hugged her and said: 'Good to see you Georgina.'

A cork popped in the kitchen and their father returned with a bottle of South African champagne – 'No French rubbish here' – and poured them each a glass.

'Here's to Georgie,' he said. beaming that great big, loving smile at her. 'Welcome home, darling.'

'Can I have some, Auntie Georgie?' pleaded Charlotte as she climbed up into Georgina's lap and attempted to wrestle the glass away from her.

'I'm not sure,' Georgina said teasingly. 'I think you're too little for champagne. Only girls who are six can have some. Are you six yet?'

'You know I am, Auntie Georgie, you sent me that pink Spanish dancing dress for my birthday. It makes me look so beautiful, doesn't it Daddy? I think I'm old enough for one sip. Pleeeease.'

246

Within minutes of setting foot in her childhood home, Georgina felt as though she had never been away. Nothing looked different, no one looked older, it was the one constant in her life, the one safe place.

The front room, the 'good' one, was kept for guests and was a lovingly tended museum to their lives. Every conceivable surface was covered with framed pictures of the children, every momentous occasion recorded – birthdays, graduations, weddings, christenings. Georgina's wedding photo had been tactfully removed years ago.

The photograph of her mother on her engagement day still took pride of place on the mantelpiece. Each day her father placed a fresh flower in the vase beside it.

The formal wingbacked chairs were placed looking out towards the back of the house, through large windows, over the veranda and on to what had been her mother's pride and joy, the garden. An ancient bougainvillaea draped itself over the fence at the back of the swimming pool; tall eucalyptus trees persisted in annoying her father by dropping leaves into the clear water.

'It's such a shame you won't be here in a month's time, Georgie,' her father said. 'I've just planted the cinerarias, and the azaleas would be out by then. They were so lovely last year. Not nearly as lovely as when your mother did it, but I do my best,' he said sadly.

'Can we go for a swim, Papa?' Violet asked, as she always did. Almost three, she had yet to grasp the idea that swimming pools were unfriendly things in the middle of winter.

'Don't be stupid, Violet,' Charlotte told her. 'It's too cold, dummy. Be quiet, I want to ask Auntie Georgie something really important. Auntie Georgie, how old are you?'

'I'll be thirty-seven this year, sweetie,' she replied, at which point Charlotte burst into tears.

'Oh, no, Auntie Georgie,' she wailed, clearly in distress.

'What is it, sweetheart?' Georgina said, cuddling the little girl to her. 'Tell me what's wrong.'

Charlotte looked up at her, tears in her eyes, and sucked back another sob, her shoulders shaking. 'You're so old now no one will want to marry you and you'll never have any babies and you'll die an old lady alone in a big house,' she said seriously.

Everyone burst out laughing.

'I thought you were bringing your children up to be politically correct, Eddie,' Georgina said to her brother.

'I try, God knows,' he said. 'I don't understand where they get these ideas from. We read all the approved books, we give them trains and cars to play with as well as dolls, and all they want to do is dress in pink and play with Barbie.'

'Why can't you marry Daddy?' Rebecca butted in.

'Because he's my brother, sweetheart, and he's already married to your mum.'

'Oh yeah, I forgot.'

'But you have to get married real soon, Auntie Georgie, or you'll be too old to have babies,' Charlotte said, starting to cry again.

'Do you want me to tell you a secret?' she whispered into Charlotte's ear and the little girl's eyes widened. She nodded her head solemnly.

'I promise I won't tell anyone, Auntie Georgie.'

'I am getting married, to an Australian man, and we're going to try and have babies,' Georgina whispered.

Charlotte jumped off her lap and shouted out: 'Auntie Georgie's getting married, Auntie Georgie's getting married! Can I be bridesmaid and have a Spanish lady dancing dress, pleeease?'

Her family looked at each other, then at Georgina with expressions somewhere between disbelief and calm acceptance. They were quite used to Georgina's suddenly announcing life-changing news. There was never any build up or forewarning with her.

'And I'm quitting my job and going to live in Australia,' she said. 'At least we'll all be closer now.'

'Well, darling, that's . . . wonderful news, isn't it, Eddie?' her sister-in-law Caroline began, always the pacifier. 'Isn't it all a bit sudden? I didn't even know you were seeing anyone. Who is he and what's he like?'

'You'll find out soon enough,' Georgina said rather sheepishly. 'We're planning to come here just before the wedding so he can meet everyone. But I expect you'll all be at the wedding anyway.

His name is Ned and he runs his father's vineyard at Yallingup, down south in Western Australia. He wanted to come over with me to tell you all, but I thought the shock might be too much for you. It's not every day your daughter announces she's about to marry a man she only met two weeks ago.'

'Nothing you do surprises us, George. Let's just hope he's better than the last drongo you married. And I hope he doesn't expect to sleep in your bedroom before the ceremony?' her father said sternly.

'Oh, Dad, for heaven's sake, I'm hardly a vestal virgin. I've been married before, remember? Don't be silly,' she said. 'You can hardly expect him to sleep in the spare bedroom.'

'It's a big decision, to give up your job *and* marry a man you hardly know *and* move to a foreign country. Are you sure about this?' he asked.

'As sure as I'll ever be about anything Dad,' she said. 'Just wait till you meet him, you'll see why.'

'But what are you going to do? If you give up your job, I mean?' Caroline asked.

'Not *if*, Caroline, when,' Georgina said. 'The honest truth is I just don't know. All I do know is that Ned would never come to London and I want to be with him. I've been thinking a lot about the job lately. I've worked my guts out for sixteen years and I've loved it, until recently. I guess I've just looked around and thought "Where the hell is my life going" In ten years' time I'll be in my forties and probably still going from one hopeless relationship to another. When you work in the kind of job I do, it's like having six lovers. The whole thing is so demanding, there's no time for a real relationship. And I want that. I want to try and have children.'

'But you've worked so hard to get where you are today,' her father said.

'And I've made it, Dad. What more do I need to achieve or prove?'

'I thought you liked working with Douglas.'

'He's changed so much. I hardly recognise the man I met when I arrived in London. Power tends to corrupt. Absolute power tends to corrupt absolutely. He's a perfect example. Douglas is so determined to become more and more powerful, he'd do almost anything to get what he wants. I'm not even sure what he believes in any more.'

'Is he still with that lovely model girl?' Caroline asked, always far more interested in gossip than in business.

'He's dumped her and run off with the daughter of one of the wealthiest men in Yorkshire, and she's just had his baby,' Georgina said. 'It's all a bit complicated because his wife, Kelly, is also pregnant. But that's his problem. My days of helping to sort out Douglas's messed up life are over.'

'Why don't you move to another company then, if it's Douglas you're disenchanted with?' her father said.

'It's the newspaper world I'm disenchanted with, Dad. Let me tell you, there's nothing sadder than a woman in her late-forties at the top of this business − no friends outside of it, no family life, working every hour God sends. It really toughens you. I don't want that to happen to me. It never stops. I got a call from our company secretary before I left Perth, saying he wants me to check up on a businessman that Tribune are about to do a deal with.

'I've got three days here, holiday, with my family whom I haven't seen for years − and they expect me to work. I want a chance at a different life, maybe writing, maybe helping to run Ned's company. Anyway, my mind's made up. I want to be with him and that's it.'


The bar was fairly sedate by journalists' standards, tucked underneath the atrium of one of the flashier shopping malls in Johannesburg. Georgina had promised Zack Priest before she left Perth that she would find out what she could about Kuper.

She had managed to track down one of her oldest friends, a crime reporter on the *Johannesburg Herald*, to fill her in on the South African businessman. If there was any dirt on anyone, Joe Lumley would know it.

He greeted her with a big hug then held her away from him. 'You look fantastic, Georgie,' he said, planting a sloppy kiss on her cheek. 'The years have been kinder to you than to me.'

And it was true. Joe was only ten years older than her but it looked like twenty. The years of late nights in the pub, chasing stories and, too often, women all over the country, had taken their toll. He had developed the characteristic body shape of a drinker: thin legs supporting an extended stomach. Georgina could not work out if his nose had grown larger through the years or if it was just the spidery broken veins that made it appear bigger. Without a family to tempt him home, he had spent most of his life in pubs indulging in his greatest love – beer.

'It's so good to see you, Joe,' she said, hugging him again. He ordered their drinks and they sat down at a small table next to the bar. It took them almost an hour to catch up on the lost years, gossiping about the people they had worked with at the *Herald*.

'I've done a bit of work on that matter you mentioned on the phone, George,' he said, taking a deep pull on his third pint. 'Kuper's a slippery character and there's not a lot I can prove, but I've got all the gossip on him.

'Like a lot of businessmen here now, he has a clean cover – multi-millionaire, diverse business interests, actively involved in government quangos, does a lot of work for children's charities. But that's just the tip of the iceberg. Underneath all that, word is he's been dealing arms to places like Sierra Leone. There's definitely a connection between him and the rebel leader Mosika. My contacts reckon he's trying to buy influence in a lot of emerging nations: aid for weapons now, lucrative business deals with the rebels once they gain power. He's a dangerous man, Georgie. Why the interest?'

'He's set to buy a share of Tribune,' she said thoughtfully.

'It doesn't make sense,' said Joe, shaking his head and staring into his beer. 'Why would he want to get involved in a foreign newspaper group? All his capital is tied up here. He's never showed any interest in the media. He'd never get the return on his money he's used to. It doesn't add up.'

'Maybe he's trying to divert some of his assets out of South Africa,' Georgina said. 'A lot of wealthy men are trying to get their money and their families out. Let's face it, Joe, Johannesburg isn't a great place to live now. It seems everyone who can get out has gone already.'

'Guys like Kuper aren't getting out,' he said, shaking his head.

'Why would they? His business is built on corruption and working the system. It's taken him decades to build up his contacts. There's no way he'd leave all that and start again.'

'Vanity?' Georgina said. 'He must be pushing sixty. A lot of men find the kudos of owning a leading newspaper quite a turn on. We both know it opens a lot of doors, especially in Britain and Europe. And, as Maxwell proved, there's a lot of cash floating around newspaper businesses.'

'I just don't buy it, George,' he told her again. 'Call it good old journalistic instinct, but I smell a rat, a big one.'

'Normally your instinct would suffice, Joe, but I need something more substantial than that.'

'There's one chance, Georgie, but it's a long shot,' he said. 'Do you remember Stuart Peteyson?' Georgina pulled a face and shook her head. 'He used to run the bureau for one of the big papers in the UK, then went over to London for a while. Came unstuck in a big way. No one really knows what happened, but it looks as though he was sacked by . . . what's his name? He's now Tribune's managing director?'

'Andy Carson?'

'That's the one. They worked together for a few years – Peteyson was running the South African operation for them during the apartheid era. He got into some trouble with a woman.'

'All very interesting, Joe, but what's that got to do with Kuper?'

'Patience, my girl, patience. I ran into Peteyson a couple of weeks ago down at the Dog and Dagger, just outside Soweto. I mean, talk about a death wish. We hardly drink there any more, it's just too damn dangerous, but Peteyson's not a man to change a lifetime's drinking habits. He was pissed but coherent, his usual state these days, and blathering on about Carson and Kuper. It didn't make much sense to me then, but maybe, just maybe, he knows something.'

'Where can we find him?' Georgina asked as she finished her wine and gathered her handbag and jacket.

'What do you mean *we*, Paleface?'

'You have to help me, Joe, please?' Georgina said, giving him her most helpless smile.

'You know when you smile at me like that I'd do anything for you, and I will try and find him, but you're not coming with me.' Georgina started to protest but Joe cut her short. 'Either I go alone or I don't go at all.'

She reached into her handbag and pulled out a tape recorder.

'For Christ's sake, George, do you think I was born yesterday?' he said crossly and slapped his coat pocket. 'Never go anywhere without my old friend. I'll tape everything and call you tomorrow.'

'Tonight, please, Joe.'

The Dog and Dagger was an English-style pub a couple of miles out of Soweto. No one in their right mind would venture in there at night. It just wasn't safe. But in Joe went. It had the stench of a place that hadn't been cleaned in years, just slopped out every night. The ashtrays were caked with layers of ash and the glass stained dark yellow, like the fingers of the middle-aged man stooped over the end of the bar.

Joe went and sat down on the stool next to him. It was only when he'd ordered his drink, and one for the other man, that the drinker looked up slowly.

'I'll be fucked,' he growled, 'if it isn't Joe Lumley. Don't often see you in here.' He pulled the pint towards him and stared into its creamy head.

Strange, Joe thought, as he eased himself up on to the bar stool. The procedure for getting information was always the same. It took time and patience and, in this case, a lot of alcohol. Peteyson was already half cut when he arrived. It was more than two hours before Joe raised the subject of Kuper.

'What's all the interest in him all of a sudden?' Peteyson asked.

'I've got a big fee to do a full investigative piece on him for an American magazine,' Joe lied. 'More money than I make in six months here. Problem is I need to get it done fairly quickly. And I need help. I'm happy to split the fee for the right information. Do you know anyone who could help me dig on him?'

Peteyson was a lush and a gambler and a womaniser – an extremely expensive combination. He was always short of money, always in debt.

'You didn't answer my question. Why all the interest in Kuper? He's just your average corrupt South African billionaire.'

'I don't write the briefs, Steve, I just take them,' Joe said dismissively. 'Do you know anyone who could help? I need info on his connections with rebel leaders. There's a lot of talk that he provides funds for rebel groups on condition that when they get into power, he then gets a monopoly on all the media, building works, banking infrastructure, car contracts to the new government, arms deals – you know the deal.'

'How much?'

'For something good – ten thousand US.'

'Make it twenty and I'll give you enough proof to bury the bastard.'

Georgina was asleep when the phone rang downstairs. She reached it at almost the same time as her father.

'It'll probably be lover boy,' he said and handed her the phone. Ned had been phoning three or four times a day since she arrived, but tonight it wasn't Ned.

'George, it's Joe. I can't quite work out what's going on, but Steve is in some kind of trouble. Personal, I think. He's been working on Kuper for a few weeks, for Carson. I've got him on tape saying Carson never paid him a penny for the information.'

'For what information, Joe?'

'He's not the most coherent of men. He's got copies of documents proving that Kuper paid money to the Sierra Leone rebel leader Mosika. Kept mumbling that he didn't get a penny for them from that bastard Carson.'

'This is incredible! You've got it all on tape?'

'Every blathering bit of it.'

'I need a copy of those documents.'

'We're meeting tomorrow night and he's promised me them then. I'm not quite sure at the moment how I'm going to square the money he wants . . .'

'Stories fall down Joe, editors lose interest. He's a big boy, he'll understand. No one pays up front. Right now all I'm interested in is the tape and the documents.'

'And I thought you were interested in me, Georgie,' he said in mock disappointment.

'I adore you, Joe. You may just have saved someone's life.'

★

The Tribune Group monthly board meeting would take place as usual at 10.30 am on Wednesday. Carson calculated that the *Sun* would need forty-eight hours from receipt of the Kuper file to publication. They'd have to do the usual checks, but they'd be gagging to run the story and discredit the boss of the second most powerful newspaper group in the country.

He had the envelope picked up by courier as Georgina left the house in Johannesburg for her flight back to London.

Georgina was anxious during the long journey to the airport. Joe had been promising for two days that he would deliver the documents before she left. Peteyson had proved to be more of a slippery customer than either of them had expected. Sober, he had questioned the wisdom of handing over documents. It was not a matter of conscience, merely of money.

In the end Georgina had withdrawn $US 5,000 and given it to Joe, as a 'down payment'. It was just enough to secure the papers and he had promised to be at the airport with them before she left.

She lingered for as long as she dared in the departure lounge before going through customs. As the last call was flashed up on the departure screen, Joe came running into the terminal.

He was sweating profusely, more from last night's drinking binge than the humidity.

'It's all there George,' he panted. She hugged him and raced off through Customs. On the plane, as she opened the envelope containing evidence that would prove Carson knew about Kuper's corrupt business dealings, Zack Priest was desperately trying to get through to Douglas.

# Chapter Twenty-one

It was Tuesday night and Douglas was home early. His head was aching and he needed to be in good form for tomorrow's board meeting. He had the Kuper deal to announce and needed approval for the proposed cuts to editorial staff. It should just be a matter of course, he had enough tame non-executive directors on the board to force it through. But at the back of his mind he was worried.

He sat on one of the enormous cream sofas in the sitting room, looking out over their private garden, Freddie lying happily at his feet. Becky handed him a glass of red wine and sat down next to him.

'Darling, what's up?' she asked.

'I can't explain it but I've got a feeling something's wrong.'

'You said the internal rumblings had stopped recently. You're just tired, darling. You look exhausted,' she said, and took his hand.

'It's when the rumblings stop that you really have to worry. It just means they've gone underground.' The phone rang several times during the evening but he decided for once to ignore it and left the answer phone on. He bathed Freddie with the help of Becky and put him to bed before they sat down to a late, light supper. She had just put the steamed chicken and pasta on the table when the phone rang again. This time no message was left, but it rang again, and again, and again.

Douglas finally grabbed the phone in frustration and yelled: 'What?' into the receiver. It was Zack, his voice quiet and apprehensive.

'Douglas, I've got some bad news, really bad news,' he started.

'I'm so sorry to have to tell you this. Have you had tomorrow's papers read over to you yet?' One of the assistant editors of the *Daily Tribune* called each night to report if there was anything of interest in the early editions, which arrived at the Tower at about 10 pm.

His sense of foreboding was suffocating. 'No, Zack, they might have called but I've been busy.'

'The *Sun* have splashed on a story about Kuper. He's crooked. They've got evidence he's been supplying millions of pounds in aid to the Sierra Leone rebel leader Mosika. Oh Christ, Douglas.'

'What's the headline?' he asked.

'"Tribune Chief in bed with the Devil".'

'And the front page, what does it look like?'

'A huge picture of you superimposed over yesterday's front page of the *Tribune*, the one with the two children dying in the refugee camp.'

'How many pages?'

'One, two and three, four and five and an editorial.'

'Fax it all to me,' he said and hung up.

Becky hadn't heard the conversation in full but she knew from the way her lover's shoulders slumped, as if in defeat, that the news was terrible. She didn't ask anything, not yet, just took him in her arms. The fax arrived in minutes and told her everything she needed to know. There was something grotesque and cruel about the way the pages of the newspaper arrived, cut in half to fit into the fax machine, slicing Douglas's head off his shoulders.

It was the unkindest picture they could have chosen. He was leering into the camera, juxtaposed with the emaciated faces of the two dying children. The leader was even more unkind.

TRIBUNE CHIEF
MUST RESIGN

*Tribune chief Douglas Holloway came to power with a pledge to clean up corruption in British newspapers. Millions of readers trusted that promise.*

Today we reveal that he has done a secret deal with a South African businessman who gave millions of pounds to a rebel army.

This army has slaughtered hundreds of innocent women and children.

In the greatest act of hypocrisy this country has seen for many years, Holloway yesterday launched an appeal to save these women and children. Save the very ones his new business partner is brutally murdering.

The canker of corruption must not be allowed to poison the honest, working-class people of this country. How can they trust a newspaper which is run by a man who does deals with the devil?

*Holloway has brought shame on the Tribune Group.*

He has acted recklessly and ruthlessly, putting profit above human lives. Now he has been exposed he must pay the price.

He must resign immediately. The readers of the *Daily Tribune* should show their disgust by boycotting the newspaper. Honesty and decency no longer exist in its pages.

*Sleaze and corruption cannot be tolerated. Do the honest thing for once in your life, Holloway, and quit.*

Becky expected Douglas to leap to the phone, demanding answers, calling for blood, but he just sat at the kitchen table, staring at the faxes in his hand.

'Carson,' was the only word he said.

Douglas slept for a couple of hours, then went downstairs to his desk overlooking the moonlit garden and started planning. One thing was clear: Carson had betrayed him. He was too experienced an operator to have overlooked the normal checks that are carried out on potential business partners. This was either negligence or malevolence, and something told him it was the latter.

He got up and went to his CD collection, the few his secretary had been able to replace, took down Verdi's *La Forza del Destino*, put it on the player and selected 'Solenne in Quest'ora'. As the track played softly in his office he indulged himself in the piece, listened to Alvaro's dying pleas to his great friend Carlos to take care of his affairs after his death. Carlos the betrayer, like Carson, was really his greatest enemy. At least I've found out before it's too late, he thought. I'm not dead yet.

Douglas remembered so clearly now Carson's offer to take care of the Kuper deal. 'You've got so much on your plate. I'd enjoy getting my teeth into it. I'll look after things personally.'

The situation had been made much worse by the Sierra Leone Appeal the *Tribune* had launched on Monday. Again that was Carson's idea. How could he have been so stupid?

He'd let his guard down. All the warnings had been there. Priest had told him again and again that Carson was not to be trusted, Georgina had warned him, but he didn't listen. Couldn't listen to the accusation that one of his closest friends had betrayed him. He thought of how they had worked together to take over the Tribune Group. Without Andy, I would not be running this company. How many times have I told him that I couldn't have done it without him? He was my friend, brooded Douglas.

He took his battered bible out of the top drawer, Machiavelli's *The Prince*, and thumbed through it. He had underlined many sections, and found the one he was looking for: 'anyone who is the cause of another's becoming powerful comes to ruin himself, because that power is either the result of cunning or force, and both these qualities are suspect to the one who has become powerful.' He hadn't suspected.

With some clever footwork, the situation could still be salvageable, he thought. He would speak to the Chairman before the board meeting and get him to keep it short. Drop the proposal for editorial cuts. Too contentious now. There was a lot of mundane business on the agenda. They would concentrate on that.

Douglas started jotting down the basis of his own defence. We must not be diverted from the good work by our enemies. It's not me they want to hurt, it's the Tribune Group. If they damage me, they damage the group. We must not give in to terrorist tactics.

He would have to discredit Kuper publicly, put out a statement that he had deliberately misled the Tribune Group, that no one could have known about his involvement with the rebel leader, that he was a master of deception.

Just let me get through today without a vote of no confidence, Douglas prayed.

By 6.15 am he had refined what he would say to each of the board members. A little early-morning lobbying was needed now.

He took out his list of board directors' home numbers and dialled the first. The answer phone was on. He left a message to call him back urgently. It wasn't until the sixth answer phone that he started to get nervous. Why were they not taking his calls? They always took his calls.

Douglas put his head in his hands. 'In doubtful times, a man will always find a scarcity of men he can trust,' he remembered.

The Drop the Dead Douglas files had arrived at the homes of the board directors minutes before 6 am that morning.

Normally Douglas would go to the Chairman's office an hour before the board meeting to run through the agenda. Today Sir Philip had called his secretary to say he was running late and would meet Douglas there. The four other executive directors' offices had their doors closed as he walked down the long corridor to the boardroom. The closed doors were made even more pointed by the fact that because the walls were glass, he could see them sitting at their desks, heads down.

When he took over the group, Douglas had insisted all offices have clear glass walls – his open office, if not open door, policy. Now they mocked him, allowed him to see something he would rather not have seen.

Only Zack Priest's door stood open and he fell in behind Douglas without a word as he walked past, silent and supportive as ever.

Gavin Matheson was there already, a copy of the *Sun* in front of him, reading avidly. Everyone else would have done so already. Douglas waited in silence until the room filled, embarrassed 'good mornings' mumbled as they arrived.

He placed his files on the long table and sat at the right hand of the Chairman. When Sir Philip arrived, some ten minutes late, he barely acknowledged Douglas.

'I would like to bring the meeting to order,' he said. 'Although it is customary to address the order of business presented on today's agenda, I feel circumstances require – no demand – that we immediately address the charges raised in this morning's *Sun* newspaper. I'm sorry, Douglas, but the board demands an explanation.'

He felt that all eyes were on him, though in fact most were kept carefully averted. Each person around the table had read the dossier which arrived at their door early that morning. Most of them knew their own job was at risk. All were angry.

'How could it be that the background of this man Kuper was not fully investigated prior to the Tribune even entering negotiations with him?' Sir Philip demanded.

'All the normal checks were done,' Douglas replied and looked across the table at Andrew Carson, who could not meet his eye. He knew there was nothing to be gained from blaming Carson. *He* was the Chief Executive, he was responsible for the deal, he ran the company – and Carson would surely deny any wrongdoing. 'Kuper is a clever man. Businessmen like him know the art of deception. We could not have known of his alleged dealings with Mosika.'

'Then how the hell did the *Sun* find out about them?' the Chairman demanded.

'This is simply another example of the *Sun* trying to undermine the Tribune Group,' Douglas began. 'It's terrorist tactics. Take out the leader and the group will be mortally wounded. This is an attack on us all and everyone here must realise . . .'

'Is . . . it . . . true?' the Chairman boomed at him, punctuating every word like a series of body blows. 'And how did the *Sun* find out the details of our deal? It has not been ratified by the board. We haven't even announced it to the City ourselves. It makes us look ridiculous.'

'I started an investigation last night into the allegations against Kuper. And let us all remember, they are still only allegations,' Douglas insisted.

'Come off it, Douglas,' Matheson broke in. 'You know as well as I do that the *Sun* would never have published that story if they weren't absolutely, 100 fucking percent sure it was true. The proof was printed in the fucking paper – the letter to the rebel leader, the bank statements.'

'They could have been forged,' he said lamely.

'And while we're on the subject of backroom deals,' Matheson said, 'it has just come to my attention that you are close to a deal with Fosters TV, to merge the Tribune Group with them and create Fosters Communications. Is that true?'

Christ, where did that come from? How could Matheson possibly know about this? 'I will not deny that I have been in discussions with Fosters. You are all fully aware of my desire, and the company's, to create a more broad-based media empire. We have discussed that goal endlessly around this very table.'

'In board terms perhaps, Douglas,' the Chairman interrupted, 'but I am not aware of any minutes which detail a specific proposal. Surely you were acting beyond your remit in taking the discussions to the stage they have now apparently reached?' And he pulled a document from a brown envelope and shoved it across the table. 'Is the information contained in this file correct? Take your time and read it carefully.'

It was a copy of the detailed financial proposal Douglas had given to Stanley Billmore at their last meeting, only a week ago.

'I have no intention of being interrogated in this manner,' Douglas said. 'I will report back to the board at the end of the day on the contents of this document.'

'I'm afraid that is simply not good enough,' the Chairman replied. 'But perhaps, since you do not feel able to answer the broader question as to the document's authenticity, you could address a simple detail contained within it. Is it true that almost half of the current board members would lose their seats under this proposal? And that you hoped to become Chief Executive of Fosters Communications?'

Douglas was silent. They knew the lot.

'Is it true?' the Chairman demanded again.

Again Douglas was silent. He could feel himself sinking, literally and spiritually. There was no way he could fight this. Someone had gone to a lot of trouble to dig his grave. His thoughts were interrupted by a woman's voice from the end of the table.

'Douglas, let me ask you a different question,' said Sarah Beauford, one of the non-executive directors. 'Today we had planned to discuss proposed cuts to editorial staff on the *Tribune* titles. The new streamlining as you call it. You know I have always had reservations about this plan. That aside, how is it that you can justify the loss of more than a hundred jobs, most at an average salary of £35,000, yet continue to employ your own

262

relative on the *Sunday Tribune* at a salary of almost four times that average?'

Douglas's head jerked up. How the hell have they found that out? He looked desperately at Priest, then at the Chairman. 'What's going on here? This is like the Spanish Inquisition. Where did you get that information from? I demand to know. Where?' And his voice rose higher and higher with every question.

'You are not in a position to demand anything,' the Chairman said. 'Would you kindly answer the question?'

'These payments are nothing to do with me. These stories were commissioned by the editors of the *Daily* and *Sunday Tribune*.'

'As it happens, I have several of the contribution print-outs here and they were all authorised by the editor of the *Sunday Tribune*,' the Chairman said, sliding a computer print-out across the table.

'This has nothing to do with me. If there is any hint of impropriety, then Georgina must be responsible,' Douglas said. Seconds later the full implication of what he had just done hit home. Without a second thought, he had betrayed Georgina to save himself.

'How convenient then that the editor of the *Sunday Tribune* is, I understand, on a flight back from Australia as we speak,' the Chairman announced.

'These are side issues,' Douglas said, desperately trying to focus their attention back on to the one issue he had a chance of winning. 'The real question here is how we salvage the reputation of the Tribune Group in the light of the Kuper accusations. We must release a statement immediately discrediting him. The most important thing now is . . .'

'I'm afraid, Douglas, there is one other issue I wish to raise,' the Chairman interrupted again. 'I understand that some weeks ago the *Sunday Tribune* was planning to run an exposé on Tony Blakehurst, the new Minister for Transport and the Environment. Could you explain to the board why that story was never run?'

'Why are you asking me this?' he replied, genuinely confused. 'The story didn't run because we didn't have enough proof. The last thing I'm going to do is allow one of my editors to land us with a massive lawsuit. And we would have lost with the evidence we had.'

'And it had nothing to do with the fact that Les Strangelove, a personal friend of yours, I believe, called Georgina and tried to blackmail her into not running the story? That he claimed the Minister had some incriminating evidence about your personal life and business affairs?'

'This is outrageous! Yes, Les Strangelove called Georgina, and yes, he said Blakehurst would expose me if the *Tribune* ran the story, but my response was completely honourable. Georgina came to me and asked me about the accusations. By then everyone knew about my relationship with Becky. I'm not proud of the way I handled that, but if every person around this table who has had an extra-marital affair were to leave right now, we wouldn't have a quorum. As for my business affairs, I told Georgina I had nothing to hide. I have always conducted my business dealings with the utmost propriety. I told her to publish and be damned.'

'Were there any witnesses to this conversation?' the Chairman asked without looking at him.

'Only Georgina.'

'A close colleague who depends upon you for her future career and who, as we have already established, is on a plane travelling back from the other side of the world. In the light of what we have heard this morning, and of the unprofessional handling of the Kuper affair, I am afraid I have no alternative but to call for a motion of no confidence. Who will second that motion?'

Matheson raised his hand. The vote was decisive. Only Zack Priest voted against.

'You can't do this to me,' Douglas said in a cold, controlled voice. 'I *am* the Tribune Group. Without me none of you would be here. Without me you are lost. The company is lost. I will not sit here another minute. I do not recognise this vote. I'm going to speak to the major shareholders immediately and have this farce of a board meeting struck from the records.'

'It seems you are forgetting, Douglas, that no individual is bigger than the Tribune Group. As it happens I took the precaution of speaking to all the major shareholders this morning before the meeting. Reluctantly they have agreed that this is the only course of action. Andrew Carson will take over as caretaker Chief Executive to handle the day to day running of the company until your replacement is formally announced. Thank you, ladies and gentlemen.' Sir Philip rose and left the room, quickly followed by the other board members.

Douglas waited until they had left, then made his way down the corridor to his office. He sat down, put his elbows on the desk and his head in his hands.

Sharon burst into Carson's office when she heard the news, ignoring his secretary's protests that he wasn't in. As indeed he wasn't.

The exhilaration in her face turned to anger as she turned on the secretary and screamed: 'Where the fuck is he?'

'Mr Carson is at a meeting out of the office.'

'What meeting? It's fucking urgent. I have to speak to him *now*, do you understand me?' Sharon said, her red curls bouncing as she stamped her foot on the floor.

'He left specific instructions that he was not to be disturbed.'

'Well, you fucking un-instruct yourself, sweetie, and tell me where he is.'

'I can't do that, Miss Hatch.'

Sharon spent the day trying to reach Carson. He never returned any of her calls. She was desperate to speak to him so he would make the announcement that she would take over the *Sunday Tribune* as well as the *Daily*. It was only a formality now. Or was it?

If this was their victory, why wasn't Carson with her to share it? The night of the taxi, his evasiveness . . . something wasn't right and she had to clear it up.

If he's too busy to take my calls, she thought, I'll just have to make him talk to me. She decided to confront him that night at the flat.

Almost an hour after Georgina had boarded the plane, she was able to use the telephone. Zack Priest had left the office and his home number was constantly engaged. When she finally got through to him, the line was bad.

'Zack, it's George,' she said more loudly than she wanted. The other passengers in business class stared at her disapprovingly.

'Have you got anything on Kuper?' was all he asked.

'Yes, Zack, I'm extremely well and had a fantastic break. And I'm in love,' she said sarcastically.

'Sorry, George. I'm afraid social niceties are the last thing on my mind at the moment,' he replied wearily.

'I've been trying to get through to you for hours. What's happening?'

'I've been in a board meeting and then on the phone to Douglas and our lawyers. The *Sun* splashed on the Kuper deal, exposing him as the very man who's been helping the rebels to kill babies, just as we launch our Save the Children of Sierra Leone campaign. The board has suspended Douglas pending an internal enquiry. It's a nightmare, George. Douglas has had it. It's over.'

'Maybe not, Zack. Maybe not,' she said and went on to explain about the tape and the documents she had with her.

'I'll meet you at the airport,' he said, new life returning to his voice. 'It may not quite be over yet.'

Georgina rested back in her seat after finishing the call. She knew there would be no sleep on this long flight, there was too much crowding her mind. While Douglas faced sacking by the board over the Kuper deal, she was aware that what she carried in her bag was enough to save him. There was no doubt in her mind that that was exactly what she would do, and pay back forever the debt she owed him.

But, quid pro quo, if she held Douglas's salvation in her hand it gave her great bargaining power. She could name her price. For the first time she felt the editorship of the *Daily Tribune* within her grasp.

She thought about Ned and she thought about the *Daily Tribune*, the job she had worked so hard for. Even she did not know which was more important to her right now.

# Chapter Twenty-two

It was the middle of the night when she felt the cramps, sharp stabbing pains in her stomach. Kelly instinctively reached across for her husband, forgetting for a moment that he would not be there, had not lain beside her for months. In that brief moment of confusion between waking and consciousness, she felt only the pain in her stomach. It took a few moments for the realisation to come flooding back. She was alone. Douglas had walked out on her. He had someone else. Their marriage was over. God how am I going to get through this on my own? she thought, and groaned aloud.

Kelly got out of bed slowly and walked to the bathroom. It was only when she switched on the light that she saw the reason for the stickiness between her legs. She was bleeding. Partly in pain, partly in fear, she doubled up and hugged herself tightly, sliding down the smooth surface of the wall and on to the comforting chill of the marble floor.

'Please, God, don't let me lose this baby,' she prayed, calling on someone she had seldom had reason to trouble before. Kelly staggered to the phone.

'Kate, please call me an ambulance,' she said as soon as her friend answered. 'I'm bleeding ... I think I'm losing the baby.' She put down the receiver and wept.

The next few hours were a blur. There were strangers in her flat wearing white overalls; a big man with tattoos on his forearms holding her hand, telling her everything would be all right but with a face which said the opposite. She felt herself being lifted on to a stretcher, slid into the back of an ambulance, that hideous siren. Then different people wheeling the trolley now, into a lift, faces looking down at her, an operating theatre.

It was as though she was seeing everything from a distance. She felt somehow detached from what was happening to her, only connected by the pain.

All Kelly remembered was praying, praying for dear life, for the dear life of her unborn child.

Kate was still at her bedside when she woke up, holding her hand, stroking her hair.

'The doctor's here,' she said as Kelly slowly opened her eyes.

'You've had a very close call, Mrs Holloway,' the young man began. 'The bleeding has stopped.'

'The baby?' she whispered.

'The baby's fine. You're going to have to really look after yourself now. Lots of rest, healthy eating, no stress. Are you related to Mrs Holloway?' he asked Kate.

'No, I'm her friend.'

'Could we have a word outside?' he said earnestly, and ushered her into the corridor. 'I'd like to talk to her husband.'

'So would she. They've just separated. He's run off with another woman. Let's just say he's not too happy about the baby.'

'I see. So who will be looking after her when she gets out of hospital?'

'I guess I will,' said Kate without thinking.

'She's very thin,' the doctor went on, 'and her blood count is unusually low. Are you aware of her having an eating disorder? Bulimia perhaps?'

Kate gasped and said: 'No, she's always been slim, she was a model, but I've never suspected anything like that. I'm sure you're wrong.'

'You're going to have to watch her very carefully. If she doesn't eat properly, it will harm the baby. It's not uncommon for women to hide their eating disorders. Hers isn't severe, or she couldn't have got pregnant in the first place. But she'll lose the baby if she doesn't take care of herself. Here's the number of the specialist at this hospital if she needs help. Just watch her.'

After he had left, Kelly returned to her friend. 'Do you know a strange thing happened to me last night,' Kelly said. 'I know my marriage is over. I thought the baby would bring us together again, but it didn't. It was too late. I know Douglas doesn't want anything to do with this child. I should have been glad that the baby was going to die, but I wasn't. I was desperate for it to live.'

Kate tried not to show her astonishment. She knew only too well her friend's manipulative attitude towards her pregnancy. She also knew of the 'offer' Douglas had made her to abort. In her heart she'd believed Kelly would take it. 'You don't have to make any decisions now, just try and rest,' she soothed.

'No, I need to explain this to you,' Kelly said anxiously. 'I *want* this baby. Not for Douglas, but for me.'

Sharon arrived home late from work and went straight to the fridge. She took out a bottle of wine and a tub of chocolate ice-cream. Tonight was not the time for thinking about waistlines, she decided. Right now she needed a little comfort.

She kicked off her shoes and curled up in her favourite armchair, spooning great globs of ice cream into her mouth and washing it down with Chardonnay the colour of sunshine.

An image of Carson flinging her money from the cab, and laughing, laughing at her, played back in her mind. She flinched at the thought of what she had done, just to please him. And at the way he had treated her. With contempt. Carson had treated her badly before, but he had always come back, contrite and hungry.

It had been days now since she had been able to contact him. He had not returned one of her calls, was out whenever she had called at the flat. Even when she left the message on his answer machine about the meeting with Georgina – no reply. She was not yet ready to admit that he had dumped her, but her gut instinct told her that was exactly what had happened.

The bastard had used her – for sex and for information, she thought angrily. Well, no one used Sharon Hatch like that and walked away. She would give him one more chance. If she could just get to see him face to face, she would know the truth.

And if he has dumped me, she thought angrily, I will get my revenge. If Douglas or the board hears how he's worked against them, Carson will be booted out of existence. No, it's not over yet, not by a long shot.

The upstairs lights were on at Carson's flat when Sharon arrived, parking her TVR Griffith nose to nose with Carson's new Jaguar. She had dressed carefully tonight, in his favourite vivid blue Versace suit, black bra and suspender belt, very short skirt to show off her stocking tops when she sat down. No point in leaving anything to the imagination.

And one thing was for sure. If it was over between them, she wanted to look her best for the grand finale.

Before getting out of the car, no driver tonight, Sharon performed her usual routine – more lipstick, a squirt of breath freshener as her last cigarette burned in the ashtray, perfume and more perfume. As she adjusted her stocking tops she realised with horror she was still wearing knickers and squirmed out of them, putting the black lace G-string in the glove box where about six other discarded pairs were stuffed. I must remember to wash them one day, she thought, and stepped out of the car.

She had rushed to the hairdresser that afternoon for a quick wash and blow dry and her hair was now a magnificent mane, framing her face with masses of red curls.

Sharon buzzed the intercom and waited. Buzzed again and waited. No one answered. She knew he was home because the lights were on. Carson was so mean he always checked the lights before leaving the flat. He was there. She called him from her mobile and got the answer phone.

The fear that had been coiling in her stomach all day started to squirm and rise, like bile. He was avoiding her. But why? On this their night of triumph. They had worked so hard to get Douglas out. Carson couldn't have done it without her. They should be celebrating. She started banging on the door and pressing the intercom at the same time, shouting up from the street.

'Andy, let me in. I'm not fucking leaving until I see you.' She rang him again, and again got the answer phone. It took almost an hour of hammering, buzzing, phoning and shouting before a rumpled Carson opened the door. Sharon seized her moment and pushed past him before he realised what was happening. She raced to the top of the stairs and into the living room. He was quick behind her.

'Sharon, it's not a good time,' he said dismissively.

'What do you mean, not a good time? This is the fucking best time of our lives! Douglas booted out, Georgina about to be sacked, you the new Chief Executive and us, us, us!' she said, walking as seductively as she could towards him on her six-inch white Shoe Express spikes. 'It's time to celebrate,' she murmured and pulled a bottle of chilled champagne from her bag. She shook it like a Grand Prix winner, popped the cork and sprayed the room with froth. 'We've won, we've won.'

Carson's face had gone white. He grabbed her by the wrist and said: 'I told you, Sharon, this is not a good time. Get out.'

The brutality of the words and the ice in his voice sobered her up. Suddenly she was thinking clearly. Not a good time, refusing to answer her calls, wouldn't open the door, hadn't touched her since she'd walked in, no sex . . . something was terribly wrong.

If in doubt, don't confront, seduce, she thought. Sharon shook back her hair and dropped her chin, looking up from beneath her fringe in an exquisite pastiche of the Princess Diana come-and-get-me-I'm-a-naughty-little-girl look. Her lips were pursed into a perfect tangerine pout. She twisted one curl around her little finger and turned her toes inwards, making herself look knock-kneed and even more vulnerable.

'Andy Wandy, don't be cross with baby,' she cooed. 'I'm sorry I made a mess. Let's kiss and make up.'

Carson just stood looking at her, shaking his head, making no move towards her.

'Do you want me on the sofa or the stairs? Let's fuck and make up. I'm sorry I was a naughty, naughty little girl. Maybe you'd better spank me.'

'I will only tell you this one more time, Sharon. Get out of my flat,' he ordered.

Instinct took over. She walked past him and up the stairs to where she knew the bedroom was. He made no move to stop her. She had never been in this room before. He had banned her from sex in the bedroom. It took her a moment to take in the surroundings, she felt disorientated by everything but especially

271

Carson's anger. Her eyes gradually focused on the softly lit room.

The naked woman in the bed was Myra Prescott. Sharon couldn't believe her eyes.

'What the fuck is she doing here?' Sharon screamed and rounded on Carson who was now standing in the doorway. 'You fucking lying bastard,' she said quietly.

'I told you it was a bad time,' he said with a smirk on his face.

'How long have you been screwing little miss politically correct, then? What's going on, you fucker?'

'I might as well tell you the good news now. Your wish has come true. As of next week, when I make the formal announcement, you will be the editor of the *Sunday Tribune*. Well, to be more precise, you will be acting editor while the board reassesses the situation. After the Diana sister fiasco, I'm not sure you can be trusted with anything. Now allow me to introduce you to the new editor of the *Daily*.'

'But Myra's a fucking Leftie feminist!' Sharon exploded. 'And she's never even worked in a fucking newspaper, let alone edited one!'

'I have made my decision,' he said coldly.

She looked over once more at the smug face of Myra Prescott. All this time she's been pretending to be my ally, Sharon thought. Her precious feminist principles, power against the men, all that crap about women looking after other women. She's fucking taken care of me, all right. Sharon walked out of the room with as much dignity as she could muster on her six-inch spike heels. She could hear Carson talking to Myra, who laughed loudly in reply.

'No need to see me out,' Sharon shouted back at him as she walked down the flight of stairs to the flat's entrance. 'I know the way.'

Moments later he heard the slam of the front door, then the roar of her car's engine.

What he did not hear was the faintest click as Sharon walked past the hall table, paused for a moment to open the lid of the antique box containing Carson's spare keys, and slid the set marked 'Flat' into her handbag.

\*

Julie had found out from the other secretaries quickly enough what had happened. She had been Douglas's personal assistant for fourteen years, had seen him through two marriages, several affairs, and now this. When the Security guards arrived to inform her that his personal possessions must be packed and removed by the end of the day, and that Andrew Carson was moving into the office tomorrow, she almost wept. But the years had taught her how to handle the most difficult of situations and, without Douglas uttering a word, she took control. Only family and close personal friends were put through on the phone, and Becky – no wives or ex-girlfriends.

At least he had the day to collect his things and did not have to suffer the ignominy other sacked staff did, of being called to the Personnel office, given their termination agreement and told to leave the building immediately.

After about an hour the phones started ringing madly: friends, colleagues, journalists from other titles trying to get a quote. It was hot news, the deposing of the Chief Executive of one of the biggest newspaper groups in the country. Julie fielded them all, no one got through. Everyone said it was urgent, everyone had to speak to him now. The solicitors from a company called Rosebud Inc. were the most persistent, but they wouldn't even say what the call was about. Julie had never heard of Rosebud Inc. so she put their names at the bottom of the long list of calls she would give her boss at the end of the day.

Douglas stood at the window overlooking the City, taking in the view the way a condemned man absorbs every detail of his last glimpse from a prison cell. The heat haze hovering around the tall buildings made everything look opaque and slightly grubby. It was lunchtime and the streets were full of people darting about or sitting in the parks, skirts and trousers pulled up to expose as much skin as possible to the sun.

The phone rang. It was Julie to say that Zack Priest wanted to see him.

'Tell him to come in,' said Douglas, and went to sit at his desk. More out of habit than curiosity, he switched on his computer and typed in the code to access the company's daily revenue intake.

'Access denied' flashed on the screen as Priest walked into his office.

'They didn't waste much time,' Douglas said bitterly. 'They've taken away my access to the system. Christ, I was only sacked half an hour ago!'

'Carson wants you out of the building as quickly as possible,' Priest said softly. 'I'm sorry, Douglas.'

'It appears I owe you an apology, Zack. You warned me about him enough times. Thank you for not saying "I told you so".'

'I didn't trust him, but I had no idea he'd go to these lengths to get rid of you. I'd lay odds that I'm out of the building within the week too. He knows I'm loyal to you. He'll want his own person in now.'

'I'm sorry, Zack. If there's anything I can do to help ...' Douglas stopped mid-sentence. What could he do to help anyone now? He would be lucky if people returned his calls. His empire had been stolen from him. Without the Tribune Group behind him Douglas Holloway would have no influence, anywhere.

'There is something,' Priest said tentatively. He had agonised over whether to tell Douglas about the evidence Georgina had found against Carson. A lawyer by training and inclination, he was naturally cautious. 'I don't want you to pin too much on it, but Georgina has been talking to people in Johannesburg about Kuper. She says she's got evidence that Carson knew Kuper was corrupt and deliberately deceived the company. I'll meet her off the plane and give you an opinion once I've studied the documents. At least we've still got a chance.'

Douglas looked up wearily. He had hardly heard what Zack had said. All he wanted now was to get home to Becky.

'Do what you have to,' he said, 'and call me at home if you get anywhere.'

The only call Douglas made on his way home was to Becky, to say he would be back at the house by three and would explain everything then. The Bentley stopped outside East Heath Road and Douglas turned to the driver: 'I won't be needing you until tomorrow morning John, around nine,' he said.

The driver looked down at his knuckles on the steering wheel.

'I'm afraid that won't be possible, sir.'

'Well, get David to pick me up then, just sort it out,' Douglas said impatiently.

'That's won't be possible either, sir. I've been instructed by Mr Carson to clear your personal possessions out of the car and leave them here. I won't be coming back. Dave won't either.'

Douglas slammed the door and strode into the house. Becky was waiting for him, sitting with Freddie in her arms on a sofa in the drawing room. She put the baby down carefully and walked across to Douglas, took him in her arms and held him, stroking his hair.

'There, there, darling,' she said, 'you're home now.' She knew there was no point in saying that everything would be all right. There would be time later, when he was ready to talk about what had happened. She led him to the sofa and sat with her arms around him. They stayed that way for almost an hour, then Douglas stood up.

'I need a drink, do you want anything?' he asked and walked to the kitchen, returning with two glasses and a bottle of champagne. He slumped down in the sofa again and said: 'I just can't believe it. That bastard. How could I have trusted him? How could I have been so blind?'

'You trusted him because he was a friend, darling. Don't blame yourself for that.'

'I'll show them. I'll show them all. I'm not finished yet, not without a last fight. Something came up today – I won't know how important it is until tomorrow. Whatever happens, I'll fight. They'll wish they never heard the name of Douglas Holloway!' he ranted like a child whose toy had been stolen. 'I'll sue them for false dismissal ... damages ... drag them through the courts. I know every shady deal that company has ever done. I know where all the bodies are buried. I'll destroy them all.'

Douglas never once stopped to consider what effect this would have on Becky. He knew she would not desert him. Of that, and only that, he was sure.

Zack Priest pushed his way through the airport crowd to get to Georgina. Taking her trolley and pushing it towards a waiting car he asked: 'Have you got them?'

'Why don't we wait until we're in the car?' she suggested. 'So we can talk it through with Douglas.'

'How did you know he'd be here?' Zack asked, surprised.

'I knew he wouldn't be able to resist coming, to see the evidence for himself. Remember I've known Douglas for a long time.'

The car was waiting outside the automatic doors and the driver opened the door for her to get in beside Douglas. Zack took the front seat. Georgina could not help noticing it was a massive comedown from his usual limousine and chauffeur.

She had never seen Douglas look so old. His face was lifeless and lined. Only his eyes burned. He greeted her with a kiss from cold lips.

'It's all here,' Georgina said, removing the envelope from her bag and handing it to him. 'Transcripts of tapes proving Carson has colluded with this South African journalist for weeks to get the dirt on Kuper, and the documents that prove Kuper is a crook.'

Douglas read the documents then handed them to Zack, who studied them carefully then turned around in the car and squeezed Georgina's knee.

'This is brilliant,' Zack said. 'I'll start preparing the deposition to the board as soon as we get back. I've a team of lawyers waiting.' He paused for a moment then asked: 'But where are the tapes? You've only got the transcripts here and they won't hold up in court. I need the original tape.'

'And you will have it, Zack. But first I need to have a conversation with Douglas. Alone.'

Zack was dropped off at the offices of Wight and Anderson, the largest corporate law company in London. He knew it would cost him his job if Carson discovered he was trying to help Douglas, but he had no choice. First, without Douglas at the helm, he was out. Second, and he hoped just as importantly, Douglas was a friend.

They had less than forty-eight hours to present the case against Carson and both men would be required to work around the clock, alongside a team of corporate lawyers.

276

'Let's have a drink, George,' Douglas said and told the driver to take them to Claridge's.

'I'd love that, but frankly I'd prefer somewhere a little less formal,' she said and smiled. 'Driver, would you take us to Christopher's in Covent Garden?'

It was early evening, too early even for the pre-theatre crowd, as Georgina led Douglas up the grand staircase of the restaurant. They took a table in the best end and she ordered a bottle of champagne.

'It's a bit early for me, George,' Douglas objected.

'I'd say it may be a bit late for you,' she said sharply. 'Humour me, have a drink for once.'

He looked at her closely for the first time since she had stepped into the car. Despite the long journey, Georgina looked radiant. There was something different about her: an extra shine to her hair, a brightness in her eyes, a friskiness even.

'You look different, George,' he said clumsily. 'What's happened to you? You're not pregnant, for God's sake?'

'Typical Douglas,' she replied teasingly. 'As soon as a woman looks happy, you immediately assume she's swelled with the joy of some man's baby. God, you're predictable.'

'Sorry,' he said weakly.

'I'm happy, that's all. I'm in love. I met him in Australia.' Georgina stopped, feeling like a foolish schoolgirl blathering about love while her boss's world was crumbling around him.

'Look, George, about that tape . . .'

'I know, you need it.'

'We both know I need it,' he said. 'What I don't understand is why you're keeping it. It's not like you.'

'Exactly. What *is* like me is to do whatever you want, all your leg work, and expect nothing for it.'

'That's not fair,' he said, hurt. 'We've always stood together, I've always looked after you, even when . . .'

'Don't do it, Douglas,' she said fiercely. 'Don't ever fucking do it again. Don't tell me how much I owe you. You've held that over my head long enough and I won't have it. Now I'm in a position to save you and the debt will be repaid. But just as I've paid you over and over for saving my life, I want payment for saving yours. And I want it up front.'

'I don't understand?'

'You will.' Georgina started to pour herself another glass of champagne when the waiter intervened.

'I will provide the tape on condition you make me editor of the *Daily Tribune*. That's what I want. Is it a deal?'

Douglas stared at her. 'Is that all you want? It was going to happen anyway, before this Kuper thing blew up. You must have heard about the Diana secret sister fiasco? Sharon is now discredited as an editor. I'd already decided to offer it to you. Other things got in the way.'

'Marvellous!' Georgina said, and withdrew an envelope from her bag. 'Then you won't mind signing this.' She placed the document before him on the table.

'What is it?' he asked.

'A contractually binding agreement that you will make me editor of the *Daily Tribune* at a salary of £250,000 a year, plus share options and performance bonuses. I believe it's the going rate for a successful editor.'

'Georgina, we don't need this. You have my word . . .'

'Once that was good enough for me, Douglas, but not any more. Times have changed. More importantly, you've changed. And so have I. Just sign it and you'll get the tape. After all, it's what you want anyway.'

On her way home in a taxi, Georgina took the signed contract out of her bag and examined it. She still wasn't sure if she wanted the job. All she knew was that she'd wanted to be offered it.

There was only one thing that bothered her. When Douglas had asked if she was pregnant, she had dismissed it automatically. There had been no need for contraception when she was with Belinda. In Australia they had both acted recklessly. Condoms were not on the agenda. On my God, what if? she thought.

She stopped a few blocks away from her flat and went to buy a pregnancy test at the pharmacy. The chemist assured her these new tests could detect pregnancy from as early as two weeks. She dropped the test into her handbag and went home.

The sound of Ned's voice on the phone when she got back was almost enough to make her forget about the *Tribune* and everything else.

'Have you resigned yet, baby?' he asked finally.

'I've walked into a storm, Ned. It just wasn't the right timing,' she explained. 'I'll do it soon, I promise.'

That night, before she went to bed, Georgina remembered the pregnancy test. She peed on to a small litmus wand and held her breath for what seemed an eternity. In fact it was only one minute, the minute that would change her life forever. She was pregnant.

# Chapter Twenty-three

It was almost midnight when the phone rang. Georgina had been sitting on the terrace of her flat, wondering why even the fragrance of the scented geraniums reminded her of eucalyptus, trying to come to terms with the fact that she was pregnant with Ned's child.

Everything was moving so quickly. Too quickly. The phone switched to answer machine and Georgina waited, expecting to hear Ned's voice. She couldn't speak to him, not yet, not until she had worked out what she wanted to do.

Instead of the soft Australian drawl she was waiting to hear, a woman's voice began: 'Georgina, this is Sharon. I need to talk to you, as soon as possible. Can you make breakfast, tomorrow, eight o'clock? I'd rather meet somewhere private. There's a restaurant at the Marriott in County Hall. No one from the *Tribune* ever goes there. It's urgent. Please be there.'

Georgina was tempted to pick up the phone. Why would Sharon-I-never-do-breakfast-Hatch be calling her and what could be so urgent? Whatever it was, it could wait, she decided. She wrapped the dressing gown tighter around her and went to bed.

She wished it had been Ned on the phone. Even if she couldn't speak to him, she longed to hear his voice, to have some contact with him. She turned on the bedside light and picked up the phone. I can't call him, she thought desperately. He'll know something's wrong.

Georgina took a photograph off the night table and lay back in bed. It was a picture of her and Ned, taken the day before she left, sitting on the veranda. The eucalyptus trees framed a sunset of pale pink and gold. For a moment she could smell the eucalyptus and strong scent of Ned's skin. She fell asleep imagining that he was holding her in his arms.

Dawn was still hours away when Georgina woke. Damn the jetlag, damn the lonely hours of darkness, she thought. Remembering Sharon's call the night before, she wondered again what could possibly make that woman call her.

Call it curiosity, whatever, I'm awake and I might as well meet the dragon, she decided.

Sharon was already waiting for her when Georgina arrived at the restaurant. She was hungry, unsure whether it was pregnancy or jetlag that had brought it on.

'Fantastic view,' Georgina said as she sat down at the window table overlooking the Houses of Parliament. As she looked back at Sharon, she was struck by something. Sharon looked different, less, well, *orange*. Her makeup was softer and there was a tiredness about her that Georgina had never seen before.

The waiter took their breakfast orders. After he'd poured the coffee Sharon looked at Georgina.

'I might as well get straight to the point,' she began. 'I've fucked up. Carson has screwed Douglas and in the process screwed me. I don't have a lot to lose.'

'What do you mean, he's screwed Douglas?'

'You know,' she said, running a hand through her red curls. 'It was Andy who sent those files to the board members, and I helped him get the dirt.'

'That's hardly a surprise, but why are you telling me this, Sharon?'

'Because I want to nail him and I want to do a deal.'

Georgina had ordered scrambled eggs and bacon. The sight of them being placed before her made her want to be violently ill. She looked at Sharon and knew there were only a few minutes before she did exactly that.

Sharon looked at her more with curiosity than concern when Georgina returned from the toilet.

'You look terrible,' she said as Georgina sat down.

'Jetlag.' Georgina looked straight ahead and focused her eyes on Big Ben to try and stop the room from spinning.

Sharon did a rapid calculation. Jetlag makes you hungry not sick. Throwing up first thing in the morning, at the very smell of food. Didn't add up.

'You're pregnant, aren't you?' Sharon didn't wait for an answer. 'I can't believe it! Just when you get the chance to land the big job, you get the baby. Life's a fuck.'

The two women sat in silence, then Georgina started to cry. The tears welled in the corners of her eyes then ran down her cheeks. She made no attempt to stop them, couldn't understand why she was crying in front of Sharon of all people, didn't care anyway.

Georgina was the first to speak: 'Did you ever regret not having kids?'

'To be honest, I never wanted them,' Sharon said in a voice that was almost unrecognisable. 'I had such a shit childhood, I'd never want to inflict that kind of pain on someone I love. My mother was hardly the maternal type and it seemed I was a constant disappointment to my father. I've had enough experience of unhappy families to last me a lifetime.'

'I'm sorry.'

'Sorry about the fact I've never had kids or sorry that you're going to have one?' she asked.

'I don't know,' Georgina sighed. 'Maybe just sorry that this whole thing is such a mess, with Douglas and the *Tribune*. Was it all worth it?'

'Fuck knows,' Sharon said. 'All I know is Douglas doesn't deserve what's happening to him and I played a big part in all of that.'

'It's a bit late in the day to be playing the contrition card, Sharon.'

'Look, I've done some shit things in my time and if it had worked out the way I wanted it to, I'd be running the whole show with Andy by now. But he double-crossed me and I'll be damned if I'm going to let the little fucker get away with it. You'll never believe who Andy plans to appoint editor of the *Tribune*?' Georgina looked up. 'Fucking Myra-call-me-a-friend-Prescott.

Right behind my back that Leftie bitch has not only been screwing Andy, she's been screwing me, her *new best friend*.'

'Don't tell me she's been trying that on with you, too?' Georgina asked, amazed. 'She told me *I* was her new best friend. Incredible! That two-faced bitch. So much for her sisterhood. At least *we* never pretended to like each other,' and they started laughing.

'Anyway, if we get Andy out, she'll be nowhere. Back to the business at hand. I want to do a deal.'

Georgina sat back in her chair. This was more like the Sharon she knew.

'I can prove that Andy set Douglas up with the Kuper deal . . .'

'Is that all?' Georgina interrupted.

'And that Andy was the one who delivered the files to the board members discrediting him.'

'And what do you want in return?'

'A job, a good job. I know I can't edit a paper for a while, but if Mandelson can come back, so can I, in time.'

'How can you prove it?' Georgina asked. 'Your word isn't going to be enough.'

Sharon thought for a moment how easy it had been to get access to Carson's flat, his computer and his records. She'd had the flat keys copied the morning after he dumped her. She had waited until he left for work and replaced the originals exactly where she had found them. He would never know. And she could gain entry to his flat any time she liked.

'I'll get the proof you need,' she said confidently.

Georgina looked at her, not with pity but with sympathy. Sharon had fought for months to destroy her, now she was asking for Georgina's help. And, strangely, Georgina wanted to help her.

Must be the hormones, she thought. I'm going soft.

The phone had rung incessantly for four days and Douglas screened all calls by leaving it on answer phone. He was sitting in his study, poring over the hundreds of pages of evidence compiled by his lawyers.

With the tape as proof of Carson's collusion, Douglas's lawyers were confident he would be reinstated within twenty-four hours.

The Tribune board had been keen to keep their problems out of the public eye, especially with an end-of-year result looming. Douglas's suspension and Carson's caretaker role had still not been publicly announced.

When Douglas's lawyers went to the Chairman with their preliminary evidence, all plans were put on hold until the outcome of the internal investigation, which would take place tomorrow.

He was disturbed by Becky calling from downstairs.

'Darling, that was Jacqueline on the phone again. She called this morning but this time she sounded really upset. She's left a number.'

It wasn't their home number, but he dialled it anyway. Jacqueline answered almost immediately, as though she was waiting.

'Jacqueline, called to gloat, did you? Bad news certainly travels fast,' he said.

'I don't know what you're talking about. How typical of you to think every phone call is about you, every crisis your own. You really are the most self-centred man I have ever known,' she said.

'I'm sure you won't be pleased to hear it,' Douglas cut in, 'but rumours of my demise are greatly exaggerated. As of tomorrow I expect to be back at the helm of the Tribune Group.'

'Actually, Douglas, I'm at the hospital.' It was only then that he noticed her voice was choked with tears not anger.

'Oh my God, what is it? Simon?' he asked in a panic.

'No, Douglas, it's not Simon.'

'Is it Jamie? Tell me it's not Jamie.'

'Douglas, the boys are fine. It's Daniel. He's in intensive care . . .' She broke off as sobs cracked her voice. 'I just can't believe it. He was so well. We were just sitting having breakfast and he collapsed.' She broke off again and cried into the phone.

Douglas waited a few minutes, partly to give her time to collect herself, partly to allow himself to take in what he had heard. He was in shock, trying to piece together the words: intensive care, Daniel, collapse.

'It's all to do with that damned rheumatic fever he had as a child,' she continued quietly. 'It damaged his heart. There was an infection, a clot or something in the brain. Oh, Douglas, what am I going to do without him? Why is life so unfair? Why did it have to be Daniel and not you?'

'I'll catch the first flight out,' he said. Becky made the arrangements. It was not until he sat back in his seat that it all began to sink in. To be losing two of the things he cared most about in the world, his brother and his career, was unthinkable. How could fortune be so cruel?

As he walked down the long bleak corridor to the intensive care ward, Douglas was struck by the fact that the last forty-eight hours had been marked by such solitary walks to disaster. He had never felt so alone, so completely stripped of those things that made him what he was. He could not even begin to contemplate life without his brother.

He stood outside the door of Daniel's room, looking in through the glass panel. His brother was surrounded by what seemed to him a million tubes and wires and machines. Jacqueline was at his bedside, holding his hand. Simon, the elder of their boys, stood beside her. Jamie, only seven years old, was sitting on the bed reading something written on a piece of paper in a child's big coloured letters.

Jacqueline looked up at him and smiled bitterly as he walked into the room. It pained Douglas to see his brother lying so still in the bed, the sheets carefully arranged around his body, his pale, thin hands stiff by his side. His body was somehow jack-knifed in the bed, slightly bent, and Douglas desperately wanted to lean over and straighten him out.

'Jamie is reading his daddy their favourite poem from A A Milne,' Jacqueline explained. 'Go on, sweetheart.'

'Do you think he can still hear me, Mummy?' the little boy asked, tears brimming in his eyes.

'He'll always be able to hear you, darling.'

Slowly Douglas looked around. Something was wrong. There was no noise, no nurses, no heartbeat on the monitor. Only stillness.

'Jacqueline, he's still alive, isn't he?'

'No. He was slipping fast. The doctors said he was brain dead, there was nothing they could do. I had them turn off the life support system an hour ago.'

'But you could have waited! You knew I was coming.'

'Yes, I did.'

'The truth is, Sharon, we all get fucked over by men, and we fuck men over,' Georgina said. They were sitting in the American Bar at the Savoy, drinking champagne.

To a casual observer, they were just two career women enjoying a drink and a gossip after work. To *The Times* diarist sitting in the corner out of their view, it was an incredible meeting.

'Were you in love with Andy?' Georgina asked quietly.

'I thought I was, in a way,' Sharon confessed. 'What a fucking fool I've been. He was just using me.'

'At least you're out of it now and can get on with your life. There are still some good men out there, believe me.'

'Yeah, and just what do you intend to do with the one you're found?'

Georgina fished another cashew out of the bowl. The bar was noisy enough, but then the pianist started to play and, unfortunately, sing in a pastiche of Frank Sinatra. Both women sat back in the booth. Georgina looked over at Sharon, who was loudly humming 'My Way' and filling in the words where she could remember them.

Part of her could not quite believe she was actually sitting here discussing her love life, with Sharon of all people. But they had been brought together in a crisis and, bizarrely, were finding a way of relating to each other.

'The truth is, I don't know. I just don't know. Anyway, more urgently, what are you going to do about Andy?'

'Fuck the bastard over, of course,' Sharon said and laughed so loudly the entire room turned to look at her. 'I've already prepared a statement that he tricked me into spying on Douglas.'

'You know that's not going to be enough,' Georgina warned. 'Why would the board take your word against his?'

'You'll have more than my word, you'll have the proof we

need to bury him. Trust me,' and Sharon started singing along with the chorus of 'New York, New York'.

The funeral was planned for Thursday, in three days' time, at the small church they had attended as boys, where they had learned their first lessons at Bible School. Douglas had no reason to return to London. Becky was flying out with Freddie tomorrow. There was no job for him to go to. As he sat on the plane to New York, he felt completely numb. He knew he was in shock, knew the pain would come, but for now there was only that awful deadness. He was haunted by images of Daniel lying jack-knifed in the hospital bed, the children crying by his side. Would they ever go away?

He tried to disentangle the strands of panic in his mind. He simply could not comprehend the loss of his brother. It was as though he had lost a part of himself. He felt like an amputee. Something crucial to his life had been taken from him, yet still he felt its phantom presence.

It was almost impossible to comprehend what life would be like without the Tribune Group. His success had given Douglas a place in the world and now he felt emasculated by its loss. Worse still was the embarrassment he felt. He didn't want to see anyone or talk to anyone. What would he say? Who was he when you took away the job? What kind of man was he? His job had defined him.

For Christ's sake, he thought angrily, you've lost your brother and maybe your job, not your life. He cleared his mind of the pain and began thinking about the meeting ahead.

Julian Stockwell from Johnson Questing had finally tracked him down, via Julie, and asked for a meeting in New York. It was good timing, as Douglas was keen to finalise the details to make Freddie the beneficiary of Rosebud Inc. Now that Daniel was dead, it was crucial to get it sorted out immediately. His brother's death had reminded Douglas sharply of how unpredictable life was. He was aware for the first time in his life of his own mortality. What if anything happened to him? He must secure his son's future.

The lawyer's offices were just off Wall Street, behind an

unimposing red-brick façade which hid a magnificent old converted home. The receptionist asked him to wait, then led him through oak-panelled hallways to Questing's private rooms.

'They're waiting for you in the meeting room,' his personal assistant said and indicated a door on the right. Douglas turned the old brass knob and stepped inside. Sitting at the table were Teddy Questing, who ran the New York operation, Jacqueline and Kelly.

'What on earth are you two doing here?' he said from the doorway. 'I thought this was a meeting about Rosebud.'

'It is, Douglas, but the situation has become slightly more complicated since you last spoke to Julian,' Flanagan said, clearly embarrassed. 'I have been trying to reach you for almost a week. I assumed your secretary had passed on my calls.'

He thought of the hundreds of people who had called during the past week, first either to commiserate or gloat over his fall from power and then to offer their condolences when they heard about his brother. He couldn't even remember seeing Questing's name, let alone Stockwell's, but had to admit he'd hardly glanced at the list.

The reason Stockwell had originally called was to alert Douglas to the fact that his wife had discovered the existence of the company and her lawyer had demanded a full account of the investments. Then the call came from his sister-in-law just the day before.

There was nothing Douglas could do but sit down and find out what they wanted, although every instinct told him it was Rosebud.

This was the first time he had seen Kelly since the disastrous board meeting. She was dressed in red, the Chanel suit she had bought about a year ago. Unlike Kelly to turn up anywhere in something so old, he thought. Jacqueline was wearing a long navy skirt and ill-fitting jacket that looked as though it came from Oxfam.

'It was very, very careless of you, darling, to leave me in such a hurry and not take the contents of your desk drawer,' Kelly began. 'It was always the only little secret between us. But when I discovered your other little secrets, your mistress and the baby, I thought it was time to end all the lies between us. I found a confusing set of accounts there from a company called Rosebud Inc. I guessed that's what you called your mistress, so I handed them over to my lawyers.'

Douglas could think of nothing to say. He was cornered and for once he decided to listen.

'It appears your brother was fond of keeping secrets from me too,' Jacqueline said bitterly. 'The night he died I couldn't sleep, haven't slept a moment since then actually, and I decided to go through his papers to see if his will was in order. We never had any secrets. Then I discovered this company worth millions of pounds. I might have known you'd be behind it, Douglas. You made Daniel lie to me. He was the sole beneficiary of Rosebud Inc. I have since discovered. He always promised me he would sort his will out, but it was nowhere to be found. I called his lawyers and they said he had never made one. That means everything he had is mine. Daniel would have wanted that money to go to his sons.'

'But he knew that money wasn't his,' Douglas protested. 'I told him a few weeks ago I was making my son Freddie the sole beneficiary. Daniel knew that. That's what he would have wanted.'

'I'm afraid I have to disagree with you there, Douglas,' Jacqueline said sweetly. 'He never mentioned that to me and as I am now his sole beneficiary, it would be a foolish thing for a mother to do to give her sons' inheritance away. My boys deserve better than that.'

'Mr Questing, this can't be right, or fair,' Douglas began. 'That's *my* money and everyone around this table knows it.'

'I'm afraid, from what I've heard so far and the documentation I have received, Mrs Holloway, well, actually, both Mrs Holloways, have a case,' Questing said.

'But my money, it's my son's money . . .' Douglas protested.

'Excuse me,' Kelly interrupted, 'but aren't we forgetting a little detail here, like *my* baby? Actually, whether you like it or not Douglas, *our* baby. I have no intention of sitting here and squabbling over money. It's so common. My lawyers can handle that. Let me just make one thing clear. I only want what's fair. Somewhere to live, support for our child and maintenance for him or her. I've started work at a publishing company, and I intend to support myself from now. After that I don't give a damn who takes the rest. You can argue that out between yourselves.' She rose elegantly from her chair, picked up her Chanel handbag and smiled at her husband.

'Goodbye, Douglas,' she said, standing over him. 'I'm sorry for our child's sake, but I don't expect I'll ever see you again.' She strode out of the room and closed the door.

# Chapter Twenty-four

Carson's chauffeur arrived punctually at 7.45 am outside the flat. With the engine running, he left the Jaguar and pressed the front door bell, then walked back to the car and stood beside it, waiting for his master.

'Good morning, John,' Carson said affably as he climbed into the back of the car.

Having been Douglas's chauffeur for years, John knew he could speak when spoken to, which was indeed a rare moment, so ventured a brave: 'Lovely weather we're having, sir.'

Carson ignored him and started leafing through the morning's edition of the *Financial Times*.

Sharon had already checked his diary with his secretary – breakfast at Simpson's in the Strand, first meeting in the office at 8.45. She waited until the tail lights of his car had disappeared around the corner, then walked across the street with her head down. Not that anyone would have taken any notice of the head-scarved woman in the long navy coat taking a set of keys from her pocket and letting herself into the flats.

The first thing that struck her was the smell, his smell, a combination of leather, musty shag pile carpet and whisky. Locking the front door again from inside, she went straight to the study, trying to force from her mind memories of the last time she had been here, bent over the chair, being pounded from behind, porn images flickering on the computer screen.

Well, if he could access hetero pornography on his computer, he could access anything, she thought.

Sharon had learned well from her little hacker friend: how to access the Internet, how to create files and store them, how to download material on to a disk.

Working quickly, she started up Carson's personal computer. Within half an hour she had downloaded enough lurid pornography for her purposes, created a personal file on his data base and poured it into a file labelled 'Tax'. Inserting a disk, she downloaded the entire Drop the Dead Douglas file, which she had found hidden in a document labelled 'Inheritance'.

Carson had clumsily tried to hide the material underneath a detailed account of the legacy he would receive when his mother died. Fortunately for Sharon, there were only eleven files on his hard disk, so finding the documents she needed was easy enough.

She ejected the first disk, labelled it, then inserted the second. This time she downloaded the pornography, then the Inheritance document into one file.

By the time the second disk was ready to eject, her hands were sweating inside the fine suede gloves. Sharon picked up the second disk and placed it with the first inside her handbag, but not before raising it to her Tangerine Sunset lips and kissing it.

Douglas was sitting in his Montreal hotel room thinking about Kelly. She had changed. He couldn't quite put his finger on it, but she was not the woman he had lived with these last years. There was a quiet strength about her, a decisiveness he had not seen before, something deeper.

He laughed outright at the thought of her getting a job. The Kelly of old would never have worked. She would have gone from one rich protector to another. It was all very puzzling.

When the phone rang, he expected it to be Jacqueline.

'Douglas, it's Zack.' He held his breath. This was the call he had been dreading, the call which would decide his future.

'It was all touch and go for a while. Georgina's evidence was crucial, but I think in the end it was Sharon who swung it. She was magnificent. I tried to keep her away from the meeting but she insisted.'

'Sharon?' Douglas asked. 'She came to the board meeting?'

'For once she had her tits tucked in, quite demure really,' Zack said with a chuckle. 'She'd already signed the statement to say that she had collected information against you on Carson's instructions.

'Then she just arrived, unannounced, with poor old Roxanne carrying a portable computer. You should have seen her, Douglas, cigarette in one hand, waving a disk in the other, excusing herself for butting in. She rigged the computer up to the big screen in the boardroom, turned the lights down and said: 'Let the show begin.'

'Up came a set of figures on the current assets of one Mrs Angela Carson: house in Dorset, flat in London, shares, Tessas, the lot. All you could see was Sharon's cigarette end glowing in the dark. 'For those of you who are in the dark, Mrs Angela Carson is Andy Carson's mother,' she said, like some kind of corny narrator.

'Then the whole file on you that had been sent to the board members came up, page after fucking page of it. You could have heard a pin drop. Actually, all you could hear was Sharon lighting another cigarette. She was dynamite.

'Then she put the lights back up and went on to explain about her affair with Carson.'

'I don't believe it!'

'Sharon was brilliant. She said she'd been duped by Carson, that he had said he had to have you watched because the board thought you were doing something illegal. He lied to her and lied to her, first about his motives and then about the affair itself, promising to leave his wife. Sharon actually started to cry as she explained she'd believed they were going to get married and have children together. You had to see it to believe it!'

'Was he at the meeting?'

'Strange that, he didn't show,' Zack said. 'I know he was due to come. I went past his door, actually your door, on my way to the meeting and Sharon was in there waving a disk at him. I don't know what she said to him, but I've never seen the bastard look like that. He was white.'

'So what now?'

'I'm delighted to be the first to tell you that you are now, or should I say still, Chief Executive of the Tribune Group.'

There was a long silence.

'Douglas, Douglas, are you there? You've won.'

Douglas had slumped back in his chair, cradling his head in his hands. He picked up the phone again and said simply: 'Thanks, Zack.'

'It's not me you've got to thank, Douglas. We'll leave it a few months before appointing Sharon Head of Light Entertainment for the new cable channel. Oh, and by the way, the board decided to act on your recommendation to make Georgina editor of the *Tribune*. They were so impressed with her they've made her editor in chief of the whole group. Answerable to no one but the Chairman,' Zack added quietly.

The day of the funeral was unbearably warm, the air thick and heavy with humidity. It seemed somehow obscene for it to be so hot. Inside the tiny wooden church the hundred friends and colleagues who had come to bury Daniel Holloway sweltered, many of them standing in the aisles and on the wooden porch. Douglas first found the graves of his parents and placed a simple bouquet of snowdrops and violets on each. His father used to tend them in the garden, his mother placed them around the house in dainty china vases. Becky stood close beside him, holding Freddie in her arms.

As he stood over his parents' graves, he thought of the vastness of his loss. Their deaths, so close together, had been expected. Both were well into their seventies. His mother had endured a long and painful battle with cancer. His father had Alzheimer's Disease.

Up until the last few months she had somehow managed to care for her husband at home, then the strain became too much and he was placed in a nursing home. Douglas had promised himself again and again that he would visit him there, but somehow never found the time.

The regular visits to Montreal to see his mother in that last year had been hard to fit into his busy schedule. Watching her die so slowly, the cancer gradually taking over her body, was unbearable. Each time he saw her she seemed reduced, physically and emotionally. He hoped one day he would be able to remember her as the strong, clever woman who had brought them up, struggling against the odds. Now, whenever he thought of her, he could only see the wasted body and frightened soul, stripped of almost everything that had made her the woman she was. Would those memories ever fade?

The doctors said his father could not properly comprehend his wife's death. For three days after the funeral, the old man hobbled around the nursing home on his crutches, asking every woman if she was his wife. When he was sure he had asked everyone, he went to bed and just stopped eating. He simply could not live without her.

Douglas felt the sweat rolling down his spine. He put his arm around Becky and held her tight. He still had her and Freddie and their home and his job. He had what was most important to him.

They waited for Jacqueline and the children, then entered the church together. Douglas closed his ears to the service and his eyes to the mahogany coffin in front of him. He had wanted to speak at his brother's funeral, had insisted on it against Jacqueline's wishes, but now he wondered if he would have the courage to do so. The back of his throat felt like iron. It was so hot he could hardly breathe, every inch of his skin was wet and stuck to his clothes. It was only when Becky gently nudged him that he realised it was time to move to the altar and speak.

'My brother loved the nineteenth-century Humanists. He especially loved this speech by Robert Green Ingersoll. He showed it to me several years ago. Perhaps Daniel had some premonition of his own death. Certainly none of us did.

*"My friends:*

*I am going to do that which the dead oft promised he would do for me.*

*The loved and loving brother, husband, father, friend died where manhood's morning almost touches noon, and while the shadows still were falling to the west.*

*He had not passed on life's highway the stone that marks the highest point, but, being weary for a moment, he lay down by the wayside and, using his burden for a pillow, fell into that dreamless sleep that kisses down his eyelids still. While yet in love with life and raptured with the world, he passed to silence and to dust.*

*Yet, after all, it may be best, just in the happiest hour of all the voyage, while eager winds are kissing every sail, to dash against the unseen rock, and in an instant hear the billows roar above a sunken ship. For, whether in midsea or 'mong the breakers of a farther shore, a wreck at last must mark the end of each and all. And every life, no matter if its hour is rich with life and every moment jewelled with joy, will, at its close, become a tragedy as sad and deep and dark as can be woven of the warp and woof of mystery and death.*

*This brave and tender man in every storm of life was oak and rock, but in the sunshine he was vine and flower. He climbed the heights and left all superstitions far below, while on his forehead fell the golden dawning of the grander day. He loved the beautiful, and was with colour, form, and music touched to tears.*

*He added to the sum of human joy; and were everyone to whom he did some loving service to bring a blossom to his grave, he would sleep tonight beneath a wilderness of flowers.*

*Life is a narrow vale between the cold and barren peaks of two eternities. We strive in vain to look beyond the heights. We cry aloud, and the only answer is the echo of our wailing cry. From the voiceless lips of the unreplying dead there comes no word; but in the night of death hope sees a star, and listening love can hear the rustle of a wing.*

*And now to you who have been chosen, from among the many men he loved, to do the last sad office for the dead, we give this sacred dust. Speech cannot contain our love. There was, there is, no greater, stronger, manlier man.'*

He read the words with passion, almost unaware of where he was, the congregation blurring in his vision. His only thought was that he was talking to his little brother, now a man, now gone.

The service ended and they followed the family out of the church. They walked in silence through the heat, the only sound the muffled crying of little Jamie, walking along with his head buried in his mother's side, Simon holding her hand on the other.

Douglas's only thought as the coffin was lowered into the ground, and bunches of violets thrown on to it, was that it was so hot, and his brother hated the heat. It was as though Daniel was being lowered alive into a baking earth oven. He couldn't bear to think of him being so hot.

The crowd slowly dispersed and Jacqueline walked up to

Becky. 'Would you take Jamie and Simon for a few minutes?' she said. 'I need to talk to Douglas.'

Jacqueline and he were now alone at the grave, still a gaping hole in the ground.

'I was going to wait,' Jacqueline began, 'but there didn't seem any point. I've lost Daniel, the boys have lost their father. I can't bear to live here without him.'

Douglas was confused. What was she saying? 'If there's anything I can do, for you or the boys, you know you only have to ask,' he said. 'I really don't want to discuss Rosebud here.'

'This has nothing to do with Rosebud, Douglas. The lawyers have taken me through Daniel's papers and there's something else they've found. He may have had a premonition about his death, but as you know he didn't leave a will. Everything he owned is now mine, including a house in East Heath Road. I must say I was surprised by that, another little secret he kept from me. Fancy my low-paid Daniel owning a multi-million-pound house in Hampstead. Whoever would have guessed? I'm looking forward to a new start in London. I'd like you and Becky out of my home by the end of the month.'

Georgina sat on the terrace of her flat, a bottle of champagne by her side and a full glass in her hand. The gentle heat of the afternoon sun had released all the scents from the lavender and mint crammed in to pots around her.

A portable phone was on the ground beside her. The same phone she had used moments before to tell Ned she was not coming back to Australia. Not yet.

For days she had agonised over her decision. It was all too hasty. If it was really love it would wait, and last. This new job was an opportunity too good to pass up. She'd worked all her life for a chance like this.

Over and over in her mind ran the eternal triangle – job, man, child.

Everything Georgina had ever wanted in her life had been offered to her at once. The only catch was, she knew she could not have them all.

The very best of Piatkus fiction is now available in paperback as well as hardcover. Piatkus paperbacks, where *every* book is special.

The prices shown above were correct at the time of going to press. However, Piatkus Books reserve the right to show new retail prices on covers which may differ from those previously advertised in the text or elsewhere.

Piatkus Books will be available from your bookshop or newsagent, or can be ordered from the following address:
Piatkus Paperbacks, PO Box 11, Falmouth, TR10 9EN
Alternatively you can fax your order to this address on 01326 374 888 or e-mail us at books@barni.avel.co.uk

Payments can be made as follows: Sterling cheque, Eurocheque, postal order (payable to Piatkus Books) or by credit card, Visa/Mastercard. Do not send cash or currency. UK and B.F.PO. customers should allow £1.00 postage and packing for the first book, 50p for the second and 30p for each additional book ordered to a maximum of £3.00 (7 books plus).

Overseas customers, including Eire, allow £2.00 for postage and packing for the first book, plus £1.00 for the second and 50p for each subsequent title ordered.

NAME (block letters) _____

ADDRESS_____

_____

I enclose my remittance for £ _____

I wish to pay by Visa/Mastercard     Expiry Date:_____

| | | | | | | | | | | | | | | | | | |
|--|--|--|--|--|--|--|--|--|--|--|--|--|--|--|--|--|--|
| | | | | | | | | | | | | | | | | | |